10/18/13

To SHKLA:

THIS ONE YOU WILL

LIKE TOO...

- N.

CHILDREN
OF PTAH

THE THIRD MANUSCRIPT OF
THE RICHARDS' TRUST

BY

W.J. CHERF

ISBN: 978-0-9834814-2-3

The cover's design is based upon the hieroglyphic text taken from Shabaka Stone that resides in the British Museum (Nr. 498, formerly Nr. 135). The transcription of lines 53-57 of the Memphite Theology was undertaken by Wim van den Dungen firsthand at the British Museum from November 2001 through October 2004. van den Dungen's commentary and discussion of the Memphite Theology can be found at: http://www.maat.sofiatopia.org/memphis.htm#41

ALSO BY W.J. CHERF

Bow Tie. The First Manuscript of the Richards' Trust

Recovery. The Second Manuscript of the Richards' Trust

ABBREVIATIONS

Breasted   James Henry Breasted. "The Philosophy of a Memphite Priest," *Zeitschrift für die Ägyptische Sprache* 39(1901) 39-54. The first critical analysis of the Shabaka Stone and its content.

C   Shorthand symbol for the speed of light. Approximately 300,000 kilometers per second or 186,000 miles a second that calculates out to about 700,000,000 miles an hour.

Darwin   Terrestrial planet-hunting mission of the European Space Agency (ESA) planned to launch sometime around 2015 (see TPF below).

Emery   Walter B. Emery. *Excavations at Saqqara 1937-1938: Hor-Aha.* Cairo 1939, esp. pp. 83-112. Ground-breaking publication about the early tombs of the First and Second Dynasty kings and their archaic script.

Faulkner   Raymond O. Faulkner. *A Concise Dictionary of Middle Egyptian.* Oxford, 1976. English language dictionary of the ancient Egyptian language. An abbreviated and selective collection of the Egyptian language.

Frankfort   Henri Frankfort, et al. *The Intellectual Adventure of Ancient Man.* Chicago, 1946. A tour de force presentation of philosophical thought throughout the ancient Near East.

GHZ   Galactic Habitation Zone. An annular region that extends between 7 and 9 kilo-parsecs from the Galactic core that widens with time and is composed of stars between eight and four billion years old. Within the GHZ, where 75% of the stars are older than our Sun, complex life may be present on the basis of four prerequisites: the presence of a host star, sufficient heavy elements to facilitate the formation of terrestrial planets, sufficient time for biological evolution, and an environment free of life-extinguishing supernovae.

Hannig Rainer Hannig. *Großes Handwörterbuch Ägyptisch-Deutsch (2800-950 v. Chr.)*. Mainz, 1995. German dictionary of ancient Egyptian. A valuable resource for most aspects of the ancient Egyptian language that includes lists of gods, kings, weights and measures, abbreviations, toponyms and maps.

Junker H. Junker. *Die Götterlehre von Memphis*, 23 (1939) APAW. Berlin, 1940. Critical discussion of the Memphite Theology.

Kaplony Peter Kaplony. *Die Inscriften der ägyptischen Frühzeit III.* (Weisbaden 1963). Most recent work on the archaic script of the ancient Egyptians.

Kees Hermann Kees. *Das Priestertum im Ägyptischen Staat vom neuen Reich bis zur Spätzeit*. Leiden, 1953, 1958. Invaluable source on the priests and priesthoods of ancient Egypt.

Petrie Hilda U. Petrie. *Egyptian Hieroglyphs of the First and Second Dynasties*. (London 1927). Useful source on the archaic script of the ancient Egyptians.

Read F.W. Read, A.C. Bryant, "A Mythological Text from Memphis," *Proceedings of the Society of Biblical Archaeology* 23(1901)160-

187. Early publication on the Shabaka Stone and its contents. Of questionable value (see Breasted above).

RUTI   *Rukovodyashiy Ukaeaniya dlya Tymporalie Eksploratsiya* (*Guidelines for Temporal Exploration*). Time travel protocol authored in former Soviet Union in 1941 by the famous Hour Glass Seminar. Chaired by the philosopher Gregor Survurov, its membership included: Victor Latysev, Byzantine papyrologist credited with first expressing concern for "the preservation of the delicate fabric of reality;" three theoretical mathematicians – Nikolai Federov, Alexandr Koslov, and Dmitrey Giga; and Pyotr Borov, theoretical engineer and quantum physicist. This document makes no reference to any political or governmental body and states that all temporal decisions must occur within the framework of an international, scientific forum outside of any religious, political, or ideological control. This apolitical ideological stance proved to be the Hour Glass Seminar's greatest achievement.

Sethe   Kurt Sethe. *Dramatische Texte zu altägyptischen Mysterienspielen.* Leipzig, 1928. Considered the best discussion of the Memphite Theology.

TPF   Terrestrial Planet Finder. NASA mission planned to launch around 2015. Due to the formidable cost of this multibillion-dollar effort, the ESA and NASA may eventually decide to join forces on a single, planet-finding project (see Darwin above).

W.J. CHERF

Wb   Adolf Erman, Hermann Grapow. *Wörterbuch der Ägyptischen Sprache*. 4th ed. 7 vols. Berlin, 1982. Primary lexicon for the ancient Egyptian language includes context, sources and a reverse Egyptian-German word list. Essential, but considered dated. Should be used in conjunction with more recent philological sources.

Wilson   John A. Wilson. "The Theology of Memphis." In *Ancient Near Eastern Texts Relating to the Old Testament*. 3rd ed. Edited by James B. Pritchard. Princeton, 1969. Most recent English translation and reappraisal of the Memphite Theology.

Forward

The realm of fiction allows extraordinary personalities the ability to mold the very landscape of their age; whereas history is that crucible wherein individuals are shaped by their times.

Without question this is a work of historical science fiction. As a consequence, it represents a blending of the above sentiment. While extraordinary personalities indeed populate its pages, they are not the dominating element; rather the story itself is what is truly important.

As one might expect within such a genre much contained within this book is without question factual in every respect. Much is also the product of the author's imagination. As with any work of historical writing, actual events and personalities are described, do appear and are referred to by name. As with any work of fiction, any similarity either to events or individuals, either living or dead, is purely coincidental.

J.W. Richards

Editor's Note

Allow me to introduce myself, my name is Paul Silas. I am both the editor and executor of the so-called Richards' Trust. So-called because the name behind the trust is a fiction. Nonetheless, I can assure you that the dynamic personality that lurks behind the *nom de plume* of Professor Joseph William Richards was a living and breathing individual of breathtaking capacity. You may accept this judgment based upon some thirty-odd years of association.

Per the instructions of the Richards' Trust, I was instructed to publish three manuscripts. It is my task as editor to make sure that this ardent desire of my colleague comes to fruition. As an editor of a university press, I do have some connections; however, due to the subject matter of these manuscripts I cannot justify their publication under our house banner. So I sought out the good graces of nonacademic publishing house. As a result of that collaboration you now hold the third and last of the series, or perhaps maybe not.

Since Professor Richards' sudden and untraceable disappearance, the trust has empowered me to sell his flat and its contents with all of the proceeds to be divided as specified below. During that process I discovered several large manila envelopes in one of the oversized drawers of Richards' desk. The literary contents I am currently puzzling over as they were never discussed with me nor were they included in the original trust. As to just what I am going to do with these "orphaned" manuscripts I am not quite sure as of yet.

Regardless, the Richards' Trust was quite specific regarding the publication of the original three manuscripts, the schedule to be followed, and what would set the entire into motion. Put simply, Professor Richards wished, in the event he could not be contacted for a continuous period of six months, that I, as his executor, was to begin the publication process on his behalf. Additionally, I have been granted full power of attorney in all matters legal.

As of this manuscript's printing my client has been missing for some five and a half years. The domestic and international traces on his whereabouts have turned up nothing. His brownstone near the university was searched early on and nothing was found amiss. The requisite layer of dust was present evenly everywhere. Our last records of Richards are in the form of his credit card and bank statements, all which indicate that his last transactions included a roundtrip ticket to Egypt and a hotel booking at the Mena House on August 30th. Here, with his splendid accommodations overlooking the Giza Plateau left untouched, the trail of Professor Joseph William Richards ends.

All advances and royalties from the publication of the three manuscripts are to be deposited into the Richards' Trust, where they will be divided equally among several designated funding instruments. Once any of these instruments reach a specified threshold, then that threshold is to be reduced by seventy-five percent and the apportioned amount is to be distributed equally in the following manner: to a preexisting offshore bank account, as seed money for the establishment of an endowed chair in Egyptian philology at Richards' home institution, and as research grant funds to a West Coast prostate cancer research institute. Once the specified thresholds are again reached, then the cycle is to begin anew with an equal apportionment of funds to the same entities. Once the copywrite limitation has been reached on the three publications, then all instruments are to clear their accounts to the above established entities in one final, lump sum deposit, and the Richards' Trust extinguished.

CHAPTER I
Meditations

By crass modern standards he might have been considered a man of smallish stature. To his contemporaries this detail had no relevance; instead his outstanding characteristics were a neatly groomed moustache and freshly shaved head. Some felt that he carried his own personal hygienic regimes to an extreme – imagine shaving the entire body and bathing three times a day! But no one could question the results of those measures as he never seemed to suffer from the maladies that afflicted the rest of the villagers: sores, worms, lice, and a whole host of gastro-intestinal ills. Dressed as he was in a simple white loincloth and wearing common sandals made from the tough, but plentiful papyrus reeds, at first blush he appeared quite average – almost plain. But anyone who chanced even to briefly converse with the man knew far, far better.

As the man sat cross-legged upon his tightly woven papyrus mat in the cooling shade of a fragrant sycamore, he found himself thinking deep thoughts as his reed brush delicately traced out graceful hieroglyphs across the papyrus roll that lay cradled on his lap. While sitting in this scribal pose, he was so deeply engrossed in the task before him that he almost missed a potentially bothersome black scorpion, which had skittered across the sun-warmed sand before him. Vaguely noting the movement, Ptah raised his eyes in quiet recognition to follow the insect's progress that led off into the shade of a nearby shrub.

So, he considered. Now why is that nocturnal creature scurrying about in the afternoon heat? What caused that?

Slowly looking around, the learned priest soon found his answer. For in the direction from whence the arachnid had come he spied a rather skinny desert cat digging into the base of a nearby clump of bush.

Ah ha! That little one was displaced and had to move on. How appropriate, and so much like me. He smiled inwardly as he too was just a wanderer looking for a safe haven.

Looking down and returning to the partially completed column of text before him, he sighed deeply.

Ah, the challenge of it all! As I carefully and unobtrusively attempt to imprint my thoughts upon this young world, all the while being constrained by its earthy, unsophisticated vocabulary and nascent script! Thoth himself would have been proud of my labors!

Sigh.

Thoth, my old friend, I haven't thought of you in years. You were indeed such a fine teacher – and a better friend.

So the priest bowed his head and silently returned to his labors. But in order to continue where he had left off, he had to reread that which he had written.

There first took form in the heart and there took shape on the tongue of the Great One the image of the god Atum. This act by the very Great One is unknowable. The Great One who gave essence to all life and things through the heart and through the tongue.

Sight, hearing, breathing, these all report to the heart, and the heart makes every understanding come forth. As to the tongue, it repeats what the heart has devised. Thus all the gods were born and the Great One's Ennead was completed. For every word of the Great One came about through what the heart devised and the tongue commanded.

So did the Great One's heart and tongue rule over all as if mere limbs of a body in order that its essence is in all things, even the mouth of the gods, all men, all cattle, all creeping things, whatever lives, thinking that whatever this essence wishes and commanding whatever this essence wishes.

As Ptah leaned back from his reading, he sighed again and considered.

I wonder just how long it will be before someone truly appreciates the meaning of these words? But whenever that moment finally occurs, then I will be assured that this world has indeed taken a considerable step forward.

But that, my dear Ptah, will probably not take generations, but tens of generations! Assuming, of course, that these words are even remembered.

*　　*　　*

While the priest sat so engrossed in these heady thoughts, his activity nonetheless did not go unnoticed, for nearby two heavily sweating farmers were getting an ambitiously early start on their bountiful harvest of emmer wheat. Barefoot, dressed only in dirty hip girdles, and with their already damp hair tied back with a carelessly braided length of grass, the pair swung their carefully crafted bone sickles, which were hafted from the ribs of a hippopotamus and edged with razor sharp chert microliths. Humming a rhythmic and age old farmers' harvesting cadence, the men seemed to sway as they worked in time with the breezes that rippled through the ripe grasses.

With a remarkable economy of motion, they first grasped a handful of stalks at their mid-length, mowed them down near ground level, and then stacking their labors crosswise to the side. An observant witness to this seductively lazy-looking process of sway, grasp, swing, and stack might have even noticed the subtle scalloped angle of each sickle's passing in the neatly trimmed stubble.

Peeking over his sweaty, dusty and chaff coated shoulder, one of the farmers spat under his breath.

"Look over there Hor. That scribbler of children's pictures is sitting in the shade, while we toil under Re's hot

3

gaze! I tell you that it just isn't right. We work, while that know-it-all priest sits! I'm so fed up that I'm tempted to remove that smoothly shaved head of his with my *hab*-tool!"

At the completion of this last statement the farmer viciously, but carelessly, swung through his handful of stalks and in the process nearly severed the tip of his left hand's little finger. Immediately letting out a howling yelp, the farmer unconsciously grabbed at his hand, cradling it against his body as tears leaked from his eyes and excruciating pain stabbed at his brain. Hor, at first wide-eyed and shocked at the sudden appearance of so much blood, staggered back and away from his now writhing comrade, who had taken up a fetal position on his side, gently rocking, moaning.

Almost instantaneously, or so it seemed, the bald-headed priest appeared at the stricken man's side with a small wicker basket that seemed to appear out of nowhere. Kneeling down next to the frightened and grieving man, the priest placed one hand on the man's sobbing shoulder, while the other began rummaging around in his basket. At his mere touch, the man began to calm; his sobs began to subside. Speaking in a quiet but urgent voice, Ptah commanded the injured man's companion with his direct gaze.

"You there, what is his name?"

"Kawab!" A distressed voice quickly answered.

"And yours?"

"Hor!"

"So Hor, make yourself useful and fetch some drinking water for your friend.

"Quickly now!"

As Hor scampered off, the priest turned back to the stricken Kawab and began to speak soothingly.

"My friend, you will survive this accident. Now, let me see what you have done to yourself so that I may see to it."

Shaking from mild shock, Kawab revealed to the priest his bloody injury.

"You are most fortunate Kawab, for I can see no befoulment."

Now pulling from his basket a small juglet with its plug bound with leather throngs to keep it securely in place, the priest quickly unbound it, glancing at his patient in order to estimate his mass, and removed from his basket a small drinking cup. Measuring out a small portion of the juglet's content into the cup, the priest then held it to Kawab's grimacing lips.

"Now Kawab, open your mouth and immediately drink this drought."

Sensing the man's hesitation, the priest gently prodded.

"Kawab, if you wish to save your finger. Drink."

Now accepting with his lips the pro-offered cup that contained a mixture of raw opium, wine and honey, the priest continued.

"Kawab, drink slowly. Try to swallow as naturally as you can. Good. Now that did not taste so bad. Did it?"

Shaking his head in tentative negation, the injured man said, "No, it did not. In fact, what was it? Sweetened wine?"

"No Kawab. It was not *just* sweetened wine. Now, give me your hand."

As the priest held the farmer's hand, he was simultaneously recording the man's wild pulse, noting his darting eyes, the shock induced pallor, and the blood flow as the open wound cleansed itself and began to clot.

Yes, quite a little mess. Ptah concluded to himself after inspecting the injury. But this man is indeed fortunate. Shaken yes, but fortunate nonetheless. Once the sedative begins to take hold and I get some water into him, then I will mend his flesh together and bind the wound with some *seshed*-strips – bandages.

About that time, Hor arrived with a small water jar, his chest heaving from running.

"I hurried as best I could Great One!"

5

Smiling to himself over Hor's chosen deferential choice of address, the priest took the jar from the man and first held it to Kawab's lips. As the man drank deeply, Ptah's clinical gaze began to notice that the man's pupils had already begun to dilate, his body to fractionally relax. Now finished, Ptah then extended the jar to Hor and stated simply.

"Drink Hor, you too are in need."

When he returned to his patient, the priest began to gather this and that from his basket all the while Hor's forearm rested elevated and across Ptah's left thigh. While now bleeding more slowly, its splatter was nonetheless all over the priest's once white kilt. With all of his kit now at the ready, the priest looked up and smiled into the curious face of Hor.

"Observe Hor. Placing an injury to a limb above the chest naturally slows the flow of blood, just as a river cannot flow uphill.

"Observe also that there is nothing foul in this wound as the blood has already cleansed the area. This is the body's natural way.

"Now we must prepare the mending of the finger and its tip with this powder that will ensure that our careful work will properly heal."

And before Hor's gaping visage, the priest sprinkled a whitish, yellowish powder over both the finger and its tip.

Intrigued and finally finding his tongue, Hor inquired.

"Most noble Ptah, what is that powder?"

Inwardly pleased at the man's question, the priest answered conversationally. "Oh, the powder is nothing special, just an even mixture of sea salt and natrum."

"But why, Great One, are such salty and bitter things so needful?"

"Because they help in the mending," the priest explained with some pleasure that this one was even curious. Might he eventually become a potential apprentice?

The actual stitching of the torn and sliced fingertip went uneventfully with Ptah working skillfully and with speed while his patient remained blissfully unaware except for the careful priest's gentle tugging and pulling with the hooked, fine copper needle.

Meanwhile the entire procedure was witnessed by Hor, who openly marveled at the copper sewing instrument, something of the like that he had only seen before used for mending fishing nets. By the time Ptah had applied the antiseptic honey ointment to the fresh stitching and the final bandaging of the repaired finger had been accomplished, Kawab, while conscious, was otherwise as limp as a sagging tree limb. Clearly, he was no longer in distress.

Now looking up to Hor, Ptah smiled again and asked.

"Well Hor, are you Kawab's neighbor?"

"Yes I am. In fact, we are brothers. I am the eldest." The man said with a straightening back and sense of obvious pride.

"Ah, I see. Well good. We must move your younger brother back to his household. Will you help me with him?"

As the pair first steadied and then supported the injured Hor between them, Ptah gently but firmly told Hor the following.

"Make sure that your brother pays a visit to my household in two days time.

"Furthermore, under no circumstances is your brother to use his injured hand for those two days, and that absolutely positively, he is not to remove the bindings – no matter how much his finger itches."

To all of these things the elder Hor readily agreed. While he certainly did not understand their importance, he nonetheless enjoyed the fact that he could now command his not so little brother around for at least the next two days.

*   *   *

Not surprisingly, this minor incident, just as with all of the many others, did not go unnoticed by the inhabitants of the

Predynastic hamlet of Mennefer, a place better known today by its Greek name – Memphis. To them, the priest with the oddly formed and sounding name was someone who freely dabbled in that new and useless fad called writing, someone remarkably knowledgeable of bodily ills and injuries, construction, and a ready source of all manner of things handy and inventive: the mud brick mold, the potter's wheel, the kiln bellows, use of beaten copper for tools and medical instruments instead of just for jewelry, irrigation channel locks, and the long handed broom. The list just went on and on. He was someone also who said strange things and formed his thoughts in curious, unpredictable, and contrary ways. But despite all of these quirky oddities, his pronouncements – no matter how illogical sounding, always seemed to eventually come to pass. Consequently, the mere mention of the name Ptah became as much a source of respect and awe as well as one that invoked a certain tinge of irrational unease. After all, how could someone be always right?

Even his arrival to their once disease-ridden cluster of crude papyrus huts had been as sudden as much as it had been a godsend. The then village elder, one known by the name Hesy, remembered that event quite clearly and had passed it down to his eldest son Issi just before that much beloved and venerable one had passed on to the West. Issi, years later and now the village elder, guarded what his father had told him with a pent up mixture of prideful knowledge and fearful anxiety.

"Issi," his father had begun.

"As I know that you will eventually inherit my station as the father-protector of our household and village, I must pass on to you something which you must know, something that you must eventually pass on to your eldest son."

At first, the young man feared that his beloved father was about to die and almost moaned aloud in that private agony known as "the weeping of the heart." But as his father spoke in that special way that father's speak to their only beloved son,

Issi quickly calmed himself and thought that what he was about to hear his father's usual litany of admonitions about this and that, what one must do and don't, what was polite and not. He could not have been more wrong.

"When I was a young man, much as you are now, a remarkable thing happened. As I best remember, it was a cool night during the growing season, two inundations before your birth blessed our household. As we do even today, your mother and I slept alone on the rooftop far away from the noise of the animals and prying eyes and ears of our neighbors.

"I will never forget that night and I say this with no disrespect to your mother's formidable talents," he said with a lecherous wink.

"Have you ever wondered why I taught you so much about the uncountable lights in the night's sky?"

"Yes, my father. I know by heart all their names and the seasons and times of their appearances. I know that the gods live there and make the sky their household. These things I know because of your instructions."

"Indeed my son. Indeed I know that you know, for my own ears have heard you teach your children their many names and the seasons and times of their appearances. But what is so marvelous is that one of the many lights in the night sky, one unimportant and without name, moved that night."

"Moved?"

"Indeed! It moved across the dark sky of the goddess Nut's vast belly as if it was the face of Re himself."

"So slowly?"

"Oh no, my son! The light moved with great swiftness and in a matter of just a few heartbeats traveled across the entire breadth of the sky!"

"Really." The son said without conviction and who was beginning to wonder just what his father's story was all about.

"Yes, really! And I am not blathering like old Kahepet does either." The ancient man added for emphasis.

"But my son, the light did not only cross the sky, it fell out of the sky as well and into the Western Desert."

Now with this last detail his son's attention was again regained.

"And?"

"And the following day a most curious thing occurred."

"And what was that 'most curious thing?'" His son automatically responded to his father's all too well-known conversational method of storytelling.

"A young boy walked out of that waste and approached our village. He was unclothed, without sandals, sunburned, and feverish due to great thirst. Your very mother cared for him, fed, and clothed him. After one day's time his fever relented and so we asked him his name, from whence he had come, and only then discovered that he could not speak. Instead, he slowly moved his lips whenever we spoke as if in imitation, but no sound came forth from his mouth. This boy with long hair the color of wheat at harvest was surely a stranger. Yet, he did not come from that part of the Western Desert where those wild traders and raiders have such hair as you yourself well know. Still, as is our custom, he was nonetheless a stranger in need who was now under our household's protection. Few of our neighbors knew of his presence at first, as the boy preferred to sit and watch us watch him, noting our every word in soundless imitation, cocking his head in total interest whenever we performed any household tasks – even the most simple.

"By the beginning of the third day, long assured that the boy was not a danger to your mother, I left for the fields in order to weed and water them. But when I had returned for the midday meal, I found my wife overjoyed and smiling broadly as she watched the boy kneading that very meal's bread dough. As for the boy, he looked up at me, smiled broadly, and greeted me by name!

"Issi, can you imagine my utter shock! Can you imagine my utter joy! I had many, many questions to ask the boy, not the least of which was my curiosity as to the whereabouts of his household!"

"But father, where is this wheat-haired boy now? I know nothing of him. I have never heard of him. And why are you telling me about this wondrous thing?"

"Well my son that is because the boy is now a grown man, a man who lives among us."

"And my father does this 'grown man who lives among us' have a name?"

"Why yes my son, he is the most noble priest Ptah."

CHAPTER II
Magic Time

Midway through the first semester of my third year as an associate professor of Egyptology, a very bright light bulb went off in my head that would truly change my life forever.

My mentor and now long time friend, John Milson, an emeritus Professor of Egyptology, had early on warned me about such personal epiphanies. He had even told me how he had trained himself to bring them on almost at will. But while Milson's "magic time" occurred only after having intensely worked for a time on a troublesome ancient text or some particularly knotty historical issue, mine actually occurred during the process itself. What Milson had not thought to consider was the extremely freewheeling nature of my young memory, a memory that had been enhanced through hypnosis and drug therapies far beyond what might be described as merely photographic. Because of these enhancements, I remember things in digital detail; meaning that I could remember a general scene one moment, analyze it, and then zoom in on a particular part of it – much the same way a portion of a particularly dense digital image can be zoomed in upon. But unlike a digital image, all five senses can be so called upon and focused.

What had kicked off this intellectual thunderstorm was my preparation for an advanced philology class in ancient Egyptian. I needed a sound and well-known narrative text for my students to chew on, one that they could research, one that would inspire them, and one that would display Egypt's legacy to the immense heritage that is Western Civilization. And for some subliminal reason I unconsciously, and to this day I do not know why, gravitated towards a religious treatise associated with the god Ptah, the patron god of Egypt's most ancient capital – the sacred city of Mennefer, ancient Memphis.

The topic in question is referred to by modern scholars as "The Memphite Theology" and upon reviewing it, I immediately decided upon making it the central focus for this particular advanced class. While the preserved epigraphical text dated from the late Twenty-Fifth Dynasty, the inscription itself was clearly a copy of a far older worm-eaten work – one perhaps originally inscribed in wood or painted on papyrus or leather, whose archaic grammar and subtle intellectual significance were not totally grasped by the artisan tasked with replicating the artifact.

Just how old the work really was has been a subject of considerable scholarly debate. The venerable James Breasted, the father of American Egyptology, first argued for a date during the early Eighteenth Dynasty. But as time passed other scholars, Sethe, Junker, and Frankfort thought otherwise. They instead dated the original text to sometime during the Egyptian Old Kingdom. And indeed the date may be even earlier than that for on a First Dynasty calcite bowl from Tarkhan, the god Ptah, the author of the treatise, was depicted as an austere smooth-headed male "dressed in a high-collared garment with a tassel holding a scepter of authority."

What struck me as particularly odd were not so much these facts, but rather something remembered. Something about what the high priest of Ptah had said at the funeral of his elder brother and my adopted father – the venerable Meryptah. I had distinctly recalled the voicing of a remarkable and moving sentiment; a notion that had remained fuzzy and a bit of out of context until I had read the fifty-third through fifty-sixth lines of "The Memphite Theology."

Line 53:
There took form in the heart [mind], there took shape on the tongue [speech] the form [image] of the god Atum. For the very great one is Ptah, (he) who gave essence [life] to all the gods through his heart [mind] and through his tongue [speech].

Line 54:

Horus came into being in him. Thoth came into being in him as Ptah. Thus the heart [mind] and tongue [speech] rule over all the limbs in order that it [heart/mind] is in every body and it [tongue/speech] is in every mouth of the gods, all men, all cattle, all creeping things, whatever lives, thinking whatever it wishes and commanding whatever it wishes.

Line 55:

His [Ptah's] Ennead is before him as heart, authoritative command, teeth, semen, lips and hands of Atum. This Ennead of Atum came into being through his semen and through his fingers. Surely, this Ennead [of Ptah] is the teeth and the lips in the mouth, proclaiming the names of all things, from which Shu and Tefnut came forth as him, and

Line 56:

which gave birth to the Ennead [of Ptah]. Sight, hearing, breathing, these all report to the heart [mind], and it [heart/mind] makes every understanding come forth. As to the tongue [speech], it repeats what the heart [mind] has devised. Thus all the gods were born and Ptah's Ennead was completed. For every word of the god came about through

Line 57:

what the heart [mind] devised and the tongue commanded.

Having consulted yet again this passage's critical scholarly commentaries by Sethe, Junker, and Erman, and the learned and insightful discussions of Breasted, Wilson, and Frankfort, I had to agree that Line 56 should have had followed Line 54. Besides, I could now easily appreciate how a harried stone cutter could have mistakenly transposed the line and then did his best to cover up it up. It was a common copyist's mistake; the simple matter of one's eyes jumping ahead and confusing similar looking characters. So was erroneously preserved the text of "The Memphite Theology" on the so-called Shabaka Stone that now resides in the British Museum.

But once I got beyond that philological transposition, the clear parallel in meaning between the Egyptian text of "The Memphite Theology" and that of the Hebrew Logos Doctrine of biblical *Genesis* seemed unmistakable, for in both texts when divinity speaks, matter is created. Without doubt I was intrigued first by the geographical proximity of the two cultures and then by how such a potential cultural sharing could have transpired. But when this Egyptologist remembered that the composition of "The Memphite Theology" was far older than that of the Israelite culture – far older by several thousand years, that was when the light bulb and the alarm bell had gone off.

In retrospect, I now realize that it really all had begun as a nagging suspicion. Something that lurked deep down buried in my subconscious, which would not go away. The concatenation of odd facts, details, and sheer coincidence were just too eye-popping, too uncanny, to dismiss blissfully to the intellectual circular file.

Yet to even seriously entertain those heartfelt funerary utterances of the high priest of Ptah, sentiments delivered from one brother on the behalf of another, the entire concept remained highly questionable, dodgy, if not an outright act of academic suicide if publically enunciated. Then again to wholly discard the notion also meant turning your back on a remarkable possibility that was just sane enough to be true, if but only from a certain point of view. That is if one could first grant the possibility of that "certain point of view," that represented nothing short of a paradigm shift in long established philological doctrine, considered to have been firmly established on a bedrock of dark Nilotic basalt.

For certain if I publically pursued the subject, I would face a summary dismissal by my drab and dourer colleagues to the dingy recesses of "von Däniken-like quackerdom." If discovered, the hounds of academic ridicule would immediately come nipping at my heels. Such a fate would no doubt begin with some form of institutional banishment insinuated via some innocuous bureaucratic sub-codicil of the faculty handbook. I could just imagine the ill-informed small talk, gossip, and acidic rancor that would then circulate within the department, which would then immediately go viral through the Internet and in quiet whispers during the many annual conferences about the clear intellectual crackup of Milson's own handpicked *Wunderkind*. For sure, the circling of ravenous turkey buzzards would be the immediate consequence. But then again, if it all turned out to be true, I reasoned that no one would be allowed even to know. The implications would be too sweeping, so outrageous, and far too unsettling for the general public's consumption.

Without question, to undertake that fateful first step I would require a stiff double shot of faith and a cast-iron stomach filled with conviction. But for me, a nonconforming conformist, as much as I relished taking on the challenge, this issue also represented a practical nightmare. This speculation, and at this point that was all it was, shook to its very foundations everything that I had learned about the grammatical nature of the ancient Egyptian language. On the other hand, employed as I was by the university's Near Eastern Institute and a quiet member of the Philology Annex as well, I realized perhaps for the first time in my young career that I indeed had much to loose.

So after forcing myself to mentally sit down and review the idea in as a detached a context as possible, I began to suspect that a subtle attempt at ancient encoding was afoot as well. After all, given all that I knew and all that I had recently gone through, what else could it be?

So I began to organize my thoughts in as an objective and rigorous a manner as I could imagine within the tomb-like quiet and dark solitude of one late, private evening. While sitting at my office desk on the second floor of the Near Eastern Institute with a freshly sharpened Nr. 2 pencil in hand and a curled, half-used up yellow legal pad before me, I divided it by habit lengthwise creating two broad columns.

Atop of the left-hand column I boldly scratched out the word "Given," while atop the right I wrote "Speculation." Then I began to list and number the myriad of the things that bedeviled my mind in search of any logic or organization that I could muster.

After about an hour's time I had put my pencil down and was staring at a single page of cogently formed arguments all neatly written and organized just so. No matter how I looked at the situation, or from which angle, my entire proposal depended upon that initial first assumption, an initial leap of faith. Any proof of my suspicions, if even attainable, would most likely remain unpublished given the magnitude of the ultimate conclusion. But my insatiable curiosity and thirst for the truth drove me onward. Besides the use of the highly classified technology necessary to gather such provocative evidence would be considered even more fantastic in the minds of an innocent public. Then I considered the potential jeopardy just using said technology to the quiet, peaceful, and well-established security of the Philology Annex, Horizon Pass, all of its staff connected with those fine institutions, not to mention the potential ripple effect upon several internationally recognized scientific bodies as well.

In short, I found myself in quite a pickle. Nonetheless, I decided to go forward and craft a draft proposal for the staff of Philology Annex to consider. Before I could do that, however, I had to somehow first convince my immediate superiors that I wasn't totally crackers either.

So this young associate professor of Egyptian philology struggled for a convincing argument that might sway his superiors into allowing him access to the temporal device in order to either prove or disprove the validity of a theory based upon an act of faith.

And so in search of that bulletproof argument, I began to reread the text on the yellow pad point by point.

*   *   *

The following is what was on Richards' yellow legal pad, which he had arranged into two columns with headers marked as "Given" and "Speculation."

Given: The ancient Egyptian god Ptah.

A well-known and universally attested figure throughout Egyptian history. His image is that of an upright mummy with a beard, bare head or tight skull cap that holds before it a staff. His attributes are those of creation, building, craftsmanship, and civilization. His ascension to divinity seems to have occurred during the early Eighteenth Dynasty as attested by the presence for the first time of the determinative symbol for divinity in his name.

Speculation:

Odds are that he was once a mortal being, who over time (i.e., by the early Eighteenth Dynasty) reached divinity, much as did the famous architect of the Step Pyramid, Imhotep, who was himself made a god sometime during the Egyptian Late Period. The precedence is there. In other words, this Ptah potentially could conceivably be found and interviewed.

Given: The role of Ptah in "The Memphite Theology."

He plays a significant role in the Memphite theological worldview as the source of formed thought, which once voiced, becomes physical reality.

Speculation:

Ptah's dominant role is a clear indication of just how old he might be, a personality who perhaps lived during the Old Kingdom − if not earlier, maybe even as far back as the Archaic or late Predynastic Periods.

Given: This god's primary attribute is that of creation via the authoritative utterance of a thought through which matter was made manifest.

In short, this is the forerunner of the Logos Doctrine of the Old Testament that was enunciated millennia before the Hebrews.

Given: □ + ⌂ + 🜊 + 𓈖

Ptah's name is constructed of three basic stem elements, if one omits the determinative suffix that signifies that the grammatical cluster is the name of a divine being. These elements are the bread loaf symbol, the box symbol, and the twisted rope or oil lamp wick symbol. These three stand for the phonetic values of p, t, and an aspirated h, respectively. At the same time, these three hieroglyphic signs in an appropriate context can have a pictographic value as well as they are traditionally understood to mean a loaf of bread, a box, and as either a twisted rope or oil lamp wick.

Speculation:

Ptah's name, as so constituted, seems to be an ancient Egyptian ideogram as formed by these commonly used signs. If so, Ptah's name could possess a hidden symbolic meaning, if one can accept the possibility that the Egyptians were capable of assigning a purely ideographic meaning to a name.

Given: ⬯ , ⬚

Many other hieroglyphic signs possess ideographic values; in this example, "mouth" and "house", respectively. However, the clustering of multiple ideographic signs to derive a collective meaning, as in the form of an anagram, has yet to be identified by scholars of Egyptian philology.

Given: □ , ⌂

Accepted philological convention states that within the canons of Egyptian grammar, the hieroglyphic signs for the bread loaf and box, when they appear as suffixes, are considered attributes of gender, for "maleness" and "femaleness" respectively, which can be assigned to any noun.

Given: 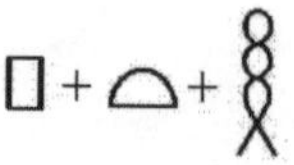

The difficult phonetic combination of these three signs is extremely rare if not unique. Additionally, this unique hieroglyphic triad appears only twice throughout the entire course of recorded Egyptian history. Once as a verb meaning "to build" or "to create" and once as the Egyptian name Ptah. This combination appears nowhere else except in compound names, as in Ptahmesou, a high priest of Ptah and in Meryptah, a high priest of Amen Re during the late Eighteenth Dynasty.

Speculation: 

Consider the ideographic meaning of the gender specific signs of the bread loaf and box followed by the hieroglyph sign that represents the twisted rope or lamp wick. Anyone with a background in biology will not interpret the sign as an image of an unraveling rope, but rather as that of a conservatively replicating DNA helix preceded by the signs for "maleness" and "femaleness".

Conclusion:

To attribute pure chance to the above glyphic combinations seems in my mind a bit of a stretch. Then when one considers the gender specific hieroglyphic signs of the bread loaf and the box that proceed the twisted rope sign in the verb "to create" and in Ptah's name, one is confronted with perhaps an extremely old truth long encoded concerning mankind's genetic heritage.

* * *

At this point in Richards' thinking, he began to come to grips with the real core question: Just who was this Ptah, this god of creation, this patron of craftsmen and civilization?

Then he had another thought.

Just where else within the Egyptian language did the suspicious unraveling rope hieroglyphic sign appear?

After a short trip to his favorite archive just down the hallway from his office, he began to amass a short list, certainly not an exhaustive one, but a list that nonetheless made for very interesting reading and which made the very hair on his arm rise. For what he had found made him pause in disbelief. The list comprised an entire family of nouns that in the main dealt with items of a biological nature.

Body or flesh
Parts of the body
Head
Throat
Ribs
Phallus
Arm pit
Menstruation
Excrement
Children

Then there were several names of divinities that really caught his attention.

Hapi – the hermaphroditic god of the Nile
Heket – the frog goddess of fertility
Hekau – the god of magic

Then he chanced upon one other unrelated, but significant noun: two twisted rope signs arrayed side by side that connoted one million units of something. When was the last time that an ancient Egyptian counted a million items? Even better, why in the world would it occur to an ancient Egyptian that an unraveling rope could imply such a vast quantity? If, however, the unraveling rope truly was a DNA strand, then he could buy that figure given all of its myriad constituent parts, not to mention that the image looked very much like two newly replicated DNA strands. Millions of units indeed!

Now sitting back deep into his office chair, Richards' head actually hurt from this by now early morning intellectual foray. So he decided to sleep on it and review it all in the morning to see whether or not it still all hung together. But that following morning, upon his review, he became even more deeply convinced of the correctness of his suspicions.

Maybe, just maybe, Akhenaten had actually been Earth's second visitor, who had attempted to leave its imprint upon mankind. Then came Ptah, who probably walked the Earth at a far earlier date, a date perhaps during the formative years of Egypt's development. Now there was a fertile seedbed out of which the children of Ptah could come forth!

*   *   *

In the end, Richards was totally convinced that he was right. Now ready to share his thoughts, he sought out his old friend and mentor John Milson. From him Richards knew that he would get a fair read, if not an outright sanity check.

CHAPTER III
Homeward Bound

Predictably, they had immediately fallen back into their same habitual routine. While it had been only a few moments since they had broke orbit, the three Surveyors busied themselves either with the internal functions of their ferry craft Redemption, its return course, or the continued monitoring of the electromagnetic emissions from the target planet. Although the latter was at present practically nil due to the current solar storm that had caused the great worldwide Black Out.

They all had admitted that if the First Scout had been recovered, then its debrief and biological integration would have been a source for much diversion. But as it now stood, with only the scout craft The Hope securely in tow, the running of its diagnostic routines would be, well, just routine. The best that the trio could do was to assess the condition of The Hope and prepare a list of needed repairs. And as the Quimbly quickly discovered, The Hope would indeed require an extensive overhaul as all of the organic interfaces were not functioning, its life support mechanisms were found decrepit, and the craft's basic operating protocols and memory banks were totally missing. These last, while noted as a mild concern of the recovery crew, were deemed useless once removed from the scout craft's hull.

Without the First Scout, however, this salvage inventory became a secondary task that once completed would be included in their next status report. As they were on the return leg of their recovery mission, there was no longer any need for stealth. Equally, there was no longer any need for the conservation of energy. So the Soss plotted an efficient course and boosted the Redemption to its terminal velocity of 0.89 C.

Still and all, it was difficult for the recovery team to simply return without the venerable First Scout. Yes, they had the "hardware" in hand and so in a sense had satisfied the directive of Survey Institute – their space-surveying community. But for the "software" that was another issue. Yes, they had gathered a significant amount of data about a new planetary species. But the fact remained that "no," they had not recovered the First Scout and the real question that tickled at all of their intellects was: "Were they even able given the current condition of The Hope?"

As to how these three intellects felt, related, or dealt with that fact is difficult to capture in mere words. The Xoxx, Soss, and Quimbly, separate species all, are very alien in both their appearance and outlook. While a kind of ethics or ethical behavior might be identified as present among them, it does not necessary follow that they thought of them as such. Similarly, our notions of religion, death, sorrow, or God are as alien to them as their species are to us. What remained unequivocally clear, however, was that the First Scout was absent. One of their own was missing. A grand tradition had ended. So, perhaps, in a sense, the loss was "felt." That something had indeed affected the trio is the fact that they spoke of it and that a lively discussion broke out on the potential merits and obstacles of attempting another "snatch and grab."

"I suggest that while the planet is so involved with the solar storms that we created, we immediately return and seek out the remains of the First Scout to the best of our ability." So went the nearly-emotional plea of the Quimbly, a member of the First Scout's own organic species.

"While that would be most ideal, in that it would satisfy all the parameters of this recovery mission, I cannot see how we could begin to accomplish such a task." Countered the Xoxx, a crystalline inorganic.

"Further," said the Soss, another crystalline inorganic, "just how would we approach, re-enter, and exit the planet's defenses without detection? Additionally, how would we find the First Scout's remains? Would doing so put the Redemption itself at risk and perhaps that we too could become the object of a future recovery mission."

"I agree." said the Xoxx, "Why jeopardize the Redemption and compound the situation with the potential loss of three more surveyors."

As for the Quimbly, a logical creature, but nonetheless an emotionally attached one, silence was its only answer, as it too recognized the futility of any return attempt.

*   *   *

While the Redemption was underway on its long, homeward-bound journey, a handful of well-informed individuals at Wright-Patterson Air Force Base were not altogether sure whether the state of the planet's security was what it should be. After all, an unknown had all too easily retrieved an extraterrestrial vehicle from right under their collective noses. In truth, those concerned were not altogether sure which was more remarkable – the actual snatch itself or the spectacular subterfuge of the unknown's near space approach. Both implied unimaginable resources and means. Given all that had occurred, a fearful agenda now appeared on the table. "Would that spacecraft return and try to recover the organic remains? And if so, should we expect some sort of an "eye-for-an-eye" retribution included in the bargain as well?"

So fanciful contingency plans were feverously outlined on white boards. After some consideration, these were further brainstormed and thrashed about into coherent and practical concepts, which became formal proposals. In the end, recommendations were prepared for presentation to a very select and special audience. These worthies, "heavies with more than a need to know," comprised a unique multinational amalgam. They were the ones who were tasked with addressing truly weighty global matters of considerable logistical and technological complexity.

But unknown to these well-meaning individuals at Wright-Patterson AFB, whose reasoned arguments would be reviewed with genuine interest by the powers that be, their delivery was well over fifty years late. For several governments and international organizations had already undertaken the formidable task – that of quietly organizing a unified planetary defense system, one that should have been obvious if one had just taken the time to notice.

First concerns for the security of Earth's own "near space" began in 1942 during the Great Los Angeles Air Raid of February 26th. At precisely 2:25 in the morning, 1,433 rounds of antiaircraft munitions began firing into the moonlit sky at fifteen to twenty highly maneuverable glowing objects. Initially thought to be Japanese bombers, their aerobatics proved otherwise.

These "lights" over Los Angeles were not to be an isolated incident. The famous European "Foo Fliers" caused considerable consternation and worry among both the Allies and Axis Forces during the Second World War. At first both sides believed the aerial phenomena to be the secret weapons of the other, but as time went by it became clear that that could not possibly be the case.

Then the events between the years 1946 and 1947 would mark an even greater period of increased unknown activity. These objects were coined "flying saucers" by the cameraman of the now famous Mount Rainier film and subsequently had captured the public's imagination with the so-called Roswell Incident. But the real capper was the unknown intruder formations that blatantly flew over the Washington, DC area in 1952. Far too many bystanders had witnessed that aerial display and the fact that the US military was totally powerless to do anything about it represented the last straw. By December 24, 1959, the Inspector General of the Air Force issued the following blunt Operations and Training Order:

> Unidentified Flying Objects . . . must be rapidly and accurately identified as serious Air Force business.

It was during the early post-Second World War era, when opposing triggers remained still well-oiled and cocked that several governments got together for a quiet chat concerning an issue of mutual interest: defense of the planet in the event of an extraterrestrial invasion. As logic would naturally dictate, the monitoring and eventual control of Earth's "near space" became the new tactical high ground. The real question was, however, who would be the first to achieve the status of Earth's protector? And so was engendered the real reason behind the "Great Space Race" of the Twentieth Century.

What became immediately clear, however, was the enormous effort that was required to safely reach "near space" and get back alive. Once the Russians and Americans had achieved orbit, a certain sense of powerlessness took over, for almost immediately an orbital cat and mouse game had commenced.

In 1964, three Russian cosmonauts reported being surrounded by a "formation of fast-moving disc-shaped objects." Two years later the Gemini XII astronauts Jim Lovell and Edwin Aldrin witnessed four UFOs linked together – almost as if they were taunting them. In that same year Representative Gerald Ford of Michigan called for and got a Congressional hearing on UFOs. Shortly thereafter, the Apollo XI astronauts Neil Armstrong, Edwin Aldrin, and Michael Collins reported seeing an unknown during the outbound leg of their epoch-making lunar mission. Their inquisitive companion reportedly moved at will and cruised effortlessly alongside their spacecraft before it suddenly rushed off.

As a result of all this activity, on June 7, 1967, the United Nations formed The Outer Space Affairs Group. Two years later, the United States Congress enacted a rather special law, 14 CFR Chapter V, Part 1211, regarding extraterrestrial exposure. In this piece of legislation, the NASA Administrator was specifically granted:

The arbitrary discretion to quarantine under armed guard any object, person, or other form of life which has been extra-terrestrially exposed.

When uncovered by the press, this piece of legislation was casually explained away as merely a sensible decontamination issue. What was left as an unspecified and open question in this otherwise extremely precise legal document was what constituted such exposure.

But perhaps the greatest step towards a unified planetary defense policy occurred on September 30th, 1971, when a treaty was signed by the United States and the Soviet Union. What is telling about this document was the surprising level of cooperation between these two bitter Cold War entities. Regardless of this harsh political reality, explicit protocols for the notification of each party were put in place.

Detection by missile warning systems of unidentified objects or in the event of signs of interference with these systems or with related communications facilities; such occurrences could create a risk of outbreak of nuclear war between the two countries.

By 1974, while many Russian and US astronauts saw and photographed UFOs during their flights, M. Robert Galley, the French Minister of Defense, stated in a radio interview on February 21st the following.

I must say that if your listeners could see for themselves the mass of reports coming in from the airborne gendarmerie, from the mobile gendarmerie, and from the gendarmerie charged with the job of conducting investigations, all of the reports are being forwarded by us to CNES (= National Center for Energy Studies), then they would see that it is all pretty disturbing. My view about the gendarmerie is that they are serious people. When they draw up a report, they don't do it haphazardly. But I must tell you that in fact the number of these gendarmerie reports is very great and they are greatly varied. The whole thing is, of course, still very fragmentary, but I must emphasize that, in this UFO business, it is essential to preserve an extremely open mind.

Then four years later, in July of 1978, Astronaut Gordon Cooper spoke with frank passion before the United Nations General Assembly.

> I believe that these extraterrestrial vehicles and their crews are visiting the planet from other planets that are more technically advanced than we are on earth. I feel that we need to have a top-level coordinated program to scientifically collect and analyze data from all over the earth concerning any type of encounter and to determine how best to interfere with these visitors in a friendly fashion.

Such addresses to the United Nations did not end with Cooper. On November 27th, 1978, Professor J. Allen Hynek stood before the Special Political Committee of the United Nations General Assembly. His subject was UFOs. Then on December 18th of that same year, the 87th Plenary Meeting of the United Nations General Assembly decided on a vote of 436 to 33 to recommend the establishment of a department or agency of the UN to coordinate and disseminate the result of research into UFOs and UFO-related phenomena.

Is it any wonder that several years later President Ronald Reagan would publicly comment on the need for the United States and the Soviet Union to join forces in order to repel any potential extraterrestrial invasions? In this light, one might ask the true purpose behind the "Star Wars" defense system.

During the early nineties, a hint at US preparedness finally saw the light of day, when the Federal Emergency Management Agency (FEMA) authored the following manual: *Fire Officer's Guide to Disaster Control*. This tamely titled work initially caused little notice in the public sector. At least not until it got out that the subject matter of its thirteenth chapter was entitled: "Enemy Attack and the UFO Potential."

In the final analysis, the public sector is not aware of the extent of our planetary preparedness or lack thereof. In a sense, we know all too well just how helpless we are. That the recovery of the Scout Craft Hope had been so artfully performed during not one but two extraordinary solar events only underlined our planet's defensive nakedness. Clearly "they" know where we are; but we don't know who they are, when they will next appear, from whence they come, much less their intentions.

CHAPTER IV
The Mabad al-Karnak Museum

Believe it or not three years had already passed since the discovery of the Treasury of Amen Re by the Dutch survey mission that was headed up by Professor Dr. Willem van der Boek. During that time hundreds of unique and precious cultural artifacts had been cleared out of the treasury's many chambers, catalogued, restored as needed and then shelved by the overworked restoration staff of the Cairo National Museum lead by Dr. Ahmed Rashid. To date, the "crown jewels" had been the intact and pristine recovery of a falcon glider frame, its hawk-headed helmet, all of its accessories, and even a papyrus manual. The world's media had been agog over them and the Egyptian nation's chest measurably swelled with pride. And why not? Manned glider flight had been pushed back, what, some 3200 years? Then as the magnitude of the find became apparent to all, a plea went out to all of the foreign archaeological missions in Egypt for help and again under the coordination of Dr. Rashid, tremendous progress had been made. But funding was still needed, for there did not exist in Egypt a large enough warehouse nor restoration facilities that could accommodate the copious tidal wave of artifacts as the clearance continued apace and seemingly without end. This is when the Egyptian Exploration and Preservation Organization, or EEPO for short, was founded. Dr. Sharil Moussa, director of the Cairo National Museum, had agreed to be its guiding light and under her direction a massive global funding campaign had born fruit.

*   *   *

As with so many of the ancient sites located throughout that open-air museum that is modern Egypt, tourist access to them is often quite literally carved out of the surrounding modern neighborhood. Tour buses by their very nature are ungainly vehicles, which require broad spaces to maneuver, park, and disgorge their heavily air-conditioned passengers. Consequently, local construction is sharply curtailed, sometimes even bulldozed back, to make room for these hordes. At day's end, the same passengers, now sunburned and dehydrated, require shade and refreshment and the local lemonade and soda vendors readily provide that latter need in the coin of an astonishing variety of currencies. Initially, these vendors sold their iced drinks and treats from their push carts; more enterprising individuals from chain-drive tricycles; then from temporary stands with coolers powered by a solitary extension cord. It was only a matter of "time" before that which was a temporary shack became permanent and with that natural development the local vendors were able to provide a modicum of shade and an ever greater variety of refreshments that were then greedily consumed. So having established their precarious plot by increments, it would be several years before the bulldozers would again come to demolish and again push back this naturally occurring economic encroachment. When a member of the press was asked about this continuous and on-going tidal process of ebb and flow, the mayor of Luxor merely shrugged his shoulders, gestured to the Nile, and compared it to the periodic and necessary dredging of an intrusive and troublesome sand bar.

The latest incarnation of this "urban renewal" to ensure an unabated flow of tourists was the construction of the vast concrete plaza of Mabad al-Karnak that was bounded by the tarmac of the Cornish al-Nile on the west and the Karnak Complex to the east. That this newly cleared area so very near and conveniently located next to the temple complex was subsequently requisitioned for the permanent site of the new Karnak Museum came as no surprise. In fact, at the grand unveiling of the museum's plan amid much fanfare lead one Egyptologist to actually quip that it just represented "the latest architectural extension to Karnak." And truer words could not have been spoken, for the rectangular footprint of the museum, built with EEPO funding and the support of the international community was precisely sited and oriented directly west of the short Avenue of the Sphinxes that stand before the First Pylon of the complex.

In the main completed three years after the Dutch discovery of the Treasury of Amen Re, the new museum's vast storage spaces and laboratory facilities for the restoration and preservation of the treasury's artifacts came just in the nick of time. Given the already strained temporary storage and restoration facilities that were quite literally throw up in months by the EEPO subsequent to that eye-popping discovery, the availability of the new Mabad al-Karnak Museum's resources quickly took up the slack. In fact, much of the initial material that had been sent to the Cairo National Museum, and in particular the Egyptian falcon glider and its kit, had been already placed within their environmentally controlled display cases.

As for the structure itself tasteful aesthetics ruled the day as its sloped exterior walls were cladded in fine limestone finished off with traditional Egyptian papyrus and lotus cornices, the whole set off with a monumental pylon entranceway that opened directly on the Cornish al-Nile. Even atop its flat-topped roof, a second pylon-shaped structure housed the facility's massive HVAC machinery, while the remainder of the roof's area was covered with a vast rippling sea of articulating solar panel arrays that tracked the sun's progress by day and provided seventy-five percent of the structure's day-time power, while its solar batteries supplied sixty-three percent of its night time needs. These solar arrays that were designed, constructed and donated by a renewable energy outfit out of Boulder, Colorado, were built to last and withstand the annual sand storms of the region. Was it any surprise when they were subsequently marketed by their proud manufacturer as the "Karnak Panel Array?"

As for the interior spaces of the Mabad al-Karnak Museum, not a square meter of its three stories of floor space was wasted. The central spine of its ground floor and basement, for example, was devoted to a full-sized replica of three main corridors of the Amen Re Treasury, complete with wooden bridging over the many simulated pit-traps along with their sometimes (again simulated) grisly remains. The many side chambers, however, were purposely built larger so as to provide not only sufficient room for the environmentally sealed displays, but also with a mind towards tourist flow. While the "treasury display" fully took up the basement and a goodly portion of the ground floor of the museum, the room that remained was devoted to the preservation of artifacts, their storage, laboratory facilities, administration, and of course the ubiquitous museum store and cafeteria.

*   *   *

"You know Sharil," Dr. Rashid said, "I am becoming ever more, day by day, a mere logistics manager. First we were scrambling just to get all the treasury material from Thebes to Cairo. Remember all of those armored security convoys? Now, we're doing the opposite as we ferry all the material back to Luxor for the new museum. Frankly, there are times when I wake up in the morning and do not know where I am. Then there is the administration of that godforsaken lottery that you instituted for the restoration and publication of the treasury material. That has become an absolute nightmare!"

Dr. Sharil Moussa, director of the Cairo National Museum and head of the EEPO could only ruefully smile at her adopted "uncle." His points were well taken, but she countered nonetheless.

"Uncle, would you like to trade places with me? I am juggling the management of the Cairo National Museum, the EEPO, and so many television, cable, PR and endorsement requests that I cannot count much less courteously address them all. And then there is this generous but insistent cosmetics' firm that wants me to be their lead 'marketing image.'"

"Now Sharil. You know that's not fair. And no, you know that I do not like the lime light. It's just that I am a simple chemist, a man who was trained to restore artifacts, and at best a part-time departmental administrator. I am not a master scheduler of shipments or a lottery diplomat by nature. And if the French Archaeological Mission starts crying foul yet again on their lottery assignments, assignments that are honestly arrived at, I fear that I might have resort to physical violence. Sharil, you just cannot imagine what absolutely petty children these French academics are! Their antics just make me want to scream!

"Uncle, believe me when I say this. I fully understand. But consider this. What a marvelous position we are in! We have the Japanese, Australians, Poles, Germans, Americans, Dutch, Austrians, Italians and French all vying to *help* us with the restoration, preservation and publication of the treasury's vast contents. We, the two of us above all, must persevere. And as for the French. Remember. They do have a legitimate grudge. We did after all allow that Dutch survey team to undertake under their very noses that investigation in their assigned archaeological preserve. Put simply, their problem is more one of embarrassment and loss of face than anything else. Here was this vast archaeological treasure trove quite literally beneath their feet and they were not aware of it. And how long have they been working in and around the Karnak complex? Frankly, all in all, I am a bit amazed at their present restraint."

Grudgingly agreeing with his superior, Rashid just silently nodded, but sheepishly nonetheless felt a whole lot better for having vented his frustrations.

As for Sharil Moussa, this was the first time that "Uncle Ahmed" had ever expressed such frustration. Recognizing this, the director of the Cairo National Museum and EEPO found herself internally sympathizing with him. He had been under quite a bit of strain. His entire staff was overloaded, stressed to the max, and frankly, quite frazzled by all the seemingly endless material that poured out of the Treasury of Amen Re on a daily basis. It really was a "rags to riches" situation and one that was totally unprecedented in the history of modern archaeology. Nonetheless, somehow, they just had to find a way to hold on.

*   *   *

Professor Dr. Willem van der Boek, whenever he got really excited, tended to unconsciously blur his conversational English into a German/English mix. He self consciously called it "Ginglish" and clearly this was one of those moments as he sat with the director of the Cairo National Museum in her remote office in the Mabad al-Karnak Museum in Luxor.

"Dr. Moussa, as ve near die completion of die clearing process of die treasury, I vould like to have Horst Villing und his team perform one last survey of die treasury's labyrinth. Vould dhat be agreeable with you and your vater?"

"Why certainly Professor van der Boek." Moussa replied with her Cambridge acquired English accent, "That would be perfectly fine. But what prompted you to so formerly and directly request of me such permission instead of my father?"

The retired Dutch Egyptologist first just shrugged his shoulders and then ran his hand across his balding head before he responded.

"Vell, first, I really do not know your vater dhat vell. Und perhaps it is just me, but I haf a feeling dhat die treasury has not quite revealed all of its secrets."

"What do you mean 'not revealed all of its secrets?'"

"Dr. Moussa, Sharil, again, perhaps it is just dhis old man's nervousness, but very little has been recovered vom die treasury dhat is manufactured of metal or vood. Instead, most of die manufactured material recovered up to now has been textiles, beer, furniture, und vine. Meanvile, ve haf found literally tons of bronze, silber und gold ingots und meters of cedar planks. It is like ve haf found a large manufacturing inventory for a factory. Frankly, I und my team suspect dhat yet another chamber ist yet to be found – a chamber dhat just might be filled with treasure dhat is made of such materials. As Horst likes to say, der Mutter load ist still out dhere somevhere und I haf to agree mit ihm."

*   *   *

Van der Boek's survey team, lead by Horst Willing, included Claude Assman and his digital cameras, Brigitte Claus – an epigrapher, Dieter Meier – civil engineer and surveyor, and Marta Rosen – van der Boek's most recent Ph.D. Candidate. Moments of prescient intuition had occurred several times among this bunch during the initial discovery, survey and clearing of the treasury. For them, it had almost become a commonplace, something to be expected, and now it again time for another such moment. And again it was Marta who saw through all the ancient subterfuge.

"Professor van der Boek, look at dhis." His graduate assistant began. "See how die central aisle of der main chamber along the south vall of Corridor B lines up? It also lines up mit die entrance of der main chamber as vell. To me, dhat suggests dhat something very big und heavy could be moved directly vom Corridor B to die center aisle of the main chamber. My guess is dhat die vall dhat the center aisle ends at is a false one."

Studying carefully the survey plot of the treasury van der Boek pinched in thought his lower lip between his thumb and forefinger.

"Ja, dhat is possible Marta. Certainly, it vould be simple to test. Or, have you already done so my clever one?"

Now blushing bright red, the graduate student just smiled.

"Ja, professor, there is a very, very cleverly disguised plug on dhat vall. Horst and I tested my theory yesterday afternoon und professor its dimensions match those of die main chamber's too!" She concluded with a slight hop on her toes.

Now glancing over at Horst with a sly smile van der Boek just said, "Vell, Marta, dhen vhat are you vaiting vor?"

*   *   *

The clearing of this latest plug strictly followed van der Boek's methodology that emphasized a careful awareness of one's place in archaeological history. All stood before the suspect wall in their full-faced masks with air bottles attached at the waist. Assman first photographed the virgin bare wall. Dieter and Horst stood by on hand with two wheel barrows and several hand brooms. Van der Boek made sure that the halogen lamps were correctly placed and out of the way.

"Okay Marta," the Dutch archaeologist called out through his mask, "make that famous first swing of yours!"

And with that said Marta swung her pick into the wall with a crash that resulted in an explosion of flying plaster. Standing back and admiring her handy work, van der Boek pronounced excitedly. "You know Marta, I dhink dhat you haf been verking out too much! Just look at the dhent dhat you haf made in dhat vall!"

And truly, it was a dent as the rubble material that had backed the plaster had given way exposing a small black hole. The event was immediately captured by Assman with three bracketed shots.

Now offering his own hand pick to Marta the archaeologist seriously said. "Now Marta, enough total destruction. Now clear dhat passage very carefully and the vay dhat I know you can."

And so the laborious teasing process began as Marta began to chip, pry, and cajole away the rest of the blocking material.

Chapter V
Palo Verde

It had been too long since the young man had visited his mom and dad, far too long he re-reminded himself. While emails and phone calls had flown fast and furious between the pair and their sole child, it had been fully a year and three-quarters since Richards had last seen them, John and Irene, face-to-face.

And that encounter had been a very strained one indeed, as the young man had "practically disappeared off the face of the earth," as his mom had so directly put it. During that long weekend, explanations were furiously invented as to why he had suddenly dropped out of football and the university. Why hadn't he regularly called or even written. What was he up to?

Now to their absolute astonishment, here he was a college professor in Egyptian philology of all things. Lands sake! It all just didn't make any sense and they were absolutely right. But in the end, he was what he was, a well-paid and quartered academic at a prestigious university. While his mother's initial ire eventually abated and transformed into brimming pride, "My son the university professor," his father's quiet and unspoken curiosity remained. Yes, he was surprised and pleased with his son's good fortune. Granted he was plenty confused about it and was just as pleased at his son's incredible accomplishment, but from a far different point of view than his beloved wife's.

As a retired United States Air Force captain, he had seen his fair share of government bureaucracy, ninety-day wonders, bullshit artists, and plain, flat liars. He had also seen firsthand what the military could really do if it wanted to, how rules and regulations could be ignored or thrown to the wind in times of expediency. Good things occasionally happened when America's brightest and bravest were put on the line. And most importantly, he knew the look, for he immediately recognized it in his son's eyes. There reflecting back at him was an extremely knowledgeable confidence that he remembered having seen only a handful of times during his long career. And that made him smile. His son had arrived. But John still heard his inner voice protest.

But at what cost?

Richards, now painted into a corner by his sense of nagging guilt, fully acknowledged and swallowed back the growing evidence of their mortal fragility. It was a fact difficult to deal with, but a reality nonetheless, in truth a natural constant that he had already dealt with once in the recent past and once again in a far more distant one. In both instances, they had elicited emotional floods. Such experiences Richards hoped would strengthen him for his own kin, when their time came.

Besides, the Thanksgiving holiday was coming up and mom made dynamite turkey dinners. Just the thought of her sausage and onion stuffing, the green peas, biscuits, and pineapple and cabbage salad made his mouth water. So without any further thought, Associate Professor Joseph Richards booked a flight from chilly and cloudy Chicago to warm and sunny Phoenix. It hadn't been a hard sell.

*   *   *

The flight in coach had been as blessedly uneventful as was the meagerness of the so-called snack. Having found his rental car in the cool shade of a sun awning in the second aisle, Richards absentmindedly scanned the proffered map while the air conditioning kicked in. Having checked out, he drove west on Interstate 10 towards his folk's home. Home: what an odd bunch of feelings welled up with that word! Home had been in New Jersey – although I was too young to remember that one. Then there were all those tours in Japan, Hawaii, Saudi

Arabia, Germany, Egypt, and now Palo Verde, that quiet little community conveniently located near Luke Air Force Base.

Yep! I'm a born and bred zoomie brat all right!

Turning south off of the interstate, his journey-starved stomach loudly growled and so the young Egyptologist stopped to temporarily fill it at a conveniently located hamburger joint.

Finding the homestead was not a problem. In fact as he was pulling onto the stark glare of the long concrete driveway flanked by neatly raked light pink gravels and desert-bred greenery, the garage door began to rise. As it did, a pair of sneakers and strong legs clad in khaki shorts began to appear. Dad was dressed in a rakish and faded Hawaiian shirt that wasn't tucked in. His dad just stood there, with his hands on his hips, grinning ear to ear.

Extending his hand, the former Air Force officer soberly stated for the record.

"Welcome home son."

"It's good to be home, Dad."

Ignoring the proffered hand, Richards instead bear-hugged him.

"Whoa boy! Save some of those bones for my chiropractor! Jesus you've gotten strong!"

"Yeah, that's just part of the program. Know what? I got my snow cones!"

"Son, you mean as in jump wings?"

"Yep!"

"Now since when does an Egyptologist need to jump out of an airplane?"

Blushing at the obvious nature of his father's question, Richards began back peddling.

"Well, Dad, surely not that often." He stated with a grin.

"Ah ha, I just knew it." John said with a certain amount of triumph in his voice.

"Knew what?" A now frowning Richards responded.

"That you went black, like deep black. Why else would you have dropped out of sight for so long without contacting us? It's the only answer." His dad stated with finality.

"Does mom know about your assessment?"

"Nope."

"It had better stay that way. I don't want her worrying unnecessarily."

"Understood and I totally agree. But since you know that I know. Can you talk about it?"

"Later, perhaps later tonight after mom goes to bed. Besides, isn't that her fried chicken that I smell?"

Then, as if on cue, the young man's stomach sounded loudly and with a fatherly slap on the back the laughter began.

Side-by-side, arm-in-arm, and thick as thieves the pair entered the garage enroute to the screened kitchen door. Then John stopped by the spare refrigerator and said.

"Gad Joey, where's my manners? You want a beer?"

"Duh, what's that?"

"Yeah, I thought so." His dad deadpanned. "By that look I can tell that you'll be in need of several!"

*   *   *

True to form, mom's fried chicken dinner had been as advertised – simply great and the table conversation had been ever better, if not gushing due to some carefully applied lubrication. While John and Joey began creating a small forest of extruded aluminum between the two of them, Irene had already polished off on her own almost two-thirds of a bottle of a red Australian Shiraz. The blush on her face had become rather obvious.

Richards noted the ancient tactic of fine food and plentiful libations, but chose to ignore who had employed it and why.

Well, he reasoned. It's about time that they found out anyways. And given dad's background, they're secure.

After the table had been cleared and dishes done, dried, and put away by the boys, a standing family rule since mom was the one who had cooked, the trio retired to the rustic, sunken great room. While mom plopped herself down with yet another glass of red wine in her favorite Early American comfy chair padded with blue and red calico fabric, Joey started a mesquite wood fire in the large field stone hearth. It wasn't long before a roaring fire partially brightened the room, smoke filled the chimney, and its aroma began to waft back in through the open screens.

"You know Joey," Irene smirked. "I suspect that there is a pyromaniac gene that you and your father share."

Coming into the room at that moment with two fresh Silver Bullets, John heard just enough to come to his son's defense.

"I heard that!" John barked with no bite. Handing over a beer to his son he then shifted gears, as he straddled his favorite foot stool.

"Well Joey. Now that your gut is filled with mom's best and half a case of Colorado's finest, what can you tell us about what you've been up to?"

"Now John!" Irene snapped. "You know that Joey will tell us what he can, when he can, in his own time."

Richards had heard this well-rehearsed routine before: the post-mortem of his first high school prom; the night that he had turned up missing on a school ski trip, because he had fallen fast asleep on the floor of the bus; the morning after his first roaring drunk; the list was a long one. But he had learned that if he came clean, after having been caught lying just once, then all was forgiven – even if the "just talk" session was oftentimes more brutally painful than any form of physical chastisement. Richards reckoned that it was his parents' relentless emphasis on personal responsibility, accountability to the law of unintended consequences, and the pursuit of doing what's right that always shamed him into toeing-the-line.

Sitting now with the warmth of the fire at his back and looking down at the golden richness of the pegged pinewood plank flooring, Richards inwardly smiled at his parents pent up curiosity and thought. Well, here we go!

The young man quietly stated in preamble.

"Okay guys, here's the deal. What I am about to tell you, no less than three sovereign governments and God knows how many agencies will throw me in the slammer for sharing, so if you even think a word of this outside of this room, don't."

By their collective looks and a telling glance shared between them, Richards knew that he had their undivided attention and so he continued while counting off his points on his fingers.

"First, those governments are: the United States, the Russian Federal Republic, and the Republic of Egypt. Some of the players include a very black and scary Army security group and an oddly-named entity called the Philology Annex. It turns out that the Annex is a front organization with lots of clout and very deep pockets funded by our government, but by which department or departments I do not know. Then there are all the scientific and technical geeks out at Wright-Patterson. Recently, I have even learned that NASA is also part of the picture.

"Okay, so where do you want me to begin?"

"Well," a wide-eyed and much impressed Irene began. "Why don't you start with how you became a university professor?"

CHAPTER VI
The Annex Papyrus

Never before in the annals of modern Egyptology had such a well preserved papyrus been recovered, much less so digitally recorded; so thoroughly examined in the infrared spectrum, and then fixed in such a pristine state. It was said – and perhaps with too much imagination – that even the document's vegetative fibers still breathed through its museum-grade glass an aroma akin to that of freshly cut hay.

The artifact in question, the Annex Papyrus, measured 13.7 meters in length – almost forty five feet. While certainly not the longest of record, it nonetheless told a most interesting story in its sixty four columns of neatly and immaculately brushed hieratic text. The document recounted the tale of a meandering traveler's journey through the heavens, complete with coordinates, time hacks, and thumbnail descriptions of all those places that had been visited. The account's author was an ancient Egyptian, a pharaoh no less, who wrote with his left hand and lived during the late Eighteenth Dynasty. In other words, the papyrus was authored some 3,250 years before the flight of the Kitty Hawk.

Needless to say, neither the papyrus nor its contents ever saw the light of day as it was immediately placed under a security embargo mandated by the scientific communities of no less than three nations: the Russian Republic, the United States, and Republic of Egypt, the latter which jealously protected the artifact and rightly so. The level of secrecy apportioned to this document allowed for only a very select few to even know of the papyrus' existence, much less be privy to its eye-popping contents.

Discovered only three years before, the Annex Papyrus was so named, because it had been found within a chamber of an artificially constructed cavern secreted in the mountains east of the modern Egyptian village of El-Amarna. When it was discovered, the papyrus lay in a tight roll neatly bound with three colored cords of linen yarn, housed within its own exquisitely carved cedar wood chest.

This cavern, referred to by its own inscriptions as the Abode of the Aten, was itself an aircraft hanger of sorts for a most remarkable flying artifice. In fact, the device was held in such regard that its original owners even came to retrieve it during the memorable worldwide Black Out. Again only a select few knew that that spectacular event itself was no accident of nature's fickle hand. Instead it had been part of a rather elaborate ruse, which had covered that bold extraterrestrial recovery of something lost, or perhaps better, something misappropriated.

To return to the document itself, the Annex Papyrus required careful study. To that end, the production of an authoritative translation – complete with literary, technical, and scientific commentaries and full facsimile work up, would task the energies of an interdisciplinary staff of compartmentalized scholars and scientists one and a half years to complete and consume over three days of computer processing time.

Naturally, few on the globe were qualified to decipher the document's neat hieratic text and even fewer were cleared to do so. Consequently, Dr. Sharil Moussa of the Egyptian Antiquities Organization – herself an expert in Egyptian hieratic, led that challenge with an American, Dr. John Milson, as her sole collaborator. Initially, Moussa had taken the lead as was logical, but as time went on and as her responsibilities elsewhere began to mount, the translation became more and more a shared burden. And in the end, it was Milson's near-encyclopedic memory, long time membership and intimate familiarity with the Philology Annex, and uncanny feel for the ancient Egyptian's language that got this truly gifted pair over the top. On the technical side the Americans generously loaned two imaginative encryption experts and three programmers from a nonexistent organization based in Langley, Virginia. For all matters astronomical, a scholar from the Russian Academy of Science, Dr. Petr Dvorak, provided all the necessary insights.

To assist in this analysis, another secretive American institution gladly offered its vast computing farm that it jealously housed in its "basement." In all some seventy-two hours, four minutes, and thirteen seconds represents a formidable amount of time when subjected to so much silicon horsepower. Yet, it was required in order to first decode and then extrapolate upon all the interstellar coordinates listed within the document, while simultaneously balancing and juggling the constant movement of the entire Milky Way Galaxy in four dimensions. Tens of variables were involved. Needless to say, some very imaginative programming was required to perform the task. The bottom line was a computational achievement – the successful plot, over time, of the breadcrumb trail of the wanderer's journey, whose place of origin was reckoned at being within a star system near our galaxy's core. As to how long he, she, or it had been on this galactic sojourn, no one could directly calculate. Nor did anyone even bother, for the duration of time was simply unimaginable in relativistic much less Earth-bound biological terms. One learned estimate, however, did reckon the duration in the thousands of years.

* * *

In all, twelve thick hardbound copies of the papyrus' translation and its many appendices were authorized for production on heavy museum-grade acid-free paper, but rarely did any of them ever see the light of day. Instead, the secure darkness of a nation's vault or security locker was the more likely prospect. But one location did possess a copy that was read, reread, and studied quite a bit by two scholars, who deservedly possessed that rarely granted "need to know." As a consequence, this particular manuscript's page corners had long since lost their crispness, having become curled, soft, and slightly frayed from constant page turning. Also, many of its pages were adorned with carefully penciled in marginalia. That such scrawled notations might be perceived by some as some sort of desecration, fear not. It's quite the usual among specialists and scholars, all the more so since these two were experts in the field as well.

Now hovering over two photographic facsimiles – one black and white and the other color of the papyrus' first column of Egyptian hieratic text, the huddled pair pointed, poked, and prodded at a cluster of its seemingly inscrutable, but beautifully written and flowing characters.

"Sharil," Milson mused, "the author of this papyrus, while composing his complex thoughts in a clearly borrowed tongue and hampered by its nontechnical vocabulary, had quite a capacity to get his message across. Still and all, he seemed to be especially fond of this rather colorful and intriguing phase: 'the subtle traces left by the seeds of the Old Ones.'"

Now pinching his lower lip in thought the white-haired emeritus professor of Egyptian philology continued a moment later.

"You know, I must admit to being a bit of a science fiction buff and this phrase sounds very much like any number of hack-kneed sci-fi plots that I have come across over the years. But coming as it does in this context, to actually read those words from a papyrus over 3,200 years old! Well, it just sends goose bumps all up and down my spine."

"I share your feelings John." The middle aged, but quite attractive Egyptian whispered.

"Well, then I suppose," The American continued, "it just might be well worth doing a search and follow up analysis of all of the instances in which this phrase appears. That might give us a better sense of what the author was referring to given the confined universe of the ancient Egyptian's vocabulary."

"That's a wonderful idea, John. I will start one immediately."

With an unconscious flick of her still raven black hair the Director of the Cairo National Museum and the papyrus' principal translator loaded a laser disk of the document's text into her laptop. After entering several commands and keystrokes, moments later, the curious couple had their answer. Fifty-six instances of the phrase with two close equivalents appeared in the editorial pop up window.

"My word!" The wide-eyed octogenarian Egyptologist gasped. "Akhenaten does seem to have been a bit obsessed."

"John, I do believe that we have really stumbled upon something." Dr. Sharil Moussa nodded in firm confirmation. "I am going to do a crosscheck on their contexts right now and then I'll print them out."

Pausing for a moment and again pinching his lower lip the American added. "Good, good. But before you do, I want to let you in on a little something that no one else knows about – save one."

"What's that?" Sharil asked with raised eyebrows while peering over her tortoiseshell reading glasses.

"It involves my colleague Joseph Richards."

"And what about Joey?" She said with an impish look on her face. "And come to think of it John, why am I not surprised?"

"Well, as you know, he does not have security access to this material. Nonetheless, about a year ago he shared with me in confidence some interesting speculations that he had come across. It's all about the god Ptah, some cognate and near cognate words, and the contents of the 'The Memphite Theology.'"

"So? What's the connection?"

"Well, it's difficult to say, but considering the text and context of the first two columns of the Annex Papyrus, there could be a lot. Because the author clearly states here that he is searching for "the great household of the Old Ones" and by following 'the subtle traces left by the seeds of the Old Ones' he hopes to find their ultimate source. In describing that ultimate source, I believe he used the Egyptian illusion of 'the first primeval mound of Atum.'"

Quickly paging back to the first column of translated text Sharil quickly confirmed.

"You're right John. But what does all of this have to do with Joey?"

"Well, Joseph believes that he has found a code to a long hidden truth. It has to do with the grammatical construction of the name Ptah and several of its many cognates. What he noted was that the god's name held two meanings: one phonemic and the other ideographic."

The Egyptian's brow furrowed in question and some confusion after the man had finished writing out the three constituent glyphs that made up Ptah's name.

"Now John, just what am I looking for? What's Joey's point?"

"Now Sharil! Shame on you! I think that you have been working with hieratic for far too long. Think simple, basic Egyptian grammar. Think ideographic and not phonemic."

After several moments Sharil exclaimed.

"John you got to be kidding!"

"Nope, not at all.

"Now let's return to the Annex Papyrus. I wouldn't be a bit surprised if the alien Akhenaten had himself been in search of such evidence, of the kind that Joseph has found, for the 'subtle traces left by the seeds of the Old Ones.'"

"Well, are you going to tell Joey about this possible linkage?"

"No, not yet. In fact, as much as I want to, I can't. He isn't cleared on this material as yet. Besides, I told him to bide his time and develop as much evidence as he could on his own. I said this not so much to hinder the lad, but rather to see just what other evidence that he might come up with. And knowing Joseph, he will find more, present it logically, will lobby for a temporal insertion, and that means that we'll again need the good will of the Egyptian Antiquities Organization."

Smiling like a Cheshire cat who had just ate the canary, the Director of the Cairo National Museum said.

"That was some sell John." She chided. "But don't you worry. My father and I will gladly assist your Joseph in any way we can, but what of the others? Especially the Russians? What will they think? And wouldn't they want a piece of the action as well?"

With a furrowed brow and a curt nod Milson allowed.

"Please accept my thanks for your and your father's unqualified support. But as always, Sharil, you have seen a wrinkle that I had not fully considered. And you're right as always. There is indeed much to think about when considering how to enlist our allies."

Despite how crazy Richards' theory seemed to be at the time, Milson had nonetheless seriously entertained it and just now for the first time shared it, for the young man's argument had been extremely compelling. At that time, some twelve months ago and before the final translation of the Annex Papyrus had been completed, he remembered with some relief how he had wisely counseled his young charge to hold his thoughts and beliefs closely to the vest. How he had encouraged Richards to pursue the issue quietly in order to build and strengthen his case. But as Milson sat with Sharil with the Annex Papyrus' translation before them, Milson now knew beyond a shadow of a doubt that his young colleague was really onto something very, very big.

*   *   *

The following is an excerpt from the Annex Papyrus.

CHILDREN OF PTAH

Column 1

Line 1: I am the first traveler of my people and joined [1] rudder man [pilot] of my celestial bark [space craft], the shining Aten [disk], The Hopeful One.

---

[1] Given the independent preliminary analysis of the Aten spacecraft, "joined" or more properly "becomes as one" could well refer to the observed organic remains that appeared to interface the pilot directly with the Aten spacecraft's internal workings.

Line 2: [I the first traveler] am a member of my people's surveyor priesthood. [2]

---

[2] Strictly speaking this is not a religious institution; more likely this is a referential illusion to a community, guild, organization, or ministry of survey. Clearly this "surveyor priesthood" has taken our current notion of the galactic habitation zone (GHZ) to a much higher level than just speculation as to what regions might be promising for "the biological evolution of complex multi-cellular life," as their technology allows the dispatch of "surveyors," a far cry from the terrestrial planet-hunting missions of Darwin and the Terrestrial Planet Finder (TPF), both of which are still in the planning stage.

Line 3: [I the first traveler] am bound to my many *kas* [doubles] within the scribal priesthood, who tirelessly record my journeys. [3]

---

[3] Again, strictly speaking, this is not a reference to religious institution, but rather a reflection of the Egyptian language and its culture. Current speculation is that all "surveyor" communications are "bound" to a record keeping organization on their home world. If correct, then this suggests layers of organizational dependencies not unlike those of NASA or the ESA.

Line 4: [I the first traveler] have traversed myriads upon myriads of stars in search of that most sacred and excellent of place whence all life first sprang forth.

Line 5: [I the first traveler] dare to seek the great house (?) of the Old Ones. [4]

---

[4] "Great house" or "*pr*" in Egyptian signified the royal palace and by logical association the king. It is also the basis for the modern word

"pharaoh." In this context, however, the word's usage seems to indicate a point of origin or source.

Line 6: [I the first traveler], [who] like a bee who seeks its hive, yearn to find that first primeval mound of Atum.[5]

---

[5] This is an allegorical reference taken from Egyptian myth concerning the world's creation as the first mound that appeared above the waters of chaos. In this context, however, this appears to be an allusion back to the first origin of life in the galaxy, the "great house of the Old Ones."

Line 7: [I the first traveler] have found during my many sojourns and in many places the subtle traces left by the seeds of the Old Ones.

Line 8: [I the first traveler] now know that this most sublime of places cannot be found here amidst the land of *Kemet* [Egypt], but [rather] [elsewhere?] among the vast and bejeweled sky, even though the subtle traces left by the seeds of the Old Ones are in truth here present and are obvious to my eyes.

Line 9: [I the first traveler] have written down this account [in order to] instruct those who will come after, so that they may know and better understand their station within a celestial kingdom [realm?], which is so vast that its understanding is as ignorant [incomprehensible?] as the bellow of a hippopotamus or the bray of a donkey at Re's first appearance. [6]

---

[6] So ends what is clearly this document's introduction. Thereafter, this document's structure and organization is that of a descriptive travel itinerary or diary with the following internal elements: distance traveled, time traveled, speed, and descriptive narrative.

Column 2

Line 1: "1 sand grain, 4 sand dunes, 7 locusts, 10 great millions,[1] 2 hundred thousands, 3 ten thousands, 7 thousand rivers.[2]

---

[1] "Sand grains," "sand dunes," "locusts," and "great million" are not conventional ancient Egyptian ciphers; rather, they seem to be both the invention and convention of the author for expressing numerical values greater than the Egyptian language could accommodate. Since the ancient Egyptians employed a decimal system of counting, it is here assumed that these new ciphers are also decimal in their position.

Consequently, their meaning should be: a "great million" = tens of millions, a "locust" = hundreds of millions, "sand dunes" = billions, and a "sand grains" = tens of billions.

(2) Given the above assumptions, this string is understood as 14,710,237,000 rivers, where 1 "river" equals 20,000 Egyptian cubits = 6.52 miles (hereafter m) = 10.5 kilometers (hereafter km). This notation then has been interpreted as a distance measurement, 304,710,237,000 rivers = 95,910,745,240 m or 154,457,488,500 km. This first distance hack, therefore, would indicate the surveyor's first location that it stopped at, one that was perhaps located in the vicinity of his home world.

Line 2: 1st season, 1st month, 12th day, 8 hours.(3)

---

(3) The ancient Egyptians divided their year into three seasons, each composed of four months that numbered thirty days each. This time stamp then could be understood as a shipboard, relativistic transit of 12 days and eight hours. Given the above mentioned distance, that would yield an average rate of 324,022,787.97 miles per hour (hereafter mph) or 521,815,839.53 kilometers an hour (hereafter kph), or about 0.463 the speed of light (hereafter C).

Line 3: As a yearling, my scribal masters [mentors?] had warned me to carefully guard my senses [emotions?] as they [too] excited my first *ka* [double] of the scribal priesthood.

Line 4: [As a yearling] still, [even] now, I am [the] same as during my first sojourn into that great wilderness amidst the gods. (4)

---

(4) This clause is a parenthetical construction and consequently constitutes an aside or break in the natural flow of the narration.

Line 5: [As a yearling] I became one with my Aten [disk] and dared to name it The Hopeful One. Many among my priesthood thought ill of this choice for my celestial bark [spacecraft], for its meaning suggested that [I] sought only selfishly for the subtle traces of the seeds of the Old Ones and not for the good of my household.

Line 6: [As a yearling] my surveyor priesthood received a message of great interest from a distant place that caused much excitement.

Line 7: [As a yearling I] was sent as my priesthood's first ambassador to answer it. After much traveling[5] [I] arrived at the appointed place.

---

[5] First reference to space travel. It, like all other such allusions that appear throughout the text, remains vague in terms of absolute distance and time. The reasons for this gloss on the part of the author are perhaps many, but the most logical explanation is a relativistic one. "After much traveling," at least in this case, refers back to the distance and time hacks of Lines 1 and 2.

Line 8: My senses [emotions?] were high in anticipation that this place was the great house of the most Old Ones.

Line 9: With much disappointment, [I] found this not to be true.

Line 10: [As a yearling, I] found [instead] a vast expanse of rock and sand all scattered throughout the sky lacking any breath of life. [6]

---

[6] This description suggests that the region described is composed of cloud debris, perhaps comparable to that of either the Eagle or Crab Nebulae.

Line 11: It was as if Apophis[7] himself had vented all of his fury upon these lands.[8]

---

[7] Apophis, the incarnation of pure and malevolent evil that inhabits the Egyptian underworld as a gigantic, flint-scaled serpent that spits fire.

[8] Strictly speaking "lands" is not meant here; rather, reference is made about an entire world or an entire star system that had come to its end.

Line 12: [As a yearling, I] now began my long search for the great house of the Old Ones."

Column 3

Line 1: "1 sand grains, 7 sand dunes, 1 locust, 70 great millions, 8 millions, 4 hundred thousands, 4 ten thousands, 6 thousand rivers.[1]

---

[1] 17,178,446,000 rivers = 112,003,467,920 m or 180,373,683, 000 km. Distance between the former and current coordinates has been

estimated at 21 light years +/- 3 due to gravitational shift and galactic rotation.

Line 2: 1st season, 1st month, 23rd day, 5th hour. [2]

---

[2] This time stamp suggests a relativistic transit of 23 days and five hours from the previous destination mentioned above in Column 2, Line 2. This would yield an average rate of 201,083,425.35 mph = 323,830,669.66 kph or about 0.29 C.

Line 3: After my first *heb-sed* transformation,[3] again my *ka* of the scribal priesthood informed me of another message that had caused much excitement among our priesthoods.[4]

---

[3] Strictly speaking, the *heb-sed* ritual of renewal was a pharaonic rite of magical rejuvenation, which usually occurred in regular cycles to ensure the strength of the king and the fertility of the land. Its usage here, therefore, must be allegorical. Apparently, the author, an organic life form of some type, experienced a biological threshold or stage of development at this time. A molting perhaps?

[4] Based upon subsequent internal evidence, the use of the term "*ka*," the Egyptian expression for an individual's "second self," again is allegorical in meaning. Apparently, the author was in communication with his "double" on his home world.

Line 4: Forthwith my *ka* bid me to hasten on my way.

Line 5: After much traveling, [I] arrived at the appointed place.

Line 6: [I] found a land made [up of] six dung balls created by the divine industry of Kheper Re[5] (all) tethered to two glorious and shining Aten's [disks] – one great red [one], one small blue [one].[6]

---

[5] This is a clever allegorical illusion to six planets with organic life. As for Kheper Re, the Egyptians believed that this dung beetle-headed god caused the movement of the sun across the heavens just as a dung beetle rolls its dung balls across the ground.

[6] This description is of a dual star system composed of a red giant and blue dwarf. The existence of such systems has been independently confirmed and observed via the Hubble Space Telescope.

Line 7: [I] listened carefully upon my arrival, but my ears were greeted only with the silence of the tomb.

Line 8: [I] traveled to each of the six dung balls and again discovered windblown wastelands bereft of any trace of life.

Line 9: [I] recorded for my *ka* that which [I] found built upon the fourth dung ball, being handsomely made of vast and endless terraces of stone. [7]

---

[7] So is recorded the author's first descriptive encounter with the remains of a civilization not of its own.

Line 10: [I] grieved mightily at their loss so great was their industry.

Line 11: [I] dutifully recorded all that [I] could find for my *ka* and his scribal priesthood.

Column 4

Line 1: [Nonetheless, I] searched on for any trace of the Old Ones and found none.

Line 2: My heart became heavy with sadness.

Line 3: [And] so unbidden [I] left that accursed and desolate place. [I] began my own search for another before it too had come to such an end.

Line 4: [I] told my *ka* of my plan to find life before, like a oil lamp, it extinguished itself and was at first rebuked as it was not thought seemly for a surveyor to go hither and thither without reason [mission?].

Line 5: [Nonetheless, I] began much traveling.

Line 6: My first *ka* of the scribal priesthood became speechless. [1]

---

[1] This statement seems to indicate that the author was cut off from all communications with home world.

Line 7: Never before had [I] been so alone within such a vast and deserted place. It became a time of much reflection and independent thought.

Line 8: After much traveling, my second *ka* of the scribal priesthood sent me a message that brought much joy to my heart.

Line 9: The surveyor priesthood and scribal priesthood had agreed to free me of their bonds.[2]

---

[2] With this fascinating statement, apparently some sort of rapprochement had been reached between these two factions of the author's home world. On the basis of the narrative's internal evidence, formerly surveyors went "hither and thither" only with permission and with a specific mission profile in mind. The author's independently-minded (rebellious?) attitude had seemingly made an impression upon the two priesthoods enough to make them reconsider their working relationship.

Line 10: [I] again was with speech.

Line 11: [I] again could share that which my eyes could perceive.

Line 12: [I] was whole again.

Line 13: My heart soared like Horus rising on the warm breath of Re."[3]

---

[3] Another allegorical reference, but this time it is to the god Horus and his animal namesake the falcon, which can be so often seen soaring upon thermals above the Egyptian Desert.

Column 5

Line 1: "1 star,[1] 50 sand grains, 2 sand dunes, 60 great millions, 9 millions, 1 hundred thousands, 2 ten thousands, and 9 thousands.[2]

---

[1] Another invented cipher of the author. "Star" seems here to indicate a number in the hundreds of billions.

[2] 152,069,129,000 rivers = 991,490,721,080 m or 1,596,725, 854,500 km. This is a location of an unnamed star system. The distance between the former and current coordinates has been estimated at 52 light years +/- 3 due to gravitational shift and galactic rotation. Without question, the author's chosen course was decidedly outbound from the galactic core on this leg, while the two prior visitations had remained nearer to the core's outer edges.

Line 2: 2nd season, 3rd month, 6th day, 4th hour.[3]

⁽³⁾ This relativistic time stamp is for a transit of 186 days and four hours from the previous destination. This would yield an average rate of 221,909,292.99 mph = 357369260.18 kph, or about 0.32 C.

Line 3: After much traveling [I] encountered cloudy and obscure [?] lands made up of many young and shining Atens [suns]. ⁽⁴⁾

⁽⁴⁾ This vivid description can be that of a galaxy in formation, similar to the many examples recorded by the Hubble Space Telescope.

Line 4: [I] found within this region a sight wondrous as if Khnum [himself] was fashioning lands upon his potter's wheel. ⁽⁵⁾

⁽⁵⁾ This is another allegorical reference, but this time to the god Khnum in his guise as creator. The grammatical opposition of "Atens" to "lands" suggests that the "fashioning" taking place is of planetary bodies.

Line 5: As [I] gazed about the ferment my senses told me that many elements of life were present [around].

Line 6: My heart again soared on the wings of Horus!

Line 7: [I] began to make a record of everything that my senses perceived so that such wonders [I] could share with the scribal priesthood. ⁽⁶⁾

⁽⁶⁾ The use of the Egyptian physiological word for "senses" most likely refers to the Aten space craft's battery of observational and recording sensors.

Line 8: After a brief time [I] came to understand that this land was as young and fresh as a panting and still bloodied newborn infant.

Line 9: [I] came to understand that the Old Ones had not passed along this river course.

Line 10: For the first time [I] came to understand that my purpose was far greater than [just] the stubborn [?] search for the Old Ones.

Column 6

Line 1: [I] came to understand that my greater purpose was to be the senses for the scribal priesthood for all things new and never before witnessed.

Line 2: This greater purpose struck [stunned?] as a revelation that [I] shared with my scribal *ka*.

Line 3: My scribal *ka* was overjoyed and encouraged me to describe all things that [I] deemed noteworthy.

Line 4: [And] so [I] began the reckoning lists of things. Things large, things small.

Line 5: From these reckoning lists [I] began to see forms and likenesses. [1]

---

[1] The meaning of this statement seems to be "[I] began to see patterns and trends."

Line 6: [From these reckoning lists, I] began to foresee that which had yet to become.

Line 7: [From these reckoning lists, I] began to build a way of assessing the way of things, what should rightly follow, and what should not rightly follow, in the natural way of things. [2]

---

[2] This statement expresses the development of a quantitative and qualitative rating or ranking system for observations made. It may seem odd that such an empirical approach was developed while in transit, but it also reflects the marked shift in the surveyor's mission profile.

Line 8: These things [reckoning lists], [I] shared with my scribal *ka*, who in turn shared them among the scribal priesthood.

Line 9: As a consequence of these sharing's, the surveyor and scribal priesthoods agreed upon a common way of understanding between the priesthoods, a way that [I] with greater ease could speak of new things with a clearness of thought that would not be mistaken. [3]

---

[3] As remarkable as it may seem, a standardized rating system for observational data seems to have been initiated by the author, discussed by the two priesthoods on home world, and only then *ex post facto* established.

Line 10: [And] to my great joy, my priesthood [as a consequence] sent forth another surveyor to explore the Great Green." [4]

---

[4] The deployment of a second surveyor is an interesting detail. Apparently, the author's priesthood and/or the scribal priesthood decided that he had not become an unmanageable asset after all and so decided to deploy a second "surveyor." Whether this second surveyor was subject to the former mission profile or not remains a matter of conjecture. "Great Green" – an illusion to the Mediterranean Sea, which to the ancient Egyptian mind was synonymous with a vast and nearly unimaginable expanse. In short, here it is used as a fitting expression for deep space.

CHAPTER VII
Musical Chairs

Once an established institution has managed to successfully last far beyond its avowed purpose, it has also by that time generated a sort of inertial mass that is diametrically opposed to any proposed flexibility or need for change. At this point the well-known mantra, "if it isn't broke, why fix it," takes over. The planned and reasoned replacement of those who are themselves considered indispensible institutions rarely if ever occur prior to their retirement. That which is well-known and familiar, even if over time it has become less than ideal, remains nonetheless a marginally useful resource when placed within a well-recognized environmental context, as in a "good old boy" or "most reliable comrade." So with people change is always hard to initiate; and so it was with a select fellowship within the scientific leadership of the Russian Federation of States.

The cleansing reorganization of that leadership clique, quite literally the "out with the old and in with the new," occurred remarkably during just one brief weekend. Equally remarkable, was the total lack of bloodshed. In many respects, this velvet power shift was initiated as the result of leveraged technology, or rather perhaps better said, the lack of it. Consider for the moment the current technological marvel known as the wireless smart phone. It, and its many clones, is ubiquitous among the under-forty generation, where instantaneous communication is an addictive drug, where thumb ligament pain has replaced the carpel tunnel syndrome. It should be noted here that dinosaurs have no thumbs.

Already well into their fourth decade of leadership, Karlov Drazinzka, the Head of the Special Projects Directorate, and Vasily Alexandrovich Ostrogorsky, the Director of Theoretical Biology, both of the Russian Ministry of Science, were fast becoming endangered species. To them letters, faxes, landlines, and desktop computers were *de rigueur*, while the novelty of a trans-Atlantic video conference was an understood event it nonetheless was considered highly invasive and so was held in dark suspicion. Add to this, that near-instantaneous translation software developed by the United States Air Force, Language Guru 3.1, which could detect a conversation's context and then match to it an appropriate linguistic idiom, was considered outright black magic. And things that were black magic were things not to be trusted, and distrust leads to paranoia.

Enter Stefan Rosovec, the newly minted Director of Advanced and Theoretical Technological Research for the Russian Academy of Sciences. Clearly, he was the new kid on the block. Just as clearly, Rosovec represented a vast generational gap, better leap, where photocopy machines and highlighters, brick phones, CRT screens, and desk top computers were considered already "old technologies."

Within the hierarchy of the Russian Academy of Sciences the real movers and shakers were three individuals: Drazinzka, Ostrogorsky, and Rosovec. While indeed Rosovec was part of this "Scipionic Circle," and while he was not usually made privy to the inner machinations of his august colleagues, their hidden plans, their true agenda, Rosovec knew from the start that he had time on his side.

After all, the relative youngster mused. "It is just a matter of opportunity."

As things usually work out, and if you are really patient, opportunities do indeed present themselves and just as often they appear in unneeded bunches. But before such opportunities can be usefully taken advantage of, careful preparation and almost arachnidian planning are required. For Rosovec, this meant finding two appropriately qualified candidates, who would replace the two dinosaurs. This also meant stretching beyond his usual social circle of collegial acquaintances, expanding his sources in the Theoretical

Biology and Special Projects Directorates, and reaching out in some more indirect ways. But by far the most ticklish part of his internal coup would be arranging just the right situation, just the right set of circumstances, which would cause the needed cascade that would lead to the inevitable.

In all, he had to review just a handful of dossiers, for Rosovec knew precisely what he was looking for: stable, bright, intellectually flexible, self-made men of his generation, much like himself. With family ties in place Stefan reckoned several factors that he could depend upon. Given the second place environment of the young Russian Federation, he wanted those who had traveled abroad on academic research scholarships, earned in the coin of pure intellectual competition. Personally, he preferred those who had gone to Germany, that marvelous marketplace of scientific heritage and nearly neutral crossroads of East and West, where scholars the world over met, worked, made lifelong friendships and contacts, and intellectually thrived. Finally, none of his candidates were the offspring of the former regime with its besotted party bosses and dulled and pampered aristocracy. Rosovec not only saw world socialism as a failure, but a cannibalistic one at that. He wanted men who could say to his face an unqualified "no" in one breath and in the very next present a viable alternative. He was looking for that quality that the West is so known for: "the ability to think outside of the box."

Next came the highly targeted interviews, which of course had to be conducted in such a way that they did not appear as such. Planned encounters at scientific conferences where the candidate had read a paper or lead a discussion panel, casual drinks during a holiday celebration, departmental family gatherings, and the like. Near the end of this very private search where Rosovec saw himself in the guise of a true "head hunter," he found two kindred spirits.

Viktor Sokolovska, a visionary biologist, first impressed him not with his impeccable credentials, but rather with his soft-spoken yet decisive undressing of an academic heckler who had had the misfortune of challenging his thesis that potential extraterrestrial life could just as easily be sulfur- or silicon-based as carbon.

After all, Sokolovska had so logically stated. "If tube worms can evolve, reproduce, and thrive in the superheated and high pressure soup that exists in Earth's abysmal trenches, then why cannot the ice encased seas of Europa produce something similar?"

Just as decisive for Rosovec was the fact that this tall, round-faced and boyish-looking Slav from the Urals was a fiercely protective family man.

Rosovec's second selection was Gregorii Popev. While highly intelligent, the man was an absolute artist on ice. Ruddy-skinned, red-haired, and powerfully built, his genes just screamed Viking and his family's long heritage of settlement along the Volga was strong evidence that that was indeed the case in this family of total red-heads. But it was in his youth as a junior-league hockey player that the qualities of discipline, teamwork, and personal commitment were etched into his very soul. Bright eyed and enthusiastic, a future in the Russian military seemed the natural fit. That was until his high aptitude in mathematics and chemistry caught the eye of the Special Projects Directorate, who had recruited him on the promise of an academic career of his choosing. Blazing his way through his the early years at the university, Popev earned a summer fellowship at a Max Plank institute outside of Munich. There, he learned his German so well that he dreamed in it and in the process integrated so well into the multicultural research staff there that he was invited back the following summer. So began Popev's career as a spy-scientist of the Directorate, who watched out for potential defectors and at the same time published in professional journals of mathematics. That his PhD thesis was in the statistical underpinnings of modern cryptography had not hurt him in the least.

Children of Ptah

*   *   *

The fall of Drazinzka and Ostrogorsky began during Rosovec's return flight from Chicago. His conversations with that Egyptologist Milson had provided much of the fodder that his mind currently was carefully plowing into the fertile soil of his imagination. The seed required for germination had come from Vesna Gregorieva, her free-spirited and independent-minded attitude, and the rather significant fact that she had survived her first temporal deployment. She was a survivor.

Why, he thought, was Gregorieva such a perceived threat to Drazinzka and Ostrogorsky that they had wished her to fail while on that last temporal mission?

That she was a woman?

Possibly and most likely. Certainly it was not because she was Alexander Piankoff's prize student. Hell, those old farts practically worshipped at the man's very feet. His final resting place beneath Lenin's own tomb supports that.

And then there is the issue of frank and honest discussion, of sharing, all that had been an absolute joy with Milson.

Well Stephan, that settles it. What is fair for the goose is fair for the gander. It is high time that I called a meeting of my own with those two old dinosaurs. At a time of my choosing, with an agenda of my own making – their replacement.

*   *   *

"Gentlemen," stated Rosovec formally, "thank you so very much for agreeing to come to this meeting."

Two silent nods from Drazinzka and Ostrogorsky were their only reply. However, Rosovec was pleased to detect a perceivable wariness in their eyes, for they were not in absolute control of the meeting's agenda, much less why they were so politely asked to attend.

After an intellectual deep breath, Rosovec began.

"So, as to why I have asked here, I can only say the following: it is time that you both retired."

At first his two near octogenarian colleagues' faces blushed with shock that was quickly replaced by amusement.

First coughing into his fist to clear his throat.

"Ahem, well, that is a most interesting assessment," Academician Drazinzka said with a thoughtful turn of his head. He then continued. "And just what prompted you, to give us, such sage career advice?"

Smiling like a man who had all four aces in his hand, Rosovec said.

"Well, for one, do you know what this is?" As he placed a small thumb drive in the middle of the conference table.

Ostrogorsky now answered.

"Not I." He stated in a reasonable and measured voice. "Should we?"

"Why yes. It is a cheap, inexpensive thumb drive. It is a 50 gigabit memory stick that I bought in Chicago for about five Euros."

Hostile silence broke out at both the use of the techno-babble vocabulary and that the object in question came from "Chicago" – that legendary home of American gangsterism.

Unaffected, Rosovec continued on in a friendly and conversational tone.

"Such things have been available in the West for at least the last, what, ten years or so."

"And your point?" Stated a very chilly Drazinzka.

Ignoring his elder colleague's attempt at turning the discussion, Rosovec just forged on.

"And do either of you know what a USB port is?"

Now Drazinzka and Ostrogorsky merely looked at one another in hope that the other knew what the young whipper-snapper was now babbling about.

Again it was Ostrogorsky who replied.

"Of what possible significance or purpose is the continuance of this discussion?"

Now looking down at his hands and sighing in mock resignation, Rosovec simply stated.

"Because, my dear colleagues, both of you are technological dinosaurs. Both the memory stick in its many incarnations and the USB have been in public use in the West for the past twenty years. Now, how is it possible that neither of you know of them, yet have any pretentions of being current with the times? How can either of you honestly say that either of you is prepared to protect the *Rodina*?"

Rosovec knew well what he was doing. And summoning the nearly divine image of the *Rodina*, the Russian Motherland, while it might not carry much if any current importance, truly was the clarion call for these two men, who as youths had literally put their lives on the proverbial line in its defense.

Now a red-faced Drazinzka simply exploded.

"You miserable, ungrateful whelp! Just what the fuck do you know about the defense of the *Rodina*! You, who gulped and stammered when I asked you if you had the stomach to order a kill! How dare you question our resolve and then evoke the Motherland!"

Slowing shaking his head from right to left and back again while gracefully wiping the spittle from his Armani suit coat with his silk handkerchief, Rosovec softly replied to the both of them.

"My dear colleagues, did you not know that your early teleconference discussions with the Americans were tapped? Were not secure? That several agencies, both domestic and foreign were privy to view them? That my predecessor was totally oblivious to this fact as well? That I shut down the tap with a special encryption of my own design? And finally, that I then shared that encryption with our American colleagues?"

Stunned shock, horror, and contempt erupted on two faces.

"Gentlemen, as the American's are so fond of saying, 'the times they are a changin',' and so must we, if our Motherland will have a ghost of a chance for a bright future. I well realize that I have royally pissed both of you off. I frankly don't give a damn. But look at what is at stake. Our future is no longer dependent upon carefully compartmentalized secrets within secrets, but rather in shared trust. I have begun that process with the shared encryption, for which our colleagues abroad were most grateful. You both have served the *Rodina* well. Now give her the service of retiring well."

At the conclusion of his prepared remarks, Rosovec reached over to his open briefcase and removed two personnel jackets. Sliding them across the conference table to their respective owners, he then said.

"Gentlemen, these fine men I think you will find most capable. That they can immediately fill your shoes as well as you do now, I sincerely doubt, but they both show much promise. At the very least consider them."

And with that, Rosovec got up and left the elder pair to their own thoughts. After several moments in silence Ostrogorsky was the first to speak.

"Now that was one gutsy pronouncement. Back in the old days, I would have shot him on the spot, if not gutted him like a sturgeon for his eggs!"

Shaking his head in surprise, his colleague merely said. "Vasily, this is uncanny. He chose the very man that I was considering. Now look at your dossier. What about you? Who did he choose?"

Now with widening eyes.

"My God! Sokolovska would not have been my first choice. He's so young. But all in all not that bad. Vasily, as much as I hate to say this, that snot-nosed bastard just might have a point. Somehow, a quiet place along the Black Sea would not be so bad during this time of season, eh?"

So had Rosovec's bloodless velvet revolution come to pass.

CHAPTER VIII
An Archaeological Bonanza

(Luxor) AP – The Egyptian Antiquities Organization announced today the historic discovery in Luxor of a treasure trove hidden within the Treasury of Amen Re by the Dutch Survey Mission.

The Director of the Egyptian Antiquities Organization, Dr. Ibrahim Moussa, who was present at the opening of the chamber, was quoted as being astounded by the find. "Today's archaeological discovery totally, and I do mean totally, eclipses that of the tomb of Tutankhamen."

The Dutch Survey Mission, lead by Professor Dr. Willem van der Boek of the Department of Egyptology at the University of Amsterdam said about the discovery, "I think that the contents of that one chamber could address Egypt's national budget for the next several years."

Ms. Marta Ann Rosen, a Ph.D. candidate in Egyptology and member of the Dutch team, reportedly was the first to suggest the location of the hidden chamber and performed the historic breakthrough. "Yes, I was there, but also was Prof. Dr. van der Boek, who supervised the entire process, and my colleagues Dieter Assman who photographed everything and Horst Willing and Dieter Meier who helped me with all the rubble. I wish to be clear: this was a total team effort."

Reporters on the scene described the chamber of the "treasure trove" as being hidden behind a camouflaged plaster wall façade within the main chamber of the Amen Re Treasury. The chamber itself was reported by the Dutch as being about 16.2 meters square and that its contents were neatly arranged in three aisles. The Dutch team reported that within the hidden "treasure trove" stood numerous gilded statues and fine furniture.

Dr. Moussa quipped that the Department of Conservation at the Karnak Museum will be busy cataloguing and processing all the new finds. "I just hope that there is sufficient floor space available to display all of the new-found riches!"

The Egyptian god Amen Re, considered by the ancients as the sun god, was the patron deity of the ancient capital city of Thebes.

CHAPTER IX
Egyptian Philology 302

There is a special excitement that courses through the bloodstream of any university campus at the start of the fall semester. For the students it is the sheer joy of getting away from home, of making new friends or renewing old ones, keg and rush parties, the start of the football season, some more parties and to a lesser degree of finding out what their classes will be like and whether their professors are professors or just advanced graduate students.

On the other side of this equation, the arrival of the fall semester for the university faculty means the return to what is prosaically called "the grind." Over is the glorious summer break devoted to that book, article, or lab research. Start the siege of litigious students that carefully examine course syllabi for loopholes both real and imagined and who are fully prepared to negotiate their grade. Legacy students, who, due to their mere genetic inheritance, fully expect immediate access to the highest levels of the academic administration. Student athletes, while appearing as corporeal entities on course rosters, become inexplicably incorporeal in the classroom. And then there are the many meetings: departmental, faculty senate, service, outreach, and did I fail to mention those absolutely "stimulating" departmental meetings. All this, and then one must prepare the lectures, grade the tests, and read the papers.

As for Associate Professor Joseph Richards, he had only three classes this semester, two Introduction to Egyptian Philology 101 courses that he had already successfully taught twice, meaning the preparation for them was already in the can, and one Advanced Egyptian Philology 302 course that was his first, and so was really jazzed about. Since Richards' reputation had spread across the campus as a tough, but fun professor, he usually pulled a head count of around twenty per Intro course and that meant a larger classroom usually scheduled over at Smith Hall. The advanced class, however, was for serious students – the real gunners, who tended to be mostly his former charges, his real fans who were eager for more. Still and all, and even for an upper level class, Richards was mildly surprised when he pulled the computer printout of the class' roster from his mail slot. No less than twelve intrepid individuals had signed up for it.

Well, he thought. Just where will this class meet? Certainly not on the second floor of the Near Eastern Institute, because none of those seminar rooms are large enough for twelve. Maybe somewhere on the first floor? I really need to talk to the departmental secretary about this, he finally concluded. Maybe Smith Hall too?

*　　*　　*

As it turned out, and after only considerable behind the scenes maneuvering on the part of one very overworked departmental secretary, the advanced Egyptian philology course was eventually slotted to an obscure seminar room on the third floor of the university's main library, itself a massive, castle-like edifice of formed concrete. Known as the "fallout shelter," here Richards would regale his students.

Unlike most other classrooms throughout the campus, this seminar room was more a cramped windowless storage closet. It was populated mostly by its long and ultramodern white plastic conference table dated *circa* 1980s complete with a swooping pedestal and matching white plastic chairs. The lone board space was a camouflaged white board hidden behind two, yes, white plastic doors. And did I mention that the walls were painted white as well? The only detail that was missing from the scene was Woody Allen and the Orgasmatron.

On Tuesday, at 10:05 in the morning, the class began with six students squeezed in on each side of the conference table, while a late registrant was left standing at one end and Richards at the other with the white board behind him.

"Well my friends, it seems that we don't rate very high with university operations." He began as smiles, a couple of chuckles, and one "No shit" broke out.

"If any of you have any better suggestions for our accommodations, just let me know. And I am serious about that. But before we get going on that item, first some housekeeping."

After completing the roll call, Richards quickly realized that the class was composed of three Classicists, six Egyptology folks, two Anthropology types, a humanities geek, and one, lone ancient history major. In short, an interesting mix and one that triggered in Richards an idea that he had been considering.

"Well," he began, "folks we have a real opportunity here. We're a small group; but we're a reasonably diverse one. So here's the deal. I want us to thoroughly investigate two epigraphical sources this semester and I want you to prepare them for publication."

To this announcement bulging eyes and exaggerated swallows were the silent response.

"At the very least, I want to produce a hard cover publication that is suitable to occupy a shelf in this very library. At the very most, I really hope that we can put together something that our very own university press can publish. And such a publication means royalties, royalties in which I will not participate in, but each of you will enjoy. Furthermore, I want this crew to work as a team, much like a large study group, who can divide and conquer. Whadda' say?"

The bulging eyes at this point began to dilate even more. The gulping and gasping had stopped, but a lone hand was raised, the hand of the humanities geek.

"What about our grades?"

"That's easy." Richards replied, "a B for a library only edition; an A for anything that we can get published."

Standing, "I'm outa' here." The humanities geek replied as he made for the door.

"Done." Rapidly replied Richards as he quickly crossed off the name on his roster and in his next breath he said.

"That's now your chair Mr. Williams. Have a seat. And before we go any further, as you're not one of my former students, where did you learn your glyphs?"

Williams, the ancient historian, now the curious focus of the room, turned white and with a bit of sweat breaking out across his forehead said.

"I...I am self-taught Professor Richards."

"I see. What did you use for your grammar textbook?"

"Ah, well, several actually. I started with Sir Alan Gardiner's, then moved on to James Allen's. Only last semester did I discover yours."

"That's impressive. So you're purely a Middle Egyptian glyph guy then?"

"That's correct. I haven't messed with either Late or Old Kingdom Egyptian at all."

"That's fine, but are you sure that you're up to what we're going to attempt in this class?"

"Yes sir. In fact, I have done some archaeological field work and I think that that might be of some help."

"Where abouts?"

"First at Tell Beer Sheva with Anson Rainey. Then at El-Amarna with Barry Kemp."

Now tilting his head a bit to the left in thought, Richards suddenly realized that he might have a real gem on his hands.

"Well, Mr. Williams. Welcome then! You will be our resident 'ancient historian and archaeologist' and the rest of us word-nerds will no doubt be coming to you for your unique perspectives!"

CHILDREN OF PTAH

*   *   *

"Well crew, the first inscription that we will be working with is the Shabaka Stone that is today housed in the British Museum. Imagine a rectangular slab of black granite roughly three by four and a half feet. The entire surface of the inscription has suffered from a circular abrasion and even some of the glyphs have been hacked out with a chisel. And as if to add further insult, a square hole was cut into the middle of it with ten crude radiating channels emanating from it.

"Now clearly this artifact started its existence as an important monument, but can any of you guess what became of it? Any ideas whatsoever?"

"Yes, Ms. Gérard."

"Does the hacked out glyphs mean that the stela was from the Amarna Period?"

"That's a logical thought, but the ancient Egyptians seemed to hack inscriptions practically during each and every period. Remember: *damnatio memoriae* was very big with your enemies. No name, no memory, no afterlife. And besides, this inscription is dated to a pharaoh of the eighth century BC."

"Next insight?"

Studious examination of fingernails.

"Come on gang, open up, and think together. You're a team. At least throw out some ideas."

And then Richards saw a sheepish smile creep across Mr. Williams face followed by his raised hand.

"Yes, Mr. Williams. What's your contribution?"

"Well, Professor Richards, while I cannot posit a reason for why the glyphs were excised, I do have a suggestion for the hole and the abrasions. Granite is a hard, igneous stone, a stone that many cultures liked to use almost exclusively in grinding mills, so my idea is that the stone was reused as part of a mill of some sort."

That "many cultures" used granite for mill stones the three Classicists vigorously nodded their heads in affirmation.

"Bingo! Mr. Williams. That is precisely what happened to this slab. Way to go. Next class we will discuss those erasures."

So ended the first class, but not before a bibliographical handout was passed around with no less than twelve sources on it and clear instructions that a five-minute oral summary was due on each for the next meeting. Let the horse-trading begin!

CHAPTER X
Decoding and Deciphering

Dr. Roy Allen Peters sat glumly at his desk. The former Director of the Materials Technology Department and Laboratory at Wright-Patterson AFB, managing head of the SNOWMAN analysis, and Chief Investigator of the Aten Spacecraft was now for all practical purposes out of a job. Needless to say, this careful and successful materials scientist pursed his lips in frustration about it. To make matters worse, it was Monday, 9:13 in the morning, and he had already finished all the paperwork for that week.

Ever since the loss of the Aten spacecraft three months ago during the worldwide Black Out, he found himself on autopilot. While the "bugs and flowers" project members were still quite busy investigating the organic remains of what they believed was once the pod's pilot, Roy, a real "hands on" kind of guy, found himself on the curb. Simply put. No Aten, no Aten Project.

Yes, he admitted to himself. We still have in our possession several minute surface samples of the craft The Hope, a handful of beautiful crystals, and the tantalizing preliminary survey of the technology aboard the Aten. And then there was always that enigmatic artifact – the SNOWMAN, an object itself recovered from the moon by the Apollo XII crew. Oh, how I wish that we could have definitively proven that SNOWMAN was from the Aten!

But all of that had been only a tease; for the entire craft had been hijacked off the base by its rightful owners before any truly serious study had been undertaken. In short, as things now stood, this brilliant mind and organizer was now trapped within a ho-hum administrative exercise as he began to wind down the Aten Project, return resources to their former posts, and finish dotting all the i's and crossing all the t's.

But at 9:16, all of those sad and sober feelings dramatically changed, when a member of the SNOWMAN analysis team, Dr. Gail Sonnenschein, paid an unannounced and breathless visit to his modest office.

What Peters initially found so remarkable about that momentous conversation was that Dr. Sonnenschein – as cool and calculating a research scientist geek that he had ever laid eyes upon, was now standing in front of his desk bouncing up and down on her tip toes. Wearing her worn neon blue Nike running shoes and white starched lab coat, Sonnenschein seemed in midflight with her dangling reading glasses in a continuous, bouncing, ascent and free fall. The image before him reminded Peters vaguely of a white ghost in perpetual vertical oscillation.

"Roy! You just will not believe what a couple of us at the lab just stumbled upon! The excited brunette from Elizabeth, New Jersey blurted out.

"You remember that component that we removed from SNOWMAN? You know, the one with a residual charge that we all thought was its hard drive? It's memory? It's brain? Well, guess what? We finally figured out what it stored!"

After a few pregnant moments of silence, Peters sat back in his chair, smiled the expectant smile of a child at Christmas Eve and said.

"Okay Gail. So what did you and your illustrious crew discover?"

With a grin as broad as a barn the expert in astro-spectrographic analysis said.

"Light Roy. It's full of light. Electromagnetic values. They all look like a series of spectrographic readings, but they're not Roy! It looks like a language! It looks like a message! It looks like they wrote in color!"

"Gail, that's extraordinary!" Said a Roy Peters now sitting forward quite literally on the edge of his chair.

"But how did you come to the conclusion that the values might represent a coherent message?"

"From the values themselves Roy! They were all suspiciously of the same amplitude except for certain markers that appeared scattered throughout with precisely null amplitudes.

"Roy, those null markers look a lot like either the beginnings or endings of a phrase. You know, like capital letters or periods. Maybe they're even used as stops, just like in old fashioned telegrams. Roy baby, we need to get some language, cryppie types in here real quick!"

*   *   *

"You know Dr. Peters," the seasoned Egyptologist wryly stated. "Your spectrographic expert is really quite a crackerjack! And what an eye for detail!"

"Yes, Professor Milson, I know, and take it from me, she's quite ingenious too. She hails from Cal Tech."

"Ah, I see." Said the philologist, coughing politely into his fist and left wondering what the significance of being a Cal Tech grad had to do with an individual's inventiveness. Clearly, he was missing some sort of "in" reference.

"Nonetheless, Dr. Sonnenschein did accurately and squarely put us on a path towards the identification and potential translation of the 'light language,' as we have come to call it. In fact, what Dr. Sonnenschein and her team found in the SNOWMAN's memory module actually contained three messages, all with the same content, but each expressed at a different electromagnetic range, one each in the infrared, visible, and ultraviolet.

"In all, with Dr. Sonnenschein's able assistance, we have been able to isolate some thirty-six distinct wavelength data values. The relationship of each across all three electromagnetic ranges is a direct one-to-one relationship proving beyond a shadow of a doubt that we are dealing with the same message content expressed in three color dialects – so to speak.

"Additionally, Dr. Sonnenschein's initial surmise that the occasional shift in amplitude, to a precisely null value, indeed strongly suggests some sort of philological beginning or end markers.

"But what we are now tasked with is an in-depth study of the message's content via multivariate analysis. What I suspect is that we'll first identify any repeats – that might be nouns, and from that any similar formations – that might indicate clausal formations, prepositional expressions, and the like."

Extremely impressed with Milson's preliminary thoughts, Peters, forming a steeple with his hands, then asked from his office chair.

"That's all well and good professor, your cryptographic approach seems very sound to me, but what isn't, is how you're going to get to the meaning of all those values. It seems to me that we require another source, a Rosetta Stone of some sort, in order to assign a specific meaning to a specific wavelength value."

Smiling down appreciatively into his hands at Peter's adroit mention of the philological foundation of modern Egyptology, Milson replied.

"Fortunately, Dr. Peters, we do have in our possession a potential shirt-tailed relative of this 'light language' of yours. And, once all of the statistical work is completed, I fully intend to put the best minds to work on an analysis of this 'light language's' message. My suspicion is that, lacking the intercept of second transmission that would provide us with further examples, we will only be able at best to get a general gist of the conversation, as it were."

Now it was Peters turn to smile a knowing smile.

"Ah, Professor Milson, I think you might be in luck."

"How so?"

"We do have a second transmission available. In fact, with the second transmission, your multivariate analysis should improve considerably, I would think."

"Indeed Dr. Peters. But where and when did you come across this second message?"

"Can't really say, just like I noticed that you didn't reveal your potential Rosetta Stone source. But nonetheless, I will make sure that the second transmission is made available to you and your people as soon as possible."

"Now that would be simply grand!" The old man beamed with undisguised enthusiasm.

*   *   *

On July 15th, 1799, a remarkable artifact was uncovered during the construction of fortifications near the Egyptian port city of Rashid along the Rosetta branch of the Nile River. The discoverer, a French Captain named Pierre-François Bouchard, realized immediately the immensity of the find, for the dark granite monument had been inscribed in no less than three languages: Greek, Demotic, and Egyptian hieroglyphs. The decree's content was immediately clear from the Greek portion of the stela, which dated to 196 BC – the reign of King Ptolemy V, and announced the repeal of taxes and the erection of statues in temples. Needless to say, the trilingual character of this monument directly led to the decipherment of a then unknown language, in this case Egyptian hieroglyphs. The formidable task was to link the Greek characters to the Egyptian hieroglyphs and fortunately the beginning of this process was greatly aided when the name Cleopatra, spelled out in Greek, was successfully equated with the same name in Egyptian hieroglyphs. It would be some twenty-three years later, in 1822, that Jean-François Champollion, and again in 1823 Thomas Young, both used this key source to decode the language system of the ancient Egyptians. And with this translation, the field of Egyptology was born. This epigraphical gold mine is called the Rosetta Stone that now resides in the British Museum for all to see.

*   *   *

Modern code breaking formally began in the ninth century, when an Arabic polymath with the name of Al-Kindi described the use of frequency analysis in decrypting secret messages. What Al-Kindi had discovered was that certain letters appear with a higher frequency of usage making the decoding of messages possible. Ever since the publication of his work entitled *A Manuscript on Deciphering Cryptographic Messages,* frequency analysis has become a basic tool for the decoding of ciphers.

For example, the most commonly used letters of the English language are E, T, N, R, O, A, I, and S, respectively. In all, they make up some sixty seven percent of the text in the English language, while the remaining eighteen letters make up the remainder. The lowest frequency letters are, not surprisingly J, K, Q, and Z, as any Scrabble player will immediately tell you. Vowels comprise some forty percent of the written English language, while the most likely pairs of letters are EN, RE, ER, and TH, which can be located anywhere in a word.

One weakness to frequency analysis is that it relies as much on linguistic knowledge as it does on statistics. In other words, it only works if a text is sufficiently long enough to produce a recognizable frequency count. But the other weakness of such analysis is that it absolutely falls flat on its face if the language is an unknown.

In the face of such a daunting challenge as the translation of an unknown language, a Kasiski Examination, first developed by Friedrich Kasiski, sometimes can be of assistance. This promising approach involves looking for strings of character values that may be repeated throughout a text. Such repetitions or patterns in words or phraseology could hint at a message's general format and the possible presence of standardized nomenclature. Repeats also give many clues as to the type of language system and the makeup of the plaintext message itself.

Similar to the Kasiski Examination is another statistical approach called the Acquaintance Algorithm, which measures the similarity of documents based upon "n-grams," which are simply long stings of continuous characters in a document. By comparing the distribution of n-grams between documents a score is computed that represents the degree of similarity between documents. Scores range from 1.0 that connotes an identical match to -1.0, which is a total mismatch. An appropriate sample size must be at least two hundred characters long. If the highest score returned is greater than 0.25, then the languages of the documents compared, whether known or unknown, are deemed to be the same.

Occasionally, cryptographers employ yet another approach that is referred to as traffic analysis. Instead of looking at the message itself, this approach examines the message's externals, which include: identified call signs or words, transmission frequencies, message volume, and of course message format. This latter detail can be very intriguing as it includes an examination of a transmission's internal divisions, in essence its stops, punctuation, delimiters, separators, spacers or fillers. In the end, externals can be a rich source of information, regardless of whether the meaning of the message can be ascertained. Externals can also give substantial clues as to organization, sophistication, and even the possible purpose of a communication.

In the final analysis, what cryptanalysts search for are patterns and repetitions between messages with similar characteristics. The goal is to determine the language used, its general system of organization, the reconstruction of decryption keys to that system, and only then the construction of the message's plaintext, or what it means.

*   *   *

As a result of the clever use of the above decoding techniques, the "light language" began to unravel and reveal its secrets. The grist of its analysis were the two recovered transmissions: one from the so-called "memory module" of the SNOWMAN artifact of unknown, but ancient date, and the transmission snagged by NORAD's Near Space Telemetry Tracking System recorded on September 29th, at 03:51:14 MT.

In the background of these two remarkable transmissions, the text of the Annex Papyrus was consulted in the belief that it might provide context and even clues as to the decryption of these transmissions, much as the Greek of the famous Rosetta Stone had for the decipherment of the ancient Egyptian language. This last represented an extremely optimistic leap of faith that Milson willingly took, for to him, there just were too many circumstantial coincidences not to try.

*   *   *

"Dr. Milson, I can confirm some of our preliminary suspicions and offer some preliminary interpretations of the "light language" transmissions."

Slowly shaking her head side to side in quiet awe Sonnenschein proudly announced with a broad grin that could have easily spanned the Hudson River. "You know professor. This language system is truly fantastic and fascinating at the same time."

"For starters, both transmissions, as we initially thought, are indeed linear pulses that contain sequentially presented content in three separate electromagnetic media, whose spectra formats were in the infrared, visible, and ultraviolet.

"Very cool. No, way cool. The why of it boggles the imagination Doc. However, it could well be a combination of concern for message clarity through transmission degradation as well as readability for three different audiences.

"As you would expect, the infrared frequency intervals are longer, while the ultraviolet are extremely short. What this of course infers, at least from a biological point of view, is the ability to see in the infrared, versus our own visible range, versus the ultraviolet. All of this represents totally different ways of perceiving photonic data that the exobiologists will simply go nuts over.

"Doc can you even just imagine what it would be like to see in ultraviolet?!?"

But before Milson could get a word in edgewise, the pumped up scientist had raced ahead without a pause. Her excitement notably ratcheting up as she shifted her mode of address from "Professor" to "Doc."

"Well Doc, we were next totally freaked to find that each of the three spectra contained precisely the same number and set of wavelength data units, but each expressed within its own frequency range.

"That said, we then decided to focus upon the message clusters themselves. What we found was that each was precisely broken up into "data packets" of sixty discrete wavelength data units separated by "null, null" or a double neutral wavelength pattern – black.

"This bundling of data into sixty discrete units suggests to me the use of a preference or cultural norm, a base-sixty, sexagesimal system. Such a system would possess a large number of conveniently sized divisors and it's one that would be quite useful in expressing fractions."

At this point in Sonnenschein's report Milson, try as he might, simply could not contain himself. Putting his hands up forming a 'T' and so signaling "Time Out," he excitedly interrupted.

"Dr. Sonnenschein, this finding of your team is truly extraordinary. The sexagesimal system is well attested in the ancient Near East. In fact, the Babylonians are the one's credited with its creation, which was then adopted by the Persian and later Ottoman Empires. Unlike most numerical systems, base-sixty is best used in measuring angles, geographical coordinates, the measurement of time, and not to be forgotten, the base-sixty system was important as well to the calculation of pi."

"You're kidding!"

"Nope, not one bit. Now, what else did your team's analysis reveal?"

Returning to her yellow legal pad of scrawled notes, a now numb Sonnenschein adjusted her glasses, found where she had left off, and continued.

"Right, ah, well, it seems that each wavelength data unit represents a precisely enunciated infrared, visible, or ultraviolet value. In all, we have found within the three spectra clusters a total of thirty-six distinct data values. Surprisingly, these wavelength data values are precisely specified out to five decimal places of amplitude – and in the case of the visible spectrum – they are defined at precisely 10.83334 nanometers. Some of my colleagues believe that the reason this precision was required was to ensure message transmission clarity over great distances. Once again, the degradation issue.

"And Doc, these data values themselves appear in groupings suggestive of linguistic constructs! We have observed groupings ranging in length from one to as many as sixteen data units."

"What do you mean by groupings? How can you define them as such?" asked Milson.

"Well that was relatively easy, for each grouping is delimited by a single "null" or neutral wavelength pattern. In essence, a "null" wavelength value, as I said before, the absence of light – utter blackness, brackets each data unit. So the transmission, if printed out on an ink jet, would appear as a riotous stream of color broken into large chunks by wide black bars and then subdivided into smaller chunks by narrow black bars. In many ways, it looks much like a bar code, but far prettier."

Now pushing back her reading glasses back to the bridge of her pug nose, Sonnenschein concluded.

"So, what we found looks very much like a highly stable language format composed of thirty-six discrete data values. Values I might add that have been found in both transmissions, which are suspected to have been transmitted during widely disparate time periods. The arrangement of these discrete data values also suggest that the linguistic makeup of the "light language" uses single values, digraphs, and perhaps even trigraphic and tetragraphic constructions. In addition, we cannot discount the distinct possibility for the presence of a sophisticated numerical system as well. If I had to guess, the double and single null divisions look a whole like paragraphs and word clusters.

"And, oh by the way, this canny use of visible light as a medium for communication first occurred to Alexander Graham Bell back in the late 1870s. He, of course, didn't have the benefit of fiber optics to realize his vision, just common twisted copper wire."

*   *   *

After working several days with Sonnenschein's analysis of the two "light language" transmissions, Milson began to truly appreciate just how much effort and sheer creative brilliance had gone into that effort. Now with the transmissions' wavelength data values transliterated into numerical equivalents, the Egyptologist began to settle into what he referred to as "his philological mode."

With the two color transmissions now transliterated into their assigned numerical values, Milson arrayed them side-by-side before him on his desk blotter. Almost immediately, the philologist began underlining several cluster patterns that were immediately obvious and even noted that they were approximately placed in the same locations.

While his job was not so much to confirm what Sonnenschein had already found, Milson was out to try and assign linguistic values to the "light language's" wavelength data units. His approach was none other than a classic linguistic approach of applying a key source text – that of the highly classified Annex Papyrus, a source that only a very few even knew of much less had access to.

Now paging through his thumb-worn copy of the papyrus' publication, the philologist began looking for promising key words or phrases. Initially, one phrase, The Hopeful One – the name of the alien Akhenaton's space craft, jumped out at him. He wrote it down. Then he latched onto the phrase "surveyor priesthood," which he loosely interpreted more as "surveyor guild" or "surveyor society" than the more strict translation of "priesthood." As he continued scanning through the text, he stopped, all the time jotting down potential ideas that might offer him keys to the decipherment of the texts.

Several hours later, the Egyptologist began to apply his suspected key words to the first transmission that was recovered from the SNOWMAN artifact. Milson deep down was tremendously excited and at the same time strangely motivated. He knew that he was breaking new ground in an area that he had never before ventured into; yet, it was nonetheless an arena that only he and he alone was uniquely suited for. At his core he freely took the intuitive leap of faith that the SNOWMAN artifact was not only contemporaneous with Akhenaten, but was also somehow connected to the Aten craft as well. And as hunches go, Milson instincts were right on. It just would take some time, sweat, and luck to prove it.

CHILDREN OF PTAH

*   *   *

"Okay, for the record, let me get this straight," the cryptographic programmer said.

"I'm to run a multivariate analysis across both of these transmission records, using these potential keys?"

"In a word, yes." The firm voice said.

"Fine professor, but what would you like me to do with those keys? How would you like me to parse these out? I need some sort of specs; otherwise, all we will be doing is wasting some very valuable computer time. And that is something that I rather not do."

"I fully understand your position, Mr. White. I can assure you that we are not going on a wild goose chase. All we need to know is the following."

*   *   *

For Milson the task of deciphering of the "light language" turned out to be a surprisingly refreshing exercise that represented the challenge of a life time. As he again carefully aligned before him side-by-side the gloriously colored printouts of the visible spectra versions of the two transmissions, he could not help but smile in awe.

We were right all along – three spectra transmissions faithfully produced in parallel. And here's what we can see.

And it's all so beautiful, all of these shaded bars, a veritable riot of distinctive hues. Truly, it's Joseph's coat of many colors! And its flow! So efficient! So logical!

And who could have ever predicted that the text would have coursed according to the ancient boustrophedon style – that marvelously quaint zigzagging style that goes from one line to the next, literally "as an ox goes," while plowing a field.

That detail totally surprised the cryptographers, but strangely it doesn't surprise me at all. It's almost as if there were purposely planted details, almost borrowings – or better – should I say legacies, for which I must remain ever vigilant.

And I sure don't want to miss any. Clearly, Joseph didn't.

*   *   *

THE "LIGHT LANGUAGE"

Preliminary Analysis

The following key, translation and commentary on the so-called "Light Language" (hereafter LL) are considered authoritative. The work of Milson [1] and Sonnenschein [2] on the plaintext reconstruction of the SNOWMAN and NORAD transmissions has been described by the cryptanalysis community as "herculean" and "downright psychic." Clearly, such unsolicited accolades have elevated these scholars into a class of their own.

---

[1] John A. Milson, Professor Emeritus of Egyptology, Near Eastern Institute, Chicago, IL.

[2] Gail Sonnenschein, Ph.D., Department of Astrophysics, Wright-Patterson AFB, Dayton, OH.

The following table key to the LL was established on the basis of observed data value frequencies and string repetitions, in addition to the brute force use of a Kasiski Examination and Acquaintance Algorithm. Once these baseline analyses were completed by Sonnenschein, Milson then employed classic linguistic substitution theory with the aid of a highly secured comparative source.

While both scholars consider their key table reliable, they also recognize that it can only become better with further samples. Therefore, the preliminary transliteration values are presented in the key table as capitals, while possible alternate values are provided in lower case.

Code Value	Visible Light Color	Wavelength (nm.)	Alphabetic Value
1	REDS	780.00000	A, aa
2	REDS	769.16666	M
3	REDS	758.33332	Y, ee
4	REDS	747.49998	B
5	REDS	736.66664	N
6	REDS	725.83330	Z, ss
7	REDS	714.99996	C
8	REDS	704.16662	O, oo
9	REDS	693.33328	1
10	REDS	682.49994	D, t
11	REDS	671.66660	P
12	REDS	660.83326	2
13	REDS	649.99992	E, ee
14	REDS	639.16658	Q
15	ORANGES	628.33324	3
16	ORANGES	617.49990	F, ph
17	ORANGES	606.66656	R, l
18	YELLOWS	595.83322	4
19	YELLOWS	584.99988	G, j
20	GREENS	574.16654	S, sh
21	GREENS	563.33320	5
22	GREENS	552.49986	H
23	GREENS	541.66652	T, d
24	GREENS	530.83318	6
25	GREENS	519.99984	I, i
26	GREENS	509.16650	U, oo
27	BLUES	498.33316	7
28	BLUES	487.49982	J
29	BLUES	476.66648	V
30	BLUES	465.83314	8
31	VIOLETS	454.99980	K, q
32	VIOLETS	444.16646	W
33	VIOLETS	433.33312	9
34	VIOLETS	422.49978	L
35	VIOLETS	411.66644	X, ch
36	VIOLETS	400.83310	0

As with all such plaintext reconstructions, a certain amount of latitude must be allowed in order to produce a smooth translation. While considered authoritative by Sonnenschein and Milson, any linguistic or statistical queries should be directed to Sonnenschein.

SNOWMAN Transmission
August 29th, 1359 B.C., 21:43:23 GMT [1]

EXTREME EMERGENCY [2]
Scout Craft HOPE [3]
Surveyor 1
Missing. Reunification of self [and] pod failed
Scout Craft HOPE recovery needed [4]
Coordinates 3948.4334.3221
Relative Time 585943.001
EXTREME EMERGENCY

---

[1] The date and time of this transmission is calculated based upon the REDEMPTION's transmission date and time formats. This transmission is based upon the following assumption: that the Pharaoh Akhenaten and Surveyor 1 were indeed one in the same individual. While this surmise is fraught with many issues, not the least the organic remains taken from the Aten space craft, the alien's telepathic relationship between these remains and those of the individual known as Akhenaten appear to be undeniable.

[2] This message is composed of six general elements: an identical header/footer that brackets the transmission; the vehicle call sign; the pilot call sign; the message body; current location coordinates; and relative temporal coordinates. It is significant that exactly the same format appears in the REDEMPTION (formerly NORAD) Transmission.

[3] It is assumed that the craft here mentioned, the HOPE, is synonymous with the craft discovered by Professor J. W. Richards in the hidden mountain hanger located east of the site of modern El-Amarna.

[4] Message content is expressed in a series of brief statements. On the basis of Milson's research, it now seems reasonable that the true identity of Surveyor 1 was that of the Pharaoh Akhenaten. However, the subsequent statement that the reunification of Surveyor 1 with "self [and] pod failed" remains unclear unless one assumes that the two were in fact one in the same individual. Nonetheless, independently derived evidence, however, strongly supports just such a hypothesis.

CHILDREN OF PTAH

REDEMPTION (formerly NORAD) Transmission
September 29th, 2004, 3:50:13 GMT [(1)]

PARTIAL RECOVERY [(2)]
Recovery Craft REDEMPTION [(3)]
Surveyors 97, 83, 90 [(4)]
Scout Craft HOPE secured, [but] compromised
Surveyor 1 not recovered
REDEMPTION enroute to Survey Community [(5)]
Are prepared to return
Awaiting instructions [(6)]
Coordinates 3944.4331.3220
Relative Time 640901.093
PARTIAL RECOVERY

[(1)] The transmission's date and time as received by NORAD precisely confirmed the independently derived numerical data structures as translated by Milson and Sonnenschein. As with the SNOWMAN text, the REDEMPTION transmission was made up of the same six elements: identical header/footer, vehicle call sign, pilot call sign, message body, location coordinates and relative temporal coordinates. The preservation of this format, despite the clearly vast span of time between the SNOWMAN and REDEMPTION transmissions suggests an institutional standard or convention.

[(2)] It should be noted that this text, "Partial Recovery," is in fact a cognate compound upon which the space craft REDEMPTION's own name is based.

[(3)] Based upon the NORAD telemetry, the size of this craft has been estimated as being five to six times that of scout craft HOPE.

[(4)] This statement implies that the REDEMPTION space craft was manned by three individuals and hence most likely represented a recovery team. It may be that the first Surveyor mentioned, 97, is the craft's communication's officer or commander.

[(5)] Since the recovery Milson's intuitive insertion of the value "Survey Community" was derived from an independent classified source has lucidly explained the relationship of Surveyor 1 with the crew of the REDEMPTION. On this basis, we assume that the recovery of the HOPE was considered a justifiable act according to near universal right of salvage and not as an act of outright aggression.

95

[6] The clear import of the REDEMPTION's transmission has been shared with the following national security agencies of the nations of the Republic of Egypt, the Russian Republic, and the United States. Since the recovery of the HOPE by the REDEMPTION and its crew, serious concerns have arisen about the organic remains removed from the scout craft's interior, which were left behind at Wright-Patterson AFB. This transmission only confirms those concerns.

Chapter XI
Egyptian Philology 302 (cont.)

"Thank you Ms. Pattersen. That was a very concise summary of what Frankfort had to say on the subject." Richards said with some pleasure.

"So, next on the docket is Mr. Kennan and Breasted's 1901 article in *Zeitschrift für die Ägyptische Sprache*. Mr. Kennan, the floor is yours."

Now with a strongly beating heart and swallowing hard Mr. Kennan, a member of the classical triumvirate, stood and very suddenly realized that all eyes were on him. So he loudly cleared his throat and began reading from his carefully prepared notes.

"Well, this is what Breasted had to say about the Shabaka Stone."

"First off, Breasted's article in *ZÄS* provides us with a good start towards an authoritative text, how to translate it, and how best to understand it. It seems that Breasted was in a bit of a hurry to publish this article as two other scholars, Bryant and Read, had just managed to beat him to the punch, literally by weeks, in another journal in the very same year. In some respects, I prefer Breasted's abbreviated analysis to the one that he had originally intended.

"Second, Breasted dated the orthography and grammar of the inscription to the early Eighteenth Dynasty, with some indications that the origin of the text might be even older, as in Middle Kingdom. This is, as we have already heard, a rather conservative position, meanwhile Bryant and Read had dated the text as far back as to the Pyramid Texts of the Fifth Dynasty.

"Third, Breasted noted that while the hieroglyphic text faced to the right of the stela, it is actually read in reverse; meaning that this is a retrograde inscription.

"Fourth, while Bryant and Read understood the stele's content as nothing more than the bumbling together of several religious texts, Breasted understood it instead as a coherent whole, a deep philosophical treatise, where the god Ptah was seen as being both the content and source of the inspiration for a kind of universal mind. From this universal mind, which the god Ptah was both content and source of content, when the universal mind thought of something, and the mouth voiced that something, then that something, that thought, that idea would come into existence."

Breaking away from his prepared text, Kennan, now a bit more relaxed and feeling his oats, elaborated extemporaneously.

"I know that all of this sounds pretty heavy, but Breasted really got into this inscription – almost like a Vulcan mind meld. In a nutshell, it seems that Ptah realized that something, the universal mind, was far bigger than he. Still, it was Ptah's job to provide ideas or content for that universal mind and then when those ideas, content, or thoughts were actually enunciated, then creation occurred. While I know that this is probably way outside our project, someone will have to look into the Logos Doctrine that is found in *Genesis* as the two are just too similar. And, we as a team just might want to make a comment, maybe just as a short footnote, as to which influenced which. Sorry about that aside, but I just had to get that off my chest.

Now returning to his notes.

"Fifth, one of the earliest investigators on this inscription was a fellow named Goodwin…"

This mention of Goodwin raised the eyebrows of his two colleagues as they certainly were very much aware of a certain Goodwin, who was also the author of a very well established Greek grammar. Clear from their faces was the question: is this the same Goodwin?

"Who made a Latin translation of a faulty reading by another scholar named Sharpe. We as a team will have to decide how far back we want to go into this inscription's historical scholarship and whether we should provide a translation of Goodwin's Latin text or just stick with a good Egyptian-English one.

"Sixth, Breasted pointedly stated that the philosophical content of this text severely taxed both the Egyptian scribe and the Egyptian language generally. Consequently, many of the deeper philosophical concepts had to be expressed in mythological terms and almost secondhand allusions.

"Seventh and finally, Breasted waxed lyrical on the qualities of Ptah that he interpreted from this text. Here are Breasted's words:

> Ptah, therefore, from the earliest times was known as the patron of the craftsman, to whom he furnished plans and designs. It was but a step further to make him the author of *all* thoughts and plans, and from the architect of the craftsman's work, he became the architect of the world."

CHAPTER XII
The Cedar Box

Within the quiet silence of his personal laboratory, the chief curator of the Cairo National Museum sighed heavily as he took in the magnificent cedar box before him. Its smooth and perfectly proportioned lines and exquisitely carved features could only be described as sublime. Working in soft cotton gloves to prevent any oils or enzymes from marring the late Eighteenth Dynasty artifact, Dr. Ahmed Rashid methodically measured its dimensions and recorded them on a small pad of paper to his left. His ability to write with his left hand had been acquired only through considerable effort. Now as the years had passed since the war that had so damaged his right, he judged his penmanship reasonably legible.

"So beautifully carved and designed," he murmured to himself. "Every dimension is so perfect. It is almost jewel-like, with every plane a complimentary facet of a greater whole."

Shaking his head slowly in true wonder, the man continued his measurements in order to flush out the artifact's log. Finished with the exterior, he dutifully measured the interior and again marveled at the precision and craftsmanship of the still mildly fragrant, ruddy red box that once held the now highly classified Annex Papyrus, which was found within the "Abode of the Aten."

Finished with his task, Rashid next scooted on his wheeled stool with his handwritten notes over to the drafting table. With the box now behind him, the curator began working on a rough diagram of the box's dimensions based on his notes. Before him lay an oversized and secured pad of centimeter graph paper that made the translation of the artifact's proportions a simple children's game of connect the dots. Finished, he sat back, viewed his effort, and frowned.

Something is amiss here, he thought. I must have miss-measured the interior. The proportions are all wrong. How could its base be so deceptively thick?

Scooting back to the lab table Rashid patiently re-measured the interior of the cedar box and this time even spoke them aloud as he wrote them down.

"Length: 35 centimeters.

"Width: 14 centimeters.

"Depth: 14 centimeters."

Spinning around back to the drafting table where he had left his first set of notes, all that Rashid could do was let out a quiet grunt.

Precisely the same, he read.

Thinking that perhaps he was becoming a bit daft in his old age, he then remeasured the exterior.

"Length: 37 centimeters.

"Width: 16 centimeters.

"Height: 18 centimeters!

Why the need for an additional two centimeters! His rational mind called. For balance to assure that the container doesn't easily turn over? Or could it be something else entirely?

I wonder...

*   *   *

"Blessings be upon you. May I speak immediately with Dr. Hosny Zaaki. This is Dr. Rashid, chief curator of the Cairo National Museum.

"Yes, yes, I'll wait."

After a momentary pause.

"Dr. Zaaki. I wish you good health as well, and, I have another small favor to ask.

"No, no this time it has nothing to do with any mummy – of that I can assure you.

Pause.

"It's a small cedar wood box.

"Yes. It's about eighteen centimeters high by thirty-seven long.

"Yes, quite small, and quite manageable you say?

"Shall I bring it over when your schedule permits?

"Today, that would be simply wonderful!

"Okay then, three o'clock it is."

*   *   *

Dr. Hosny Zaaki hung up the phone immediately regretting that he had so quickly agreed to again help out Rashid. The last time that the chief of radiology had done so had been most unsettling. It was all that hush-hush business surrounding that mummy and its curiously amputated right hand. And then that staged interview with the museum director himself, who requested his silence on the entire matter.

Most irregular, most irregular indeed, Zaaki grumbled to himself, and now this latest request to x-ray what sounds like a simple shoe box!

While staring at his telephone, the radiologist had to finally admit to himself why he had so readily agreed to squeeze Rashid into his already busy daily schedule. It was sheer curiosity. If this box was as mysterious as that ancient and decrepit old mummy that Rashid had brought over before, then he wanted to be in on the ground floor on this latest escapade – even if he was again sworn not to breathe a word of it. Then it all hit the middle aged Egyptian technician right between the eyes. As much as he hated to admit it, his current professional life totally lacked a whit of excitement, mystery, and uncertainly. If anything, it was the exact opposite: clinical, sterile, and mundane. With that personal insight squarely placed before his consciousness, Zaaki smiled, rose from his desk chair, and began to whistle a jaunty tune as he left to finish his rounds.

*   *   *

In the half darkness of the office two men spoke in hushed, almost pious whispers, while the only illumination glowed from behind several large x-ray positives that hung against a wall viewer.

"If I did not see it with my own eyes I would not have believed it!"

"Nor I," said Rashid breathlessly. "It must be some sort of secret compartment in the base."

"Indeed, and now that we know that it is there, our challenge is to figure out how to open it."

"Hmmm," said Zaaki as he tilted his head this way and that before the screen. "You know, my dear colleague, if you look carefully, here and here, you can just make out two parallel lines. It looks to me that a portion of the base is really a panel that slides out."

"Dr. Zaaki! You're absolutely right! How did you spot those faint lines?"

Smiling, Zaaki said, "Years and years of experience reading hairline and green splint fractures Dr. Rashid."

"Simply remarkable, but what do you make of the compartment's contents?"

With squinted eyes behind his tethered glasses, the radiologist said, "I really don't know. It appears to be a rectangular object. It almost looks like film or a clear plastic sheet of some kind."

Taking off his thick reading glasses and rubbing the bridge of his nose Rashid said.

"You know, Hosny, I am no longer a young man. Such surprises are beginning to take their toll. So, may I invite you over to my laboratory? When, of course, you are able to schedule it. I think that it would be most appropriate that you should be one of the first to see just what that object is. After all, you found the compartment."

"Thank you Ahmed. I would be most delighted to accompany you back to the museum. Just allow me to call my wife to let her know that I will be late for dinner."

*   *   *

After some trial attempts, all it took in the end was some gentle, but specifically applied thumb pressure to the center leading edge of the container's base. As it slid open, both men swore in retrospect that they had caught the elusive scent of distant antiquity. With the panel removed, the pair now peered down at a strange sight. Fitted perfectly within the hidden compartment's dimensions lay a thin and diaphanous material that was covered with lines upon lines of beautifully formed bars of color. To say that Zaaki and Rashid were stunned would be an understatement.

Finally Zaaki whispered. "I am almost afraid to breathe."

"As am I," relied the curator. "It appears to be made of an extremely delicate almost transparent material. I dare not remove it. Instead, help me with that camera stand so that I can properly record this moment."

In all, it took Rashid only about thirty seconds to digitally record the base's contents. As a matter of course he used no flash, but instead shot eight bracketed images using varying focal lengths. Finished, he carefully resealed the base and only then did he noticeably take a deep breath himself.

"Well, that was quick," remarked Zaaki.

"Had to be so. I do not wish to unnecessarily jeopardize that artifact – whatever it is."

Picking up the cedar box in his cotton gloved hands, Rashid immediately placed it back in his personal safe, closing its door and spinning its dial.

Returning to his partner-in-crime, Rashid smiled and said.

"I find it simply remarkable how well camouflaged that panel was, using the wood's own grain to hid its existence. But enough about that. Let's project those images on the wall over there and see if we can together figure out just what we saw."

After an hour of discussion, they still didn't know what all the beautiful colors represented. But several familiar ideas did come to mind: bar codes, genetic gel strips, and color wheels. But that was as far as their speculations would go. They did note, however, the odd banding of the colorful bars was made up of every color of the rainbow. However, their jointly grumbling stomachs were cause enough to call it a day – albeit, a very interesting and exciting one.

*   *   *

That night neither Zaaki nor Rashid could sleep a wink. The radiologist found his rational mind was awash in contradictions. What was the material made of? What did all the colors mean? Why was it hidden so? Just how old was the box?

As for the curator, he wondered just how to present this new and curious tidbit of Akhenaten's legacy to the museum director, Dr. Sharil Moussa. His concern was not that she would not know what to do, but the curator was feeling some institutional guilt at having rushed ahead with his investigation so impulsively, and then again involving Zaaki, without her specific permission to do so.

*   *   *

Dr. Ahmed Rashid had known Sharil since she had been a young girl. In fact, he was considered a close professional uncle. It was easy to remember her running here and there in the shadow of her father, all the while he was inspecting archaeological sites and tombs. As she grew up, Sharil had excelled in her classes, became her father's personal assistant, and as a consequence went to Cambridge to secure her degrees. Upon returning to Egypt, her father, who was the Director of the Cairo National Museum, and so it was only natural that he should have his daughter at his side, quite literally in the thick of it. At her father's promotion to the head of the Egyptian Antiquities Organization, she emerged the natural choice for the new director of the Cairo National Museum in a bureaucracy typically dominated by males.

So as soon as Rashid had settled himself the following morning, he called his director with the news. As he was placing the receiver into its cradle, the curator could already hear the quick steps of the director's heels through his open transom. Instinctively, his stomach began to knot and a light film of perspiration began to form on his cleanly shaven upper lip.

Stopping briefly to deliver a gentle knock on his door, Sharil then burst into Rashid's office and exclaimed.

"Uncle! Please show me the slides!"

Having prepared precisely for this most reasonable of requests, Rashid flipped on his already running projector in the office's dim light.

Sharil's reaction was not what Rashid had expected, for she silently stood before the projected image with both hands covering her mouth and nose as if in an act of Christian prayer.

Still quite stunned, she slowly turned away and faced Rashid.

Well, here it comes, he fearfully thought.

"Uncle, where is the cedar box?"

"In my personal safe, right here." He said indicating to his left.

"And of the x-ray films, where are they?"

"Also here in the safe."

At this point Sharil paused as her eyes lost focus of their immediate surroundings. Then she continued.

"Uncle, you did precisely the right thing. You're instincts to pursue your investigation were totally within your purview as this museum's chief curator. But I do have one question: just who took the x-rays?"

"Dr. Hosny Zaaki, the chief radiologist at the El Kahera Medical Center. And if I may anticipate your next question, the answer is no, he does not know of this artifact's provenience. Just that it had a hidden compartment."

"Did he see the hidden contents with his own eyes?"

"Yes he has, and I felt that it was only the right thing to do at the time. As you know, your father knows his father. And besides, he has remained silent to this very day about Meryptah's x-rays as well."

Now pinching her lower lip between her thumb and forefinger in thought the director concluded.

"Uncle, you were absolutely right. I remember my father telling me about Dr. Zaaki. Since he trusts him, I see absolutely no reason why I should not as well."

Now sitting down before his desk with her eyes all aglow and with her hands all tied up in a bunch just as they did as a young girl whenever he had showed her an exceptionally interesting find, Sharil whispered.

"Uncle, may I now see your discovery?"

*   *   *

The phone rang and a very groggy man with a dry and hoarse voice said, "Hello?"

"Hello John? Did I wake you up?"

If it had not been for Sharil's distinctive voice, one Professor Dr. John Milson would have been extremely cross at the voice sent from half way around the world.

"Well Sharil, as a matter of fact yes, yes, you did, but I'm fully awake now. Just what do I owe the pleasure?"

Smiling to herself at the professor's quick recovery, Sharil could not contain herself any longer.

"John, do you remember that beautiful cedar box that contained the Annex Papyrus?"

"Ah yes, why yes I do."

Now speaking as slowly and clearly as she could Sharil began.

"Well, Dr. Ahmed Rashid, our chief curator, discovered today that it had a false bottom, that the base of the box had a secret compartment. When he opened it up he found within it – now brace yourself John, he found a message written only in colors."

A pregnant pause passed.

"John? John are you there?"

"Yes Sharil. Yes I am. To say the least this is stunning news. Is the artifact in question in a secure place?"

"Absolutely, positively so. But the real reason that I called John is that the four best digital images of the document are now sitting in your encrypted email."

"What! You've got to be kidding!"

"No John, I'm not. Now go back to sleep. You need your rest."

And then before she hung up she mischievously added.

"And don't let the bed bugs bite!"

*   *   *

Needless to say, Milson didn't sleep a wink for the rest of that night and early morning. He was suddenly like a kid on Christmas Eve with a pound of sugar coursing through his veins. No better, like a graduate student with a fresh pot of strong coffee in his gut. Regardless of which metaphor that you prefer, going back to sleep after Sharil's phone call was no longer an option, so Milson instead burned the literal midnight oil and toiled over a rough translation of the cedar box's hidden message. By 4:38 in the morning, Chicago time, he had his translation of the visible spectrum's five sentences, which he immediately emailed back to Sharil. Without question, the text's import shook the retired Egyptologist to his very core.

> When you find this message, then that is a good beginning, for you are both observant of form and cunning of mind. If you can understand my words, then you are already wise to the ways of the stars. I am the First Surveyor of the Survey Institute and am the author of the roll that is contained within this fine cedar wood chest. I have no doubt that you have read the tale of my many sojourns among the stars. While I have looked long for the subtle traces left by the seeds of the Old Ones, I have failed. Perhaps you will not.

Now back in bed a quite tired, but very satisfied Milson began to ponder yet again the First Surveyor's words and their meaning. While laying there in the dark with his hands behind his head, the aged Egyptologist suddenly realized that Richards' quest for Ptah had gained an even greater importance.

"Now wouldn't it be grand if Ptah was one of the Old Ones!"

Just before he finally slipped off to sleep, a smile formed on his face as he murmured to himself.

"And I think that it is high time that Joseph is fully brought up to speed on all of these developments. Hell, he was more right than the rest of us!"

CHAPTER XIII
The Teleconference

While over the past years' real time intercontinental teleconferences had occurred quite often, they nonetheless still retained a special, even novel quality about them. On the one hand the distances alone, spanning nine time zones, were so seamlessly and instantaneously bridged that the effect was as if you were chatting over the fence to your next door neighbor. On the other, the similarly seamless and instantaneous translation software that allowed for such effortless communications seemed to be the stuff of the Great Merlin himself. Even so, the medium was the product of several upgrades and two revisions that allowed for many nuances and colloquial expressions to be accurately understood. That the United States Air Force had incongruously provided both the means – the geostationary communications satellites, and the method – Language Guru 3.1, only added spice to the mix.

The two scientific panels, one in Chicago and the other in Moscow, had been initially and blissfully ignorant of their benefactor's lack of respect for their privacy. But in time the two groups had figured out the score that they were not totally alone in their deliberations. The solution provided by the Russians had been to add their own electronic "tweaks" in the form of one time, encryption pads of 256, and later 1024 density levels. As a result of the pad usage, it was quickly discovered that those embarrassing leaks didn't seem to happen with quite same unnerving frequency.

So was reached a *status quo* of sorts for the past two years between this select user community and an American military institution. The USAF knew well that if they chose to suddenly deny these scientific panels access to their communications satellite and its translation software, then that denial would have been an outright admittance of their past chicanery. Now so thoroughly trapped in a web of their very own making, the teleconferences continued, and one might add, now to the distinct benefit of the scientific panels.

"Fool me once, shame on you. Fool me twice, shame on me."

* * *

"So in essence Professor Milson," the Russian formally reiterated, "your people believe that another temporal excursion is justified."

"That is correct, Academician Rosovec. In fact, it would represent a fact finding mission more than anything else. All activities undertaken would be in strict accord with the *RUTI* mandates."

"Most encouraging," he said dryly. "And just when and where do you expect to find these facts that you are looking for?"

"The ancient records refer to temple repositories, what we moderns might regard as archival libraries. The ancients actually called such places the House of Life, or *per ankh*, after their god Thoth, the patron of writing and learned pursuits. We believe that there, within one or several of such collections, Dr. Richards should be able to confirm his suspicions."

"And for the record, would you remind us again just what Dr. Richards is looking for?"

"Why certainly Academician Rosovec," said Milson warming to the subject. "He's looking for any evidence that the ancient Egyptian god Ptah was once in fact a living being."

"Please excuse me Professor Milson, for I do not wish to appear dense, but such an apparently mundane academic request seems to suggest that there is a greater point to be made, especially when one considers the technical resources required and the stringent *RUTI* mandates regarding any such deployment. So just why is the identification of the god Ptah with a mortal man of such importance?"

"Because Academician Rosovec, we suspect that the life form who we know as Akhenaton was himself searching for evidence of this man, or more probably, for evidence of his kind."

"Or evidence of his kind." The Russian allowed as he slowly sat back into his chair allowing his last statement to hang theatrically in the air.

"So now the shoe falls. Professor. Let us speak candidly. Just what is so special about this god Ptah?"

"Well Academician Rosovec, I suspect that as the Director of Advanced and Theoretical Technological Research for the Russian Academy of Sciences that you may have had some exposure to genetics in a university class or two?"

To which Milson received a brief nod in confirmation, who then continued.

"I know for sure that Academician Sokolovska, to your right, certainly has. So what I am about to share with you should not be all that shocking. Now please give me a moment, while I sketch something out for you."

As a thinning head of white hair bent over towards the video camera's lens, the Egyptologist furiously began to draw several large images across his yellow legal pad. Meanwhile, the handsome Russian in his early forties was struggling not to smile at the dog and pony show that his friend in Chicago was putting on for the benefit of his two new colleagues.

That cagey American! Just what is he up to? This meeting that was clearly of his making, as that Brit Young and haughty physicist Jung have yet to say a word! And then here comes Milson's ploy for me to tease out of him all the details. Why not just come out with it? Why all the games? But knowing John, all of this will be well worth the ride. I just wonder if this fellow plays chess?

Now finished, Milson held up his pad lengthwise and held it towards the transmitting camera.

"Academician Rosovec, would you direct your technician to zoom in on this image?"

Silently nodding from his end, the Russian scientist turned to someone off camera and signaled to them with two pinching fingers.

The initial look of total bafflement on the faces of the three-man Russian panel was complete. Then the new Head of the Special Projects Directorate, Academician Gregorii Popov, who was sitting to Rosovec's left, piped up.

"These appear to be Egyptian hieroglyphics, Professor Milson. Am I correct?"

"Indeed they are Academician Popev." Milson's disembodied voice answered to the powerfully built, red-haired administrator. He then directed his attention towards the other newly appointed director of the prestigious Institute of Theoretical Biology, Viktor Sokolovska, who sat at Rosovec's right.

"Academician Sokolovska, I know that you are a biologist and from what I hear a very good one. Now I wish you to think like one.

"Please note," Milson began by indicating each character with this pencil. "These four Egyptian hieroglyphs make up the name of the god Ptah. For now let us ignore this last one of a seated figure here and instead concentrate on the first three."

After a brief explanation of the grammatical import of the three signs, the round Slavic face of the tall biologist became impassive and went blank as he continued to focus upon the three images before him. Then his eyes fractionally blinked, and then widen as his brown-haired head began to tilt slightly to the left. But before he provided his answer to the visual puzzle placed before him, he again noticeably blinked, swallowed several times, and then whispered his reply.

"But Professor Milson," the biologist gasped, "can that be possible?"

Milson beaming off camera with exuberant energy simply said. "Why not? Your interpretation of these glyphs is precisely the same as ours. And by the way, this revelation, when combined with the startling data gleaned from the Annex Papyrus, almost makes this deployment an imperative. Additionally, I now wish to seek permission from your panel to fully brief Dr. Richards on the contents of the Annex Papyrus and our recent results on the 'light language' as well."

CHAPTER XIV
Good News

Milson always was of the belief that good news should be shared quickly. So following the immensely successful teleconference with their Russian colleagues, Milson found himself briskly walking with purpose over to the Near Eastern Institute in search of his departmental colleague Richards. Bounding up the steps of the lion-headed stone staircase that leads to the institute's second floor, it didn't take long for the octogenarian to find his quarry in the archive.

Reining in his adrenalin and standing at the threshold, Milson took in the view. The rapidly fading light of the early evening had already begun to transform the vast chamber's many peaked stain glass windows into dark sword blades. The soft glow of the many reading lamps that adorned each of the long and massive study tables beckoned with a warming, cozy quality. The heady smell of ink, paper, and leather from the priceless research collection filled his nostrils. And of course unbidden, came to Milson that first image of when he had first approached Richards with his most remarkable career offer. In fact, the man immediately recognized that his young colleague was even ensconced at the very same table, off to the left, feet up on a neighboring chair, deeply immersed in his reading. Glancing about and seeing the silent archive otherwise unoccupied, he entered.

"Good evening Joseph." He gently began.

Startled, Richards banged his right knee against the bottom of the table, the sound of which then reverberated off the stone arched ceiling and the beautifully painted crossbeams decorated in multicolored hieroglyphs.

"Jesus Doc! You just did it again! My heart and knees just can't take it."

Pulling out a neighboring chair, Milson sat down with a satisfied smile.

Richards, instantly noting it, quipped.

"Okay John. I know that evil shit-eating grin of yours. What's up that's got you in such a darn good mood?"

Milson countered.

"Well, so what's a young stud like you doing here on a Friday night burning the midnight oil? Cramming for midterms?"

Glancing defensively at his watch, Richards stated.

"It's still early. It's only six-thirty. Now, what's up my friend?"

Knowing that he couldn't sit on the news any longer the emeritus professor of Egyptology opened up the flood gates.

"Well Joseph, I've got some good news. Our people and the Russians have authorized a deployment for the expressed purpose of finding out just who Ptah was. And oh yes, the Egyptians are friendly to the idea as well."

From Milson's point of view, Richards' reaction was a classic, down to the sagging jaw line and instantly distant and glazed eyes. Finally finding his tongue, Richards whispered.

"You've got to be kidding."

"Nope."

"What's the catch?"

"No catch."

"I go solo?"

"Nope, Gregorieva tags along."

"Half expected that. The Russians must have insisted as I'll bet that they are more than just curious as well."

Milson then leaned forward in a conspiratorial manner.

"Joseph my boy, sad as this may seem to you, the Soap Bubble is not yours and yours alone to do with as you please. Gregorieva needs to build up her field experience. Besides, we all agreed to the buddy system a long time ago for a reason. Remember?"

"Yeah, I suppose you're right." He reconsidered with a half-hearted and lop-sided grin. "So when do we get to go?"

"Not so fast my young colleague, for there is much, much more that you should be made aware of."

"Such as?" Richards queried.

"Do you remember that exquisite cedar chest that was found in the Aten's hanger?"

"Yep. What about it? Didn't it contain a papyrus?"

"It certainly did and what a very interesting papyrus it was, for it was immaculately brushed by Akhenaten himself."

"You've got to be kidding! Can you tell me what it was about?"

"Now I certainly can. I fact I have just been granted permission to do so. A copy of its translation and many supporting appendices is in my office's safe. You can read it there and there only. Understood?"

"Yes sir."

"Furthermore, to return to that cedar chest again, it was discovered that it had a false bottom. Within that hidden compartment was found a small semitransparent sheet of material covered with striations of color. As it turns out, those striations were not random, but instead represented a totally new, very alien language, specifically, Akhenaten's native tongue. But the story gets even better. Remember the worldwide Black Out?"

"How couldn't I! It was like living in the medieval period, candles and all. Christ! It was near social anarchy!"

"Well Joseph, that black out was engineered, I repeat, engineered by an alien recovery craft that snatched the Aten right off Wright-Patterson Air Force Base."

"No shit!" Richards said in a hushed whisper.

"Yes shit. And on the way out of our atmosphere that same craft sent an outbound message, a message that was also written in color and NORAD somehow managed to record it.

"And so my dear colleague, while we knew that Akhenaten was indeed an alien, we had no clue what he was –

an alien surveyor of worlds, solar systems and galaxies. The Annex Papyrus says so. The hidden message in the cedar chest says so. And the 'light language' transmission that we snagged only confirms it.

"But the best part Joseph is that the alien that we know as Akhenaten was specifically looking for something, desperately and obsessively looking for something. And that something was what it called 'the seeds of the Old Ones.' Joseph, it was searching the universe for none other than the First Source of Life. And Joseph, your observations about the grammatical construction of Ptah's name sure looks to me like the name of an Old One."

*   *   *

About the same time that Milson was bringing Richards up to speed, Vesna Gregorieva was dripping wet with sweat. Despite what the glamour magazines might say that "woman glow, men perspire, and only horses sweat," Gregorieva's body nonetheless streamed with moisture as her exposed skin left steamy vapor trails in the chilly morning air. Long lopping jogs did that to her. And with the cleansing that only a good exercise can offer, so too her mind began to clear, but not totally.

That son-of-a-bitch! She fumed as she stretched out her lithe dancer's frame against the side of a convenient tree trunk. A male passerby visibly winced at what he saw Gregorieva doing. The long hamstring stretch began with her heel firmly planted on the tree's trunk high above her head all the while she embraced the extended limb with her face to her knee.

Rosovec promised to keep in touch and now it has been, what, nearly a full year of silence. All the while I train and mindlessly ape repeatedly those language tapes of my dearest Sasha.

At the thought of Alexander Piankoff, once and former mentor, Gregorieva's heart immediately softened and her eyes took on a misty look as she continued to cool down.

My beloved Sasha, you who knew of my love, but who chose to remain removed, but still near, still supportive. You who I would have gladly traded fates.

Now blinking back tears at the memory of the man's sudden passing, the young Russian unconsciously flexed the muscles of her graceful jaw line.

Be strong. Be patient. She chided herself. Sasha would not have approved.

Tired and finished with the familiar support of her favorite tree, the mid-twenty-something temporal agent strode purposefully back to her flat with her hands buried deeply into the pockets of her one-piece Nike jogging suit.

From about a block away, the course of these innocent events had not gone unnoticed.

"So, she runs daily?" said the handsome, black-haired man from behind the Zeiss binoculars.

"Yes sir."

"Well in that outfit she sure looks like an impala. How far and how long does she run? Do you know?"

"Yes sir. She holds to a very predictable jogging schedule. Distances range from five to nine kilometers. Times, well, I do not have those at my fingertips, but I'm told that her pace would kill an ordinary man."

"Well, well. It seems that our dear Vesna possesses a driven spirit. While that's good that could just as well be bad. How current is she on her language skills?"

"Excellent Academician Rosovec, I believe that she has committed to memory the entire suite of conversational ancient Egyptian that Major General Piankoff built."

"You're kidding!"

"Not at all sir. I say this with some confidence as she interacts with the program's many lessons, far too quickly."

"So what you are telling me is that this knife has been honed so sharp that it is in danger of becoming dull?"

"Yes sir. Gregorieva is sorely in need of some practical stimulation."

"Does she have an intimate partner?"

"No sir, none that we are aware of."

"Huh. So do you believe her to be ready for a deployment? That is, or course, if such an occasion might providentially present itself?"

"Without question, Academician Rosovec! In fact, 'that would be just what the doctor ordered,' or so goes that American expression."

"Yes captain. Yes, I believe that you are absolutely right."

* * *

Vesna's immediate reaction to the direct transpolar flight from Moscow to Chicago, now her third such round trip, was no different than the first. Her excitement just brimmed and bubbled over. Her anticipation of another temporal field operation, her second, was cause for joyful fulfillment. She had worked hard on her language skills; she had toned and trained her body to the point that her resting pulse was that of a dead man. Even more strangely, although she could never admit it to her Muscovite handlers, she dearly missed her colleagues at the Philology Annex. After all, they and only they truly understood all that she had gone through, all that she had sacrificed, to come so far so fast.

But really deep down, she missed most of all of those impassioned conversations with John Milson – such a remarkable man trapped within an aged and nearly cadaverous body.

What a shame. He's so much like my Sasha, but so very different as well.

And then there was Richards. The mere thought of that man brought on a blender-like swirl of emotions that simply refused to coalesce. His coolness, self-absorption, stubbornness, single-mindedness, and self-restraint above all else drove the Russian crazy – not to mention that strong sexual pull that she had to admit was undeniable. In many ways Richards was her exact analogue: a competent alpha-male and an utterly reliable loner with a strong idealistic streak that she judged almost quaint. In short, that realization cut the Russian to the core.

Now just how can that be? She asked herself.

CHAPTER XV
Horizon Pass

"You know Charlie. I really think that these latest tweaks just might change everything," quipped the ninety-two year old genius, Dr. Peter Borov, as he gently sat back into his thickly padded desk chair that nicely cushioned his lanky and all too bony jogger's physique.

His Cal Tech-trained interlocutor, easily his junior by some fifty-odd years who was being groomed as his successor, just slowly and thoughtfully nodded his chin.

"And," Borov continued while pointing his finger towards the ceiling in emphasis, "these developments will also mean that the Soap Bubble VI's power requirements will fall as well. I have just calculated that we can finally do away with that ungainly backpack cell in favor of a nickel-cadmium rechargeable. While it's my bet that initially it will be a bit less of a bulky burden, at least it won't be that nuclear monstrosity anymore! What a security risk that was! It caused a near heart attack for Tuna Cartwright each and every time he went into the field with it."

"Have to agree with you again Doc." The relative youngster said with another nod that moved much of his long, sun-bleached mane in a slow swing. But Charlie O'Brian Naysmithe wasn't finished quite yet.

"On top of that, Little Beast II's size and weight has also dropped to that of a laptop. While we have retained its flexible wafer panels and boards, we have redesigned them using self-assembled monolayers just 1.0 nanometers thick, instead of the former fifteen, much less the typical sixty five. And with that new cluster of microchips, the unit now puts out a computational speed in the 6.7 to 7.5 gigahertz range. That will give us unprecedented tower modulation and synchronization, not to mention an improvement in calibrating the temporal coordinates."

Now leaning forward across the desk, the younger man gestured to his older colleague as he warmed to the subject.

"But the really best part is again the reduced power requirements. Nadine English's innovative idea of routing all the heat generated from the microchip array to a miniaturized heat exchanger actually produces a mild trickle charge back to the power pack. She estimates that that innovation alone will extend the nominal four hour run time of the cell by some fourteen minutes. Not much, but that's nice padding before the cell's gage dips into the yellow. And knowing Tuna Cartwright, he will be really jazzed about that as well."

"Indeed, Charlie, indeed." The well-seasoned Russian immigrant beamed. Besides, that old Louisiana cracker will now finally have fewer beefs about the power pack's mass, and I quote, 'It's like lugg'n an entire frick'n frig on my back,' in that hysterical dialect of his. I just can't wait to see his face when he sees all the weight reductions and miniaturizations that we have made!"

Just what this unlikely pair of savants was discussing was the extensive introduction of self-building carbon nanotube technology augmented with next generation micro-processing into Borov's first and only love, a temporal distortion device, fondly called the Soap Bubble. Already with its earlier versions, especially Marks IV, V and V-A, two men and one woman had successfully journeyed back into time and returned without significant incident. That is, if one discounts one broken ankle, a nasty case of riverine parasite that proved fatal upon a totally botched modern diagnosis, and the oddly variable, but blessedly brief "post drop syndrome," or PDS for short.

This last item Doc Allen, Horizon Pass' first and only resident physician, was trying his best to track down. Curiously, the syndrome seemed to affect only the males, while the lone female noted absolutely no adverse effects whatsoever from the Soap Bubble's finely tuned electromagnetic field and polarizing ionic streams. Nonetheless, the syndrome had troubled the late Piankoff to the point that he had briefly lost consciousness on one drop. As his limp form landed, so had he awkwardly broken his ankle. For young Richards, Piankoff's first and only temporal field assistant and now successor, the expression of his symptoms seemed to rise and fall in intensity for no apparent rhyme or reason. Currently, the ruddy, freckled-faced, and sandy haired Oklahoma native was stumped by the syndrome and was mad as hell about it. Yet for some reason, Vesna Gregorieva, Richards' current assistant, seemed entirely immune to PDS and no one could figure out why.

So for Borov, each and every tweak, as he so fondly put it, represented his best efforts at refining a process and hopefully minimizing, if not removing entirely, the adverse affects that temporal travel seemed to have on the male of the species. But down deep, he knew that the human body – itself an electrochemical engine, was not really designed to pass through such a highly focused electromagnetic and quantum field that the Soap Bubble's drop ring created. He knew that the reversible polarizing ion cannons that streamed forth during each and every drop and retrieval had helped to smooth that transition, PDS still remained an operational hazard – at least for males.

"You know Charlie, about PDS and Piankoff's and Richards' struggles with it, Stephen Hawking just might have been right all along."

"You mean about his remarks on time travel, chronology protection, and quantum level effects?"

"Exactly. We know that time travel into the past is not only possible given a classical physical model and Einstein's General Theory of Relativity, but demonstrably practical. What PDS may be then is the quantum penalty on our physiology. In essence, PDS may be Nature's price for us dropping into the past and a warning not to create a paradox."

"So Doc, what do you think Hawking would say if he knew about the *RUTI* that you and the Hour Glass Seminar cooked up back in 1940?"

A thoughtful pause.

"Well Charlie, probably two things. On the one hand, he would probably agree with the document's theoretical underpinnings, but would thoroughly doubt whether time travel could be practically implemented. On the other, I can only just paraphrase what he has already said on the subject."

"If time travel is possible, then why haven't we been overrun by tourists from the future?"

*   *   *

"You know Doc, I've been thinking. It would be really neat that if just prior to a jump we could drop a small leather pouch through the ring." Richards said.

"Okay Joseph, but what's in the pouch?" Borov reasonably asked.

"Some pocket money, traveling money – an assortment of small copper and gold rings of various weights."

"Well, that's an interesting request. But you know as well as I that you never drop with any metal on you. That's why we replaced all the fillings in Piankoff and Gregorieva with porcelain ones specifically because of that. But I get what you're saying. Almost a mini-drop, the pouch alone, just prior to the main drop with no human contact. It sounds reasonable. Let me look into it for you."

"Thanks Doc, I knew that you would understand."

*   *   *

"Charlie, it's time that I share something with you that has been on my plate for some time.

"Yeah. Why don't you just come right over to my office?

"Thanks."

As Borov hug up the phone, he continued to stare blankly at the plump green file folder already long faded along its edges. Even its many top security stamps were worn as was the label that indicated its content: CRYSTAL BALL.

Golly, the scientist thought, it's been a long time since I last looked into that disaster that was the Philadelphia Experiment. All those men so horribly mutilated. All those men lost. I guess that it is finally time to see what and if there is anything that we can do.

Shortly after the completion of those somber thoughts, there came a knock on his office door's frame and there stood Naysmithe, a six foot something string bean with large kind brown eyes and a shock of sun-drenched hair.

"You rang Doc?"

"Yep, I did. Take a chair Charlie because this might take some time to explain."

As Naysmithe was just getting settled into his chair, Borov began.

"First off, have you ever heard of the Philadelphia Experiment?"

"Nope." Said the physicist cautiously. "Should I have?"

"Naw, not really, the entire incident has been rather publically denied, declared a hoax, and relegated to the circular file by the Department of the Navy, and in particular, by its Office of Naval Research."

"Then why Peter do you have that shit-eating grin on your face? How come I get the sense that this experiment, or whatever it was, isn't dead quite yet?"

"Am I that obvious Charlie?" Asked the nonagenarian.

"'fraid so."

"Okay, here's the straight skinny on the Philadelphia Experiment at least as far as the Office of Naval Research is concerned. They deny it categorically. They even have the entire crew in their pocket. But back during World War II, the development of good naval camouflage was a really high priority as submarine warfare was really taking a toll on Allied shipping. So there was a big push on to do something about a ship's visibility. The British approached the issue with lots of paint, as in camouflaging schemes that decorated a ship's outer hull. Alternating light and grays, dark and grays, all applied in random-appearing vertical stripes. The whole idea was to visually break up a ship's profile. As you can imagine, that plan did not work out so well, because oil-based paint is hardly adaptive. Then, somewhere along the line a certain scientist, who had been tasked on another naval project, apparently heard some scuttlebutt about the issue, expressed his interest in assisting, got an idea, and then pitched it to the Navy."

"Now before you jump to any conclusions, I can tell you that that certain scientist was not me, but it might as well could have been. Instead, it was none other than Albert Einstein himself. His idea was audacious. Render a vessel invisible by bending the visible light around it. Slick huh?"

With his chin buried in his palm Naysmithe sarcastically quipped.

"To do that would have taken a bunch of energy to pull it off."

"Yes indeed it would have, but back in 1943 it was apparently doable as the experiment proved successful, even if it was only a partial success. They had indeed achieved invisibility, even to the point that there was a hole in the water that represented the displacement of the ship's hull."

"Okay, it was a partial success. So what really happened?"

"Charlie, very nasty things. While the vessel itself sustained no damage whatsoever, the same could not be said of its skeleton crew. As you well know yourself, exposure to electromagnetic fields wrecks havoc on the highly delicate electro-chemical human envelope. Just look at what Piankoff and now Joey have been going through with our own tiny field. Can you begin to imagine how big a field it would take to light up an entire destroyer escort? Christ all mighty, what were they thinking?"

Pause.

"Peter, what sort of nasty things?" Naysmithe quietly probed.

"Spontaneous human combustion, severe disorientation and nausea, and then there was the induced madness."

"Jesus."

"No shit."

"But what has this to do with us?" Naysmithe now wanted to know.

"Well, directly, not much. But several of the crew went missing."

"What do you mean by 'missing'?"

"Well, it was reported that for some of the crew the agony was so bad they did the logical thing and jumped overboard. But when they jumped, they didn't hit the water. They just disappeared. My best guess is that they went *somewhen*. In fact, among the initial arguments put forward in support of my early research was a plea by the Navy Department to make an attempt to retrieve those lost sailors."

"Ah ha, now I see the connection. Those duplicitous bastards! Deny the whole thing out of one corner of their mouth and then beg for help with the other."

"Precisely. So what I am now going to do is entrust you with this file. Read it cover to cover. It's a real toss salad of 'official' Navy press and some real quackery. I guarantee you that it contains some pretty scary stuff, especially considering what we know about electromagnetic fields. Basically, I want you to figure out whether or not we can mount some sort of retrieval effort, or even if such a thing would even be feasible. Got it?"

"Yep."

Now raising his index finger for emphasis.

"And Charlie, I want you to know that I do not consider this a wild goose chase."

"Got it."

*   *   *

"Doc, no matter how many different ways I have looked at this problem, I just cannot see an opening. Instead, all I see are opportunities for a security breech to occur." Then shaking his head in negation. "And if we're not creating a paradox outright, then the risk is just too high security-wise."

Borov frowning at that news then said. "Okay Charlie, I hear you. But you also sound really frustrated. Now humor me with all of your concerns."

"Alright then, consider the following. Richards and Gregorieva drop into a secure site somewhere in or near to the Philadelphia area, but yet to be identified. Somehow they locate the test area, but how do they gain access to it? Then, assuming that they get in somehow, once within the parameter, what are they to do? Even if they get in, how do they get out? Yes, Richards' ability to recollect is stellar, but regardless that will require a long debrief. Granted, for Gregorieva and her background in physics, that would be easier. Bottom line: I'm sorry, but the security net would be just too tight around such an event and the personnel involved too well known to suddenly introduce two new faces. On top of that there is nowhere for them to disappear or blend in as they did so well in antiquity. Add to that the wartime paranoia and the 'shoot first and ask questions later' mentality. Doc, this is a fool's errand."

Borov sat quietly in his office chair for several moments deep in thought. Finally, he bestirred himself.

"So, according to your analysis, we need to locate a safe house/drop point. Next, we need to locate the test area. Then, we need to provide our assets with security papers of sufficient weight to overcome all question. Furthermore, our assets need enough background training to back up any possible objections to their presence at the test site. Believe it or not Charlie, I know someone who can help us with almost all of these objections that you have raised. The only real outlier is the safe house/drop point. There, we are clearly on our own.

"Now while as much as I do not want to expose our temporal assets to any more risk than necessary, the fact remains that the Soap Bubble exists in large part due to those who supported a retrieval effort. To those supporters, I am indebted. So Charlie, let's push forward on this. That means we need to get that someone I mentioned up to speed on what we need. And oh by the way, that means that they also need to be cleared on the Soap Bubble and *RUTI* as well."

Resigned sigh.

"Charlie. No one ever said that this job would be easy."

CHAPTER XVI
Passing the Baton

To say that Charles Abraham "Tuna" Cartwright had not seen a thing or two during his varied and sundry military career would have been an understatement. In some respects, it was almost as if he had been bred for the challenge. His family's proud military tradition stretched back to the Civil War, where his great-grandfather had survived the Battle at Antietam Creek. A member of General A.P. Hill's "Light Division," he had arrived from Harper's Ferry at a very timely moment. His own words penned in a letter after that encounter stated

> I was flat tuckered out after the ford of the Potomac and quick march from Harper's Ferry. We was all hungry with blisters for feet. We fought like demons, but the sun seemed almost to go backwards, and it appeared as if night would never come.

Following that great national upheaval, the Cartwright family moved from Virginia to Louisiana as the prospects there were deemed to be better. Tuna's grandfather, however, remained a restless youth and spurned the family's fishing business as "smelly, dirty, boring and unmanly." And so in 1898 Grandpa Cartwright hitched a ride as a deck hand on a ship bound for Corpus Christi, Texas, because he had heard talk about adventurous doings – the formation of an all volunteer cavalry, in a far away and exotic place called San Antonio. Having never seen an American Indian, having sparse experience at best on horseback, Grandpa Cartwright nonetheless joined and became a member of the Rough Riders and even took part in the Battle at Las Guásimas, Cuba.

Father Cartwright, who was born in 1905, totally missed the First World War, but was the first of the family to enter

Annapolis. Upon his graduation with commission, he selected to no one's shock something that was old and new: mechanized cavalry. Quite literally, he saw the transition from horse flesh to steel and gasoline. Thoroughly loving things mechanical and the reek of diesel, pa soon found himself shoulder-to-shoulder as a staff officer assigned to a fellow named George Smith Patton, Jr., whom he served faithfully.

Tuna, the last of three brothers, who was born in 1940 followed the family tradition and graduated from Annapolis in 1956 in the very midst of the Cold War. His older brother John, following the family tradition, went into the cavalry with the V Corp stationed at the Fulda Gap. Tuna instead selected a more security-, language-, and technology-based career and quickly found himself stationed in White Sands. There, the young Army officer first met Dr. Peter Borov and in practically no time earned that scientist's respect, when Tuna single-handedly "assisted" that good doctor during an epoch-making tug-of-war between a prehistoric raptor and Roscoe the hamster.

That instance of quick assistance and resourcefulness was never forgotten by Borov. In fact, it actually formed the basis for a life-long friendship between the two men. While Borov remained an unwed and secluded émigré within his adopted country, Tuna had nonetheless made that time memorable with frequent trips to Louisiana to "just go fishin.'" And as time went on and as the Soup Bubble Project grew, so did Tuna in his security responsibilities, his understanding of the technology involved, and the transformation of his "school of fish" from a purely static into a fully deployable security force.

Now with Borov approaching his ninety-second birthday, Tuna reached his sixty-fifth and as hard as it was to admit to himself, this tough old fish was forced to confront reality. While still sharp of mind and strong of body, Tuna needed to find someone who could replace him in the field, while he would provide support from the sidelines. When Tuna first brought up the issue with Borov, the discussion, while necessary, had been a tearful one.

* * *

Standing before his men in his freshly starched desert cammies with knife edges for pleats, his polarized desert Ray Ban's and a freshly buzzed haircut, Commander Charles Abraham "Tuna" Cartwright had this to say.

"After much discussion and considerable thought," Tuna announced formally to his amassed security force, "it has been decided that Sgt. Patrick Doyle Callahan, now First Lieutenant Callahan, will henceforth lead and command this fine unit in the field. Frankly gentlemen, it has been deemed that I am far more valuable sitting on my ass in support of you-all, instead of humping my sorry ass just trying to keep up with you."

First initial shock, and then good-hearted laughter, broke out among the troops.

"Gentlemen, I promise you that I will remain your backstop behind the scenes. Furthermore, it's no secret to anyone here that "Calli" is one outstanding officer. It was just his bad luck to have been my active second for so long. Now is his time. Now is my time to find better ways, methods, and yes, toys, for you-all to play with."

Tuna then briefly paused to gather himself fearing that a tear might escape from beneath the lower edges of his shades.

"I just wish to say, officially, just how proud I am of each and every one of you. How each and every one of you has individually and collectively pushed the envelope well beyond the limits.

"Damn I am so proud of you-all! And before I dismiss you-all, I just wish to point out that behind me are four kegs of cold beer that will shortly require your careful scrutiny and attention to detail. I do not know how they got here. I do not know who paid for them. But I do damn well know that this promotion ceremony has made me damn thirsty.

"That is all.

"Dismissed."

Chapter XVII
CRYSTAL BALL

When Doc Borov said that the CRYSTAL BALL file would make for some scary reading, he wasn't kidding. By the time that Naysmithe had scanned his way through its contents for the third time, his notes had filled up the entire second page of his legal yellow pad. Many of those notations ended with an exclamation mark.

While the general concept mimicked the energizing of the Soap Bubble's drop ring, the ham-handed wartime approach adopted by the Office of Naval Research had been reckless in the extreme. Whereas the framework of Borov's theoretical concept of the early Soap Bubble had been backed up with a gradual technological development based on careful and incremental steps, the Philadelphia Experiment had been conducted based on the big bang approach not to mention the grotesquely needless and heedless exposure of American servicemen. Trying to imagine the physiological impact of the exposure time within such an immense electro-magnetic field, Naysmithe mentally gasped.

Next, Naysmithe went into Einstein's background. He was searching for the scientist's motive and potential for opportunity and what he discovered really opened his eyes. It turns out that in correspondence to a friend dated to August 13, 1943, only two months prior to the alleged dock-side experiment, the scientist mentioned that he had established

Closer relations with the Navy and the Office of Scientific Research and Development in Washington.

Upon further investigation Naysmithe found out that that organization's director, none other than Dr. Vannevar Bush, wrote that

> Some friends of Einstein visited me and told me that he was disturbed because he was not active in the war effort. I accordingly appointed him a member of a committee where it seemed to me his particular skills would be most likely to be of service.

What really surprised Naysmithe was that the aforementioned committee itself did not have a name and what it was tasked with was itself a security mystery. But from what he could ascertain the mysterious committee was highly "unlikely to have been concerned with nuclear research." Okay then, the physicist thought, if Einstein's assistance was not of a nuclear nature, then what else could he have been involved with? After some thought, Naysmithe concluded that could only be his interest in the relationship between gravitation and electro-magnetism, a relationship that he had first published in 1928. Something that he called the Unified Field Theory.

As to what this theory was about, Einstein was kind enough to explain in layman's terms in an article that appeared in the *Daily Chronicle* of January 26, 1929.

> For years it has been my greatest ambition to resolve the duality of natural laws into unity. This duality lies in the fact that sets of laws – those which control gravitation and those of magnetism...Many physicists have suspected that two sets of laws must be based upon one general law, but neither experiment nor theory has, until now, succeeded in formulating this law. I believe now that I have found a proper form. I have thought out a special construction which is differentiated from that of my relativity theory, through certain conditions. These conditions bring under the same mathematical equations the laws which govern the electromagnetic field and those which

govern the field of gravitation...The relativity theory reduced to one formula all laws which govern space, time and gravitation, and thus it corresponded to the demand for simplification of our physical concepts. The purpose of my work is to further this simplification, and particularly to reduce to one formula the explanation of the field of gravity and of the field of electromagnetism. For this reason I call it a contribution to "a unified field theory."

Now digging a bit deeper, Naysmithe then discovered that while Einstein was attached to the above mentioned mystery committee, the Navy's Bureau of Ordnance had also hired him stipulating that

His naval assignment will be on a part-time contractual basis and he will continue his association with the Institute for Advanced Study, Princeton, N.J., where most of his studies on behalf of the Bureau of Ordnance will be undertaken.

Now searching the records of the General Services Administration, Naysmithe found himself staring at Einstein's Special Service Contracts with the Department of the Navy. Among them he noted that Einstein was listed as a "Scientist" from May 31, 1943 through June 30, 1944. Then as a "Technicist" from July 1, 1944 through June 30, 1945. And finally as a "Consultant for Research on Explosives" from July 1, 1945 through June 30, 1946. So, Naysmithe concluded, it was very possible that a highly motivated Einstein could have indeed been involved with the Navy's Philadelphia Experiment that occurred in October of 1943. Additionally, the physicist strongly suspected that the Bureau of Ordnance was just providing a bureaucratic smokescreen.

Now sitting back deeply into his office chair, Naysmithe knew what the official Naval Intelligence documentation told him and what the real truth might be. But to get to the heart of the matter, he would need to risk boots on the ground both to witness the event – if it had ever occurred, and if it did, to gather as much technical detail as possible. When armed with such data, then and only then could a potential response be outlined for Peter.

The weightiness of the realization that he would have to risk two temporal field operatives in order to even judge the feasibility of whether others might be retrieved was overwhelming. And then it dawned on him that Borov had been shouldering precisely such risks for how long now? Some eleven years worth first with Piankoff, then Richards and Piankoff, and now Gregorieva and Richards. Suddenly, the physics behind the marvel that was the Soap Bubble seemed inconsequential, when pitted against the human risk involved, not to mention the many concerns as outlined in the *RUTI*.

Quietly he asked himself. Charlie, do you have the guts to authorize a deployment? Or are you just a caretaker of some really far out machinery? Or better, are you just some fancy-dancy electrical repairman?

Then another thought hit him squarely between the eyes. So this is why Borov had waited so long before confronting this project. He could not do it himself out of fear of a paradox, so he had to send someone else. And that someone else is most probably me! After all, who else would know what to look for?

*　　*　　*

It was nearing the end of another day and Borov was looking forward to an early evening jog to blow out all the cobwebs. But those thoughts were dashed to pieces by an all too familiar rap on his door frame.

"Have a minute Dr. Borov?" While the lanky physicist took a seat.

"Why yes, yes I do Charlie. Why so formal?"

"Because I took to heart what you said about that file on the Philadelphia Experiment. And I believe that I have a possible angle on it."

"You do!"

"Yep, but I guarantee that you will not like it one bit."

"Try me." The elder cautiously said.

"First, we need someone to witness the actual event. Second, that someone needs to be a physicist. And third, I'm volunteering."

Smiling broadly, Borov shook his head and said. "Totally out of the question Charlie. You're my successor, remember? You're far too valuable and certainly are hardly expendable. In short, no way Jose. Period. End of story."

"Funny. I thought that you would say something like that. But what other choice do we have? If we are to formulate a retrieval plan, we need eyes on target and someone to gather data. Otherwise, we're sunk."

"Charlie, you are overlooking something seminal. Gregorieva's university major was physics. She possesses a knowledge of how the Soap Bubble operates that far surpasses that of Richards. Much as I like Joey, he dumb as a stone when it comes to an appreciation of quantum mechanics. Not so with Vesna. So if your eventual plan is to send the two of them, then I would suggest that you put together a laundry list for Gregorieva."

Throughout this snap analysis, Naysmithe was awed by the fact that Borov had accepted his plan to deploy and reconnoiter so readily and apparently his face had given that fact away.

"You know Charlie." Borov said with a gentle smile. "When our Russian colleagues first shared with us Gregorieva's dossier, I immediately flagged her undergraduate major as more than just a nice to have. In fact, when I first saw it, I immediately realized the possibilities. If anything, Charlie, I want you to know that we are on totally the same wavelength.

"As for the temporal insertion itself, we will have to do some very careful research and planning. We'll need authentic identities, papers, Navy uniforms, currency, a safe house, and a suitable drop location. Above all, we have to wait for Gregorieva's hair to grow out, because women of the 1940's, even in the military, did have hair."

"You know Doc, this scenario goes way beyond the resources of the Philology Annex. We need to immerse our temporal assets in the news of the period, its history, and a whole raft of mundane stuff as well if they are going to pass muster."

"Yes, I know. And in anticipation of that need, we have already secured a small microfilm library of both national and regional newspapers, *Life* magazine, and an expert in the period to 'tutor' our charges. In fact, we even have at our disposal several 'period' automobiles for them to drive around in and get used to. But I think that the most challenging aspect of Gregorieva's and Richards' preparation will be the little things. Stuff like the way women were treated back then and yet were expected to somehow make do. This goes way beyond Rosie the Riveter. 'Seen but not heard' really only begins to cover it. Fortunately, our 'expert' will be able to communicate that rather well."

"And just who is this 'expert' of yours?" Naysmithe asked.

"Thought you would never ask. She's Professor Emeritus Mildred Hayes. Not only is Millie Hayes a scientist, she's also a physicist as well, who lived through those times in a very personal way. You see Charlie, I first met Millie while I was a young man at Princeton. A finer person you will never meet. But don't get into an argument with her, you'll sure as hell loose."

*　　*　　*

CHILDREN OF PTAH

Mildred Elizabeth Hayes was born in Manhattan, Kansas, on a beautiful summer Saturday afternoon. The year was 1920 and it would be another fifty-odd years before the town's motto would become "The Little Apple." Millie was a late surprise to a Presbyterian marriage. Her father Jacob was a secondary school science teacher and their church's organist. Her mother Margaret was the second daughter of a local grain farming family. As for Millie she enjoyed a loving, protective and structured childhood. She got reasonably good marks in primary and secondary school, and so when the time came she was encouraged to enroll at the local college in town – Kansas State College of Agriculture and Applied Science, today's Kansas State University. Much to her parents surprise Millie excelled at mathematics of all things, which opened up for her the wonders of engineering and physics. Given the primary agricultural thrust of that institution in the early 1940's, engineering usually meant well drilling, and physics the theoretical design of well pumps. But because of the course of World War II Millie had nonetheless flourished in a trendy and new fangled field called nuclear physics. In due course Millie was nominated by her departmental chair and subsequently received a full but modest post-graduate scholarship to the University of Chicago. She was, after all, a woman.

Chicago was a big step for Millie, for it meant leaving home for the first time in her life. The trek took almost a week by train as she and her father traveled through such exciting places as Kansas City, St. Louis, and Springfield before finally arriving in Chicago. Union Station proved to be an overwhelming, busy, and noisy introduction to that City of Big Shoulders. To say that the pair was frazzled and travel weary would be an understatement. After an entertaining taxi ride, the two-some were then introduced to a vast university campus built of Gothic stone architecture shrouded in the dappled shade of ancient trees.

Their arrival on campus during the fall of 1942 in many ways made them witnesses, in a sense, to the first isolation of the element plutonium and the creation of the first artificial, self-sustained nuclear reaction. While standing before the Student Union with its archway heavily guarded by its many leering gargoyles, little did Millie know that within a week's time she would meet the likes of the ever patient and helpful Enrico Fermi, who immediately introduced her to the newest arrival on the physic's faculty, Dr. Maria Goeppert Mayer. Mayer, who represented her family's seventh straight generational professor, was some fourteen years Millie's senior, but from the very start Mayer took the shy and eager numbers' cruncher under her wing and made Millie her graduate assistant. Now working closely with Mayer, Millie was immediately immersed in the bleeding edge developments of her chosen specialty. Even the ever suspicious Hungarian physicist Edward Teller fell to Millie's sincerity of spirit and even liked to quip, "That's Miss Millie from Manhattan, after whom the (Manhattan) Project is so aptly named."

* * *

After Millie's first whirl-wind year of post-graduate study in Chicago, it was deemed useful by Fermi and Mayer that she should spend her next year as a research fellow at the Institute for Advanced Study in Princeton, New Jersey. And so she again packed her trunk. This incredible academic opportunity of course meant another train ride adventure, this time from Chicago to Philadelphia and from there to Princeton. Again her father joined her mostly to satisfy Millie's very worried mother, but privately Jacob Hayes had long pined to travel himself and now he again had his chance. Besides, he was very curious about this place called Princeton.

* * *

As frenetic as Chicago's Union Station had been, the Princeton Junction Station was quaintly idyllic in its diminutive size and open atmosphere. The rail stop was more a simple platform roofed in tasteful gray slate, the whole supported by a steel framework painted in a dark green. It was quite a change from Chicago's indoor train stadium. Also, the first smells of Princeton were not those of harsh diesel exhaust tinged vaguely with the ammonia reek of rat urine, but rather that of sweet honeysuckle bushes the whole shaded in vast and spreading locust trees, birch, and elm.

Now standing on the platform and turning on their heels while they decided as to which way to go next, a neatly groomed young man wearing an outlandish coat decorated in alternating black and orange vertical stripes boldly greeted Millie and Jacob.

"Excuse me, but are you perhaps Mr. Jacob Hayes and Miss Mildred Hayes?"

The weary travelers, taken somewhat aback at both the odd sight and clipped Eastern greeting, took some time before their collective tongues found their function. Then, successfully finding them, they simultaneously answered.

"Yes, that's us." Quickly followed by. "And who are you?"

"Ah yes. Quite. My name is Peter Simon. The Institute's director sent me to fetch your baggage, escort you to Fuld Hall, and get you settled in. My automobile is parked right outside." Now lifting with a slight grunt Millie's trunk by its handle. "Ah, kindly follow me."

Now a bit wide-eyed and taken aback, Millie and Jacob just numbly followed the young man as he began to lug the trunk across the railroad platform towards the exit's staircase, thumping his way down as he pulled on the heavy trunk.

*   *   *

"I trust that you found your accommodations in Fuld Hall satisfactory?" asked Franklin Ridgeway Aydelotte, the then director of the Institute for Advanced Study.

"Oh, yes sir. Most cozy." Replied a nearly breathless Millie.

"And Mr. Simon. Was he helpful?"

"Oh, yes sir, and strong too. He could actually move my trunk."

"I see. Marvelous. Now as for your presence here at the Institute, both Professors Fermi and Mayer were most effusive in their recommendations, stating that your capacity for mathematics was quite remarkable and that you are particularly interested in nuclear physics. Do I have that right?"

"Oh, yes sir. But I do not think of myself as 'remarkable' in any way."

Now smiling kindly, the former president of Swarthmore College eyes' softened as he was pleasantly surprised by the humility of that statement from one so young and yet so highly recommended.

Now folding his hands on the desk before him, the director began.

"You know, Miss Hayes, you have to help me out a bit here. I am just an English major by training. Would you be so kind and explain to this avid reader of Elizabethan literature just what you find so fascinating about numbers and nuclear theory?"

And so gently began the final vetting and approval interview between a second-year graduate student and an Oxford trained Hoosier. Twenty-three minutes later, Aydelotte, with some embarrassment, found himself in a poise of rapt attention with his elbows forward on his desk and his head in his hands as he had carefully listened to each and every word. When Millie had finished, he felt transformed. Aydelotte just could not put his finger on how it had all happened. Was it her Midwestern dialect that had subconsciously so tugged at his Indiana roots, or was it the invoking of common sense analogies for intricate concepts? Regardless, never before had anyone so effortlessly and clearly explained to him that intricate matrix that was the marriage between mathematics and physics.

Now rubbing his chin in thought.

Damnation! Fermi and Mayer were spot on. This young lady is an absolute genius! And what a breath of fresh air! I now know just the person with whom she would work with for the coming year. Besides, he needs some stimulation and perhaps some of Miss Hayes' innocent clarity as well. Now just who should I contact to arrange for a proper introduction?

*   *   *

"112 Mercer Street, 11:00 am sharp" said Aydelotte's crabbed handwritten note. Millie, ever one for an adventure, began her walk from Fuld Hall to Olden Lane where she turned left. Continuing on for four blocks she passed Ober, Haslet, and Battle Road before finally arriving at Mercer Street. Millie then turned right, went by Springdale Road and then three quarters the way down the next block.

On the right stood 112 Mercer. It was a white clapboard and shuttered two-story house with an inviting four pillared open front porch. The walkway up from the sidewalk was short and the fragrance of flowers on the porch filled the air. In all, her journey had only taken her twenty-two minutes, but its impact would last a lifetime.

Excited beyond all imagination, Millie firmly rapped three times on the right wooden panel of the front screen door with a white gloved hand. She then waited what seemed to be an eternity, but was only about twenty seconds.

It first began as a rustling of paper, a brief curse in German, and then a middle aged man with a shock of gray hair and the bluest of blue eyes that she had ever seen appeared at the door.

In what sounded like a thick German accent the gentleman said. "Hallo, may I help you?"

"Yes you may." Millie replied. "My name is Mildred Hayes and I have an appointment to see Professor Einstein."

Now tilting his head slightly to the left and opening the door wide in greeting, the man said with a broad smile.

"Ah yes, so you are. Professor Einstein is indeed expecting you. By the way, please allow me to introduce myself. I am he."

*   *   *

The initial briefing took place in a secured conference room on the second basement level of the Philology Annex. It began early on a Saturday morning and because it was during the academic year, Richards' suspected that it was either someone's idea of a joke or a late-breaking crisis.

As usual, the Egyptologist had arrived fifteen minutes early. When Gregorieva arrived five minutes later, he then knew that the meeting was not a joke.

"Okay," she laconically stated, "this better be good," as she plopped down next to Richards with her fresh Starbucks grande.

And then they waited in silence.

Precisely five minutes past seven, the two temporal agents were joined by a crisp elderly lady dressed in a gray pinstriped pant suit. Walking briskly around the seated twosome, she headed immediately for the lectern at the end of the conference table. Once there, she began to settle herself in by first removing two identical looking manila file folders, her reading glasses, and what looked like lecture notes. Now with her half-glasses in position atop the bridge of her nose and her hands clasped behind her back, the five foot something began.

"Good morning. I am Professor Mildred Hayes. I am a nuclear physicist by inclination and trade. But today I have been asked by Peter Borov to be a historian of sorts. You see, there is a very good possibility that your next drop will take place in AD 1943, a time that I am well acquainted with."

While that statement was delivered, their lecturer had moved from behind the table's lectern to stand directly across from them. The effect was telling.

"By the totally vacant looks on your faces, I can see that this is all news to you." Hayes stated with a wry smile as she handed each one of the identical manila folders.

"What I have just shared with each of you is something that I have been gathering over the past twenty-one years. If I were you I would thoroughly familiarize myself with the contents of your folders. And you will see soon enough why."

"So without any further ado, let us begin."

*   *   *

Frankly, Richards just did not know where all the time had gone for suddenly housekeeping had arrived with lunch. Professor Mildred Hayes, now just Millie, had held them spellbound for the past four and a half hours, pausing only occasionally to daintily sip some water from her Mickey Mouse plastic cup. And what a story is was.

"So Millie, the Navy covered up the entire experiment with a twin ship and crew with the same name? Did I get that right?" Richards queried with his mouth half full of a delicious Philly cheese steak sandwich.

"Indeed you did Joseph. And from what I have been able to divine, that bureaucratic trick itself was almost as difficult to orchestrate as the experiment!"

And then Gregorieva offered an insight.

"You mentioned that while the experiment was being conducted that there were reports of a greenish fog surrounding the ship's hull. Is that correct?"

"Indeed young lady, that is correct."

"Well, could it be that the current that was passing through the hull was high enough that the surrounding layer of sea water was actually in the process of desalinizing, thereby producing a diluted chlorine gas?"

With a broad smile, Hayes answered.

"Now that is a most interesting observation! And one, I might add, that I have not heard before. Excellent Vesna. I can see that you did not forget your chemistry."

Now shifting gears in his head, Richards opined.

"Alright, if I got this straight, we are to drop into Philly, observe the experiment, and get back. Is that it?" Said an almost incredulous Richards.

Scrunching up her face in thought, Millie responded.

"Initially Joseph, I suspect so. Confirmation that the event occurred is the primary goal. But once that has been made, there is a very, very strong desire within the Navy to see if you can retrieve the four lost seamen, who jumped overboard and into the *somewhen*."

"But how could we do that?" the Russian broke in. "We do not know what the temporal calibration would be for a field as big as a ship, much less the power levels achieved."

With her eyes smiling, no brightly twinkling at Gregorieva's insight, Hayes then said.

"Yes, yes indeed Peter was right about you Vesna. You truly do possess a keen scientific mind. But what would you say if I told you that if you could somehow measure the field itself? What would that buy you?"

"I really don't know. I would have to first perform such a test with the Soap Bubble and then correlate that field measurement against a know calibration."

"Precisely my dear, precisely."

Then Richards' eyes got really big.

"Wait a minute here! You mean that you want us to somehow measure that ship's field!"

"Precisely young man, that's exactly what I want you to do."

"Well, to do that we will need to get really close to the ship. What about its security? Can we even do that? What sort of equipment would we need to accomplish that?"

After a brief pause, Millie just smiled that marvelous smile of hers and said. "You will do the measurements with a special probe that I was tasked to construct, while I was at Princeton."

"A probe! Bringing that through the drop ring will be a major infraction of the *RUTI*. What if it gets lost or something? You'll never get authorization for that."

Again smiling with her eyes.

"Joseph you are absolutely correct about the probe not going through the ring. But have you considered what if the probe was already there, in essence waiting for you, in the *somewhen*?"

To this revelation Richards' jaw just sagged.

Then Gregorieva had a thought.

"What really bothers me about all of this is getting so close to such a powerful field and then penetrating it. Wouldn't we need some sort of insulation or grounding to protect us?"

Yet again smiling with her eyes.

"Indeed Vesna, insulation would be highly recommended, but a pair of rubber boots, gloves, and flash goggles should do the trick quite nicely."

Richards then with a dark look on his face asked.

"Okay Millie. Come clean. Just where is this probe?"

"Well Joseph, I was wondering when you would come around to that minor issue. It's in Princeton."

"Princeton. As in Princeton, New Jersey?"

"Why yes."

"And how big is this 'probe thing?' Bigger or smaller than a bread box?"

Now taking a deep breath and looking down at her hands Millie answered.

"Oh, very much bigger. In fact Joseph, it looks very much like a fishing pole."

Richards quickly interrogated.

"How long?"

"Six and one half feet in length." And then Millie added. "Joseph, it only weighs about five pounds in total."

"So to summarize," Richards began by counting off his fingers. "We drop somewhere in Princeton. Next, we temporarily 'borrow' a fishing pole. We take the train to Philly. From the train station we take a taxi to the docks. We locate the secured area. We present our papers. We get in. We watch the experiment. We somehow get permission to probe the field. We note down the field strength. Then we catch a taxi from the docks back to the Philly train station and from there catch a train back to Princeton. We return the 'borrowed' probe. Then we are retrieved. Have I left out anything?" He finished blinking his eyes with a broad smile of total disbelief.

"Dr. Hayes," Richards coolly concluded, "do you know just how nuts this all is?"

"Sadly, yes. I know that it is quite ambitious." She said in a quiet voice.

*   *   *

"Millie, I really don't know how to ask this, but I just have to. You said that you were 'tasked to construct' the Hayes Device. Did I hear that right?" Richards queried.

Again smiling with her eyes, Millie answered. "Why yes indeed Joseph. You did hear that right."

"Okay then," Richards said as he warmed to the topic, "if that is indeed the case, then precisely who 'tasked' you to do so?"

"Now Joseph, what a penetrating question; it was Professor Einstein. Who else? He wanted to measure the strength of the Eldridge's field and use that data to further his research. I was initially slotted to perform that measurement, but in the end at the last minute I was not allowed to participate, and so the task was made merely optional. Boy was I peeved! Here I had built the probe, been briefed on all the experiment's particulars, its security measures and passwords, and because I was not a Ph.D., I did not get my chance."

Now with wide eyes Richards continued.

"Okay, fine. But Millie, why did you decide 'to hide' your device in the corner of an abandon office of all places?"

Now grinning ear-to-ear, the seasoned physicist again answered. "Joseph, Joseph, such an inquisitive mind you have. You would have made such a fine scientist. But to answer your question, again it was Albert's idea. He has always been a big believer in hiding that which is secret in plain sight. But if I might anticipate your logical next question, the answer to it is demonstrably 'yes,' Albert and I did work together quite a bit and he openly shared with me his first and only true love – his unfinished Unified Field Theory, which the Philadelphia Experiment was a direct, practical, although crude demonstration. But what neither of us could have anticipated was the intersection of that theory with dear Peter Borov's fine work. Little did either of us know that we would have a potential opportunity for a rescue effort."

Now sitting back in his chair, Richards smelling a rat, squinted his eyes, and said. "Millie, what's really going on here?"

With a waning smile on her face and eyes about to burst out in tears Millie just said. "Joseph. One of the lost sailors was my big brother."

CHAPTER XVIII
Thursday, October 28th, 1943

In many respects, the drop authorized by the membership of the Philology Annex within the Princeton University campus was brilliant. Why? In one respect, there were locations within the campus that had not changed one iota since 1943. In another, there existed an uncanny parallelism between this drop site and a much frequented other, if only someone had wanted to make it.

Under the cover story that specified the sudden need for a minor architectural renovation, the University Chapel, a magnificent cruciform Tudor gothic structure, was closed to the public for several days while needful repairs were undertaken, in which gaudy yellow construction tape Xs decorated and blocked every entranceway. Calli Callahan's troops further secured the interior and the university's own campus security patrolled the exterior. A hastily constructed PVC scaffolding, platform and boom with extraction rope and pulley were erected in the open space immediately before the altar. Beneath the scaffolding, the portable Soap Bubble Mark VI was setup, double-checked, and was judged ready to go. The whole was then tented over in plastic sheeting to give the appearance of a construction project in progress. This last had been Calli's idea. After all, he reasoned, who knew when the deacon just might demand to innocently peek in on the welfare of his chapel?

As in the past, the two temporal agents could not wear any metal on their persons during a drop. So, a canvas bag was procured into which went Richards' military belt and buckle, his wristwatch, his fountain pen, his officer's hat and his rolled up jacket with its brass buttons and medals. Gregorieva's contribution to the pre-drop bag included her wristwatch and purse.

Since the drop was timed to occur at 2:30 in the morning on Wednesday, October 27th, few thought that any would witness the event on the other side. But just to make sure, Sergeant "Ozzy" Osgood first "peeked" by inserting his plastic optical device through the Soap Bubble's field. And, as expected, nothing was seen, not even a hungry church mouse.

Taking up their usual position on the platform of the scaffolding, Richards and Gregorieva patiently watched as the drop ring began its operational ascent. Almost on cue, the dancer could feel the static charge begin to cling to her stockings and dress. With the ring in place floating about five feet above the sacristy's marble flooring, Osgood again did his visual check and gestured a "thumbs up" to Callahan.

"Okay Dr. Richards, you can drop the bag now."

And with that permission, the canvas bag disappeared into the silvery field.

Noting no abnormalities with the field, the ion cannons, or power pack, Callahan then said. "Okay Ms. Gregorieva, you are free to drop."

And Vesna stepped off the platform and also disappeared. After about a twenty second pause, Callahan then quipped with a smile. "Okay Most Noble Mayneken, it's your turn, travel well."

Richards, ever the smart ass smiled, saluted the lieutenant, and fell out of his time.

*   *   *

Following the deliciously slippery feeling of the field, Vesna expertly performed a Fort Bragg-approved drop and roll landing onto a smooth marble floor. Shortly thereafter, Richards landed with a thud followed by an involuntary grunt.

"Jesus! Just once it would be nice to drop without all the purple haze."

"Shhh. Watch your manners." She hissed. "Besides, you shouldn't blaspheme in church." Gregorieva teased him, but clearly evident in Gregorieva's voice was her concern about

Richards' ongoing physiological reaction after passing through the drop field. And in this instance, it took him a full two minutes to uncross his eyes.

Still flat on his back, Richards looked into the darkness and finally whispered. "Are we alone?"

"It appears to be so."

Now sitting up.

"Good. Now let's find some pews, stretch out, and grab some sleep as we're really gonna' need it tomorrow.

* * *

Trying to sleep on a narrow wooden pew can be best likened to trying to snooze on the edge of a cliff. It just was not going to happen. With its hard, unforgiving, and narrow surface and with Richards' broad shoulders the best that he could do was rest on his side. Gregorieva, however, given her petite dancer's build, simply curled up and quickly nodded off. Consequently, it was no surprise that it was Richards who first noticed the change in the chapel's interior lighting as the early morning sky had begun to lighten. And he was glad for it as the colored light seemed to warm him spiritually as it slowly revealed itself through the tall gothic panes. Now taking the time to notice, Richards could not believe how many separate pieces of colored glass went into just one of those magnificent windows. Just how long he mused on this discovery he really didn't know, but the very next thing that he heard was of Gregorieva creaking her body up and off of her pew.

Now looking down on the still prone American, the Russian said.

"Never again will I suggest that we sleep on a pew."

"Why?" Came the innocent reply.

"Because you snore! That's why."

* * *

CHILDREN OF PTAH

Their secondary concern was making the 7:28 scheduled train to Trenton with a change to Philadelphia, while their immediate one involved a minor campus detour. Fortunately, the Physics Department at Guyot Hall was located a scant three blocks away down Washington Road from the chapel. Also, fortunately, at 6:13 in the morning, few souls were out and about in the early morning gloom and the castle-like façade of Guyot was easy enough to pick out. Their goal was Room M27 on the Mezzanine Level. Ascending the red granite steps of the northern main entrance, they then climbed to the next floor, turned to their right and quickly found the specified room. And like the main entrance door, it too was unlocked. In fact, its wooden door didn't even have a lock – just a simple door knob and latch. Once within they found a dusty and cramped academic office. Now filled with a helter-skelter of boxes – some opened some not, they all appeared to be filled with bureaucratic debris just as Millie had described it. And there in the corner, again as recollected by Millie, stood a longish six foot cardboard tube about five inches in diameter and just like its surroundings, was filthy dirty with grime and dust. Grabbing the box quickly, the American and Russian then made their way out of the building and back to Washington Road.

It was now 6:22 and the pair quickly settled into their long walk to the Princeton Junction Station. In retrospect, they may not have made their train, if it were not for a kindly milkman in his truck, who gave them a lift all the way to the station.

When Richards offered the man a tip, the milkman just laughed it off and said.

"Ah, heck, it's the least that I can do for you two naval officers! Now just do me a favor and go out and kill some Japs and Jerries!"

*   *   *

155

Ticket now in hand and waiting on the platform on this early weekday morning, the temporal agents quickly discovered that they were the only military personnel in this cigarette smoking crowd of commuters. Certainly they were the only ones on the platform with a six foot tube that could have been easily mistaken for a rocket canister. Not really used to being stared at the pair stayed to themselves, talking quietly, and wishing that the train would soon arrive so that they could perhaps catch some uninterrupted shut eye. Nonetheless, eyes peered at them over folded morning newspapers. And given that all the commuters were male and that the Princeton population itself had not yet become a co-ed institution, Gregorieva's presence had been duly noted.

"John, would you look at all those decorations that young guy has on his chest. I'll bet you that that man's a hero."

"I wonder if they are from the Princeton Battery?"

"Naw, those are Navy uniforms Joe. They're probably just returning to their ship in Philly. Besides, there's no dames out at the Battery."

"Do you think that they are part of some secret military project here in Princeton? Just look at that tube that the naval officer is holding."

"To hell with the tube Bruce, you just gotta' check out that dame! Those are some legs."

Blessedly, before this cauldron of small town gossip could reach critical mass, the train arrived.

*   *   *

The train ride to Trenton turned out to be a non-event. Once at Trenton, the transfer over to the Philadelphia connection went smoothly enough. As the pair caught a cat nap the time just seemed to fly by and before they knew it they had arrived in Pennsylvania Station at 9:07. Now in Philly, the two naval officers quickly blended in as the station was brimming with military personnel going here, there, and seemingly everywhere at once.

As for their nearly mum Italian taxi cab driver, their naval uniforms did not impress him nor did their six foot tube, just the fare to drive them over to the naval yard.

With their feet once again on the ground, Richards lead and Gregorieva followed as they oriented themselves and began to follow the memorized directions that Millie had so rigorously drilled into them. Again, almost immediately they were lost within the hundreds of men and women who were employed in the yards, but as they neared their goal the crush of humanity had thinned out considerably.

The dock area in question that included the mooring of the destroyer escort USS Eldridge 173 had been cordoned off with two layers of cyclone fencing topped with barbed wire. Between the two fences guards patrolled with high strung German shepherds. Access to the secured area, they had been told, was made through a dockside warehouse that partially shielded the highly protected area from view. So they headed straight for the landward entrance to Warehouse Dock 37 and just as Millie had said, there stood two solidly built Marines, who flanked the warehouse's lone entrance. At their approach, the soldiers stiffened slightly at seeing Richards' rank of commander, but their eyes widened in disbelief upon seeing Gregorieva's lieutenant's bars.

The sergeant on the right stated crisply, "IDs if you please."

Knowing that this was just part of the drill, both officers silently handed over their military identity cards.

Next, the sergeant asked, "Commander Richards, what's in the tube?"

Richards answered curtly, "That's classified Marine. But if you really want to know, we're here to do some fishing."

The sergeant, registering the coded words, just nodded his head and opened the heavy metal door allowing them to pass through.

Once inside the temporal agents found themselves in a long and narrow hallway without any windows that was freshly painted battleship gray. At the other end of this security corridor was another door, another set of Marines, and another inspection of their papers. This time, however, Richards did open up the tube so its contents could be viewed. After the resealing of the tube, the Marine on the left, who had carefully watched his partner, put the temporal agents through the drill, finally announced.

"Commander Richards, Lieutenant Gregg, you may proceed. However, as I do not recall having seen either of you at this facility before, I must inform you that you must first report to your respective cloak rooms for your protective gear before entering the secured area."

"Thank you Sergeant," Richards said with a short nod.

As the pair moved off, each to their own changing rooms, both nonetheless felt the eyes of the two Marines on them.

While the temporal agents moved off to don their protective gear as directed, the antennae of Marine Sergeant Jeremy Brown commenced to twitch. It was not that he hadn't noticed that Lieutenant Gregg possessed one hell of a smoking chassis; instead, it was that Commander Richards was just such a cool customer. At first he could not put his finger on it, but Brown knew beyond a shadow of a doubt that Richards was one dangerous cat. In response to this extremely visceral reaction, the Marine picked up his field phone and gave it several vicious cranks on its charging handle. As he waited for an answer on the other end of the line, Marine Sergeant Alvin Green asked.

"Okay Jerry. What's got your hackles up?"

"I really don't know, but those two just don't shake out."

"Their papers were correct in all respects. They knew the passwords. They were even on the list. So again, what gives Jer?"

Scowling at his partner, Brown simply said.

"That guy gives me the creeps."

Then the telephone connection came through and Brown said.

"This is Sergeant Jeremy Brown over at Warehouse Dock 37. Sorry to trouble you sir, but I just had two jokers pass through here free and clear with some sort of a scientific device."

"Yeah, precisely."

"Commander Joseph Richards and Lieutenant Valery Gregg."

"Yeah, you heard me right. She's a lieutenant. Don't that beat all!"

"Their papers are all in order, but Richards gave me a really bad feeling. Put 'em through the ringer for me will ya'."

"Thanks major."

*   *   *

When they emerged from their respective cloak rooms, both were clothed in white lab coats over their uniforms, rubber boots over their shoes, heavy rubber laboratory gloves, and oversized flash goggles around their necks. Additionally, all metal was left behind with the attendant who gave each of them a paper chit so that they could retrieve those articles. Also left behind was the cardboard tube, while Richards was allowed to proceed with the probe itself.

For some totally ridiculous reason Richards, garbed as he was, felt as if he had just entered some B-rated black and white horror movie. Cradling the probe horizontally in his arms, Millie's carefully enunciated instructions began to scroll across his mind.

"Now Joseph," she began, "the probe, or Hayes Device, is just that, a probe. Think of it as just a heavily insulated lightning rod with a glass dialed read out at the handle end and the actual conductive rod or probe at the other. While the probe end is inserted directly into the outer boundary layer of the electromagnetic field, you will be holding on to this heavily insulated handle. What will be critical is the actual reading that you will get. The three position calibration toggle will help you to narrow the reading down. Remember Joseph: we're measuring the intensity of the electromagnetic field in watts. So when you toggle on position one – the one on the far left, it reads as kilowatts, the middle position, as megawatts, and the one on the far right, as gigawatts. For example, the Soap Bubble puts out about fifty seven watts of energy. I suspect that your initial reading may jump around at first, but then will settle out and remain steady. And when it settles out, just remember that reading!"

*   *   *

Once they left their locker rooms, the pair was directed by Marine personnel to a door that opened directly to the area of Dock 37 and the moored image of the bow of the destroyer escort USS Eldridge. Before it and along the water's edge were some twenty-odd white lab coats milling nervously about. Standing back from all of this expectant activity, Richards and Gregorieva began recording everything before them. The lone gray hulk of the bow, the massive hemp ropes that held the massive ship in place, even the sea gulls that were perched atop the communication masts.

Then one of the lab coats, having seen Richards with the probe, excitedly began to gesture to him, waving him over to the very edge of the ship's bow.

"You there! Yes you! You're late! Now get over here and take your damn reading already!"

As Richards quickly stepped forward he said.

"Sorry. I did not realize that the experiment had already begun."

Now with his hands on his hips, the fuzz ball grunted.

"It hasn't you idiot! I just want you to calibrate the Hayes' Device before we flip the switch. And just who the hell are you?"

"Commander Richards from Dr. Bush's office. And this is Lieutenant Gregg, my assistant." Richards deadpanned.

"Okay *Commander*, take your measurement and then just try to stay out of the way." He cracked as he simultaneously gave Gregorieva a look of absolute distain.

Nodding submissively, Richards extended the correct end of the probe to almost touching the hull, while he flipped through the toggle switches positions. Finishing he flatly stated.

"I've got zero readings throughout the probe's spectrum."

The nervously expectant fuzzy-headed lab coat exclaimed. "Excellent! Just excellent! Now stand back as we begin the power up sequence. By the way, *Commander*, you got here just in the nick of time."

Again obedient to this scientist's directions, Richards then almost robotically stepped back to rejoin Gregorieva to remark.

"I wonder who that is?"

"I do not recognize him, but I really want to smack him."

After the passage of nearly thirty-five minutes, the same exuberant lab coat began enumerating a rather long check list that meant nothing to Richards, but Gregorieva provided him with a whispered commentary.

"That fuzz ball has just ordered the release of all electrical circuit safeguards...the generators aboard the ship are charging...apparently they have to reach some sort of threshold before they throw the switch...hang on to your hat...can you feel all that static electricity in the air...okay, it's show time, they just threw the switch!

*   *   *

The air first began to reek of ozone and then the ship just, suddenly, wasn't there. To say that the effect was shocking would have been an understatement. As the lab coats moved forward, several of them began pointing to the hole in the water, more a depression that was formed by the underside of the ship's hull. Then, after about ten seconds into the experiment Richards was again waved over by the fuzz ball to probe the field, which he did. Millie was absolutely correct, the field's strength was not constant, but rather was oscillating over a broad span on the megawatt calibration setting. Gregorieva, now at his side, called out, "Thirty seconds."

Remember this, Richards commanded his enhanced memory.

After the passage of the first minute, the probe settled down between thirty and forty megawatts. Gregorieva again called out, "Sixty seconds."

At this point in the experiment, a greenish-yellow mist had begun to form at the bottom of the depression in the water. Seeing this development, Gregorieva whispered to Richards.

"Joey look!" She said breathlessly. "The field is indeed desalinizing the water around the ship's hull. I just knew it!"

"Uh huh." Was all that he could manage as he was concentrating on the probe's dial.

"I read now a steady forty-one megawatts." Richards announced.

Gregorieva then called out, "ninety seconds."

And then the inhuman screaming began.

*   *   *

As the experiment was initially planned to run a full fifteen minutes, the execution of an emergency shutdown after only ninety seconds left the lab coats shocked, confused and panicked. Two minutes later, the field was finally shut down somehow by those onboard, but the bloodcurdling screams had not. If anything, those agonized exhalations were decreasing only in strength and volume, ominous in their obvious meaning.

Seemingly out of nowhere naval medics burdened with gear arrived and quite literally stormed the ship's lone zigzagging debarkation ramp. Along the dock, all was chaos. The lab coats were running all around, shouting this, and screaming that. The fuzz ball, however, just stood before the ship's bow like a statue with his mouth open.

Richards, recognizing an opportunity, merely stated the obvious. "It's time to go." And Gregorieva did not argue.

Stripping out of their protective gear and getting back their personal effects, the pair with the probe again in its cardboard tube made for the second security station and while passing straight through it received some very sullen stares from the two Marines.

The biggest challenge that they could have had at the dock yards was just finding a taxi. Here Gregorieva's alluring wave and legs came in handy and in the process really pissed off three naval officers as "their" taxi quickly veered away from them!

*　　*　　*

Just after that providential taxi ride began, the field phone back in the secured area of Dock 37 rang only twice before Sergeant Brown quickly picked up the receiver.

"Sergeant Brown here."

"Sergeant Brown. This is Major Casey over at Arlington."

"What's the good news sir?" Brown asked with an expectant voice.

"You were absolutely right sergeant! Both Richards and Gregg are total unknowns. I repeat, total unknowns. Apprehend them at all costs!"

"Are you absolutely sure sir?" Brown cried out in absolute disbelief.

"Absolutely, sergeant. Where are they now?"

"They just left the secured area of the dock in a rush a couple of minutes ago. And they had that scientific instrument with them as well. They're already gone sir!"

*   *   *

The adrenaline crash hit them on the taxi ride back to the Philly train station. Gregorieva nearly collapsed. Richards was seriously buzzed. Fortunately, the driver said not a thing, although that hadn't prevented him from wondering why these two were so bushed when it was only 11:57 in the morning. Probably too much caterwauling last night he concluded to himself with a smile.

The train ride back to the Princeton Junction Station was blessedly a non-event. Even the return of the probe back to its rightful place in the corner of Room M27 went unnoticed by the now very much awake male campus population. But what did require their attention was the state of their stomachs and so the pair walked past the chapel to Nassau Street. And following their collective noses, the American and the Russian settled down for an all American lunch of cheese burgers, fries and two chocolate shakes. With their stomachs now satisfied, and full knowing that a serious food coma was in the making, they made their way slowly back to the University Chapel for their scheduled early morning pickup.

It was late afternoon as they approached the chapel and they were greeted with the heaven-sent sounds of its Mander-Skinner organ and the voices of an all male choir in the midst of a rehearsal. Smiling at each other, it almost seemed like "a job a well done" and "welcome home."

CHAPTER XIX
Bangor, ME

After the Princeton drop, it would be the following June before Gregorieva and Richards judged themselves ready for their drop into Eighteenth Dynasty Thebes. While both were already fit as fiddles, the darkening of their skin in the high altitude New Mexican desert could not be rushed. Besides Doc Allen, the chief physician of the Horizon Pass facility, wisely recognized that the pair sorely needed some quiet time to "bond" some more. While perhaps not obvious to the temporal agents, this red-headed Oklahoman noted at their arrival as there was a scratchy sort of psychic friction between them. This condition Doc Allen had immediately diagnosed was a cross between intense resentment and rut. As a superb judge of character and observer of the human condition, the folksy physician had to admit that he saw this one coming. For ever since the pair had returned from their first drop, he had sensed that something quite visceral, quite personal, had occurred between them. It took little imagination as to just what that something was, especially given the American's chiseled frame and the Russian's taunt and lithe dancer's body.

As two figures emerged from the blowing dust of the unmarked helicopter's backwash, a strong voice managed to reach them as the near-deafening whoop, whoop, whoop of the craft began to diminish.

"Welcome back to Horizon Pass, my dear colleagues!" greeted the ebullient director of the facility, one Dr. Peter Borov, with the silent and ever observant Doc Allen in tow.

"Just where does he get all that energy?" Queried Gregorieva under her breath.

"Well Vesna, he is the reason why we're here." Said Richards. "This whole complex, the Philology Annex, the

165

whole shebang is his brain child." Continued Richards in an unnecessary explanation.

Borov, stepping forward to the pair, who each carried a single black shoulder duffle, spread his arms wide.

"Ms. Gregorieva! You look simply radiant. And I see that you survived the helicopter ride this time! Well done."

The comment brought a slight wince of embarrassment to Gregorieva who had tried very hard to forget her previous bout with air sickness.

"And Dr. Richards, as always, you look as hungry as a 'young lion!'" Said the old scientist, purposely punning on the translation of Richards' Egyptian name of Mayneken – "young lion."

"Welcome back folks." Was all that Allen added as he followed the others back towards the hidden entrance to the underground complex. To a casual observer, the entrance was a heavily weathered, ramshackle wooden shack built up against a near-vertical rock outcropping in the middle of a glorious mountain valley. Once inside, all were scanned, processed, and moved safely inside the primary security vestibule within that rocky fortress. Then Borov quietly but firmly commanded.

"Okay you two, I know the drill. It's been a long day for the both of you. Now go get fed, showered, and immediately hit the sack. You'll need it. Also, you'll find your daily schedules posted in your quarters. Read them. Now off you go."

The two then split up as they were lead to their assigned billets by the installation's security personnel, Doc Allen just shook his head and said.

"You know what, Peter?"

"What?"

"I think that Vesna and Joey have a thing goin'."

"Yeah? Well I have news for you. There's no thinking needed. I know that there is as sure as I'm standing here."

"What makes you so sure?"

166

"I noted the fresh beard burn on Vesna's neck after they returned from their first drop."

"Damnation! I missed that." Allen said.

"So did I, but remind me, Doc, to compliment Colonel Cartwright, that ragin' Cajun, on that canny observation."

"Doesn't he have three daughters in college?"

"Yep, and that's why I suspect he even noticed it at all."

*　　*　　*

When the secured speaker phone connection completed and their distant colleague announced himself, both Gregorieva and Richards smiled, but for very different reasons. The Russian fractionally softened, because the firm and kindly voice reminded her of her late Sasha – Alexander Piankoff. For the American, that voice was his mentor, colleague, and sometimes beer drinking partner-in-crime. After all the polite talk was over, Milson cut to the chase.

"Okay, here's the deal. Joseph, this is your big chance so don't blow it."

Gregorieva's quick glance towards Richards was missed by the absent Egyptologist. *Just what is he up to now?*

"You and Ms. Gregorieva are going to do some very low profile poking around into your favorite subject, the god Ptah." Milson said into his office speaker phone in Chicago. "What that means is that a brief social visit to Prince Horemheb may be in order, but isn't necessary. According to the date of your insertion, he will be still busy preparing for the return of the royal court to Thebes.

"What you'll want to do is to somehow arrange for a meeting with Meryptah's successor. As best I know, that could well be a man by the name of Nebneteru. So keep your ears open. What you initially want to do is gain access to the library archives of the Amen Re Temple itself.

"Ms. Gregorieva, do not be surprised if it is referred to as *per ankh*, or the House of Life. Joseph will fill you in on that detail."

So this drop was his idea? Gregorieva noted with some curiosity.

"With luck, Joseph, you might find some clues to your mysterious Ptah."

Definitely his idea!

"In fact, I would not be at all surprised that a follow up drop might be in order so that the two of you can go to Memphis and visit the archives of the Temple of Ptah itself."

And another mission too!

"But for now, let's just keep this insertion as discrete and as brief as possible. In other words, no more than two days time – relative. Do you have any questions?"

"I have just one Professor Milson," the Russian purred. "I was under the impression that permission for a temporal drop was not easily granted. Yet, why are we endangering the current timeline, not to mention risking the rules of the *RUTI* with such a seemingly casual mission?"

While Milson answered the Russian's question politely, it was with a firm coolness that Richards had never before heard from the man. It had steel in it.

"Ms. Gregorieva. This carefully planned and calculated drop is hardly a frivolous tourist excursion. In fact, the permission to undertake it was enthusiastically sanctioned by your superiors."

With that message delivered, the Russian physically jerked her head back from the speaker at hearing the steel in it. Its implied content was practically an intellectual slap in the face. Her superiors did not want her to know! It had nothing to do at all with Joey's usual penchant for understatement and secretiveness.

Then Milson noticeably softened his next words.

"I well know, Vesna, that you have not been briefed on just what this mission is looking for. That was intentionally done, believe it or not, for your own protection. That decision was not ours. It was the desire of your superiors. At the very same time, I want to assure you that your role as Joseph's teammate has been in no way diminished. In fact, we are depending upon you to bring him back."

What!

Seeming to psychically read the Russian's turbulent emotional condition across the thousands of miles that separated them, Milson pressed on while the line remained silent at Horizon Pass.

"You know, Vesna, despite what your superiors might wish, you are nonetheless an extremely observant, bright, and gifted woman. You know this. Joseph knows this. I know it. Quite frankly, you and Joseph must continue to work seamlessly together and be allowed the freedom to share your thoughts. Otherwise, your team's effectiveness and safety will be placed in jeopardy. And might I add your team has already proved itself to be a lethal commodity.

"Now, as distasteful as the wishes of your superiors may seem, you must consider their point of view as well – no matter how paranoid that point of view may appear. The fact remains you are an integral part of this deployment. Also, I strongly suspect that several very enlightening discussions will occur while you're away. I fully encourage this as I do not want to jeopardize either the mission or the trust that each of you have developed for one another.

"Joseph. Do you clearly understand what I am unofficially advocating?"

"Loud and clear."

*   *   *

This was the first time that Richards had ever been deployed from Holloman Air Force Base in the "special," but plain-jane looking Gulf Stream V. While he had flown into this base located near the backwater New Mexican town of Alamogordo several times, this flight would be a long haul direct to Luxor, Egypt. As a consequence, he wasn't surprised to see that the plane had been outfitted with two external fuel tanks. These were attached to custom hard points located near the plane's wing roots just outside the landing gear bays. The presence of such tanks was deemed unnecessary for flights within the forty-eight states. However, the presence of such tanks stuck out like an eyesore, for no normal commercial jet would typically have access to them.

Richards stopped briefly to gaze down the length of the aircraft, while he supervised the load of the Little Beast II and the portable version of the Soap Bubble VI. As he did so the Egyptologist unconsciously sighed as he took in its subtle lines and even subtler additions. As his trained eyes swept across the aircraft, he smugly noted the two shrouded fiberglass gun ports nestled into the bottom third of the forward cowling and the almost pregnant bulging of the fuselage that began its swell just aft of the nose landing gear compartment. Because of this ventral swelling, the plane's landing gear had to be extended a full two feet to provide for the proper clearances, while its cargo carrying capacity had effectively tripled. But at its thickest point beneath the wings, the bulge's skin had three parallel seams that betrayed the presence of doors to a non-pressurized bay, which could accommodate a variety of nifty items that ranged from a photo reconnaissance and ground mapping radar suite to a rotary missile launcher.

Moving on aft Richards then noted the tall T-shaped tail, the dual engine pods attached at the rear of the fuselage and the graceful sweep of its wings that ended in canards. The aircraft looked like it was doing its civilian-rated top end of .87 mach just sitting on the tarmac. But Richards knew better, for the enlarged engine housings and flares concealed special Pratt & Whitney F119 engines with directable thrust-vectoring nozzles. Fitted with these powerful engines, the Gulf Stream's top end climbed to 1.6 mach and its ability to turn and maneuver rose to in excess of seven Gs. Ending at the aircraft's extended and pointed tail section, the American also knew that six defensive circular chaff dispensers and antimissile flare ports were secreted there, again hidden by their fiberglass shrouds.

One detail that was not at all obvious to a casual eye was the plane's paint and registration markings. Once airborne, the copilot with a flip of a switch could trickle a low voltage charge throughout the plane's outer skin that allowed the surface to subtly change color and shadings in order to mimic its immediate surroundings. While in flight, the plane's surface was said to shimmer or ripple as it passed by and through clouds, all the while its surface coating automatically adjusted itself. Similarly, the copilot could at will alter the lettering of the craft's registration markings, clearly going one step further than the rotating license plate brackets of James Bond's Aston Martin DB-5. Such aerial camouflage and bureaucratic tomfoolery were considered necessary for the plane's survival.

Although hardly a fighter jet, this heavily modified Gulf Stream's beefed up airframe was the closest thing to it in terms of speed, maneuverability, ceiling, range, and lethalness. Needless to say all of these additions, at least in the crew's mind, were sorely needed advantages that might even up the already long odds on their survival. After all, who would expect to encounter a self-camouflaging commercial business jet that was more maneuverable than most governments' military aircraft? Not to mention, a civilian looking plane that could pack air-to-air missiles and a pair of M-61A1 20mm multi-barrel cannon bored sighted at five hundred yards? The logic was: if one 20mm cannon was good enough for an F-16, then two for the Gulf Stream were better.

As for Gregorieva, she too noted Richards' thousand foot stare, the long distance setup, and caught a knowing wink from Richards as he followed her up the plane's extended staircase. Upon entering the cabin, the Russian could only shake her head and smile at its remarkable transformation. Gutted of the usual interior commercial baffles and compartments to its inner skin and painted in a light tan color, the revised cabin interior seemed absolutely cavernous. Seating, however, was pure military transport. Comfortable, safe, but butt ugly with quick release aluminum frames entwined with olive green webbing, massive but comfortable head and neck padding, with five-point harnesses to restrain you firmly in place. In all, sixteen such nests were arranged in two staggered rows around a common central aisle. General interior lighting was battle station red with convenient reading lights mounted into the interior hull accompanied by three practical, grounded, twelve-volt outlets. Additional storage was provided next to each seat with more olive green webbing in addition to generous tie-down opportunities in the form of hull-mounted rings, hooks, and Velcro strapping.

Other interior changes included the removal of the civilian cockpit door and the insertion of a Plexiglas sunroof into the cockpit's overhead escape hatch. Its purpose had seemed odd to Gregorieva until Richards had explained that a roof mounted, flush-fitting trapdoor located to the right of it was for the aerial refueling receptacle.

Seldom appreciated by the general public was the outfitting of this plane's head with a pressurized and vacuum sealed toilet seat. While flimflam politicians have often railed for decades on the supposedly wasteful spending of the military on such items, the simple fact of the matter is, "Do you want your aircraft's honey pot emptying, while you're flying inverted?"

*   *   *

"Welcome back Ms. Gregorieva!" piped a cheerful voice from the cockpit.

CHILDREN OF PTAH

Whirling around the Russian automatically smiled in the direction of the greeting. Getting her bearings, she spotted an airman with shortly-cropped blond hair and wearing a headset as he waved from the forward compartment. Briefly waving back in reply, Vesna returned to the stowing of her gear in the provided webbing.

Americans! She thought. They're all so friendly. Why is that?

Meanwhile Lieutenant Dale "Airedale" Foster did not turn away. Instead, he just continued to savor the view of the Russian's backside.

What a body!

Breaking his impeccable concentration on the target rich environment was his senior, who was sitting next to him.

In a low voice, Captain Johnny "Black" Jones mumbled. "Well Airedale, if you continue to hold that position your neck will surely break. Now quit thinking with your dick and get your sorry ass back to the preflight checklist."

Now somewhat chastised, Airedale said. "Yes sir, Captain! I'm back to the here and now. But Captain, you got to admit, that we're ferrying some mighty fine cargo back there."

"Airedale, that is the most sensible thing that you have said all day. Now get cracking and get me some fuel specs for Bangor."

"Bangor? As in Bangor, Maine? As in nothing but trees and hard cider?"

"Yeah, we're swapping out there. Just got a change of orders over the rio. We're not going transatlantic."

"Aw, heck! I was looking forward to some sightseeing. See some pyramids. Get some pictures."

"Crap Airedale, don't you know anything? Don't you ever watch the *Discovery Channel*? Luxor doesn't have any pyramids. Just a bunch of royal tombs and some of temples."

*   *   *

For the crew's passengers the flight from New Mexico to Bangor had been a nonevent. The pair read, but mostly slept during the glass-smooth ride. Richards, before he drifted off for a second time, realized what it was. His body was preparing him for the battle to come. Besides, the warm glow of the red lighting against the light tan interior gave the sense of being inside a womb and so subliminally calmed the Egyptologist.

The landing at Bangor's air base was as smooth as well, and Richards might have slept right through the turn around. Gregorieva, however, had been wide awake reading Erik Hornung's book on the history of Egyptian religion that her partner had thoughtfully provided her. As the plane's tanks were topped off and the new crew began their checklists, a third group opened up the plane's belly and immediately began turning air wrenches that resulted in several bumping and clanking noises. At this point, Richards awoke and did so in a sleepy, grumpy mood.

"Jesus! What the hell is going on anyways?"

"I don't know." Gregorieva replied evenly. "They have only been at it for about thirty seconds."

"Whose they?"

"I suppose your military."

"Whadda' ya' mean? We're on the ground?" Blurted out the still disoriented American.

"Yes we're on the ground and, well, four men with a large object on wheels just rolled up to the belly of the plane and got to work."

With Richards now looking out one of the window ports, he asked.

"Did you see what it was?"

"You mean on the motorized wheeled racking?"

"Yeah, the dolly. It's called a dolly."

"No, I didn't. It had a tarp over it."

Richards, now as his head cleared asked.

"Huh."

"Did we get some new drivers?"

"Drivers?"

"Yeah, pilots."

"Why yes, yes we did. In fact, they're settling into the cockpit right now."

At this point, Richards was now fully awake as he began to hastily piece together all the facts. The newest, latest and greatest version of the Soap Bubble was aboard. The Bangor refueling stop wasn't at all necessary, but was done anyways supposedly to top off the tanks. A fresh flight crew had arrived. And some modifications were now being made within the bay. He didn't like it. He didn't like it one bit. All the measures frankly smelled like nothing but trouble.

$$* \quad * \quad *$$

While piracy on the high seas is an ancient and well understood profession long governed by international law, air piracy on the other hand is a distinctly modern phenomenon. Initially, it all began with hijackings between the United States and Cuba, but these puddle-jumping excursions quickly developed into an ever more dangerous trend that escalated far beyond hijackings and hostage-taking to outright terrorist acts of senseless carnage committed upon national entities.

"I want the plane and its contents recovered intact." The electronically altered voice said.

Listening carefully with a bowed head to this seemingly simple statement, the man could not believe what he was hearing. What was being requested was a massive undertaking.

"And what of the flight crew and its passengers?"

"We wish no survivors."

A grunt followed by a pregnant pause. Then the man countered.

"What you ask will be very expensive."

"That is not an issue."

"How much time do we have to prepare?"

"Three weeks time – no more."

"You can't be serious!"

"If you cannot deliver what we require we will go elsewhere."

A brief, tense, and sweaty pause.

"Okay. Transmit the details. In four hours time call back and we will discuss particulars."

CHAPTER XX
The End of a Busy Day

As the shadows lengthened across the valley with the impending sunset, Ptah sat physically exhausted and mentally drained before his modest house constructed of courses of white washed mud brick. His was the only in the village with bundled papyrus reed columns that supported the house's broad expanse of flat roof. His was the only in the village with a woven reed doorway that rolled up. His was the only in the village with a fired mud brick flooring. But typically at day's end, the man could be found sitting before his doorway facing west as the sun bathed his façade in a ruddy pink glow. The lighting effect was so intense that all the gore and spatter of the day's labors that found their way on the man's kilt seemed to disappear.

Sitting on a folding wicker camp stool with his ankles crossed and hands leaning forward heavily on his knees, Ptah watched the sun set through his eye lids. As he did, he marveled at the delicate blood vessel traceries of that membrane. He even imagined that he could actually see his blood flowing through them. As he continued to find his center and relax, the priest's breathing began to slow, his aching muscles unknotted and his mind cleared. As this daily ritual took hold, a peaceful half smile creased his face as he reviewed the day's events, what he had observed, and what he had learned about this most promising culture.

Quite a day, my good friend, he said to himself, while sitting in the semi-trance-like state luxuriating in the fading warm bath of the sun. First, some worthwhile writing. Then it was Kawab's finger that required attention – and what a mess that was! Finally, my assistance with the successful birthing of a healthy baby girl. That detestable midwife surely wanted my head for all my interference. With her water already broken, the infant was trapped practically sideways in the canal. The mother was at risk. I did what was needful. Nothing more. And so our tiny community grows anew practically with every passing moon. How, I do not know, given the generally wretched housing and sanitary conditions, not to mention their perverse reluctance to accept change. But nonetheless, we are now one more and change is slowly taking place.

Sigh.

That satisfied sigh seemed to deflate the man, but as he did so, he also sensed that he was being observed. It was one of those funny feelings that people become aware of and eventually become accustomed to. Some call it "the sixth sense." Ptah understood the situation somewhat differently, for him this was a sort of game. His first five senses were extremely acute and his ears easily picked up the quiet rustle of clothing and the crunching of the small bare feet on sand. The bottoms of his feet and backside had similarly registered the vibrations of those footfalls. His nostrils had picked up a new and invasive scent.

What's this I hear? A lightly hesitant, but curious footfall. It almost has a stalking rhythm to it. Yes, it seems to be that of a child.

But the priest's sixth was very well developed and what he read was young, unfettered, and fearless curiosity. My visitor is definitely a child – a female child. Her name is Hathor. She's the youngest daughter of the household of the farmer Hor. She was the inquisitive one at today's birthing, the one with the intelligent eyes that seemed to miss nothing. She had even dared a giggle at the midwife's noisy and heated departure from the scene.

So without opening his eyes, Ptah quietly spoke to his unseen little visitor.

"So, most beautiful and curious Hathor, why do you sneak up on me like the blessed Isis' own cat?"

Smiling inwardly after hearing a quick and audible gasp that was followed up with an equally quick and undisguised giggle, the little girl of six inundations blurted out.

"That's not fair. You were peeking!"

"No lovely Hathor, I was not. Your approach was as noisy as a rampaging ox. I heard you quite clearly."

"That's not true! I was being really quiet."

"And how quiet is quiet, fair one?"

"Well, today I caught bare-handed two ducks!" She said with considerable pride.

"Two ducks you say?"

"Yes, they were two pretty males too! And Mother says that I can have all their feathers."

Still with his eyes closed, the priest turned towards the voice of this brave huntress of water fowl.

"And your mother is going to cook them for this evening's meal?"

"Yes! She's roasting them right now."

Now slowly opening his eyes the priest beheld his charming visitor.

"So, I see that your voice did truthfully say that you are beautiful, Hathor. But you have yet to answer my question – why have you come to visit me?"

"I witnessed the birthing of Nebet's little baby girl today. I found it interesting, especially the way you helped the woman breathe to fight her pains, the way you massaged her tummy to help the baby come forth, and then the way you caught the baby when it finally came out."

"You noticed all of that?"

"Yes, I did." The girl stated with pride. "But why did you first clamp off the blue birthing cord with the papyrus twine and not just cut the baby free? Why did you hold the baby upside down by its ankles? Why did you suck on the baby's nose? And what was that you spat out?"

"Well Hathor, I can see that you have many questions, but I can also see that you are very observant, in fact, far more so than some of your elders."

To this compliment, the little girl beamed and said. "Why did the midwife Taneter suddenly leave in such a rage? What did you say to her?"

"Yes, I can see. You did observe much! Now Hathor, what would you say if the next time that there is a birthing that you would be my assistant?"

"Could I?"

"Well, first I must speak with your father about this, for I must first train you if you are to be my assistant at such birthings. Are you prepared to work hard Hathor? There are many things to learn, many things to look for, many things to consider.

"Yes! Yes! I would love to be your assistant!"

"Well, Hathor, your enthusiasm tells me that you are indeed interested. I will speak with your father tomorrow regarding this subject. Now, scoot! Off with you! It's time for you to join your family's evening meal."

With that the scamp ran off bounding like a young gazelle so full of new found energy.

As for Ptah, he could only smile. I believe indeed that I have found my first apprentice!

*   *   *

It was the extraordinary ability to focus upon a task that caused her mentor to smile as Hathor's dexterous fingers rapidly and neatly stitched up the tear in the calf-skin pouch. Finishing with a lock stitch, the now eight-year-old bent her head and bit off the heavy thread.

Ptah then voiced a mild admonishment.

CHILDREN OF PTAH

"Now Hathor, how should you have trimmed that thread? Certainly not with your teeth. Have you not remembered my many instructions concerning infections?"

With a downcast look, the young girl's shoulders slumped and then she sighed.

"I am sorry teacher. I was in a rush to complete the task and I just forgot."

Smiling with his eyes Ptah gestured for the pouch, examined it, and declared.

"My apprentice, these stitches are smooth, tight and regular. I am most pleased with your pouch and so should you as well. Now, fashion for it a shoulder strap so that you may effortlessly carry it."

Now grinning ear-to-ear at her teacher's praise, the young girl immediately applied herself to the task of the shoulder strap.

*　　*　　*

Today promised to be a grand day, both for the very pregnant mother and for Hathor as well. While the relief of a sound birthing was much to be welcomed, this medical event also was to be Hathor's first to perform on her own. In many ways, it represented her final medical examination as she had already proved her dexterity in mending living flesh, mixing and dispensing sedatives, and the setting of broken limbs. While she well knew that her teacher Ptah would be standing near, Hathor was determined to see this birthing through.

*　　*　　*

It was during my 121st inundation, as my life's course was reckoned among my adopted kin, that a certain sense of accomplishment was reached. Already had I outlived two generations and in so doing had managed to provide not only an uncommon sense of continuity to the community of Mennefer, but also helped establish the basis of a potentially viable cultural identity – one that eventually might lead to a stable civilization. But only time will tell as the long length of this snake-like land sorely needs one head, a unifying force, to bring "all of its parts" together into one coherent whole. Yet, I remain optimistic as there are indications that just such forces are afoot. With the expansion and extension of our agricultural lands through a carefully maintained irrigation plan, food is now not only plentiful, but in abundance and it is this abundance that has spurred on the germ of exchange and commerce. While difficult at times to perceive, it is precisely the impetus of news from far away, the gossip of foreign traders, their seemingly odd ways of do things, the fabrics of their clothing, the design of their storage jars, and even the shape of their sails that have challenged their very core beliefs, habits, and norms of the inhabitants of Mennefer. No longer can my adopted kin remain in blissful isolation, all the while thinking that they occupied the very center of the universe. Contact with cultures outside of the immediate river valley will be their crucial first step towards the formation of civilization.

But just getting them past the point where food was no longer a hand-to-mouth imperative to their existence was quite a strain. The norms of personal hygiene alone required continuous reinforcement and brutally harsh lessons if those norms were not followed. Then, hand-in-hand with hygiene formed the explanations of why this lead to that, which quite naturally led to the nascent development of practical medicine and pharmacology. Apprentices had been identified and trained, because as the population continued to grow, I, one individual, simply could not provide the care needed to take up the challenge.

As a curious consequence of contact with the outside world, suddenly the value of the written word, or most commonly, the personalized seal stamp, became a thing of practical utility, a commonplace. Here to, there were several bright-eyed individuals I trained in the ways of the glyphs, those who provide their neighbors with such seal stamps, for a price. While there are currently only two *bona fide* "scribes" in our village, of which the recording of business transactions takes up most of their time, I have encouraged them nonetheless to scribble about other subjects as well. So, again in time, beyond the practical desire for recordkeeping, maybe even a literature of sorts might evolve.

The role that I play in all of this development is, and always has been, a passive one. Acceptance of something new has to be a personal decision, much like when one sees for the first time your neighbor sweeping out their house with a long-handled broom, instead of doing so bent over with the more traditional short-handled hand brush. A novel tool or advantageous method has to be seen, demonstrated, and proven many times over before its acceptance can take place.

And while I cannot always be that first impetus, I know that my many writings will be. For, on this day of my 121st inundation, I, Ptah, have almost completed my corpus of writings that will hopefully guide this young culture into a glorious future. I have already prepared my tomb, although I do not believe that I will be in need of it in the near future. I have trained two assistants as best as I am able in many of the subjects that my scrolls contain. They know full well what their responsibilities are and the legacy that they bare as they represent the very foundation of this young culture that dares to be a civilization. In these practical times, where rampant superstition must be gradually snuffed out, practical designations of rank are needed. And so, I have given these two assistants of mine the rank of "Great in their execution of handiwork." After all, not only do they know what is contained in my scrolls, it is their duty to preserve them as well.

Ah, my beloved scrolls! Sadly they are not yet complete as I still have one in my belly so to speak. Oddly, I have sought to compose and complete this scroll many times, but as I age, it too changes. While its title "On the Heart and Tongue" has remained firm, the form of its content has not. So I must think further on this.

CHAPTER XXI
Death of a Legend

The passing of a colleague that you have known for a lifetime is never easy. Words like "inevitable" and "mortal" never seem to fit the bill nor can adequately explain away the event. On top of that, some folks just seem to be timeless. They always seem to be there, practically granite-like institutions unto themselves, always ready to impart prescient nuggets of insight and wisdom gained through their long experience. Their very absence from the scene is what is most shocking, most unnerving, most unusual. And if that colleague was one who had earned your respect, your admiration, and dare I say, perhaps even your friendship, then the loss is only so much the greater.

So it was with the passing of Dr. Peter Borov, a man who had devoted his entire life to his research and to the people who had made it all possible. Borov was a man who had never wed, yet who was much loved. He had never driven a car, yet had spent his entire life moving objects around at beyond the speed of light. To the government that so generously supported him, he was a ghostly cipher, a man without a Social Security Number, a bank account or a credit card. Yet he was a man who through his extraordinary intellectual brilliance and natural administrative savvy was able to move mountains, transform a solitary natural feature into the Horizon Pass facility, reroute energy from the Hoover Dam to power it, all to better understand and transit time itself. If there ever was a real "Dr. Who," it was Peter Borov. If there ever was a time to affix the title "Legend" to a man, here it is.

Officially, or as best as anyone could tell, after some ninety-two years, four months, and seven days, Borov had expired peacefully in his sleep. That he had intended to go for his traditional morning run was apparent to anyone as his

185

shoes, jogging suit, socks and underwear were all neatly laid out and waiting. On that day his online day planner had him scheduled for an early morning meeting with his protégé Charlie Naysmithe to go over several proposed tweaks to the Soap Bubble's calibration programming and three conference calls. A luncheon date with Doc Allen and Nurse Stewart was next to be followed with a post-meal nap, another meeting with Naysmithe about some nifty idea that Tuna Cartwright had cooked up, followed by some administrative paperwork, and finally, a perusal of his daily email to round out the day.

Always prepared, one of Borov's last wishes was to have his ashes scattered along the many jogging trails that wound around the neighborhood of Horizon Pass to be followed by a "wild ass party," his very words, to take place at that research facility. It was no secret. Borov liked his Coors cold and Jack neat. Another request was that a one-time, lump sum be deposited into the accounts of the children of Willard Libby, the inventor of the radiocarbon dating technique. This took some doing as all four of the Libby's girls had married and had to be tracked down. Each deposit was accompanied with a letter sent via registered mail, which explained that the Department of Energy was eternally in their father's debt and would they be so kind and accept on this small token of their government's gratitude to the tune of $250,000 tax-free. To Colonel Charles Abraham "Tuna" Cartwright, "the raging Cajun," Borov left all of his much-beloved fly fishing gear full knowing that that native of Louisiana would put them all to good use. To Doc Allen the Russian émigré bequeathed title to several acres of land located near the Colorado town of Rifle complete with its own trout stream. To his young colleague and successor Charlie Naysmithe, the wily scientist willed him a framed, but still highly classified black and white picture of a grinning young Borov sticking a paper straw into the electromagnetic field of the original Soap Bubble prototype. Affixed to the wooden frame was a modest brass plate with the words, "Charlie: I double-dog dare you to top this!" And finally, Peter Borov addressed a sealed personal letter to be delivered to one Millie Hayes. Within it was contained a sincere promise.

* * *

Several items were really bugging Charlie Naysmithe. The first was the fact that the late Peter Borov had squarely placed in his lap the entire CRYSTAL BALL project. Beating the odds, Richards and Gregorieva had successfully pulled off their preliminary reconnaissance mission and had returned with the all important field data. When the prodigious field strength of forty-one megawatts as achieved in Philadelphia had been run through the Soap Bubble's calibration computer, it computed a time long, long ago – as in tens of thousands of years. In fact, the date suggested went far beyond the current calibration software's current calibration. In other word, the plus or minus deviation was quite wide and in order to make heads or tails of the entire situation, a full reworking of the software based on the USS Eldridge's parameters would be necessary. While the physicist was willing to pursue this reworking of the software, seeing it as principally a matter of scale, he still was not all that eager to pursue it. Why? Partly because Charlie Naysmithe discovered that he really did not have the stomach to craft a solution for the CRYSTAL BALL project, partly because he believed that in his heart of hearts that this effort wasn't his responsibility to pursue, and partly that he did not want to face the enormous responsibility of redeploying two temporal agents on a potential wild goose chase.

But in spite of all of his qualms about the CRYSTAL BALL project, what really turned the tide on Charlie's commitment to solve it was the discovery in his email box of a copy of Borov's letter to Dr. Millie Hayes. Having read and reread that email, Naysmithe now understood all too well the full burden that had been placed upon his shoulders.

*   *   *

"Well Toby," Naysmithe said, "the way that this software can be recalibrated is to use the Soap Bubble's field strength and its calibration as a relative proportion. You know what I mean? If Soap Bubble data is 'x,' then the Eldridge data has to be 'x plus whatever.'"

"I agree with you totally Doc. I'll just proportionally amp up the calibration to the Eldridge's levels, run the calibration and compare it to the Soap Bubble's baseline. That will give us a rough place to start from. Thereafter it will be all about tweaking the sensitivity of both calibration programs. Trust me Doc, I'm all over this one like white on rice."

"Thanks Toby," said Naysmithe, "I knew that I could count on you."

CHAPTER XXII
Return to Thebes

Despite Richards' radar being on full alert since their takeoff from Bangor, the second leg of the flight had gone without a hitch. Even the touchdown at Luxor was as silky smooth as any zoomie could have made it. However, what really bugged Richards was that all of his attempts at chatting up the flight crew had been met with only a polite, but near stony silence. What he did find out was that their drivers were professional US Air Force, probably fighter pilots, and definitely not members of the Air Guard. Their shoulder patches boldly said so: Maineiacs – 101st Air Wing.

These guys are all business.

This he read as another bad sign that something was up and someone far up the ladder was definitely concerned.

*   *   *

As had become tradition, a rickety pickup truck with a rock crunching tranny roared up the tarmac as soon as the Gulf Stream braked to a halt and its chocks put in place. Jumping out of its cab, strode forward a soldier who stopped at the rear of the tailgate. Grinning ear to ear and squinting in the bright sunlight out from under a tan bush hat stood First Lieutenant "Calli" Callahan. Dressed in impeccably starched desert cammie chocolate chips, Calli was their new driver, protector, and general all-round nurse maid. And he was specifically told by his august predecessor to remind them of that fact every moment of every day.

While extending his hand in greeting first to Richards, the tall former forward from Indiana declared.

"Dr. Richards, welcome back to Luxor, Sir. I am pleased to see that you are still looking fit."

Then briefly acknowledging the Russian.

"Ms. Gregorieva, you look simply outstanding!"

Then turning to them both with his hands on his hips, the soldier continued.

"But just what took you two pantywaists so long to get here? Huh? Like I have all day to nurse maid you two? Maybe Tuna did, but I won't!"

"Now shake a leg, load up your gear, and get in the cab."

As Richards and Gregorieva did as they were told, the American quietly murmured. "Well Vesna, I can tell that Lieutenant Callahan has been fully briefed by Tuna."

*   *   *

As with all previous drops, it had become tradition that the field operatives themselves erect the temporal equipment and run through setup checklists. In many respects it made sense, much as the walk-around preflight drill that pilots perform on their airframes.

"If your life depends on it, then you better well check it!" Was the order of the day.

The new portable Soap Bubble VI consisted of the improved and greatly reduced in size Little Beast II computer, three superconducting towers and their ion cannons, the central drop ring, yards of heavy-duty power cabling and electrical junctions, all enabled by a power pack, which remained about the size of an average backpack, but now was non-nuclear. As the late Borov had predicted, Callahan was simply ecstatic over that fact. All in all, the entire rig consisted of far less equipment than any garage rock and roll band would have required.

This drop, as with all the previous, took place within the most sacred holy of holies of the god Amen Re during the early morning hours. Literally located deep within the bowels of the Karnak Temple, special arrangements had been made in advance with the Egyptian Antiquities Service and the Egyptian Tourist Bureau to establish the first level of security. Needless to say such arrangements did not directly disrupt the ongoing Dutch Expedition's clearance of the Amen Re Treasury and the conservation work of the French Archaeological Mission, but would impact the near daily performed "Sound and Light" shows.

Partly in an effort to mollify the Egyptian Tourist Bureau, Callahan and his shadowy security force, which provided the airtight second level security cordon, immediately tore down the Soap Bubble once a drop was completed. This same group would then re-erect it for the drop team's retrieval – again during the early morning hours. While a tedious task, the exposure of the team and its priceless equipment was greatly reduced, and besides, the Tourism Bureau was now oblivious to their early morning presence and only lost two evening's gate receipts. Another important part of the setup process was the erection of crude wooden scaffolding around the Soap Bubble equipment that provided a platform for Gregorieva and Richards to drop from. A long since commandeered sailing rig, rope, and ancient pulley acted as the retrieval crane. These elements too had to be dismantled as well at every drop or retrieval and then secreted away from curious eyes.

*　　*　　*

The institution of the *per ankh*, literally "the house of life," is an extremely ancient one that dates back to at least the Third Dynasty if not older. It, along with the *kha en seshretou*, "the hall of papyrus rolls," and *per medjat*, "the house of book rolls," represents the ancient precursor of the modern library. Just as today, such archival collections came into existence as a direct result of the invention of writing and out of the need to save that which was considered valuable. Typically, the contents of *kha en seshretou* and *per medjat* included practical administrative and legal documents of all kinds – such as land surveys, deeds, licenses, and tax records. As one might expect, such collections have been found within administrative contexts, royal palaces, and even private households.

On the other hand, collections contained within the *per ankh* tended more towards the academic, including medical, mathematical, astronomical, architectural, and even historical records of a sort. Also found within the *per ankh* would be a class of texts that could be best described under the rubric of religiously oriented, such as cultic donations, temple trade agreements, priestly documents, and what may be considered philosophical or religious treatises particular to a region's divinity. The original text of "The Memphite Theology" would be a good example of the latter. In the main, therefore, the *per ankh* was typically a temple repository of predominately non-administrative records, more oriented towards "that [which] might be most useful for the development of the mind." Needless to say such "useful" collections associated with a region's principal temple found themselves under the care and protection of its priesthood, many of which we might consider a teaching faculty of sorts. While the *per ankh* were not public institutions, they were directly associated with the temple's scribal school. The Egyptian literature even advises young people to visit these institutions in order to learn, confirming that "one book is more precious than a palace or a chapel." Such a synergy between recorded knowledge and literary pedagogy was a natural fit for a temple's *per ankh* and is directly comparable to medieval European monastery libraries and their schools. Regardless of what sort of document that was stored, it could be recorded on either papyrus, animal skin, on tablets of wood, metal, or even stone.

CHILDREN OF PTAH

*　　*　　*

The drop into the holy-of-holies of the Great God went successfully. As both of the temporal field agents did, they experienced that uniquely slippery sensation as they passed through the field. As had become habit, Gregorieva went first, who immediately retrieved the small neck pouch of "traveling money" that her colleague had dropped first through the ring. Richards, who soon followed, landed safely despite the fact that he took almost a full minute to collect his senses as the PDS was again rearing its ugly head. But once Richards' head cleared, the heady incense of the sanctuary and the smell of its scented oil lamps immediately assaulted him. Finally opening his eyes, he found Gregorieva sitting next to him, hovering with undisguised concern in her eyes.

"My brother, are you well?"

Quickly recovering, Richards replied, "Yes, my sister. I am now well. We better be on our way."

"Here, first place this pouch around your neck."

"Yes, I somehow had already forgotten that."

Once having squeezed through the massive portal of the sanctuary so as to not sound off its alarm gongs, the pair quietly padded into the interior of the temple proper, but before leaving it, Richards instead took Gregorieva on a quick tour, whispering an explanation here, pointing out a detail there. Fortunately, the fullness of the moon provided some light through the many clerestory window slits, but they were clearly not enough as the many strategically located floor oil lamps attested. These floor lamps were cannily timed to burn only during the evening and darkest morning hours, since their carefully braided linen wicks were of a certain specified length.

Throughout this private tour the Russian dancer tried hard not to gawk and gap at the rich splendor on display, the riot of color, and of course just the sheer scale of it all. Nonetheless, Gregorieva began to appreciate the reason behind Richards' intense immersion into this corner of the ancient world and his chosen persona and social ways became far more understandable – being almost Russian in flavor. But there was more.

Yes! She thought. This is how my dear Sasha must have understood it as well!

With the tour ending at where they had begun, before the portal of the inner-most sanctuary, Richards then lead Gregorieva off towards his favored side exit guarded by the shadow of the black granite statue of Sekhmet. Once again under the bright early morning stars of the Theban capital a sudden realization came to the pair – they could not go to the handy and nearby household of Meryptah and sleep until dawn rise as it was now occupied by his successor, the priest Nebneteru, who they had yet to meet. Instead the pair made their way through and out of the vast sacred precincts of Karnak and walked south beyond the Luxor Temple to the household of Prince Horemheb. Upon arriving there, and finding no one awake, the pair just quietly slipped into the guest quarters and made themselves comfortable. Tired by the stress of the drop and the long walk, sleep came swiftly, but before it did, the brother and sister pair bedded down on opposite sides of the room just in case they were discovered before they rose.

And it is well that they had, as the morning arrived all too soon, and their surprise presence was noted by one of the housekeepers. Not knowing who the two were, the still sleepy-eyed houseman Nesi almost sounded the alarm, but thought the better of it and instead reported his discovery directly to Horemheb himself.

"What's this Nesi? You tell me that two strangers have spent the night under my roof without my knowledge? Take me to them immediately!" commanded the suddenly agitated prince.

Storming through his household close on the heels of his houseman the still groggy prince was quite a sight to behold.

Now standing at the threshold of the guest room, Horemheb could see two deeply slumbering forms in the dawning light.

"Well!" He murmured. "So it's true."

Then one stirred, rolling over onto his side and in the process baring his much-scared back. Seeing this, the prince smiled, just shook his head, and backed out of the room's entrance. Now facing his houseman in the hallway, Horemheb whispered conspiratorially.

"Nesi. You have done well. That is just my adopted brother and his sister. Leave them be, but at dawn make sure that they are up in time for the first meal." Now patting the man on the back, the prince wandered off scratching his unshaven head and thinking about his morning toilet.

Mayneken! You rogue! Just when my brother did you arrive?

* * *

As Richards and Gregorieva appeared at the first meal of the day all freshly scrubbed and shaved, a beaming Horemheb greeted them warmly at his groaning table.

"Good morning my noble brother and sister," the prince announced.

Smiling back sheepishly the pair simultaneously said, "Thank you," accompanied with a slight bow from their waists.

"Sit and refresh yourselves!" indicated Horemheb with an expansive wave of his arm. "And to what do I owe the pleasure of your presence this very early morning?" then queried the prince with a bit of sarcasm.

"A task mainly," Richards answered instantly all business, "but in particular we wish to pay a visit to the new high priest of Amen, a man named Nebneteru I am told. Do you know of him?"

"Well enough," said the prince noting his brother's serious tone, "but if I am to succeed with the revival of Thebes, I suppose that it is high-time that we meet. What have you in mind my brother?"

"Well then, perhaps we should pay the high priest a visit together. Present to him a united front as it were and then see with our eyes and note with our minds."

"Mayneken, are you always so calculating so early in the day?"

*   *   *

The walk from the prince's household to the comparatively modest abode of the High Priest of Amen Re went uneventfully. Along the way, however, Richards noted several of Horemheb's restorations and civic improvements to neighborhood wells and midden sites. But when they arrived at the Luxor Temple complex, its pools had been totally restored and gardens were again in full bloom. Seeing this, Gregorieva stood mesmerized before one particularly dense floral arrangement that was nothing short of a riot of color and mist of fragrance. This prompted Richards to compliment the young prince.

"My brother," he began, "I see that while I have been away that much progress has been made towards the restoration of blessed Thebes."

Smirking at the observation, Horemheb answered, while noting Gregorieva's floral attention. "Such as it is. The planting of flowers is one thing, but the local wells have just been completed and are finally functioning as they should. In fact, the mayor of Thebes, Sennufer, with my help has installed several local men, who report directly to him, to manage it all. They are responsible for upkeep and appearance of their neighborhoods. It has worked well, especially since I have personally rewarded only those neighborhoods who please me the best."

Smiling now with genuine pleasure and gripping the prince across his shoulders, Richards said. "I am very pleased my brother, but rewards as well?"

"Thank you," the prince replied, "but I had to offer rewards as finding strong backs are no longer an easy task. Just wait until you see what that high priest has done with the restoration of the temple. You will better understand!"

*   *   *

After the trio gained entrance into the Karnak complex, the smell of fresh mud, plaster, and drying white wash filled their noses. The sounds of stone mason's chisels and mallets, wood being sawed, hammers hammering pegs, and choruses of work gangs filled the air along with their ubiquitous dust clouds. In short, a full renewal was underway everywhere.

As they approached the household of the new high priest, all was very familiar except for the recent application of a coat of white wash. What was truly interesting was that the high priest himself was sitting in the shade of his porch on a folding chair with a camp table before him with several scrolls, an ink well, and several writing brushes standing upright in a small jar. Standing before the seated high priest were two foremen and a very exercised conversation was taken place.

"Fascinating." Said Richards.

"Indeed." Agreed Horemheb.

"Now I can see why you have been bribing the local managers to stay put in their neighborhoods."

"In fact," the prince explained, "the high priest has been so pressed for labor that he has successfully hired away most of the artisans and craftsmen from that accursed city to the north."

"Really…"

"Indeed." The prince said with a wry smile.

At this point in their conversation, the two foremen stormed off in a huff with their heads down, while furiously cursing under their breath. Looking up, the high priest wearily waved the trio over with a look on his face that almost read: "Take a number."

However, at their nearing approach Nebneteru quickly recognized Horemheb, smiled, and rose from his stool to greet them.

"Noble prince! What a blessed surprise. At first glance I thought that I had yet another labor issue to pass judgment upon."

Grasping each other's forearms the prince and high priest greeted each other. Then, turning, Horemheb announced his companions.

"Great one, I wish to present my adopted brother and *sem*-priest of Ptah, Mayneken and his sister Maatkare." Both of whom then politely bowed in the direction of the high priest.

"Mayneken?" said Nebneteru, "would you be the same Mayneken, the adopted son of my predecessor Meryptah?"

"Great one, you do honor to my adopted father's memory," purred Richards.

Taken aback by the deference given by such an impressive looking priest and his sister, the high priest said.

"The sun is high. Come and refresh yourselves within my humble house. After that insolent confrontation, my throat has become thirsty."

*   *   *

To Richards careful eye, not much had changed within his adopted father's household. The same spartan furnishings were still in place; only here and there were noted some minor personal touches. A call to the houseman was promptly answered and several cool jars of beer immediately appeared to the four-some seated around the low dining table. Breaking the seal on one of the jars, the houseman poured out its contents into four frothing ceramic cups. Once passed around and shared with all, the high priest then toasted his guests.

"May Thebes rise again from its doldrums to a far greater glory; may the royal court shortly return; and, may a strong pharaoh stride forth!" After which, Nebneteru drained his mug.

Immediately recognizing a kindred spirit, the trio drained theirs as well. For Gregorieva, the beer, while delicious, she found it to be also surprisingly chewy. Richards, ever the social barbarian, just drank deeply and then burped. Nonetheless, this reflex exhalation brought a broad grin to the high priest's face.

"Now, that was most refreshing! Mose, pour us another round!" commanded the high priest.

After taking several more swallows and allowing a relaxed sigh, the high priest rather pointedly got down to business.

"So Horemheb, how much progress have you made with your many restoration projects?"

"I am making headway, but am having some difficulty finding enough laborers. Do you have any suggestions?"

Now realizing that the prince had seen his rather impromptu meeting with his foremen, the high priest again sighed and just shook his head.

"I find it remarkable those men with once nearly starving families have now decided that the largess of the Great God is no longer sufficient to silence their bellies."

"Send your troublemakers to me," the prince said, "and then we will see what happens."

Then the high priest and the prince shared a look, one very hard to interpret, but one that communicated enough agreement that the two then simultaneously nodded to the other.

Then turning to Richards and Gregorieva, Nebneteru said.

"Noble Mayneken," and with a slight bow with his head, "and the most beautiful Maatkare, I have heard many tales about you and your master Piankhotep from the prince here and also from the Osiris Meryptah himself. Is it true that you are an ambassador, a warrior-priest, and seer as well?"

With a smile, Richards answered. "Perhaps noble one. If you are referring to my blessed father who has gone West, then absolutely in every respect. But if you are referring to my princely brother Horemheb, then most absolutely in every respect."

With this clever reply, Horemheb loudly guffawed.

"My brother, as always, a master of understatement!"

Now allowing himself to totally focus upon the sultry image of Maatkare the high priest asked.

"And of you my lady, is it also true that you are your own brother's assistant in these matters?"

"Indeed, great one, in absolutely every respect."

Now chuckling at her pun.

"And so it should be."

After the third round of beer, Richards sought out and finally found his opportunity to pitch his personal request to the high priest.

"Noble Nebneteru, is it true that the Great Hidden One Amen Re's complex possesses its own *per ankh,* one beyond compare?"

A bit surprised by this sudden turn in an otherwise casual conversation, the high priest nonetheless found the opportunity to puff-up like a hen.

"Why yes, Mayneken, indeed such a marvelous collection exists. What is your interest in it?"

"I seek wisdom, great one, wisdom. The Osiris Meryptah had once spoken of it. Is it even possible that I and my sister may visit it?"

"Without question," came the immediate reply from the now slightly inebriated high priest. In fact, the high priest thought that the request was such a commonplace. Then he wondered why such a powerful seer, the personal ambassador of the Nefertiti, and adopted son of his predecessor even had thought to ask. The sheer fact that Mayneken had requested his permission was as stunning as the fact that it was made in the spirit of respect for his station. Strangely, the high priest felt humbled by the simple request. Finally finding his tongue, Nebneteru said.

"In fact, I will instruct a certain Merimaat, my most trusted assistant, to be your guide. When do you wish to go?"

*　*　*

The following day, just after the first meal, Gregorieva and Richards appeared at the entrance of the Karnak complex and waiting for them at that agreed upon place and time was a young priest, no more than perhaps some twenty inundations old. Rail thin, but wearing a broad tooth-gapped grin at their approach, the priest welcomed them with a slight bow from the waist.

"Greetings most noble Mayneken and Maatkare! I am Merimaat, second prophet of the Great Hidden One, Amen Re. I am here to escort you to our *per ankh*. Please follow me."

That carefully rehearsed script having been said the priest then immediately turned and began striding off towards the interior of the vast complex. A bit startled by the abrupt efficiency of their guide, the pair blinked and then almost broke into a quick jog to catch up. After a series of quick turns between several newly repaired mud brick structures the group passed behind a partially tented courtyard that was filled with about twenty furiously scribbling scribal students, who were transcribing a text being read aloud by their priest-instructor. Acknowledging their quiet passage with a quick bow of his head, the instructor's voice did not break in its rhythmic delivery. The students, who were bent over and sitting on woven mats, did not notice the visitors' passage. To Richards, himself a teacher of the ancient Egyptian language, the academic task was an interesting one and one that he had to try out the next time he was in the classroom himself.

The opposite side of the courtyard led to an entrance into a massive limestone structure. Once out of the intense sun and into the interior's shady coolness, the pair involuntarily shivered, looked about blinking until their eyes had adjusted, and then found the smiling Merimaat waiting for them next to a sizable cedar wood double doorway.

"Here most noble ones is the *per ankh* of the Great Hidden One. It, of course, is at your disposal at any time. Allow me to introduce you to its caretaker, the master of the secrets of the *per ankh*."

Turning towards the central break in the cedar doors Merimaat pushed with both hands, one placed on each door, opening the entrance way wide and in so doing released a fragrant puff of air that greeted their noses, which smelled like fresh-cut hay.

Once inside, Merimaat quietly closed the doors while Gregorieva and Richards stood wide-eyed and with their mouths ajar. In many ways, the *per ankh* was in terms of scale the size of a typical Wisconsin barn's interior: some two stories high by fifty feet wide by one hundred deep – all gently lit by broad clerestory window slats along the entire roofline. Standing where they were, the central interior had a sunken level that was reached after a short flight of steps, which contained two parallel rows of long low tables with an aisle between. At the end of each table was an open basket filled with highly polished river stones. Meanwhile, the raised level of the chamber's outer walls was covered with a nearly continuous cedar wood structure that best resembled a widely spaced, crisscrossing diagonal framework. Within each diamond-shaped space, lay easily ten to fifteen tightly bound papyrus rolls.

CHILDREN OF PTAH

What a papyrologist's dream! Thought Richards, who then rather quickly amended the thought. No, what a treasure!

Meanwhile, Gregorieva was roughly calculating what this temple's treasure-trove contained.

Eight sections per side. Five against the rear wall. Thirteen nooks per section. Figure ten rolls per section. That calculates out to about 2700 rolls at a minimum! Hopefully, we will not have to search each and every one.

Totally forgetting Merimaat's offer of introduction to the library's master of secrets, Richards wandered off to the right towards the nearest section, tilted his head to one side, and instantly saw how the papyri of one nook was identified.

Ah ha! So that's how they do it!

Each roll has its own wooden tag attached with a linen yarn-like string. And so many tags!

Now looking down the sightline of the right side's eight sections.

My God! He thought as he gently fingered a single wooden tag with the tip of his finger. All these id tags look like so many delicate wind chimes!

At this point, a purposely loud throat clearing abruptly snapped both of the temporal agents back to the here and now.

"Merimaat!" Bellowed the library's master. "Just who are these two gaping donkeys? And you over there. Don't touch that!"

The source of the indignation came from a small, very lean, and elderly priest who stood no more than five feet tall. With eyes that blazed with sheer territorial wrath and a left hand that held a stout staff, Richards rather suddenly found himself directly confronted by this mighty mite quite literally nose to, well, chest. Gregorieva, who was standing over on the other side of the library, simply froze in place.

"Just who are you, you muscle-bound oaf! And how dare you touch my collection!"

Richards' reaction to this confrontation was mixed between immediate recognition and impish curiosity. For the priest before him reminded him of a very stern Sister of Mercy that had once chastised him in fourth grade. The real question was just how far he could push back this imperious individual without losing all access to his collection.

While Richards was pondering his next course of action, Merimaat just observed from across the library.

Well, this should be good as the venerable master of the secrets is in his usual feisty form. But I just wonder what this well-scared Mayneken will do? By the look on his face he is clearly considering his options and now he is actually smiling!

Richards, for his part, had decided that the best course of action was to totally surrender before the elderly priest and so very slowly got down on his right knee, bent forward his head, and exposed the back of his neck in total submission.

"Most venerable one and Master of the Secrets of Amen Re's own *per ankh*," intoned Richards to the man's feet. "I am Mayneken, *sem*-priest of the great god of the White Wall, a student of ancient wisdom. I and my sister Maatkare seek your permission to consult your vast archive of knowledge."

At the surprisingly submissive posture and deferential tone of this *sem*-priest of Ptah of all things, the caretaker was taken aback and caught at a loss for words. Never before had anyone shown him such respect, and, surely one so nobly scared.

By the Great Hidden One! The master of the secrets thought. What sort of dire misfortune so disfigured this young one?

Now finding his tongue, the master formally said. "Well. Rise student of ancient wisdom. You are correct. My collection is indeed vast."

Then in an act of grudging apology the master asked.

"Just what is it that you and your sister seek? Perhaps I may be of some assistance."

So began the basis of a working relationship between the master of the secrets of the *per ankh* and the temporal agents. Polite questions were asked; slowly warming answers were offered. As the master began to walk the pair around the library explaining its contents and organization, Mayneken followed respectfully behind and to the right with his hands behind his back. His sister flanked the master librarian to his left, choosing to remain silent unless directly addressed. To all of this Merimaat recorded with eyes of disbelief.

It is no wonder that Mayneken is the Great Queen's own ambassador!

*   *   *

After about thirty minutes of a most fascinating tour Richards found himself salivating over the many topics and treatises that quite literally boggled his mind. Organized in a logical manner, the master clearly indicated where several works that dealt with astronomy were placed. Easily twenty rolls were devoted to pharmacology, chemistry, and medicine all grouped together. Others contained the temple's architectural plans that included many pious donation documents. Twenty-six rolls were none other than the original Asiatic campaign journals of Thutmose III from which the text of his monumental inscriptions had been culled. Several king lists of clearly ancient age, multiple copies of the annual calendar, recent pharaonic decrees, and a whole section by itself held the historical works that included the many Theban campaigns against the Hyksos. But by far the greatest collection was of a literary nature, which fully took up over one half of the entire library: myths, religious litanies, funerary texts, hymns, biographical works, and finally those that were of a purely secular bent.

While standing before the section of medical papyri, Richards inquired. "Does the work of the royal physician Ankhmes reside here?"

Surprised, but pleased with the question, the keeper instantly replied in the affirmative and even indicated where the massive roll's resting place was located.

"And venerable master, do you know whether the blessed Osiris Meryptah ever wrote a manual on how to ride the winds of Amen Re?"

The absolute surprise at this last inquiry could not in any way be contained on the master librarian's face nor in his stammered reply.

"Why, why, how most noble one, could you know of such a sacred document?"

With a knowing smile, Richards said. "Because I am the adopted son of the venerable Osiris Meryptah, and because I buried him near the most sacred precincts of Memphis, in the very shadow of the Osiris Djoser's own pyramid."

Quickly glancing over towards the still silent Merimaat with hard eyes, the master of the secrets deeply sighed and then addressed Mayneken with a surprisingly gentle, almost whispered voice.

"Most noble Mayneken, please accept my deepest apologies for my rank ignorance. I did not know of this. I was just told that a priest and priestess wished a tour of the *per ankh*. The Osiris Meryptah, the most holy and kind man that I have ever known, was a very good and close friend."

Richards, now understanding, pitched his voice to the master librarian alone. "And should I understand that your kind assessment of my father would not include that silently spying jackal over there?"

Keeping his eyes lowered, the keeper quietly responded. "Most certainly noble one."

At this quiet and brief conversation Merimaat's eyes narrowed in suspicion. Now what's this? Just what is that imperious librarian up to now? And what is this talk of a manual to ride the winds? How absurd! No wait! What have I not been told! Thought the now suddenly paranoid priest.

CHILDREN OF PTAH

Richards, subliminally noting a change in their tour guide with the unconscious shuffling of the second prophet's feet, then stated loudly enough for all to hear.

"Master of the secrets of the *per ankh* of Amen Re, what is your name?"

"Seti, most noble one," replied the librarian now with a respectful bow of his head.

"Venerable Seti, my sister Maatkare and I are seeking the written works of the god Ptah and his description of the first days of the Primeval Mound. Does your marvelous and vast collection contain such?"

"Sadly, no most noble Mayneken, but I do suspect that I know where you can find what you seek. I have a good acquaintance at the city of the Great White Wall, Memphis. He is the master of the secrets of the *per ankh* at the Great Temple of Ptah. It is to him that you must ask your question."

"And to whom should we go?"

"Why, most noble one, you probably already know one of the high priests of Ptah already, the younger brother of the Osiris Meryptah himself – Ptahmesou. His colleague is Pahamneter."

With that revelation, Richards realized that the master librarian was right, for the *per ankh* of Amen Re would not logically contain a single work that could be attributed to Ptah. In hindsight that made considerable sense to the Egyptologist, especially since the entire theological doctrine of Ptah was a direct competitor to that of Amen Re. And that meant that Gregorieva and he had a journey north to make.

Now taking Richards by the elbow, Seti steered him over to one of the corner bins of scrolls. Reaching up and pointing.

"Ah, here is what you seek, noble Mayneken. This is the very scroll that your adopted father had ordered to be created. It is entitled: 'On Mastering the Winds of Amen Re.'"

"Venerable Seti," Richards now asked, "is it possible to have a copy made of my father's creation?"

With a bow of his hairless head the master murmured with the pleasure of purpose.

"Most assuredly noble Mayneken. Consider your request completed before the sun sets."

*   *   *

It never failed to amaze Richards the sheer influence of his ambassadorial ring. That, followed by a gentle and reasonable tone, seemed to grant the Egyptologist with the ability to move mountains at will. In this instance, it was the quick procurement of a swift, comfortable and well-stocked river boat that was free of lice and fleas. Then again, allowed the American, perhaps it might have been the devastating allure of his sister that had turned the boatman's knees into mush. Or, perhaps it was just the two gold rings from his pouch. Then again maybe it was the silent machinations of his adopted brother, Prince Horemheb, who was presently overcome not only with tasks surrounding the care and feeding of the newly arriving royal court, but also the renovation of the royal palace on the Western Bank of the river. Regardless, that very afternoon the pair pushed off into the northern current enroute to Memphis.

Traveling along a river's current at a rate that only Nature determines grants one ample opportunity to day dream, think deep thoughts, and just dose. For the boatman, his job is merely to gently guide his tiller around the many islets, sandbars, territorial hippopotami, and other river craft, all the while dozing with one eye open. For the two temporal agents, both products of our modern world, they had to consciously relax and accept the fact that they could not just jump on a jet, grab a car, or reserve an air conditioned berth on the overnight train. For Gregorieva, a dancer and avid jogger, confinement aboard the small boat was a very real challenge. While she had done tolerably well on the day and a half trip to Akhetaten,

CHILDREN OF PTAH

Memphis was almost another two full days beyond that. She fully realized that she would have to find something to occupy her mind both for this trip and the return journey. In the end it would be nothing more than an exercise in patience.

For Richards it was different. He just turned on his enhanced and near-digital internal recording and absorbed everything and anything of interest. And what he saw was a sublime canvas. A winding ribbon of water that gradually made its way through an ancient land speckled with river craft coming, going, and crossing their path. A continuous northern breeze that refreshed, cooled, and even managed to keep most of the ever-tumbling swarms of river gnats at bay. Mesmerizing flocks of birds that shimmered in the cloudless African sun like kaleidoscopic pinwheels of color. Lazily swaying date palm fronds laden with their fruit. Silent, expressionless and unblinking crocodiles basked in the sun along the river bank and amid the clumps of fragrant papyrus reeds. Vast floating mats of ducks that at a moment's notice would stir, take to the sky, and fill it with their fluttering wings only to suddenly turn as one, pivot in the air, and settle anew. The rhythmic creaking of a *shaduf*'s pivot as a farmer endlessly lifted water from the river to the raised irrigation channels of his field. The caterwauling joy of children chasing helter-skelter after several newborn piglets. The heady wafting aromas of blooming lotus and acacia. The friendly waves from southbound river craft with their rectangular sails bulging and straining in the wind. Yes, travel along the river under the shade of the hot sun was a nearly-hypnotic, sleepy time when the subtle gurgle of the passing water along the hull first tugged at your eyelids and then conspired to keep them closed. And everywhere there was the sight and rich smell of the renewed black earth, the musty reek of the Nile's rich silt that stained both the river and its banks as far inland as the recent inundation.

W.J. CHERF

*   *   *

The pair sensed that they were nearing Memphis because the river traffic had become noticeably denser. Not in the way gridlock suddenly "happens" on a modern highway, but rather in the gradual increase of river-born craft to the point where the tiller man had to now keep both eyes open. As they coasted by the nearly abandoned wharves and marketplace of Akhetaten had been a total nonevent, countless other townships, nowhere mentioned in the modern archaeological record, passed by their bow. In the end, it was the distinct smell of many cooking fires that really provided the first clue that civilization was about to appear before them, around just the next river bend.

Consider. Memphis was an old city even by Egyptian standards, while in comparison the establishment of Thebes had been a relatively recent phenomenon. While archaeologists state that Memphis was first founded on the western bank of the river sometime in the prehistoric mists of the Predynastic Period, it really was even older than that. After all, it was here, at Mennefer, "the enduring and beautiful (place)," that the legendary Egyptian King Narmer (or Menes according to some modern scholars) supposedly established Egypt's first capital following his unification of the upper valley and lower delta regions of this long, ribbon-like land. Located as it was at the southern end of the Nile Delta, this highly strategic site hence earned the nickname the Great White Wall after its towering and crenellated fortifications. It was here, at Memphis that the Third Dynasty Pharaoh Djoser ruled, who is credited with the construction of the massive Step Pyramid – Egypt's first, and its surrounding mortuary complex at Sakkara. It was here too, at Memphis, that the powerful pharaohs of the Fourth Dynasty reigned. These god-kings built in ever increasing magnificence a seemingly endless series of pyramid complexes along the western plateau overlooking the Nile at Abusir, Sakkara, and Dashour. But the pinnacle edifice was that of the Pharaoh Khufu – the Great Pyramid at Giza. And it was here as well, at Memphis that the city's patron god, Ptah, resided in his magnificent temple.

As the river boat glided past that last bend in the river, the Great White Wall appeared on the left bank and while this was a "true" city, Richards and Gregorieva had never before seen anything like it. It surpassed Disney Land and Disney World and Universal all put together. It was like flying over downtown Chicago, New York, San Francisco or Paris for the very first time – on a clear night. Arrayed before them was a proper urban complex complete with sprawling mud brick suburbs that long ago outgrew the confines of the massive fortification circuit that contained a labyrinthine limestone temple complex at its center. Along the city's whole river front was the port of Perunefer, "happy journey," with its many warehouses, factories, workshops, principal marketplace, docks and landing areas. On the left upslope and beyond the city, the simply extraordinary funerary architecture of the Old Kingdom stood in bold relief against the late afternoon sky from the raised desert plateau: pyramids of various slopes, pyramids in collapse, big pyramids, little pyramids, pyramids perfect in every way, and even an experimental bent one as well. The tableau was truly surreal for the land of the living and the land of the dead could not have been more clearly defined and so neatly divided by the distinct line of cultivated black mud, *kemet*, and dry red desert sand, *deshret*. It is this clear dichotomy of life and death that so defined the Egyptian psyche.

* * *

As the boat approached the busy and frenetic atmosphere of the city's port Richards once again confirmed with the man at the tiller that their stay would unfortunately be a brief one and that his immediate availability for departure, either day or night, would be well-worth his time. Again, bobbing his head in agreement and clearly with visions of golden "sugar plum fairies" dancing in his head, the pair disembarked with an over-the-shoulder wave and headed directly for the main marketplace that was located a short walk away.

"Damn I need a bath and a shave. I flat out stink!" Richards said. "I need to find a groomer."

While taking in an appreciating deep breath.

"Then, I am going to absolutely gorge myself on sweet breads and grilled beef. I am starved!"

Managing to smile and chuckle at the same time Gregorieva quietly cracked. "I agree my brother, you do stink and you do need a groomer. And as for your empty stomach, it has been talking to me incessantly since early this morning. Kindly fill that beggar to silence it's mouth. In the meantime, I suppose a bath would be most refreshing. Where shall we meet up?"

Pausing near a public well that was getting a steady business, Richards just tilted his head towards it and said.

"My dear sister, will that delicious well over there do?"

*   *   *

By the time that the temporal agents again met up, bathed, shaved, and fed it was nearing early evening and the marketplace itself was fast becoming a ghost town as the locals had retreated to their homes and the cooking fires of the evening meal. By sundown, Richards knew that most would be bedding down upon their roofs to escape the heat and to better benefit from the evening's cooling breezes.

Quickly realizing the situation, the twosome struck out towards the city's center in search of the Great Temple of Ptah, its high priest, and hopefully a grant of hospitality for the night. Now threading their way through the warren maze that was the port's warehouse district they headed by sheer reckoning towards the nearest gateway of the city's fortifications. Taking care not to step into any of the manure or any of the questionable fluids and other debris that seemed to stream down and clutter up the center of the streets, it did not take them long before just such a gated portal was located. Passing through the massively huge mud brick barrier and its wooden gate leaves, Richards unconsciously measured their girth at twenty-two meters at the base. Once inside, just as any tourist would, he stopped to look up and estimated their height at about thirty meters with engaged staircases that gave access to the wall's parapets.

Observing this academic interest and mistaking it for something else and most likely something sinister, a bored and self-important soldier directly challenged Richards before he saw Gregorieva who was following in his wake.

"You there! Yes you, you gawking son-of-a-donkey. Just what are you doing?" Officiously bellowed the soldier and in the process alerting several of his squad who were lounging around.

Stopping dead in his tracks, blinking twice, and now slowly turning towards the direction of the clear insult, Richards' jaw muscles, clearly exercised, gritted out a slow smile that was not reflected in his dark eyes that had locked onto the soldier. Somehow, Gregorieva now saw, Richards said through his teeth.

"Who asks?"

The soldier, seeing the scared back, the muscular frame that carried them, and now facing Richards directly, stopped where he was. He then drew out his bronze sword with a quick metallic hiss full thinking that he was now in total command. The overly self-confident are that way and in the process oftentimes they unwittingly blunder across that imaginary line that they never really intended to cross.

"I do not answer questions you befouled oxen. You do!"

"Fine." The American answered with a curled upper lip.

And ever so slowly Richards raised his ripped right arm and extended his fist towards the soldier, and in a quiet voice challenged him.

"Do you recognize this ring?"

At this point in the confrontation, Gregorieva had taken up a defensive position with her back to Richards as no less than six armed soldiers had now surrounded them.

The soldier just glared back and belligerent silence was his reply, so Richards repeated, now with far greater volume that carried a clear command force.

"This royal ambassadorial ring?"

The shock of that statement visibly shook the now wide-eyed soldier and caused the rest of his colleagues to shuffle their feet as they stepped back.

Still holding the soldier's gaze and slowly lowering his arm to his side as if it were a dangerous weapon, Richards then turned on his heel and walked right through the encirclement and in the process scattered it as if the soldiers were nothing more than a hutch of rabbits, so did they quickly scurry to get out of his way with Gregorieva in tow.

Now briskly storming off and slowly allowing the heat of the moment to dissipate, after a few moments, Gregorieva chose to break the silence.

"That was close my brother. Well done. But my dear ambassador, I do not think that you made many friends today."

*   *   *

It did not take long before they practically ran into the white washed enclosure wall of the Great Temple of Ptah. In many respects, the Egyptian name for it, *Hout-ka-Ptah*, "the Castle of the *ka* of Ptah," says it all. It is purported that when the late Hellenistic Egyptian historian Manetho translated *Hut-ka-Ptah* into Greek, which when it was Latinized for the Romans became ÆGYPTUS, the very origin of the English word for Egypt today. Regardless, the layout and appearance of the temple's enclosure seems to have been inspired by the Memphite outer circuit, consequently the temple complex of Ptah was surrounded by thick and tall mud brick walls complete with decorative crenellations running along its crest. Not seeing a gate, the pair began to walk to the right near the wall's base in search of one and after several minutes, as luck would have it, the monumental limestone entrance pylon was found.

Again Richards went into recording mode as precious little has been preserved of this magnificent structure. To begin, and leading up to the monumental limestone pylon itself, the paved stone entrance way was flanked by no less than twenty-two alabaster sphinxes, only one of which has managed to survive to this day. Measuring some twenty-six feet long by thirteen wide and weighing in around ninety tons each, while uninscribed, their graceful and delicate facial profiles strongly suggested that they were the pious donations of the female Pharaoh Hatshepsut. Next, the pylon had engaged within its niches eight magnificent red granite statues of the god, each painted with a realism that took one's breath away. Standing some forty feet tall their weight could only be estimated as around two hundred tons each. Because they were of red granite that meant that their origin was in the Aswan area, some five hundred miles to the south. On either side of the monumental entrance gate stood two towering cedar wood poles that each supported its own bright yellow pennant that slowly fluttered in the breeze. As for the pylon itself, it remained unpainted exposing its natural color and displaying its unblemished and seamless texture, so unlike the mud brick enclosure wall that was white washed to a brilliantly blinding gloss. Looking up Richards judged the pylon's height at easily one hundred feet by three hundred wide with a magnificent forty foot high cedar wood gateway that was decorated with thick and substantial bronze bands and rivets. Fortunately, the gates were still open and had not been closed for the evening, being guarded only by two young *wab*-priests.

Stopping to share a look of relief, Richards and Gregorieva approached the priests, performed a short bow, and quietly requested an audience with the high priest Ptahmesou. Surprised by the request, they were asked just who they were. In response, Richards, again speaking for the two of them, identified themselves by name and with full titles. Looking at each other with genuine surprise, one of the priests immediately excused himself, while the other graciously offered to share with the pair the cool shade within the pylon's entrance.

Surprisingly, their announcement did not take long as the other *wab*-priest returned quite a bit winded.

Now from a deep bow the young priest blurted out.

"Most noble ones" (gasp) "I have been instructed to escort you to our guest quarters where you can dust your feet in preparation for the evening meal." (gasp) "The great one would be overjoyed, of course, assuming that your travels thus far have not been too strenuous, if you could join him at his household."

Smiling Richards replied.

"Dear priest, kindly tell the great one that I and my sister would be most pleased to accept his most generous invitation to join him at the evening meal. You may now lead us to our quarters."

Gregorieva then said in a whisper that only Richards could hear.

"Ah, now that's my brother the ambassador."

*   *   *

Now refreshed yet again, but luxuriating nonetheless in that squeaky clean feel, Richards and Gregorieva, while individually fetched by a priest and priestess, yet somehow managed to arrive at the high priest's household at the same time. Clearly, some sort of practiced temple etiquette and protocol was at work. Still and all, Gregorieva managed to look even more beautiful than ever and she knew it, catching Richards appraising glance, which she returned with a wicked little grin.

Ah yes. The Egyptologist thought. I can already see who is going to be the object of tonight's dinner conversation.

*　　*　　*

The household of the high priest of the god Ptah was a surprisingly modest affair, being by Richards' best estimate only about two-thirds the size of his adopted father's house. Nonetheless, what it did not have in absolute size, it more than made up for in efficient design and comfort. Located as it was deep within the cramped confines of the temple complex, Ptahmesou's house was a two-story construction with the latrine, kitchen, and servants' quarters on the ground floor and the high priest's private quarters and dining area on the second. To their surprise, the pair was directed to a wood ladder that led up to the roof where a framed awning provided shade and yet took advantage of a remarkably cooling breeze. In the shade of the awning's center was laid out the evening meal on a low groaning board, around which were arranged several gaily colored goose down pillows. As usual, Richards took in all the gustatory details with his near-digital memory and in the process recorded no less than four different cheeses, roasted quail and dove, several delicious dipping sauces, fresh loaves of bread, two different sweet breads, some cooked perch, and fresh sliced yellow onion all arranged just so amid clusters of fragrant flowers.

With arms extended wide, the elderly Ptahmesou greeted them.

"Welcome my nephew to my household. My heart is overjoyed at your presence! However, I must apologize that my colleague Pahamneter could not be here as well." Said the old man as he embraced Richards.

"And, by the gods, who is this most lovely flower? Your wife, Mayneken?"

Smiling broadly the Egyptologist said. "No, my uncle, this is Maatkare, my sister."

Now embracing Gregorieva as a father would his own daughter, the high priest said. "Welcome to my household as well most beautiful Maatkare. For I have not had such a fine woman as you in my home since my beloved Tia went West."

Now extending his arms wide. "Please, all, sit and be well."

As if on cue two young priests magically appeared with two sealed jugs of beer. Once all their ceramic mugs had been filled the host then rose and delivered the following dinner toast.

"May Egypt be healed, may Egypt again be led by a righteous pharaoh observant of Maat, and may all things that my guests seek, may they be found."

And with that all three drank deeply and Richards, ever and always the barbarian, immediately burped, which brought an immediate smile of satisfaction and pleasure to Ptahmesou.

"Ah Mayneken, ever the polite ambassador."

Now grinning from ear to ear.

"Not really, my uncle, that was just the fine beer speaking."

Now chuckling at Richards' clever pun, their host commanded.

"Now, let us fill our stomachs before we attend to the needs of the mind. Please, begin."

CHILDREN OF PTAH

*   *   *

"Now Mayneken, my nephew and the much-loved adopted son of my eldest brother, the Osiris Meryptah, what caused you to travel all the way here from far distant Thebes?"

Richards, with his mouth full of soon-to-be non-existent sweet bread, nodded to Gregorieva for help. Gregorieva, seeing Richards plight, and then wondering just where does he put it all, firmly took hold of the reins.

"Noble Ptahmesou, as I see that my brother ever the ambassador, is currently fully engaged in negotiations with a sweet bread, may I answer that question for him? As we both seek the same."

"By all means most beautiful Maatkare!" The high priest encouraged, now very pleased to legitimately focus upon her image.

"We seek permission from you to visit the *per ankh* of the Ptah, for we wish to study his wisdom, and if it is permitted, to even copy that which is needful to us. The why of this is clear. We find the creation myth of Amen to be, let us say, lacking in intellectual rigor, while we have heard that of Ptah requires discipline of thought before it is put into words."

Ptahmesou sat spellbound during this brief and so cleverly constructed allusion to "The Memphite Theology" of creation. Then, blinking back into the here and now, the elderly high priest realized that while he had been totally smitten by Maatkare's beauty, he was now totally fascinated by her intellectual acumen. Finding his tongue he replied.

"But of course, Maatkare! I freely grant you and Mayneken access to our most treasured *per ankh*. But from your words it seems to my ears that you have already found what you seek."

Then catching himself, the high priest restated his answer. "But what is it that you two truly seek? Surely it is not just wisdom alone, but perhaps something more?"

"My dear Ptahmesou," the Russian said, "your instinct and insight are honed to a very sharp edge indeed! While I do not wish to sound blasphemous in the very presence, in the very house of the high priest of Ptah, truly "he who is great in the execution of handiwork," we seek evidence of the man Ptah."

Taken by Maatkare's clear deference to his station even to the use of his high religious title, Ptahmesou knew precisely what the beautiful one was seeking, for it was something that he himself once had been inquisitive about. For Ptahmesou, he knew that the divinity of Ptah was a recent event. His careful examination of the scrolls had indicated so, as the sacred writing of his name had not even included the sign of divinity until relatively recently. And then there was the stoic, no austere image of the god: a bearded mummified form standing straight and tall wearing a simple tight skull cap, while holding the staves of life (*ankh*), stability (*djed*), and power (*w3s*) before him. Never and nowhere is there any evidence of high station much less divinity – at least until recently. Making up his mind, the high priest said.

"What you have said Maatkare has held my interest as well. This evening you and your brother will be my household guests. Tomorrow, I must share with you what I have found regarding this matter."

*   *   *

After the morning meal, Ptahmesou, true to his word, took the pair deep within the labyrinthine confines of the Great Temple. After many confusing turns and passageways they at last arrived before a simple cedar door that opened at the high priest's gentle pull. Before entering, the high priest bent down and took from within a small recess near the door jamb a palm-sized oil lamp that he promptly lit. Once within the small windowless chamber the heady smell of papyrus greeted them.

CHILDREN OF PTAH

Much like the *per ankh* of Amen Re this one too had its central copying tables, three arranged end to end with a small wicker basket at one end that was filled with large, smooth, river stones and at the other, nearest the door, lay several more of the diminutive oil lamps. Lighting two of them, the high priest passed these on wordlessly to his companions and then continued on deeper into the chamber. Arriving at the rear wall of the chamber, Ptahmesou then turned to face Mayneken and Maatkare.

"What is behind you is just one *per ankh* of this temple. As you can see, there are no classrooms nearby and so frankly it is seldom frequented. As to what it contains that is so rarely consulted, are the ancient sun litanies that formerly were part of the *per ankh* at the Great Temple of Heliopolis, which regrettably is now in considerable disrepair due to recent, unfortunate events. It is sincerely hoped that the *next* pharaoh will restore that which has been left to decay and the cruelty of common thieves."

Now in a more conversational tone, the high priest continued. "As I said, this is just one of our *per ankhs*, but in spite of its rather distastefully ignorant contents, it is nonetheless the most important. I say this because there is only one way to it. In fact, I would estimate that it would take the two of you perhaps a full day to find your way back into the sunlight."

Now pausing for a moment Ptahmesou asked Mayneken with a firm directness. "Noble Mayneken, ambassador to Queen Nefertiti, adopted son of my own elder brother, and adopted brother of Prince Horemheb, just how true is your heart?"

"Why, great one, as true as one of Maat's own feathers."

"And you Maatkare, just how true is your heart?"

Bowing her head slightly, the Russian responded. "Great one, the very same as my brother."

Returning to the American and apparently satisfied with his answer, Ptahmesou now queried. "Noble Mayneken, what are the principle qualities of Ptah?"

Now feeling as if he was in the midst of his PhD oral examination all over again, Richards first thought and then carefully replied.

"Craftsmanship and creation. His thoughts, once so crafted, and then spoken, created all things."

Smiling a smile of true satisfaction, Ptahmesou said. "Well spoken Mayneken, for behold what Ptah has created."

With those words, the high priest handed his oil lamp to Richards, turned to face the blank wall that was behind him, gave it a gentle push, and a dark rectangular opening appeared!

Holy shit! Screamed Richards' mind. Just what is it with these Egyptians and their hidden passages!

Now entering a dark and cramped passage the flickering light of Ptahmesou's oil lamp quickly indicated that he had already begun descending stone steps at the end of the entrance passage. After seventy-two steps, which clearly cut through at least two layers of sedimentary rock, they arrived at a small chamber filled with stale air slightly sweetened. And Richards unconsciously said.

"Myrrh!"

"Indeed Mayneken. For this is the very tomb of Ptah himself!

Stunned by the high priest's words the Russian and American immediately began scanning their location. The burial chamber was formed as a perfect cube that was rough-cut into the living bedrock, in this case an extremely fine and dense limestone. Before them, that is directly facing what Richards considered the descending passage, was a simple, unadorned rectangular wooden coffin that rested upon a raised pedestal, itself carved from the living rock.

Examining it closely, Richards noted. "It is not constructed of cedar wood as is right and proper."

CHILDREN OF PTAH

"Indeed Mayneken, your eyes are attentive ones. It is made of common tamarisk, the material of commoners, but see its clever design. Made of narrow planks as it is, it is both strong and light in weight."

Upon hearing this, Richards began to wonder and then dared to voice his thoughts.

"My uncle, just how do you know such details? And more to the point, just how do you know that Ptah himself resides within?"

At first pretending outrage at such a blasphemy, inwardly Ptahmesou was very pleased, very pleased indeed, for in his distant youth, when he was first initiated as one of the high priests of Ptah, those were practically the same sentiments that he had expressed. And now allowing Mayneken some embarrassment at his all too blunt a question the priest finally relented with a smile.

"Because my nephew I too as a young man once asked very much the same question of my elders."

Shocked at the personal revelation, Richards blurted out.

"Uncle! Please accept my deepest apology for my ignorant tongue. I truly meant no offense."

"Among us no offense was received. And besides, do you think that Ptah himself would have been offended by such a logical question? I think not. Now, Maatkare, come here and assist me. You of delicate hands and fingers, so that I may prove to your doubting and muscle-bound brother that Ptah himself here resides."

Now indicating with the fingernail of his right little finger, Ptahmesou continued.

Note here Maatkare, the tiny square along the wood's edge?

"Yes, right there. Tease it out with your fingernail no more than the width of your thumb."

Working very carefully, both Gregorieva and Richards were soon surprised that indeed a wooden plug slowly began to emerge from the coffin's upper edge.

"Excellent Maatkare! Now see here, here, and here along this edge? There are three more. Carefully, extract those as well, while I busy myself with the other side."

After about ten minutes time all eight of the carefully camouflaged wooden locking pins had been pulled out.

"Now Maatkare, do you see where I have my hands positioned? Do likewise on your side.

"Good. Now very gently, lift."

And as one the wooden coffin lid rose about five inches, then ten, then fully to chest height.

"Now Mayneken. Peer into the face of Ptah."

As Richards indeed stepped forward, the light of his oil lamp fell across an extremely old and fully intact mummy, a mummy that was wrapped in a most peculiar way, but one that was extremely precise. But the most curious aspect of the mummy were its hands, each carefully wrapped, each finger individually swaddled; both hands formed in such a way as they held before the mummy a simple wooden staff that ended in a Y-shaped forked end.

Richards forgetting himself simply observed. "By the gods, he is holding a common snake-stick for a staff!"

"Indeed again, my nephew, you powers of observation are most acute. My predecessor said that in his time that there must have been a surfeit of snakes, so much so, that he was buried with his favorite staff so that he could have use of it in the afterlife. In fact, it is so even today, for during the harvest, a watchman with such a staff and an ax guards over the harvesters as they tend to very often encounter cobras, vipers and dangerous snakes that seem to spit a poisonous fire."

Then after a brief pause of several moments.

"Are you now convinced Mayneken?" said the high priest.

"Yes my uncle. I now believe."

"Good. Now Maatkare, you have been too patient, help me reseal the coffin."

224

CHILDREN OF PTAH

With considerable care, the high priest and the Russian placed and then reinserted all eight of the locking wooden coffin's lid pins. And while they were doing so, Richards began to explore further in the darkness the contents of the chamber.

To the right (as one entered the chamber) were arranged along the wall several plain lidded chests meant to contain linens, unguents, and common domestic toiletries. However, along the opposite wall stood the now very familiar wickerwork cabinetry made up of diamond-shaped spaces filled with rolls of papyrus, each roll wrapped in leather and bound in three places with twine. Affixed to the end of each roll on a short twine was a ceramic label etched in extremely archaic hieroglyphs.

Fearing even to breathe, Richards with extremely delicacy lifted up one of the labels to his oil lamp's radiance with just the pad of his forefinger and read.

"On Mending Wounds."

Moving on to another space, he read.

"The Belly of Nut." In essence, "The stars of the sky."

Upon sampling another niche, Richards found.

"On Writing."

Now on his knees and totally heedless to the thick dust that had accumulated on the tomb chamber's floor, Richards barely choked out.

"On The Heart and Tongue."

And so Richards went on and on, examining each and every one of the papyri labels, reading them aloud. As he had expected, each niche or niches contained treatises devoted to a general subject, but there were not really all that many, just: medicine and pharmacology, astronomy, grammar, philosophy, architecture, chemistry, metallurgy, and agriculture. Remarkably, there appeared to be absolutely no mention either of religion or magic.

Stunned and with eyes grown weary from the poor illumination of his oil lamp, Richards simply announced to his uncle.

"I have seen sufficient. My head hurts."

Ptahmesou replied with a grunt. "As it should. But my nephew, do you not even want to read even one of Ptah's books?"

Richards in total shock at such a suggestion blurted out. "But they are so old, to touch one, much less attempt to unroll one would turn it to dust!"

"Nonsense," said the elderly priest. "Each of these rolls is a mere copy, an exact copy I might add, of its predecessor. During my tenure as high priest I have restored them all. That means that I have read them all as well and I can say with some authority that some indeed are quite interesting. So my nephew, I will ask you once again, which one would you like to read?"

Confronted with such a choice, the American felt almost trapped, much like a kid with a dollar in his pocket peering into the window of a vast candy store. But after a moment's consideration, he gently lifted away the roll with the title: "On The Heart and Tongue."

Ptahmesou, taking the roll and examining its label, just smiled a pleased and knowing smile as he handed it to Gregorieva.

"Maatkare, would you be so kind and gently carry this to the surface for your oafish brother?"

And so the trio then left the chamber and ascended the seventy-two steps, stopping once for Ptahmesou to catch his breath, and returned to the seldom-used *per ankh*.

Upon closing the hidden passage's door, the high priest took the roll from Gregorieva' hand, carefully placed it on the end of the near table, untied it, and began to slowly unroll it, taking from the open wicker several of the smoothed stones to hold the papyrus down to prevent it from rolling up upon itself. It wasn't very long before the full length of the papyrus was exposed, nearly all twelve feet of it. In all Richards counted thirteen panels of neatly brushed text each about six inches wide by eight inches tall. Between each of the panels of text was what looked like a four inch space.

At this point, Ptahmesou pointed out to them a curious phrase located at the end of the text.

"Mayneken, note this cipher. "It reads: '142nd Inundation.' Each of Ptah's books has one and each cipher is different. To my mind I understand it as: 'This roll was completed in my 142nd inundation.'"

"But great one," Gregorieva gasped, "is it even possible for one to live so old?"

Smiling up at her question, Ptahmesou replied. "Remember Maatkare, we are discussing a man who has become a god. Anything is possible."

Now returning to the start of the roll, the high priest continued his commentary.

"Note that I have as accurately as possible copied what had been preserved on its predecessor. The characters are recognizable, but are very old ones nonetheless. The patterns of speech too are curious, but with time and experience they become understandable. To be perfectly honest Mayneken and Maatkare, when I copied my first roll I was totally baffled."

In the light of now five oil lamps the papyrus was fully illuminated and Richards' eagerness broke through.

"My uncle, may I attempt reading it?"

"Absolutely my son," as he stepped away from the tables to give the American room.

At this point Richards knew exactly what he was going to do, memorize the entire text character by character. And if he had to do so twice, or even thrice, then so be it.

*　　*　　*

Following his memorization of the ancient text, Ptahmesou approached Richards with an interesting proposal.

"My dear nephew, as the adopted son of my elder brother I hold you nearly in the same regard as I would my own son, if I had been so blessed. "You have now seen the tomb of Ptah, gazed upon his face, and even have read his very words. As I am an old man, would you consider taking my place when that time comes? I am quite sure that my colleague Pahamneter would immediately agree to such an arrangement."

Richards, stunned, did not know how to respond. Yes, the family ties made sense. Yes, he had in essence gone through the initiation that every high priest of Ptah had to perform. But, a high priest of Ptah?

"My uncle, your suggestion carries with it the burden of a great responsibility. I am speechless."

"As you should properly be my nephew. And your reference to responsibility is precisely why I made the suggestion. Think on it noble Mayneken. That is all that this old man requires."

*　　*　　*

Their return to Thebes went uneventfully; the retrieval likewise. For Gregorieva, the impact of what she had just experienced was not as great as it had been for Richards. But what truly impressed her, was Richards own reaction to Ptah's tomb. The words "stunned," "numb," and "flabbergasted" seemed to fall far short of the mark, but at least approximated what she had witnessed in her partner. For Richards everything had become a blur as he endlessly played and replayed back in his head the significance of all of the archaic hieroglyphic labels, even though upon leaving the crypt Ptahmesou had allowed him to make a careful list of them all.

The vast corpus of knowledge that it represented was truly awe inspiring in the extreme. Then there was that simply marvelous philosophical text "On the Heart and Tongue" that was so filled with double meanings. And finally there was Ptahmesou's offer to succeed him as one of the high priests of Ptah. In the end, Richards reckoned that this deployment had been a complete success, for he had, in essence, been allowed to peer upon the god's own face, visit the god's own private library, read one of the god's own books, even held in his hand a copy of the god's own library's card catalogue, and on top of that had a job offer to boot.

CHAPTER XXIII
Aerial Encounter

All systems read nominal aboard the westbound Gulf Stream V as it left in its wake the airspace of the Mediterranean and the Straits of Gibraltar. At a cruising speed of six hundred knots, it didn't take long for the Canary Islands to quickly fall astern. The open and cloudless skies of the North Atlantic beckoned while the white jet attempted to outrun the daily course of the sun. In another time, Ra might not have been pleased with such a prideful, human act.

For the experienced flight crew, they all knew that while the flight was an extremely high-security VIP ferry with some very strange looking equipment stowed aboard, it was nonetheless a ferry. This translated for them a quick puddle jump that was going to be a yawning no-brainer. To relieve their utter boredom, the pair switched off every half hour to hit the head, suck down water, nibble on chow, or listen to some music.

At this precise moment, Captain Josh "Boomer" Blake was doing just that – sitting back in his seat, humming along with a U2 hit through his Bose headphones. Meanwhile, his copilot, Rich "Go Fast" Stansbury, was busy checking fuel levels, making sure that the pumps were redistributing it correctly, noting that the radar was at the moment clear, even though they were squarely within an international commercial flight corridor. As further cover for the flight, Go Fast had even inserted a 747 signature chip into the transponder.

Craning his neck around, Go Fast saw that the red cabin lights were on dim. Peering into the artificial gloom, he confirmed that their fatigued passengers were still fast asleep and all securely strapped in.

Grunting in satisfaction to that observation more to himself than to his colleague Go Fast murmured. "Those two have been out like a light since takeoff. Must be nice."

"What's that?" Asked Boomer.

"Ah, nothing Sir. I was just checking on our special cargo."

"Yeah, I know what you mean. But since we weren't told, it's best that we don't ask. Even more so as they're in unmarked Air Force flight suits. Ya' know what I mean?"

"Yep."

While Go Fast knew that his superior was dead on, the copilot, who had been an ex-A10 Warthog driver, was curious nonetheless and his mind began to wander. After all, he lived to fly in the weeds and then pound the crap out of whatever had been in his sights. Action was in his blood. Ever since his much beloved and tiger-toothed Hog had been mothballed by some congressional budget committee, the only ride he could get in this man's Air Force was driving this glorified shuttle. Without a doubt Go Fast respected the Gulf Stream's enhanced performance envelope, he had often wondered about what it could really do if and when that time came. The drills, checklists, and simulations were one thing. But just how would it stand up in a real aerial fur ball?

*   *   *

Just as Go Fast was ruminating on his beloved and long lost Hog, a predator began to stalk the Gulf Stream V just beyond the margin of its radar envelope. While not completely stealth, the stalking aircraft's attributes had many advantages as much of its fuselage had been reworked. Its narrow head-on cross-section gave the hostile airframe just enough of an edge to fire its self-guiding weaponry well within range of its unsuspecting target. At 35,000 feet of altitude, the crippling of the commercial jet was all that was required. Its mayday would be heard, which would cause its logical diversion to the nearest available landing strip and that meant Iceland. Once on the ground, the rest of the mission would be accomplished. This last part, the pilot did not know about. All he knew was that at a precisely designated location he was to fire a very special, long range, air-to-air, heat-seeking missile.

As the pilot began his careful countdown to launch, several rivulets of nervous perspiration snaked down the sides of his face, which pooled against the creases of his skin and oxygen mask. Focusing upon his radar attack screen, at the appropriate moment a gentle pressure was applied to the joy stick's firing stud. With a sudden whoosh and shudder to the airframe the missile left the right wing rail. Following his instructions to the letter, he dutifully tracked its fiery course first visually and then on his green screen. For a moment a brief pang of guilt flitted through his consciousness, but that was swiftly swatted down like a pesky fly.

I must confirm this strike, he thought as he simultaneously counted down to the missile's impact.

*　　*　　*

The commercial jet was not as dumb nor as defenseless as its predator thought. For as soon as the missile ignited, the bloom of its heat signature was immediately recognized by the countermeasures array located in the aircraft's enlarged tail section. A split second later Go Fast's headset began screaming into his ears the insistent missile alert tone.

Deedle, Deedle, Deedle!

Reacting, the copilot slapped Boomer's shoulder and quickly pointed to the incoming green batwing symbol on the threat radar's screen. With an immediate grunt of "Holy Shit" from Boomer, both pilots began their preparations.

With a quick hoarse whisper Boomer said, "Plan A."

"Affirmative," a wide-eyed Go Fast responded as he yet again unconsciously tugged down on his shoulder harnesses and jettisoned the plane's external auxiliary fuel tanks.

He then thought to say to Boomer over their own cabin radio, "I just hope that our cargo are really belted in."

"If they're not, then they'll be so much toast. "Executing A now!"

"Roger!"

*   *   *

To the pilot of the predator, it seemed like an eternity for his long range missile to reach its target. He knew that at this distance the burn would take a full twenty-four seconds before impact. In a live aerial combat situation that duration represented an eternity, but this was hardly the case.

From the point of view of the missile, its onboard radar had acquired the commercial jet while still on the wing's rail. Only when it was in thermal range would the nitrogen cooled seeker head detect the Gulf Stream V's heat signature and take over its guidance. That occurred fifteen seconds after launch as the heat signature had quickly resolved into two quite distinct infrared heat sources. Only one meaningful question remained. Which engine pod would receive the full brunt of the swiftly flying missile's kinetic impact?

*   *   *

At precisely ten seconds before impact, Boomer viciously banked, jerked the stick hard to port, simultaneously vectoring the afterburners at full military power into a looping dive. The immediate sensation was that the aircraft was turning so quickly that it was side slipping, which it in fact it was. At the same time, Go Fast ejected a full fusillade of six antimissile flares and a cloud of aluminum chaff for good measure in an effort to hide the evasive maneuver.

For Richards and Gregorieva, they instantly awoke at the sudden maneuver only to find themselves pressed up against their restraints in a disorienting free fall. Surprised stomachs do not do well in such conditions and the Russian did not disappoint as she immediately decorated the cabin with her last meal.

To the rapidly closing inbound missile, the target had suddenly bloomed into a far too tempting six mini-suns and so flew on straight through the reflective aluminum cloud, searched out one of the radiant flares, missed it, and ignored totally its true target. Now dumb as a stone and without a heat source to lock on to, the missile continued on until it flamed out, and eventually fell harmlessly into the frigid water of the North Atlantic.

Snapping out of the power roll and dive, Boomer now pulled up on the stick, felt the Gs rapidly building, while his flight suit automatically squeezed the blood out of his legs and into his thorax. Meanwhile Go Fast had unsafed the forward guns, turned on the plane's surface camouflage, and powered up the rotary missile launcher in the belly. By the time Boomer had brought around the Gulf Stream V to face the hostile head on and from below, Go Fast had the bomb-bay doors open, the launcher ready to fire, and had acquired their target.

"I have tone!" The gee-ladened copilot grunted out.

"Fire two and bracket." Boomer grunted back.

"Fox one, Fox two away!" And out from under the Gulf Stream V two very deadly air-to-air infrared and self-guiding radar missiles streaked out on two white smoky plumes.

CHILDREN OF PTAH

*   *   *

The pilot of the predator aircraft was suddenly confused. At impact, his radar had detected a sudden radar bloom with multiple heat signatures. He positively knew that missile had no warhead. It was meant to only shred one of the jet's engines. Did the plane actually explode?

That notion, however, quickly was rejected as his own missile threat detection system began screaming into his helmet's headphones.

Missiles?!? Two of them?!? But from where?

The combined closing rate of the predator aircraft and the Gulf Stream V's missiles was about Mach 4. And then in an instant the predator was no more.

"Total splash, no chute," Go Fast barely choked out in awe.

"Sweet! That sucker never saw it coming," said Boomer. Now hitting the deck and bugging out. Go Fast. We clear?"

"Roger, only God's own angels are on the scope."

"Roger, squelch the transponder and kill radio. No emissions. We're going invisible."

"And Go Fast."

"Yes sir?"

"Nice shooting, you really must have learned something as a Hog driving ground pounder."

"Thank you sir. But what just happened to us? And why?"

"Go Fast, I really don't know the why. But I do know that something really fishy is going on. That missile's signature was Russian. I wouldn't be surprised if it wasn't a medium or long range Alamo. Those critters have proximity fuses. And that fuse never went off."

"A dude maybe?"

Smirking under his mask Boomer said. "Yeah, right, a lone striker going after a private jet with a sophisticated dude. Go Fast, face it. That missile was not meant to kill, but to maim, cripple us. Think about it. What would a fragged engine do to us? Probable cabin decompression. We would survive because we have masks. Our cargo doesn't and so they buy the farm. Then our control surfaces would be affected, because of fragging to our hydraulics all over the place."

"Where the hell would we have put down – the Canaries?"

Glancing quickly at his charts, Boomer smirked again.

"Nope. You know, Go Fast, it looks like somebody wanted us to pay a visit to Iceland. Most likely Keflavik in particular. It has four military grade runways. It's located near Reykjavik too. This whole incident stinks to high heaven."

"How so?"

"Assuming catastrophic decompression, that leaves us alive. And why go to all the effort? To capture us? Nope. It has to be all that special gear that we stored aboard that they are after."

"Who were they?"

"Damn, Go Fast! How the hell do I know!"

Pause.

"Once we're on the deck get on the sitcom scrambler and call in this incident right quick. Inquiring minds will want to know."

As Boomer peeled back his oxygen mask from his sweat-soaked face, he took one breath of seeming relief, gagged, and barked to no one in particular.

"Damn this aircraft stinks to high heaven!"

* * *

It took some moments before the static of the heavily secured connection cleared and began to ring the phone at the other end.

"May I speak with Dr. Young please?

"He's in an important meeting you say?

"Well, would you be so kind and immediately inform the good doctor that an attempt has been made on his wife's life?"

At the recognition of the message a gasping intake of breath was clearly heard from the receiver quickly followed by some quick words of disbelief.

"Yes, that is correct. An attempt has been made on his wife's life. Please tell him that in precisely those words.

"No madam, this is not some sort of sick joke.

"My name? Mr. Daniel Smith.

"No madam, that really is my name."

With that the phone was put on hold, catching the powerfully moving cords and chorus of the *Carmina Burana* in full gale. By the airman's own watch, a well worn and battle scarred Timex, it took a full four minutes before the tone of a now secured telephone line came alive, this time with a nearly wheezing male voice.

"Yes. Hello? This is Dr. Young. What's all this about an attempt on my wife's life?"

"Not to worry Dr. Young. Your wife is safe and sound. But established security protocol demanded that I inform you of just that fact. This is Lieutenant Daniel R. Smith, United States Air Force."

Pausing to take in the enormity of the message, Dr. Paul Young, Dean of Humanities, cradled the receiver against his neck as he groped for his handkerchief. Now dabbing his sweating upper lip, he thought to ask.

"Ah, 'Leftenant Smith,' may I ask where my wife was so threatened?"

"While enroute westbound over the Big Puddle."

The sheer enormity of that almost flippant statement physically staggered the academic, who now was leaning against a conveniently close paneled wall. Quickly gathering himself, he coolly said.

"Ah yes, quite. And what was the nature of the threat?"

"An air-to-air missile."

"Really, and what is the status of the assailant?"

"Splashed."

"And my wife, you say that she has arrived home safely?"

"Indeed sir, she has, although her drivers and cargo were a bit upset. But all in all are no worse for wear."

"Well that's really good news! But was the, ah, assailant, acting on his own?"

"No sir. Five others were picked up in Iceland at the Keflavik Airport as the result of a surprise security sweep of the area."

"I see. Well, Leftenant Smith that is very interesting news and thank ever so much for the call. I'm going to rush off right now to see after her. Thanks ever again calling. Good day."

*　　*　　*

As the dean hung up the secure phone, he visibly sagged against the conference room's wall with glazed eyes, or as they say in the profession, with a classic thousand foot stare. His secretary, who had remained at his side throughout the conversation, of course pitied the man, but for all the wrong reasons. Placing her hand delicately upon his forearm she offered,

"Dr. Young, should I cancel the rest of the day's appointments?"

"Yes, Mrs. Gundersen. Yes, please do. That would be just marvelous."

With that, Young levered himself off of the ancient oak paneling and strode purposefully to his magisterial desk. Crossing the expanse of Persian rug, he sat down with a thump into the soft leather of his high winged chair.

Damnation! He silently fumed. The absolute utter brazen gall of it all! Someone has actually tried to hijack the Soap Bubble! I would have never believed it if I hadn't heard it myself. Someone actually tried to force down our jet and plunder it! And of all places – Iceland! Jesus H. Christ! And then Air Force security types actually bagged five of the blighters as well! Well, I certainly hope that they wring them dry for information and then very slowly wring their necks for good measure!

*　　*　　*

Once the good Dean of Humanities finally got his wits about him he made an encrypted call to his New Mexican colleague. After the hiss of the encryption had cleared off the line Young said.

"Hello, may I speak to Dr. Naysmithe, please?"

Pause as the connection completed.

"Why Paul, what a surprise!"

"Surprise indeed," the Brit dryly added. "I am sorry to say that I must deliver some very bad news. Someone took a shot at stealing the Soap Bubble."

Pause of reflection.

"Was it our Slavic colleagues perhaps?"

"All indications at this time strongly suggest so, unfortunately. And here I thought that the new group held such promise."

"Well, yes, but did it ever occur to you that those inexperienced 'youngsters' over there might have felt the need to sow some wild oats and make their mark as well?"

"Never thought of that…that's quite a prescient point of view."

"Paul, may I make a firm suggestion?"

"By all means!"

"The next time that we take the Soap Bubble out of the barn, let's heighten the security level a bit. On the tactical side I will discuss this with Lieutenant Callahan, but on the technical side, I want 24/7 satellite imagery on our side as well. No wait. Scratch that. Heck, we'll do even better if we get a Predator drone tasked to overfly the site."

CHAPTER XXIV
The Debrief

It was perhaps appropriate that they sat in their institution's own archive discussing the contents of another library. As it was after all a Friday, and past sundown at that, they had the room to themselves. As the younger spoke, the elder listened.

"You know John, you would not believe it possible, but old Ptahmesou had had the duty, no privilege, to mind Ptah's own library collection! In the process of making fresh copies, he had read the entire corpus, and along the way had grasped the archaic grammar *and* the author's many contextual nuances."

Now sighing deeply, it was clear to Milson that Richards had been deeply moved by the experience. And with the fragrant papyrus card catalogue in front of him he could at least attempt to imagine the emotion of the moment. But what fascinated Milson the most was the archaic text before him, recalled by the enhanced memory by his young colleague.

"Joseph, do you think that you could locate Ptah's tomb?" Milson softly inquired.

"Well, I really don't know. Perhaps if we got really lucky with ground penetrating radar, but wouldn't it be under water anyway?"

"Hmm, good point. Well regardless, think on it Joseph. At the very least it might be worth a try, don't you think?" Milson prodded.

"Now Joseph, getting back to this text, 'On The Heart and Tongue,' are you absolutely sure that you got it right?"

"You bet Doc. And to make doubly sure that I would, I read it twice, much to the amusement of Ptahmesou and growing impatience of Gregorieva, who unbeknownst to us with that teeny tiny dancer's bladder of hers was under some considerable distress."

Smiling in a wistful way, Milson said. "So Joseph. How did she do?"

"Just great John. She's such a counterbalance to me. It seems that whenever I would falter, she was right on her game and vice-versa. As a team we are quite formidable."

"No doubt." Quipped the elderly scholar as he unconsciously tapped his fore finger against his chin. "Now, do you feel up to walking me through this text?"

"Not a problem John. But my sight translation will be a bit rough as I have detected several potential levels of meaning that can really skew its understanding. In fact, this one document just might be two, the obvious one and its second hidden beneath the surface of the first."

"Well Joseph," said Milson, "it would not be the first time that such a message was so encoded."

*　　*　　*

Meanwhile, half a world away a similar debriefing was taking place.

"So, Ms. Gregorieva, allow me to summarize your last adventure. First, you dropped in on the household of Prince Horemheb, who then introduced you and the American to the new high priest of Amen Re, whose name was, let's see now, Nebneteru. He then passed you off to his second named, ah, Merimaat, who then introduced you to the keeper of the *per ankh*, a man named Seshi. Is that correct?"

"No sir. That's Seti."

"Ah yes. Seti it is then. Splendid. Now once in the *per ankh* how many papyrus scrolls did you estimate again that it contained?"

"Approximately 2700."

"You don't say…"

"Are you again implying that I miscount?"

"Oh no, Ms. Gregorieva. I just did not know that the ancients had that many things to write about. Perhaps your scroll count was more like 250, eh?"

"No you ignorant ass, I said 2700!"

"I see. Well, to continue with your imaginative narrative, the American then skillfully enlisted, ah, Neshi's assistance, the keeper you say of the *per ankh*. To what end do you suppose?"

"The librarian's name was Seti! And I do not suppose anything you imbecile. Joseph secured the name of the high priest of Ptah from him, a priest called Ptahmesou, who arranged for our admittance into their *per ankh*."

*   *   *

The debriefing room, where Gregorieva and her persistent interrogator now sat, had installed within it remote biosensors, hidden microphones, and a two-way mirror through which a digit camera was recording the entire session.

"So," Rosovec said. "How long have they been at it?"

"Two days, sir," the technician responded to his superior.

"And do you have any preliminary impressions?" the bureaucrat asked.

"I do not know what you mean sir."

A bit thick this one is, Rosovec thought and so he reworded his query.

"Do you have any gut sense as to whether Gregorieva is telling us the truth, or, is she just telling us a fairy tale?"

"Well sir, she has been consistent and unwavering in her story and its many interesting details. According to her body temperature and skin moisture levels, I would say that she thinks that she is being totally truthful. However, she is right on the edge with Captain Pushkin. Her reactions to his well-known talent for sarcasm have reached levels that I would have thought would have led to serious concern for his physical safety."

"You don't say," the bureaucrat said with a grin. "Well, that's my lioness!"

CHAPTER XXV
Second Teleconference

Once again it had been the Americans who had extended the invitation to their Russian colleagues for a long distance video chat. And once again the US Air Force, now long rendered totally powerless to eves' drop, had permitted the use of their language translation software and satellites in the future hope that one day they would again regain the high ground.

The American panel consisted of John Milson, Egyptologist, Paul Young, Dean of Humanities, and a new personality, a certain Mr. Smith. As soon as the video feed had stabilized the Russian contingent of Academicians Rosovec, Sokolovska, and Popev had immediately taken note of the new face on their colleague's panel.

While both Young and Smith remained mute and with strangely neutral, almost serious faces, Milson in contrast appeared surprisingly animated and confirmed that impression by starting things off in a lively manner.

"So good again to see you gentlemen and thank you for adjusting your schedules so quickly to meet with us! Today I am joined by Dean Young and…Mr. Smith.

So the cipher has a name, thought Rosovec.

"By now I hope that you have been able to digest the contents of the brief that we sent to you and no doubt you have dovetailed those details with those of your own field operative."

Now just what is John so happy about? Groused Rosovec. What is he about to sell us this time?

"This last deployment, initiated by Dr. Richards, we have judged to be a total success and on the basis of the data before you, we hope that you think so as well. Additionally, please allow me to say a few words regarding the performance in the field by your Ms. Gregorieva. I believe that there is currently a military expression that is very apt and that expression is 'outstanding!' And that is precisely how we think she has performed. And we hope that you feel the same."

Where is this going John? Rosovec now fretted behind his placid smile as he waited for the dreaded "but," "however," or proverbial shoe to fall.

"In particular," Milson continued, "I wish to draw your attention to our original contention regarding the individual named Ptah. Specifically, three items stand out. First, the simply amazing breadth and depth of his academic industry as evidenced by the fifty-sixty papyrus scrolls seen by our field operatives and that he is credited as being the author of. Frankly, the range and scope of them simply boggles the imagination. Second, regarding his purported longevity, specifically the paleographic evidence as reported that he lived at least 142 years, fully three times the norm for that period, is noteworthy. Finally, given the deep and multifaceted philosophical content of the text entitled, 'On the Heart and Tongue,' I personally find this document as a compelling argument for a follow up deployment, this time to a much older period in Egyptian history, in the hope that our field operatives can find and interview the man literally face-to-face."

Ah ha! Triumphantly thought Rosovec. Milson is lobbying for another go at Ptah!

And then Milson continued.

"However…"

What's this?!? Thought Rosovec.

"Before we plan much less any of us commit to another deployment, we will have to address a rather disturbing matter regarding the security of the temporal device known as the Soap Bubble."

At the mention of security of the temporal device two of the Russians shared a rather damning quick glance, while one remained totally oblivious.

"Mr. Smith, regarding this matter, I believe that you have a few words to share with us."

First clearing his throat into his right fist, Mr. Smith sat up erectly in his chair and began.

Definitely a military type from the posture and haircut Rosovec immediately surmised in spite of the rather tweedy academic garb.

"Gentlemen, my full name is Daniel S. Smith and I am a Lieutenant in the United States Air Force, Department of Intelligence. What I am about to share with you should be considered of the utmost secrecy and handled in an appropriately responsible manner."

Military indeed! Realized Rosovec whose hands had now begun to perspire.

"On the return leg of the last deployment of the temporal device known as the Soap Bubble, the aircraft that carried the temporal device, field operatives, and aircraft personnel was attacked at 35,000 feet by an unknown aircraft employing a heat-seeking air-to-air missile."

While this dissertation was taking place both Milson and Young were carefully watching the Russians collective and individual reactions.

"The missile used in the attack, has been identified by its telemetry as either a medium- or long-range Vympel R-27TE, also known by its NATO designation as the AA-10 Alamo. The missile in question has been current in the Russian arsenal since 1985, has a range of 60 kilometers, travels at 3.5 MACH or better, and usually carries a 39 kilogram thermite warhead. It is the weapon of choice specifically designed for the Russian MIG, SU, and YAK fighter airframes.

"I mentioned that this missile usually carries a 39 kilogram thermite warhead. What I did not mention was that this particular missile's design included a detonation proximity fuse in the event that the missile lost its infrared lock. In this attack, however, a lone unknown attacked our aircraft and a one missile was fired. That missile was a purpose-built dude, meaning, that its warhead had been removed, even its proximity fuse had been deleted."

At this point, Mr. Smith again cleared his throat into his fist.

"Clearly, the missile employed was being used as a kinetic weapon only. It was not meant to kill, but rather to cripple. If the missile had stuck one of the aircraft's engine pods, the kinetic energy of that event would have destroyed that engine pod, caused catastrophic decompression to the airframe, and a high probability of damage to the airframe's hydraulic and electrical systems."

Pause to swallow.

"Once so injured, the flight crew, who would have survived the decompression due to their oxygen masks, would have headed directly to the nearest military airfield available. That airfield was on Iceland, and in particular Keflavik, a military airfield located near that island's capital city of Reykjavik.

"Following these facts, an emergency security sweep immediately took place at Keflavik and five suspects were quickly apprehended. They are now being intensively interrogated. Here are their photos.

Pause to raise a placard with the photos. Now continuing to speak from behind the raised cardboard.

"In summary, a planned, premeditated air attack occurred over the Atlantic Ocean within a heavily trafficked commercial aircraft corridor. Furthermore, the attack's purpose was to cripple the airframe, in the process killing all of the passengers, and forcing an emergency landing at a preordained location. Once on the ground, the aforementioned accomplices, for we believe them to be precisely that, cleverly camouflaged as emergency ground crew, were to first kill the flight crew and then secure the temporal device."

At this point, Mr. Smith lowered the photo placard collected his notes, sat back deep into his seat, folded his hands on the conference desk, and just stared back unblinking into the video camera's red eye.

Milson and Young clearly saw it together and confirmed the fact of what they saw. Wide-eyed confusion and horror was painted on the face of Sokolovska, while Rosovec looked on with a sigh of sad indifference. But Popev had been classic, he looked absolutely like a kid caught with his hand in the cookie jar.

Silence.

Now leaning forward Rosovec quietly asked.

"What is the disposition of the unknown?"

Mr. Smith leaned forward into his microphone and simply said. "Eliminated."

Silence.

At this point Young took over.

"Gentlemen, this incident is very serious. Very few know of the existence of the temporal device. Fewer knew of its recent deployment to Egypt. Even fewer still of its scheduled return transit. In order to put this operation together implies considerable foreknowledge. The ability to put a fighter aircraft into the air and with a modified missile to boot suggests considerable resources. May I suggest a good, old fashioned, Christian examination of conscience?"

And with that said, Young looked to the cameraman and drew his finger across his throat in that universal signal to cut the transmission.

Damnation! The Brit thought with immense satisfaction. I have always wanted to do that!

*　　*　　*

Now looking at a snowy screen instead of their American counterparts, Rosovec asked the technician if their audio was live and immediately received a negative head shake. Then he said with considerable understatement.

"Well, that could have gone better."

"Better!" Nearly shrieked Sokolovska. "Just what the hell is going on here?"

"Apparently," voiced Popev, "someone tried to hijack the temporal device and failed miserably."

"Was it us!" Sokolovska next demanded.

"No, it wasn't us." Assured Popev to his exercised colleague.

"Well then, God damn it! Who was it?"

"It was a Syrian asset." Rosovec quietly said.

"A Syrian asset! Under whose direction!" Screamed Sokolovska.

"Isn't it rather obvious?" Popev lazily slurred.

Silence.

Then Sokolovska chose to state what was truly obvious. "We're screwed. No, worse. We're really screwed."

Silence.

"Perhaps," said a now contemplative Popev. "But what I want to know is how that Syrian asset failed. Why a highly reliable heat-seeking missile somehow missed. And the real question, what eliminated the asset itself."

*   *   *

"Well, do you think that they will ever 'fess up?" Milson mused with his chin in hand.

"Most doubtful." Grumbled a now introspective Young. "And the true pity of it all is the simple fact that they felt the need to steal something, instead of asking us if we were willing to share."

"Paul, a rather nasty thought just crossed by mind. If they were so audacious to plan the hijack of the Soap Bubble once, what's going to prevent them from trying again?"

"Believe it or not John, Charlie Naysmithe and I have already had that discussion and appropriate measures are being taken. But I also share your concerns actually more for young Joseph than that damn machine."

Pause.

"You know Paul," Milson began, "it would really behoove us to somehow get Gregorieva out of Russia ASAP."

"Now that is a novel idea John. Imagine. Us on the offensive for once. What a wonderful idea, but one that we are not capable of dealing with. Who do you think that we should ask?" the Dean of Humanities responded.

"Paul, you really have me there, but I do know that we should not leave that girl high and dry."

"Agreed and I just realized something. Do we not have access to a rather special airplane? And since it was your idea to begin with, do you feel up to a quick flight off to Moscow?"

"For Gregorieva's sake, definitely." Firmly stated Milson with conviction.

"The real issue," Milson said, "is how do we quietly get in contact with her? And then, once Stateside, we must confront the entire question of her papers. That will require help from the State Department. But once we somehow even get in contact with her, then whose palm do we need to grease just to get her safely on the plane?"

"John, you are of course assuming that she even wants to emigrate." Young pointed out.

"Damn, you're right. We'll have to somehow find out."

CHAPTER XXVI
Toby Richter's Football

"Doctor Naysmithe, the calibration of the Eldridge data has been completed." Toby Richter soberly announced. "Given the size of the destroyer escort and the forty-one megawatts of energy that were reported, the calculated target date that came out of the Little Beast II was Monday, September 19th, 19754 BC. However, I have some serious reservations about the accuracy of that date."

Naysmithe, now leaning back in this office chair with his hands behind his head, simply asked. "What's troubling you Toby?"

"Well Doc it's really quite simple. If you consider the field configuration of the Soap Bubble, it's really, practically speaking, a two dimensional plane contained with its drop ring. But when we consider the Eldridge's field, we have a three dimensional field that is only approximately defined by the ship's hull and superstructure. What's bugging me is this basic dimensional difference between the fields themselves. I just do not know whether the configured shape of a field will somehow skew its calibration. Frankly sir, I have no experience whatsoever calibrating such a field."

"Toby, I see your point. And your point is a theoretically important one. But I ask you, how would you approach this issue from an experimental point-of-view? In other words, how would you test for a difference in calibration due to a field's configuration?"

Full knowing that Naysmithe would ask him just that, Toby had already done his homework and even had something in mind.

"Well Doc, I have been thinking about that very thing. And what I came up with is an oval-shaped field bubble, itself defined by either electromagnets or lasers."

Pleased both with Toby's aggressive inventiveness he said with some encouragement. "Will a mockup cost us an arm and a leg?"

"Naw, my team will just reuse stuff available in the SCRAP HEAP."

"Good. Now get to work."

"You got it Doc!"

*　　*　　*

Toby Richter hailed out of New Brunswick, New Jersey and consequently did his undergraduate work in engineering at Rutgers University. From there, he got into MIT where the he fought, scraped, and scratched his way to an MS specializing in electromagnetic field propagation. Without question, at least in Naysmithe's opinion, the ginger-headed Toby was the go-to guy for the calibration of the Eldridge's data.

Free to create within his own "play pen" laboratory, Toby had a real knack at fixing stuff, cobbling together stuff, and making discarded stuff perform far beyond their original purpose and specs. His much beloved "scrap heap" had provided countless internal mockups that often worked better than most dedicated first generation prototypes. It was claimed that the EM (electromagnetic) whiz could make a bent paperclip dance on the head of a pin. So Naysmithe eagerly awaited what Toby would come up with.

Three days later the physicist heard a familiar knock on his door frame. Looking up, there was Toby with an absolutely shit-eating grin on his face.

"Got a moment Doc?"

Looking up from his paperwork, Naysmithe smiled and immediately was intrigued as to what Toby had to say.

"Yeah sure, anything would be better than this garbage, what's up."

"Want to come down to my play pen for a look see?"

CHILDREN OF PTAH

Grinning ear to ear, the lanky physicist from San Diego bounded out of his chair and followed his colleague. As they threaded their way through a warren of cubicles they finally arrived at a shielded laboratory door where Toby handed a pair of flash goggles to Naysmithe with a sly smile.

While the door had proudly announced SCRAP HEAP, once inside the EM laboratory it was all business. From the get go, since organization was the order of the day and since Naysmithe had always just marveled at the spotlessly maintained environment, he consequently never blinked whenever Toby had ever put in a requisition for some new equipment.

On the right from floor to ceiling stood racking of brightly colored and clearly labeled bins. Some columns were small, some medium in size, and those over to the far right near the corner large. Basically, what Toby did with each and every discarded computer, printer, scanner, phone, test instrument, and gadget that Horizon Pass had consumed was to totally break them down to their bare chassis. Screws, nuts, bolts, washers, zip ties, and other sorts of fasteners were all carefully segregated. Reusable chassis material went into the large bins. Electrical connections went over there next to the circuit boards. On the left of the lab stood one continuous neutrally grounded work bench that was studded with electrical outlets and even sported a small vise near one end's edge. The work bench was deep, almost a full thirty inches, which provided lots of room for tinkering and set up. Above the bench, again about thirty inches above its surface, shelving continued vertically to the ceiling. Here the SCRAP HEAP "stored" the fully stripped and gutted outer plastic and metal shells of computer towers, old key boards, fax machines, you name it. On the back wall of the work bench one could easily identify practically any kind of electrical or mechanical tool, several kinds of soldering guns, a small TIG welder, hot glue guns, you name it again. Finally, lined up tight against the back wall of the SCRAP HEAP were arrayed just about any kind of electrical measurement and calibration equipment imaginable.

At the center of the SCRAP HEAP was a slightly raised and perfectly leveled two by two meter rubberized platform. Standing in its center was a scratch built mockup table made of thick black Lexan that was hot glued together. In itself, it was a beautifully made and conceived construct. Firmly bolted to its Lexan surface was a large electromagnet about the size of a grapefruit with its wiring threaded neatly down and through the table's surface that connected to the 220 amp outlet at the rubberized platform's center. Surrounding the magnet were two elliptically shaped wire loops that were joined at their ends. The wire loops, oriented at ninety degrees to one another, represented a downsized model of the keel and superstructure and two gunnels of the Eldridge. This "skeleton" was then supported by two uprights that were also bolted into the Lexan surface. These uprights were then connected to the separate electrical leads of a small portable electrical generator on wheels.

At entering the SCRAP HEAP, Toby did not say a word and instead just let Naysmithe take a look at the lab's centerpiece. After two slow circuits of careful examination, Naysmithe smiled and declared.

"Well Toby, this looks very much like Borov's first prototype of the Soap Bubble, but only in three dimensions. Does it work?"

"Yep. Thought that you would never ask. Mind your flash goggles."

And once both scientists got their optical protection in place, Toby flipped the power switch on the portable unit. After about ten seconds the magnet in the center began to wobble, then get fuzzy, and then, suddenly could not be seen as it was now enveloped in a silvery field shaped just like a football.

"Damn that is cool Toby!" Naysmithe exclaimed. "Looks to me that we have here a for real three dimensional Soap Bubble field. Most impressive. Have you calibrated it yet?"

"Come on Doc! We just got the field up and running about an hour ago." But now with his hands up in surrender. "Don't worry, calibration trials will begin tomorrow. But frankly, we have a problem. How can we probe from inside the field out? I can't fathom it."

With his chin now buried in the palm of his hand, Naysmithe pondered and then said. "I have an idea Toby, why don't you probe the inside of the football first and see what you get. You just might be surprised."

CHAPTER XXVII
A Question of Penetration

Milson's innocent question about pursuing the location of Ptah's tomb had set off a firestorm in Richards' head. While by no means a card-carrying archaeologist, the Egyptologist was not blind either to just what he might be up against and so he sought out someone that he hoped might be able to help clear up some issues. Thumbing through the faculty directory, Richards began trolling for inspiration, and for some reason that to this very day he could not explain, the Department of Geology had just jumped out at him. Fearlessly, he then picked up the phone and called the departmental secretary with his pencil and directory at the ready.

"Hello, this is Professor Richards over at the Near Eastern Institute. How are you today?"

"Well that's great. I have a question for you and perhaps you just might be able to help me out. Who on your faculty has archaeological experience?"

"Uh huh. Yes, yes, okay. Got it! Thanks so much!"

Now looking down at his directory, thanks to the helpful secretary, he now had four names ticked off.

Next, he went online to check them out. What Richards was looking for was archaeological field experience and youth. Those criteria immediately aced out three of the four, so he then focused in on the lone name standing: Associate Professor Jeremy L. Larsson.

"Hmm. He looks interesting and might be a good fit. Let's find out."

Looking down at his watch Richards saw a potential opportunity, so he dialed Larsson's office number and got an answer.

"Ah, hello. This is Professor Richards over at the Near Eastern Institute. How are you today?"

CHILDREN OF PTAH

*　　*　　*

As Richards waited for his luncheon date to arrive at the Faculty Club a certain Ms. Kelly from the Philology Annex had emerged from the long line at the salad bar and practically ran into him. Now juggling her mounded salad plate, purse, and iced tea, Richards reached out and deftly plucked the plate out of her hands with both of his.

"Well hello stranger." He said.

Now regaining her balance and with her freed hand now available, the strawberry blond just stroked his cheek and purred.

"Give me back my salad, you thief, or your dead meat."

"Dinner tonight?" He said with a slightly playful tilt of the head.

"How about Friday." She said.

"Done. Pick you up at seven?" He said with his eyebrows raised in anticipation.

"6:30. Pick me up at the Annex. And you're still dead meat." She said with a devastating smile as she retrieved her salad plate and then smoldered her way over to an available table for two.

Richards just shook his head. It's been too long.

At that precise moment in time a youngish face entered the club with sandy-colored hair and striking blue eyes. Looking around for his luncheon date, Richards waved to him and introduced himself.

Now seated with their food choices and the preliminaries out of the way, Larsson cut to the chase.

"Okay. So what's an Egyptologist want with a geologist?"

"A geologist that's really a geophysicist with archaeological field experience. Is that correct?" Richards sparred back.

"Okay, but a geophysicist with archaeological field experience in the Shetland Islands. So where's the connection?"

"Well, while Memphis, Egypt is surely not the Shetland Islands, the weather there in the early spring has got to be better. Frankly, I need some advice. What are my remote sensing options in a fluvial area?"

"Ah, so that's it. Well, depending on how homogeneous the soil is, and whether it doesn't include any clay or moisture, probably pretty good. Just how deep do you want to go?"

"Now that is a really good question as I really don't know, but surely no deeper than ten meters."

"Ten meters you say. That's a lot of material to penetrate. Just what are you trying to locate? Walls, houses, tombs, what?"

"Well, several inscriptions mention a hidden descending passage to a tomb that was supposedly located underneath a temple." Richards invented and then continued.

"This tomb is purported to contain a library of papyrus rolls, an ancient burial, and of course associated grave goods. Given that we know the general footprint of the temple, the search area is relatively well known."

"Do you know anything about the geology of the area?"

"Well, we suspect that the tomb's chamber was cut relatively deep, maybe as deep as the third layer of limestone in the area. The ancient inscription mentioned seventy two steps down, or about twenty five feet. But that was in antiquity. I have no idea how deep the current overburden might be."

"So, let me see if I fully understand you. You have an ancient temple and somewhere under it is your suspected tomb. In antiquity you know that it is about twenty five feet beneath the surface. So what you are really looking for is not the tomb itself, but the mouth of its entrance shaft. Is that correct?"

"Yeah, you're right. You're absolutely right!"

"Okay. So what you are now trying to remote sense is probably a rectangular feature that is buried under who knows how much overburden."

"Yeah, that's it."

"Richards that is quite a tall order to solve with remote sensing. Consider for the moment the following. A tomb located beneath a temple would have covering it: first blocks of stone, potentially mud bricks, then the debris of multiple habitation levels if the site was abandoned for any amount of time. Remote sensing can see through homogenous material to bedrock or until it encounters a non-homogeneous layer. Think of it in these terms. Remote sensing will pass right through fluvial silts, right through decayed habitation debris and even potentially deteriorated mud brick remains, but it cannot go through stone blocks. It can detect them, where they are and in what arrangement, but cannot go through them to detect a rectangular feature. That's what dirt archaeology is for."

Pausing for a minute, the geophysicist continued.

"In essence, remote sensing can tell you where to dig and how deep you have to go to get there."

"Okay," Richards countered, "clearly I have some homework to do. But how long would it take to perform the remote sensing of a site, say about four acres in size?"

"Using ground penetrating radar, a couple of days to do a really good job of it. That would produce some potentially slick 3D imagery. What's really critical is the ability to walk across the entire area with few if any obstacles, like structures, railroad tracks, roads and the like in the way. The reason for that is that the entire area has to be walked in an unbroken grid pattern. GPR, ground penetrating radar, will tells us what's about three to four meters down. A magnetic gradiometer, however, would tell us a little more, maybe three to five meters down. Much beyond five meters, remote sensing becomes more macro, more general and less specific, in what it can successfully see."

"Okay, I now understand. What sort of information would you need to start?"

"You're not kidding about this are you."

"Nope."

A sigh from the geophysicist.

"Well for a start, I would have to examine some 1:50,000 geological maps of the area in question in order to get a preliminary read on what the substructure might be composed of. Next, we'd need some surface photos of the area to see whether there are a lot of surface obstacles that might be in the way of a proper survey. Then, assuming that we got all the governmental paperwork out of the way that would allow us to even do the tomographic survey, a core boring would be very helpful, because that would give us a vertical slice of the immediate subsoils. By the way, all bets are off when we encounter the water table. And that goes for dirt archaeology too."

"So," Richards concluded, "are you interested?"

"Yeah, I am. Shoot me an email of the area's coordinates and I'll take a peek at some maps. Then I'll get back to you in a couple of days."

"Perfect."

"Oh, and thanks for lunch!"

*   *   *

Now finished with her salad, Ms. Kelly, wondering where that hunk Richards was and why he had not joined her, began to scan the club's tables.

I thought that I had sunk the hook deeply enough, apparently not.

Then seeing the object of her lust on the other side of the club with another faculty member, she unconsciously pouted her lips.

Dude, you are so dead meat!

CHILDREN OF PTAH

*　　*　　*

Dear Prof. Richards:

I have some good news and some bad news. First the bad: the Memphis area, generally, is situated squarely in the flood plain of the Nile and given the current water table situation since the construction of the Aswan High Dam, I really do not think that anything below three meters is going to be dry. Now for the good news, depending upon which formations are located immediately below the temple area, we might be able to at least locate the tomb's entrance passage. Not much, but that's the best that I can do with so little data.

Best regards,

J.L. Larsson.

*　　*　　*

Richards read and then reread Larsson's email in an attempt to grasp its significance. So, what does he mean that the area is potentially underwater, yet the location of the entrance might be found? Reaching for the phone, the Egyptologist decided to "reach out and touch someone" for clarification.

"Hello Jeremy, Joseph Richards here. How are you doing?"

Pause.

"Uh-huh, great.

"Well, I'm calling about that cryptic email that you just sent me.

Pause.

"Yeah, that one.

Pause.

"So, if I understand you, we need a drill rig to figure out where the water table is?"

Pause.

"Uh-huh. So how difficult is that to do?"

Pause.

"Uh-huh. Could we contract that to be done? Or do we have to be on site?"

Pause.

"Uh-huh. Yeah. Let me get back to you. Bye."

Richards sitting back into his office chair was now beginning to have some doubts about Dr. Larsson's motivation, or better, the apparent lack thereof. On the other hand, and to be absolutely fair, Larsson really had no clue just how motivated Richards was, who was now looking at his watch while making some rapid calculations. Now smiling, the Egyptologist again reached for his phone, dialed, and then waited for the connection. On the third ring, he hit pay dirt.

"Joey! What a pleasant surprise! I was just about to leave for the day and here I receive a call from one of the world's most preeminent Egyptian philologists! So how are you?"

So auspiciously began the conversation with the Director of the Cairo National Museum and the sole daughter of the director of the Egyptian Antiquities Service.

"As always, so many questions! But thank you Sharil, I am just fine. How's your father?"

"He is my loving father as always, thank you, and as you can imagine, he is busier than a baker during a famine."

Chuckling over the Egyptian's translation of the idiom, Richards finally got down to what was on his mind.

"Sharil, do you know if anyone is doing any survey work in the Memphis area?"

"Why yes, Joey, there are several teams currently working in the area. But Joey, Memphis or Sakkara?

"Memphis, specifically, is anyone working at or near the Temple of Ptah?"

"Actually yes there is and you already know him."

"Okay, I give, who?"

"Do you remember a certain German civil engineer who used to be on a certain Dutch excavation of a certain treasury?" Sharil teased.

"Horst Willing?"

"The very same. It seems that his business began booming on the continent, because of his notoriety with the Amen Re Treasury. But Joey! He has caught the archaeology bug, and so while his business is slow during the European winter months, he's over here having the time of his life. Why don't you give him a call?"

Richards' paused briefly in shock at his luck.

"You bet I will."

Now a bit sheepishly.

"Would you happen to have his number?"

Clearly smiling at the other end, Sharil coyly responded.

"It will cost you a dinner at the Mena House."

"DONE!"

"My, that was easy. I really must remember to play my cards better!" Sharil laughed. "Okay Dr. Richards, I know when I am being shaken down. Here it is."

* * *

Richards, with a feeling like the rush a gambler gets at a hot Las Vegas table, immediately called Willing's cell number as soon as he was off the phone with Sharil Moussa.

While he waited for the connection to be made, he realized that this month's phone bill was really going to freak out the departmental secretary.

"Villing hier."

"Horst, ich bin Joey! Vieh gehts!"

So the raucous conversation began between two close colleagues half a world apart. Bound by their nearest in age, shared sweat, and unbelievable archaeological success, these two had become near inseparable beer drinking buddies as well. In fact, during one particularly exuberant evening, the pair had even sworn to *Brüdershaft* as well!

And what a conversation it was, for as it turned out Willing was on contract with the Austrian Archaeological Mission to provide an updated surface survey of the Temple of Ptah and to perform some subsurface soundings, which were underway. After a good ten minute rant, Richards' secured the promise of a detailed email within the next week to ten days.

With his phone now back in its cradle, Richards swore that he saw it smoking.

* * *

True to form Willing had lied. His email with its several attachments appeared only two days later in Richards email. While the email popped up quickly enough on his screen, the Egyptologist found that he could not pull up any of the attachments as all of them, which were very large in terms of space, also carried a very unfamiliar .dfx suffix.

Nonetheless, Richards had Horst's precise summary of those supporting technical documents in the email's text before him.

Lieber Joey!

It was great to hear from you and I sincerely hope that we will again soon work together. Naturally, such heavy labor will require proper refreshment and my Austrian colleagues have solved that issue rather nicely!

CHILDREN OF PTAH

Regarding all of your questions about the Temple of Ptah surface and subsurface survey, I have attached four CAD-CAM files that contain all the technical information that you requested. CAD1 is the surface survey of the entire temple precinct. CAD2 is the raw data of the subsurface scan that we performed with a GPR device (GSSI) within the NE sector of the temple's precinct. CAD3 is the CAD2 data analyzed in three dimensions. CAD4 is the electromagnetic conductivity data display that looks like a colorful topographical map – because it is, but of the subsoil.

The results, in summary, are: 1) the subsurface water table in the NE sector of the temple precinct is calculated as 7.2 meters below the modern surface; 2) the NE sector has clear evidence of many subsurface architectural features that first appear at circa 1.2 meters, many are parallel features that strongly look like limestone foundation courses, others seem to be fallen stone blocks; 3) there was only one small rectangular feature at circa 2.1 meters in the NE sector. It is partially obscured by fallen stone blocks. This feature and its coordinates are clearly noted in the attached plans, both surface and subsurface.

Good hunting my friend!

--HW

Now smiling to himself, Richards crafted an email to Larsson with the attachments requesting whether he knew what they were and whether he could kindly print them out and perhaps interpret their content. While Horst had already provided that information in his email, the Egyptologist now wanted to see whether Larsson could do the same and so off went the email into the Ether.

Richards thought, now just how quickly will Larsson respond? As fast as Willing?

Now reaching for his calculator, Richards did some fast figuring on his yellow legal pad.

Water table at 7.2 meters is about 23.5 feet down from the modern surface. Parallel stone foundations begin at about 1.2 meters, or about four feet below the modern surface. So, the ancient surface sort of equals the top of the foundation stones. Evidence of the rectangular descending tomb passage is at 2.1 meters, or about seven feet below the modern surface. Ptah's tomb had seventy two steps with a rise of about five inches. That equals about thirty feet to the floor of Ptah's tomb from the ancient surface. So, at a maximum, about nine feet of water to the tomb's floor. Could sump pumps clear that much water?

CHAPTER XXVIII
Leaving on a Jet Plane

To shake the chill out of his bones, an average and very unremarkable business man headed for the coffee shop. Having purchased a black grande-sized cup of Columbian Supremo, he held it in both hands warming them as he climbed to the far quieter second floor of the establishment and then settled himself into an even quieter corner table. Taking a sip he sighed with his eyes closed as he fully enjoyed the coffee's aroma and the effect of its heat on his internals. Sighing again, he reached into the vest pocket of his Moscow-tailored three-piece wool suit, extracted his cell phone, and dialed.

"Hello?"

"Is this Vesna Gregorieva?" the business man said in impeccable Russian with a St. Petersburg accent.

"Da."

"I am a friend of a friend of Joey and John and they would very much like you to make a quick visit."

"Oh?"

"Da. I am having a delicious coffee right now at the Coffee Bean that used to be the Philippov bakery at Pushkinskaya 56. It's just the next block over from your flat. Do you know of it?"

"Da."

"Well, the beautiful gilt ceiling remains, but little else. Can you be here in fifteen minutes? I will even buy you a coffee. You will find me on the second floor."

'Da, I will be there in fifteen minutes. And, my friend of a friend of Joey and John, what is your name?"

"Names right now are not important, but I know your face. In fifteen minutes then."

*   *   *

"Ms. Gregorieva I presume?" Said the elderly man dressed in the dark and slightly wrinkled suit.

A tentative nod was her only guarded response.

"Frankly, your photo does not do you credit." Two twinkling blue eyes noted. Now reaching across the tiny coffee table and extending his open hand, the man added.

"Ms. Gregorieva, both Professors Milson and Richards send their very best."

Taking his hand, Gregorieva noted that it was warm and dry. His sparsely populated pate was dry as well just as was his cleanly shaved upper lip.

Absolutely no signs of stress, Vesna thought. Either he is very, very good or just sincere. Well, we'll see.

"So Mr. Friend of a Friend of Joey and John, what is this all about?"

Smiling warmly and in the process clearly exposing his very Western cared for teeth, the man said.

"Well, Ms. Gregorieva, put simply, your friends are very concerned about your future. So much so, that they have asked their government to make you a one-time offer."

Now understanding the situation a little bit better, Gregorieva, with her eyes now slightly slitted, almost dared to ask what that offer might be, but was preempted by the man.

"Do you have your papers with you?"

"Why yes, always. Why?"

"Well, I have been instructed to immediately escort you to Domodedovo Airport, where you will be quickly processed as an American VIP. Shortly thereafter you will board a very special airplane that I have been told that you know quite well. I am told that you have even lost your cookies on it."

"Lost my cook…! Oh, yes, that did happen." Blushing bright red now unconsciously moving her right hand to cover her mouth.

"Ms. Gregorieva. To be very blunt, the time is now for your decision. Upon landing, you will be granted asylum, a new identity, and will become a permanent member of the Philology Annex with a suitable salary. May I have your decision?" As he now quickly looked at his watch.

Gaping like a beached catfish, Vesna was confused and overwhelmed.

"But what about…"

"Ms. Gregorieva," the man quietly interrupted, "your life is in jeopardy. Joey and John sent me to make this offer. I can only make this offer once. Now, what is your decision?"

"But I have to pack…"

"Ms. Gregorieva," again quietly interrupting, "I was told that you were stubborn, but they did not tell me that you were stupid as well. For the last time, what is your decision?"

"Do you have a car?"

"Now that's my girl!"

*   *   *

The pair arrived at the airport twenty-seven minutes later, and then the man drove right past the passenger terminal. Gregorieva, noting this, felt her heart rate spike even higher than it had already been. Turning right into a small unloading area, Gregorieva then saw that this was a private terminal, most likely frequented by heads of state, corporate heads, and the like. Stopping at the curb before the set of sliding glass doors, the man now turned in his seat to face her said.

"Ms. Gregorieva this is as far as I go. Now please walk through those doors. Once inside, go directly to the service desk that you can see from here, and request, in as haughty a manner as you can muster, the diplomatic envoy. Now Vesna, off with you, and the best of luck."

Following to the very letter the man's instructions, Gregorieva got out of his car, immediately she adopted the strut of a runway model, and boldly approached the service desk that was manned by a woman. At her brisk approach the receptionist just looked up with a smile.

"May I be of assistance?"

"Of course. I wish to see the diplomatic envoy, immediately!"

"And who may I say is making this request?"

"Gregorieva, Vesna M."

"Thank you Ms. Gregorieva. One moment please." The receptionist efficiently said as she simultaneously pressed a button on her phone console. First listening, the receptionist then announced into her stalk-microphone that a certain Ms. Gregorieva had arrived and who she wished to see.

Now looking up into Gregorieva's face and noting her features and coloration, the receptionist, still listening, blinked, and then ended the connection. Removing her headset she then stood and said. "Ms. Gregorieva, if you would be so kind, please follow me."

By Gregorieva's own count, once they left the reception area, they walked through two doorways, one hallway, and directly into the cold interior of an enclosed aircraft hanger, where a very familiar white aircraft waited with its door open and stairway extended. What the Russian did not notice, the aircraft sported two auxiliary fuel tanks and tail markings of CH190.

Stopping at the bottom of the staircase, the receptionist smiled and wished Gregorieva a pleasant journey. Vesna, mounting the stairs, quickly entered the familiar tan interior that was stripped of its civilian seats and interior. Now within its warmth, a very good friend greeted her with open arms and said.

"Welcome home Vesna! Now quickly get seated so that we can get the hell out of here."

During these preliminaries, the copilot thumbed the speed dial on his cell phone and once the connection was made said.

"Hello Jerry?"

"Yeah, this is Go Fast, how are you?

"Yeah, we got the package and thanks for the prompt delivery.

Pause.

"Yeah, she's no doubt quite a classy chassis.

"Uh-huh.

"Bye' now. You do the same."

* * *

"I know, Vesna, that all of this last minute 'cloak and dagger' stuff may be a bit much, but it was deemed necessary especially given recent events." Milson explained after their aircraft had leveled out.

"Recent events?"

"Indeed." Milson continued. "You see Vesna, you and Joseph should not be alive."

Gregorieva's reacted to this revelation with considerable shock and confusion.

"Do you remember your last flight back from Egypt, the one with all the sudden turbulence?"

A nodding head answered.

"Well, that was not turbulence." While pointing down with his finger at the airframe, Milson continued. "This very plane was fired upon by an air-to-air missile from an unknown aircraft. What you and Joseph experienced was the emergency evasive action of the two pilots, who by the way, are flying this plane right now."

"Who shot at us!?!"

"That, Vesna, is the real sixty-four dollar question. We do not know for sure, but we have some very strong suspicions. But I think that you should know what those suspicions are. First off, the missile that was fired did not have a warhead. It was a dud, but a dud on purpose that was intended to cripple this aircraft by taking out one of its engines. In the process, the shrapnel from that kinetic impact would have killed both you and Joseph. The aircraft, now crippled, was to land on a military airfield in Iceland, where other members of the plot were to kill the pilots and then steal the Soap Bubble. In short, the entire affair was about stealing the Soap Bubble. There were to be no survivors."

"But who…"

"Vesna, you are a very bright woman. Now consider: who even knows about the Soap Bubble outside of those at the Philology Annex and Horizon Pass? Who knew that you and Joseph had been deployed? And who knew roughly when you were returning?"

As Milson watched Gregorieva's face he saw it transform from deep concentration, to suspicion, to absolute, flushed rage.

"Those bastards!"

"Yes. And that is precisely what we thought too. And in a conference call two days ago we told your former colleagues precisely what we thought. And so Vesna, here you are."

* * *

Flight CH190 left Moscow's airspace and seamlessly entered the southwest air corridor per its flight plan enroute to Geneva, Switzerland, via Belarus, Poland, with a scheduled refueling stop in Prague. However, the aircraft's transponder failed just south of Smolensk, only some 230 miles from Moscow.

"Okay Go Fast, let's pull that transponder and go black."
Pause.

"Roger-dodger Boomer. Transponder pulled."

"Okay. Now put in the computer a route to Kiev. Make it look vanilla at no more than thirty-five angels."

"Roger."
Pause.

"Computing. Navigation is responding."

Pause.

"Turning now to bearing two-zero-zero."

"Okay, now change our tail numbers to GR166."

"Roger. Changing tail to GR166."

Pause.

"Done."

"Okay, reprogram that transponder to GR166 and execute."

"Roger."

Pause.

"We're now GR166."

Pause.

"Boomer. Are we going to Athens? Maybe to do some site seeing. Drink some Ouzo?"

"Nope. Just disappearing real fast for our good friends out back."

"Roger-dodger. Disappearing fast."

*   *   *

It was considered one of the most secure vaults in Moscow, oddly located as it was deep within the Russian Academy of Sciences. The chamber surely was one of the dreariest – even by former Soviet standards. Its air still stank of acrid cigarette smoke that seemed to permeate the bunker. Visually it was wasteland: no windows, no artwork, no framed party paraphernalia broke the monotony of its crude plasterwork and dirty tan walls – only several dirty shadowed squares where the party paraphernalia used to hang. The corner lighting emanated from very special halogen pedestal lamps, and the harsh halogen glare seemed only to highlight the ceiling's near-wavy surface imperfections, poorly repaired cracks, smudges, and chance cobwebs. Nonetheless, the lamps served their purpose as each gave off a different, barely audible harmonic. When taken together, each, so precisely located, overlapped at the centrally located table in such a way as to effectively muffle any and all conversion, should the room be somehow, someway, bugged.

At the vault's center – the focus of the aural dampening, was a round table surrounded by six generously padded chairs. Today only three were occupied.

"Thank you for coming on such short notice." Rosovec said with a voice that shook with emotion.

"Gentlemen. It seems that we have totally underestimated our American colleagues. Yesterday afternoon, Vesna Gregorieva boarded a private aircraft with Swiss registration whose flight plan indicated that it was bound for Geneva. Then south of Smolensk the aircraft disappeared off of the radar. It missed its scheduled refueling in Prague as well.

"Our people in Geneva, who were immediately dispatched to that airport, report that the aircraft never arrived. Therefore, I can only conclude that the Americans have offered our temporal operative, Ms. Vesna Gregorieva, asylum.

"As you probably well know, Ms. Gregorieva was our last link, our last bit of leverage with the Americans. So now our participation in all future temporal field operations has been totally rendered null and void."

Damn can that Milson play chess! Rosovec raged.

CHAPTER XXIX
Hard Science, Harder Decisions

"You were right Doc, the environment of the enclosed EM field itself was the key – it provided neutral, contemporaneous data. When those four sailors jumped overboard they indeed were deposited in another time, for when they jumped, they went through the field. This we now know because calibration samples secured by first piercing the field and then exiting it on its opposite side provided our temporal data. And that temporal data was the same as with a two dimensional EM field. So this entire exercise has been useful only from the point-of-view of confirmation."

Smiling and examining his hands at the same time Naysmithe merely said. "Mr. Richter, independent confirmation is what science is all about. You did not waste either your team's time or any of the resources of Horizon Pass. Instead, you were participating in hard science. Period. End of Story."

Not at all pleased that he had just proved a negative, Toby Richter just grunted in surly response.

"Okay, Doc. I'm good with that. Now, what's our next step?"

"Well, first of all, are we absolutely sure of the Eldridge's temporal data?"

"Absolutely. We ran it four times with four independent calibration probes at a two sigma standard of deviation. Even at that level, the differences between the temporal data was within a range of less than three seconds."

Now with raised eyebrows the physicist commented. "Damn. That is pretty tight. So tell me Toby, if you were me, would you be willing to authorize a deployment based on that data?"

"Doc, that's not fair. That decision is way above my pay grade, but based on the temporal data analysis itself, I'd say yes, the data is rock solid."

"Thanks Toby. Trust me when I say that many people are in your debt."

*   *   *

Professor Ernst Jung hated these suddenly called evening get-togethers at the Philology Annex. First it was all the cloak and dagger about using the hidden side entrance in the alleyway. Close behind that were the adolescent passwords that were required. But most of all, Jung's own conscience was beginning to unravel. Just sending people back into the *somewhen* was stressful enough, but the authorization of plague and assassination – no let's call it by its real name, murder, was just too much for the aging physicist. And then there was the issue of Richards and Gregorieva. Both were such fine individuals, he could not bear to send either of them off into harm's way again. And to add to all of that dirty business, was the issue of Piankoff's and now young Richards' PDS – post-drop syndrome and no one, not even Doc Allen, had a clue as to what caused it or what its downstream ramifications might mean.

Having made his way through the hidden entranceway, having recited his stupid passwords, and having hung up his winter coat in the cloak room, Jung again discovered that he was late, yet again for the meeting.

Send them all to hell, he viciously thought as he made his entrance.

Dean Young, fussing once again at Jung's tardy behavior, was shocked when the physicist, who had registered his "look," merely gave him the finger as he sat down in the lone vacancy in the back of the conference room.

My! I don't believe that I deserved that! Young bristled.

"Well then, now that we are all 'finally' here, we can begin. First off, thank you all for coming on such a short notice this evening. Fortunately, we have only one agenda item that requires our consideration. Specifically, should we deploy the Soap Bubble to Philadelphia in an attempted retrieval of the four lost sailors of the CRYSTAL BALL incident? Is there any discussion?"

Immediately Jung belligerently stood up and rather forcefully announced. "Indeed, I do have something to say."

Young coolly recognized the physicist and responded. "Professor Jung, you have the floor."

As the roomful of colleagues turned as one to face the physicist, Jung opened his arms wide as if to embrace the entire gathering of some twenty-odd individuals.

"This proposed deployment to Philadelphia in the attempt to potentially retrieve four American sailors, while a nice and fuzzy, patriotic feel good sort of emotional exercise, is nonetheless a fool's errand and here's why. Let us imagine that the sailor's survived their jump. What then are we to do with them? Bring them back to our current temporal horizon? I don't think so. Alright then, return them to their own temporal horizon? Again, I don't think so.

"My dear colleagues, to date we have risked much together. Sent men, and now even a woman, back in time multiple times and without any apparent incident. To say that we have been most fortunate would be an understatement.

"But consider our current agenda item. It goes contrary to the *RUTI* in so many ways and it gives my head a migraine just considering them all. If we undertake this cockamamie gambit, then why shouldn't we go back and save Piankoff as well while we're at it!

"Sadly, in the final analysis, sometimes some things just have to be left well enough alone."

Naturally, such a damning opening statement caused much discussion. Some even accused the physicist of being a heartless old fart without a whit of humanity left in his godforsaken soul. But when the time came to call the question, a vote was taken and it wasn't even close: 18-2. The requested authorization for the Philadelphia deployment had been denied and all because of a thoughtful physicist who had just reread the *RUTI*.

* * *

The unwelcomed task of letting Millie Hayes know that the retrieval attempt for her big brother had not been approved had naturally fallen to Charlie Naysmithe, and as a consequence, his shoulders sagged yet another couple of inches under that burden.

Damn you Peter! Damn you to hell's perdition for having selected me as your successor!

CHAPTER XXX
Shock & Awe

Much to Richards' surprise, late that very afternoon he got a phone call from one very surprised geophysicist.

"Dr. Richards! This is Jeremy Larsson. I just got through reading your email and where did you get these outstanding AutoCAD images?"

Richards now playing dumb just said. "You mean you were able to print them out? They had some mysterious file suffix that I could not open."

"Print them out!" Larsson nearly shrieked. "Hell, yes, I did and they are gorgeous! But where did you get these anyways?"

Richards now smiling. "From a German civil engineering firm that is working with the Austrian Archaeological Mission in Egypt. But can you interpret them?

"Not a problem. Where's your office located on campus? I'll be right over."

Larsson hung up his phone so fast that Richards' was not even able to respond to his hurried question in the affirmative nor provide him with proper directions to his office.

*   *   *

While enroute on foot to the Near Eastern Institute, Larsson noisily berated himself for not realizing that an Egyptologist would have been located in such an obvious place. Then a thin sweat began to form on his forehead as he replayed his early impressions of Richards, his questions, and the nearly haughty manner that he had treated him, and then when he had practically blown him off on the phone.

Jesus! I gave him a laundry list and then he delivered big time and in just four days! Jesus! This guy clearly has some real pull and here I'm playing mind games with him! You total idiot! You total fucking idiot!

And then the nickel really dropped.

Damnation Jeremy! This is the same guy that was all over the cable channels with that Egyptian treasury discovery! And here I am playing games with his guy! Jeremy boy, you must be fucking nuts!

*　　*　　*

By the time one very humbled Jeremy L. Larsson, Associate Professor of Geophysics, timidly knocked on Richards' office door, he had totally flagellated himself several times over. Upon hearing an "Enter," he twisted the brass door knob, strode in with his best smile, and thought. Show Time!

Richards, now looking up in anticipation, first saw Larsson and then the large cardboard map tube under his arm. His first thought. Yes!

"Jeremy I see that you have something under your arm. Are they that big?"

"Yes they are."

"Okay then, let's go down the hall to the archives where we can easily spread them out."

Standing, Richards surprised Larsson as he went to one of his nearly bare book shelves and grabbed a handful of smoothed river stones and then said, "Follow me."

Now in the NEI archive, a place that Larsson had never before seen, the vast expanse of long maplewood tables now made sense to him as each of his colored plots were indeed huge, as in thirty six by seventy two inches.

Now struggling with flattening out the first plot, Richards gently eased Larsson aside as he quietly placed four stones at each of the plot's corners. Finished, and now smiling to himself with satisfaction, the Egyptologist asked Larsson if the plot was correctly oriented. Finding out that it was, the pair then flattened out the other three the same way.

Unable to control his inquisitiveness, Larsson asked.

"Dr. Richards, those stones were brilliant. Where did you get the idea?"

Smiling again, Richards said. "First off Jeremy, my name is Joey, okay? Second off, we often work with fragile papyri. Papyri come in rolls just like these mammoth plots. Ergo, the smooth stones."

"Very cool idea." Was the best that the geophysicist could muster.

"Okay Jeremy, you have the floor."

And so the young geophysicist did, and did masterfully, as he carefully explained the plots' scales, legends with their many symbols and colors, and coordinate system. He began with the surface survey, remarked on the size of the Temple of Ptah's footprint, the plot's many features, and even felt the need to comment on the accuracy of it.

"You know, this Willing Technik, GmbH must really be some outfit, as the purported survey accuracy is really quite good. Just look at all of these sighting landmarks. See all of these ghosted in triangles. They all overlap on at least two shared points. This is really excellent work.

"Now look up here in their designated NE quadrant. They have helpfully marked in the location of a small subsurface rectangular feature. I wonder why?"

From Richards point of view, Horst's location of the subsurface rectangular feature was dead on to what he had assumed by dead reckoning as it was situated just inside the temple's outer wall. So that meant that the tomb itself was located in the bedrock beneath the temple's very foundation stones. Clever. But then another thought came to Richards. So which came first? The tomb or the temple that seems to have been built over it?

At this point Jeremy had stopped his description and at first wondered why Richards had not answered his rhetorical question of "Why?" But when he saw that far away look in the Egyptologist's eyes as he examined the plot, he immediately knew that there was indeed something very significant about that tiny subsurface rectangle. And so he respectfully waited for Richards to return to the here and now.

Finally snapping out of his momentary reverie, Richards found Jeremy quietly watching him with a smile on his face.

"Yeah? So what's up?" He asked.

"You dude. You were like totally mesmerized over that plot. So what's up with that subsurface feature in the NE quadrant that has you so jazzed? Is that the tomb you were talking about?"

Now chuckling as if he was just caught with his hand in a cookie jar, Richards quietly answered.

"Jeremy my man, that subsurface feature could just well be that tomb that I was talking about."

"You're kidding!"

"Nope. Now tell me about the other plots."

CHAPTER XXXI
"On the Heart and Tongue"

To craft an authoritative translation of an ancient text requires a tremendous amount energy, patience, philological skill and literary creativity. While a graphical recognition scanner can assign the appropriate Latin transliteration to any given Egyptian hieroglyph, it is the application of the grammar behind the language that provides meaning to the otherwise amorphous collection of symbols. But even then, context can still trump grammar and turn it completely on its head, just as much as the sometimes peculiar, sometimes erroneous, grammatical usage of a scribe. Still, in the final analysis, it is the imperative of each and every philologist to provide a clear and understandable translation of a text that is sometimes itself poorly understood, its context unclear, and the meaning of its symbols a matter of conjecture.

In the case of the extremely archaic text "On the Heart and Tongue" this last was precisely the case. The simple fact is that Middle Egyptian, the language of the Middle Kingdom of Egyptian history, is itself so well understood today is precisely because the Egyptians themselves had rigorously scrubbed it of all of its archaic anachronisms, odd spellings and usages, and out-of-date characters. But once that process was completed the newly standardized Egyptian language again began its slow evolution into what is today referred to as Late Egyptian, the language of the Egyptian Late Period, a language rife with intrusive foreign words and the consequent invention of new characters to accommodate those new foreign sounds. Nonetheless, the core grammar of Late Egyptian is well understood as it is firmly grounded on its Middle Egyptian predecessor.

Such is not the case, however, with the Egyptian language of the Archaic Period and the subsequent Old Kingdom. These periods were one of linguistic invention, experimentation, and anything but standardization. While the characters used during in Middle Egyptian may count as many as 350, during the Archaic Period and Old Kingdom that number could be conservatively placed at around 1250 including possible variants. Add to that, the language's grammatical basis was extremely fluid early on and only by the beginning of the Old Kingdom did a grammatical foundation of sorts begin to coalesce. Consequently, documents that originate from the Archaic Period typically are short, pictographic messages devoid of prepositional phrases, complex verbal constructions, adverbs, and subordinate clauses.

That said, Ptah's scroll "On the Heart and Tongue" was remarkable precisely because it was not a short, pictographic message; rather, it was a long continuous text composed of characters well understood and others merely familiar using a grammar that followed the convention peculiar to its author. In short, to quote Milson's words.

"Oh what fun."

And to add to this "fun" is the fact that there are precious few published sources on the Archaic Egyptian hieroglyphic characters themselves, precisely three, one by Hilda Petrie, another by Walter B. Emery, and more recently one by Peter Kaplony. Not exactly the number that you would suppose.

*   *   *

"Well Joseph, I see that you have written out the text with ample room for character transcription. Good. Let's begin there."

After about an hour the two scholars had successfully filled in all the Latin equivalents to their corresponding Egyptian glyphs and with only having to consult the works of Petrie, Emery and Kaplony a handful of times.

"Now do you see what I mean John? We could conceivably translate this text in at least two ways. It is almost as if we have two texts here: one a surface text and the other one that is hidden beneath. So, how are we to proceed so that we don't drive ourselves totally nuts?"

"Well Joseph, did you know that I am a mystery and science fiction buff?"

"Nope."

"Do you read any?"

"Nope."

"Well shame on you, you really should. Those genres really free your mind and in some instances help a great deal, because what this text reminds me of is a book called *The Third Translation*. While I found the book to be a real disappointment, its premise just might help us here. So let's start by crafting the vanilla surface text first and refrain from any overly clever grammatical convolutions or deep finesses of meaning. Then, when we get through with that, we'll dig into all of the possible secondary meanings and compose the second. Sound good?"

*   *   *

Around half past noon, Richards stomach sounded off as the industrious pair had just completed the rough vanilla draft. Milson, not one to miss lunch either, looked up and stated the obvious. "Joseph, it's time to take a break and grab some grub. Let's go to the Faculty club. My treat." And so off they went to walk the short two blocks from the Near Eastern Institute.

Now in the open air and enjoying the crisp sunshine of a late October day their collective brains began a rejuvenation process as they chattered about the upcoming Chicago Bears game against Green Bay and the temperature of Richards' classes. Once inside the warmth and pleasant aromas of the club, Richards' stomach again made its displeasure known and so he nixed the salad bar in favor of the daily plate special of roast beef, potatoes, veggies and garlic bread. Meanwhile, Milson already had his salad plate piled high with an amusing assortment of items and was about to head to the cashier when he almost quite literally ran into Ms. Kelly, the secretary at the Philology Annex. Blushing a bit and apologizing profusely, the good professor then attempted to escape, but not before the secretary had made a request.

"Professor Milson, do you mind if I joined you for lunch?" A still flustered Milson managed to say. "As much as I would like just that, unfortunately Dr. Richards and I have a lot on our minds right now and need to talk about a lot of rather dreary shop. Besides, Ms. Kelly," Milson continued as he dared to gaze into her dreamy green eyes. "You do have such an effect on young Richards. Not necessarily a bad thing mind you, but not exactly a good thing either during a serious discussion. I am truly sorry. Perhaps some other time."

Damn! Kelly smiled. That's twice now that I haven't been able to corner that hunk Richards for lunch!

* * *

Refreshed, satisfied and back at the NEI their labors on the vanilla plain text was firming up quite nicely and that in spite of the fact that several philological details were missing, items like: definite and indefinite articles, conjunctions, noun determinatives, prepositions, and adverbial expressions. To get a sense of what Milson and Richards were attempting to reconstruct consider this famous line from *My Fair Lady*.

The rain in Spain lies mainly in the plain.

If we remove from this sentence that which is grammatically missing in Archaic Egyptian, then the sentence would look like this.

CHILDREN OF PTAH

rain - Spain - lies - plain.

Consequently, in order to derive just the vanilla translation of Ptah's Archaic Egyptian text required of Milson and Richards a multitude of conjectures based upon context and common sense. These then produced several possible readings of a given line that would result in several possible meanings. Regardless, the intrepid team plowed on and by four o'clock had produced a possible vanilla translation that they could live with. And perhaps to no surprise, the content expressed contained heavy doses of Egyptian mythology that was interesting only in that it revealed the state of Egyptian theological thinking at such an early date, a date that pushed back current academic thinking on the subject by some two to three hundred years. In other words, the text represented a clear declaration of the ancient Egyptians' religious and cosmographical framework as it existed around 3300 BC.

The vanilla content also included the earliest known references to what would be later considered the necessary divine qualities of a pharaoh: the *hu* – command, *sia* – intellect, and *maat* – sense of balance and order. The remainder dealt with details about the *man* Ptah and his two assistants, who carried the titles "excellent in their mastery of handiwork," which clearly represented the precursors for the later two high priests of the *god* Ptah. Striking throughout the text was the total absence of divinity attached to Ptah and even Ptah's place within the theological framework of the time.

With that task now behind them, the pair now began to play with the meaning of those words, began plugging in a known secondary or metaphysical meanings in place of the vanilla ones. The challenge before them was, if I read this word here as meaning this, what is the effect on the reading on this word over there? Then the pair was challenged to discern a flow, purpose, or theme to this alternative text for that would itself provide a possible context for the assignment of alternative meanings. Scratching their collective heads, Milson and Richards soon recognized that with so many possibilities that this process would take some time and careful consideration. And then Richards remembered something.

"John, do you remember that comment that you made about how cool it would be to find Ptah's tomb?"

"Vaguely, yes I do, now that I think about it."

"Well, hold on to your hat, but I think that our friend Horst Willing has found its entrance for us."

"You've got to be kidding!"

"Nope."

"And if we're really lucky, perhaps some of Ptah's other scrolls are preserved, which means that we could leverage them and begin to reconstruct his grammatical style."

"That could take some time Joseph."

"Yep. You're right. But all those budding graduate students out there in Egyptian philology need something to chew on."

CHAPTER XXXII
Jackals and Hounds

The planning session for the proposed drop in search of the man named Ptah included serious new considerations, for a drop as far back as the Egyptian Archaic Period required two new dimensions: a change of location and the discovery of a suitably secure drop point. The Temple of Amen Re and its holy of holies, the current drop point for the past seven temporal insertions, did not exist in the Archaic Period. Further, little was known about Thebes as well during that distant period. Consequently, logic argued for a new drop point located somewhere near archaic Mennefer. But where? And then arose the obvious question as to whether that new drop point would be a secure one.

It was a fact that a precedence of sorts had been established with the initial two solo drops by Piankoff back in the cowboy days of the Soap Bubble's calibration, when both drops had occurred fortunately unobserved in broad daylight and in the open Egyptian desert. By the current operational standards adopted by the Philology Annex and Horizon Pass facilities, however, such a ragged disregard of the *RUTI* principles was now totally unacceptable. Still, it was argued that the available technology could successfully provide pre-drop security for just such a daylight, open desert drop, just as it had so often within the Temple of Amen Re's holy of holies.

In the end it was decided that tests with the portable Soap Bubble VI should be performed within the late Third Dynasty Step Pyramid Complex located nearby and to the west of Memphis atop the Sakkara plateau. Not surprisingly, permission for both the tests and the use of the archaeological site was formally requested from the Director of Egyptian Antiquities and that it was quickly approved with the lone caveat that the tests were to occur during the first week of

August, a time of notorious heat and low tourism. And so it was agreed that come late summer, Richards, Gregorieva, and Calli Callahan's security unit would be so deployed.

*   *   *

For Richards it was just like the good old days as their very special Gulf Steam V made its landing at the Cairo International Airport. Okay, sort of, because they landed at the newly renovated Cairo International Airport. Nevertheless, as had long become custom, an ancient truck and its tail gate greeted Richards and Gregorieva at the military side of the airport's tarmac.

As he descended the short stairs of the aircraft, Richards immediately noted with a smile and a shake of the head that the truck's right tail light was still inoperable, its Arabic license plate still dangled by one wire. Then per the script, an animated US soldier in desert cammie's pressed to a knife's edge jumped out of the truck's cab and greeted the pair.

"Well, hello again! And don't you two just make a pair! As a broad grin stretched across Calli Callahan's face.

"Okay, enough with all this sweet talking. You know the drill. Now get your gear into this here fancy limo like pronto yesterday!"

Moments later, now underway with Gregorieva sitting on the poorly padded hump, Calli expertly maneuvered the rickety old Chevy through the airport's checkpoints and soon was making his way south towards modern Memphis. Along the way, the obligatory near-misses provided moments of thrill and fear that one usually associates with carnival rides. For Cairo's 24/7 traffic such was *de rigueur*, and as a result, the Russian dancer several times unconsciously grabbed Richards left bicep for support, while Calli used his horn, flashed his lights, crashed his truck's gears either to downshift or upshift, and generally ignored his brakes altogether. As perspiration streamed down everyone's face in the early August heat, the frenetic driving of Calli at least provided them with a steady breeze that made it tolerable.

High noon in Memphis was a time where the ill-fed and near feral town dogs commandeered all available shade, family store fronts were shuttered, and the insufferable heat rendered the roadside guard huts uninhabitable. Consequently, and true to form, Calli just drove right on through them all and was not challenged until he reached the bus parking lot at the Step Pyramid itself. Parking his rig near the southeastern entrance of the complex, one of his unit had appeared as if by magic out of the shadow of a wall's niche carrying a stubby-shaped weapon. He appeared to be in full body armor and was wearing a goggle-eyed Darth Vader helmet. Striding forward, he handed in through the passenger window three ice cold plastic bottles of water. Not saying a word, all three chugged their twelve ounces of sorely needed refreshment right there and then on the spot. Richards, per the usual drill, burped, and then creaked open his door as he watched the soldier return to his post. Once in place, he saw what looked like a shimmer and then the soldier seemed to just, simply, disappear.

Noting Richards' attentive stare, Calli whispered. "Adaptive camouflage."

"Wow, it's really effective."

"Yep, but the gear is really a bitch in this heat. They rotate in and out every hour and a half. Tuna is working with the egg-heads back at Horizon Pass to do something about it."

As for Gregorieva, she too just stood and stared in total disbelief.

Turning back to the rear of the truck, the threesome noted that four other soldiers had "appeared" and were unloading the Soap Bubble's pylons. Gregorieva grabbed their personal packs, while Richards beat Calli to the battery pack, which left him with only the Little Beast II computer that he tucked under his arm. And that was good news, for at least today

Richards wouldn't have to put up with Callahan bitching about "humping that God-forsaken back pack around!"

*　　*　　*

Testing began at nine pm and the first location chosen was within the colonnaded entranceway of the Step Pyramid complex. With the four pylons and their ion cannons in position, Richards input the date of August 8th, noon local, 3200 BC into the Little Beast. The portable battery pack, now a non-nuclear, began to give off a subliminal hum and the ceramic drop ring began to rise to its nominal operating height. Once reached, newly minted Sgt. Glen "Ozzy" Osgood, looked to Richards, got an affirmative head shake, and then attempted to stick the plastic lens of his cobra-headed probe into the silvery sheen of the Mark VI's temporal field. The key word here is "attempted" as Ozzy could not penetrate the field no matter where he probed around the entire diameter of the drop ring.

"Zilch Lieutenant Callahan. Looks like solid rock. We need to try another location."

And so it went that entire evening and on into the early morning hours; all the locations tested had encountered solid rock. The frustrating conclusion was that the entire area of the Step Pyramids' inner court area had been leveled and upon further consideration probably was also the limestone quarry for the Step Pyramid itself, the surrounding temenos wall, and all of the inner courts' many structures. This conclusion made even more sense as their early morning satellite status report had confirmed that the entire Sakkara plateau was part of the Mokattam Formation that was well known for its fine limestone.

"Okay, so tomorrow we gotta' find somewhere that is not all rock." Richards needlessly concluded. Looking around and then focusing on the western side of the complex he said.

"You know Calli, and I know that you will not like this, but we are going to have to go outside the walls of this complex, somewhere out west that-a-way into the open desert."

"Yeah, unfortunately I have to agree with you. But I still don't have to like the situation one bit."

*   *   *

Rosovec was sitting at his desk struggling to justify his very existence, when his private line began to ring. That is the one that did not first pass through the interrogation of his private secretary. Immediately lifting the receiver to his ear, Rosovec heard the distinctive hiss of the encryption handshake. Once that cleared, he said.

"Rosovec here."

"Director, this is Popev. Are you available? The excited voice said.

"What's up?"

"Something very interesting has just occurred that you may find of interest. Something that I cannot discuss over this line."

"Really!"

"Your place or mine?"

Rosovec, now looking down at his watch, decided to be gracious; besides, what pressing business did he have to do?

"I'll be over in ten minutes."

*   *   *

Secretly Rosovec was very pleased to have an excuse to leave his bureaucrat prison. Besides, the walk over to the neighboring building was invigorating and exciting as well as the director's imagination began to run wild wondering just what the hell had Popev so wound up.

*　　*　　*

"So okay my friend, what's up that has you so excited." Rosovec said.

"About one hour ago, we picked up a satellite transmission from Egypt, from the Memphis area, that while encrypted, was of an encryption that we well recognize. Upon its decipherment, it was found to be a conversation between our former colleagues at Horizon Pass and presumably their team in the field."

"You don't say…"

"Yes, Stephan. It looks like they have dared to field the Soap Bubble again and this time on their own."

"Interesting, most interesting, but it's early August! My God it must be an oven there! Then seamlessly shifting gears. "So what are our options?"

"None immediately, but in twelve hours time we could have a snatch and grab team in the area. Are you game?"

"Yes I am, but let's stop and think about this for a moment. In the meantime, call up your operations chief-of-staff."

*　　*　　*

The following evening but now out in the open desert to the west of the Step Pyramid complex, the drop point survey team hit pay dirt on their first try and great relief. As the fiber optic probe did its thing, "Ozzy" Osgood estimated that the surface on the other side was about four feet and so the drop to the "other side" really wasn't, being more like a deep wade in the surf, meaning that the temporal agents would have to literally drop to their knees and then crawl away from beneath the Soap Bubble's aperture.

Once this successful test was completed members of the team marked the location of the pylons with pneumatically embedded surveyors' marks into the exposed bedrock and recorded the site's precise GPS location. The many reports of the pneumatic gun seemed to noisily echo forever off the western walls of the Step Pyramid Complex.

As the wrap up of that task was almost completed, Calli suddenly turned his head away to better listen to his headset. Just as one of the soldiers was about to embed yet another surveyor's mark, Calli quickly squatted down next to the man and showed him a fist, which instantly froze the soldier in place. Then Calli said in a quiet, but quiet clear command voice.

"Kill the flashlights and everybody get down. We have unexpected company!"

Calli and his three immediate soldiers dropped to their bellies, while Richards rather roughly pulled a confused and unresponsive Gregorieva to the ground. Starting to complain as to what was going on, Richards just clamped his hand over her mouth and whispered into her right ear one word: "silence." Now wide-eyed, the former Russian nodded in understanding and only then did Richards uncover her mouth. As he did so, Richards just barely heard the lieutenant communicating with the rest of his security squad through his helmet's stalk microphone.

"Sitrep. All report in pronto."

A longish pause occurred while he listened to his unit that was scattered about in the dark desert. After enunciating a quick series of enigmatic sounding commands, he then turned to his men and the two temporal field agents and whispered.

"Okay, here's the drill. We, as a unit, are going to belly-crawl as quickly and quietly as we can west into the desert. Richards, you take the battery pack. Gregorieva, you take the computer. Anderson, you have the hula hoop. We leave the pylons and cables in place as bait. Johnson and Emmett, you take point. Anderson and I'll follow with the civvies. Make sure that you task your goggles to night vision and infrared. Okay everybody, move out."

*   *   *

It is just remarkable how slowly one's progress can be when imitating a snake or lizard, but that is precisely what the six were doing while trying to put some distance between the erected and now abandoned pylons and whoever else was out there in the darkness. All the while during their crawl Calli was in constant contact with the rest of his team, who were currently repositioning themselves per his direction to form a kill sack with the pylons as its center. After all, Calli reasoned that was what they were after, the technology and not the personnel.

As their group approached a modest rise in the desert terrain Calli called a halt beneath the ridge, paired the two civilians with one each of his men and ordered them to quietly dig shallow slit-like depressions that they could easily slip their bodies into. The idea being more to lessen their silhouettes than to provide for their protection. That housekeeping chore out of the way left Calli and Anderson to find slightly forward positions in order to cover their charges and plug the kill sack at their end.

With all settled into their newly acquired positions, Calli ran another check on his unit's secured tactical radio net and found out that the "bad guys" had departed from their initial skirmish line and had advanced from the western limits of the Step Pyramid Complex into four three-man teams who were now leapfrog advancing in and out of the desert terrain. That quick shift in tactics alone told the Irishman that the opposition were real pros. It also told him that they most likely had communications and night gear vision too, so it was a good thing that all of his troopers were in shallow depressions so as not to give themselves away. But their real advantages lay with their adaptive camouflage suits that in essence made men invisible and the night and infrared sensing of their goggle-eyed Darth Vader helmets that provided uncanny vision.

At this point Calli rolled onto his side and pulled out of one of his thigh pockets what looked like a Blackberry. Now shielding its glowing red graphics in his hands, the real time overhead drone imagery that was displayed showed all the "good guys" in green and the "bad guys" in red and from what Calli could see, the reds were almost totally within the greens' envelope.

Apparently the "bad guys" either had really good intel or were just very lucky as they clearly were slowly converging upon the pylons' location. Then, Calli suddenly realized that it must have been the pneumatic gun reports that had initially gave away their position and probably nothing more. Returning to his sat screen, he then saw that the "bad guys" had stopped dead in their tracks as if something had spooked them, but by then it was already too late as he whispered a simple word into his stalk mike.

"Execute."

And almost as one six of Calli's team who had clear sights on target began firing in well-disciplined, three-shot sequences with their silenced weapons. To Richards, what he heard sounded like the three-beat staccato of heavily muffled coughs, which were promptly answered with similarly suppressed returns, but the fire fight did not long last.

Calli, who had watched the entire envelopment with his tiny screen before his eyes, could actually see the heat signatures of his adversaries slowly blur and then dim as their blood spilled into the desert's sand and rock. Only after all twelve "bad guy" images had dimmed into almost nothing did Calli command.

"Move in."

Then, on second thought, he quietly said into the darkness behind him. "Richards, Gregorieva. I gotta' go. Stay put until we come back to get you. Got that?"

"Da."

"Yes sir."

*　　*　　*

"So who were they?" Richards asked Calli.

"Well, and Ms. Gregorieva you had better listen up as well, as best as I can figure right now the "bad guys" were Russians. Several of them even carried the shield and lightning bolt tattoo of the Spetsnatz. By their movements alone they were clearly a well-trained and professional team. Their silenced automatic weapons appear to be Czech in origin with filed off serial numbers. They did have night vision goggles, communications and GPS gear. By their kit alone I would estimate them to be some sort of governmental swat team. So far no documents or identification papers of any kind have been found on them. That fact alone makes them black ops. So that means that we have to evac this area ASAP. I already have called the Delta Force commander at Heliopolis for some helicopters to pick us up and them as well. They should be here shortly."

And with those words said, Richards could already make out the sound of a distant whoop, whoop, whoop across the clear, cool desert night air.

*　　*　　*

Before Calli boarded his designated helicopter that contained the Soap Bubble gear and all the dead "bad guys" in their body bags, he had to make a quick call.

"Charlie, this is Calli." Lieutenant Callahan said from the Sakkara Desert to Dr. Charles Naysmithe in New Mexico over the one-time encrypted satellite phone.

"Yeah Calli, what's up."

"Nothing much, just that our survey got really busy this evening."

"How so?"

"Got a visit from some hostile estate developers."

"REALLY!?!"

"Yep, but our door locks held up just fine, just as fine as you and Tuna said they would. Calli out."

*   *   *

"Daaa?" Said a half asleep Rosovec into the telephone receiver next to his bed.

"I am very sorry Stephan to trouble you at such an early hour, but we have lost contact with our first team in Egypt." Popev said.

Now fully awake, Rosovec hissed. "Just how can that happen?!?"

"I really do not know, but the backup team could not even locate their bodies, much less the item that they were tasked to find. They did, however, find many shell casings and several extensive blood spoors."

Pause.

"So the Americans got away again." Rosovec concluded.

"Da, and I also have a suspicion that we were expected as well."

"What?!?"

"Stephan, it is only a suspicion. But during last night's operation, the American's made two, quick satellite phone calls, both with two separate encryption's that were undecipherable. Yet, the night before, they practically broadcasted their location with an old and very well understood encryption. Consider Stephan: on the basis of that first transmission, we chose to act. And now we must face the fact that the Americans know positively that the old encryption has been compromised, and perhaps more telling, that we were willing to act. Stephan, we are playing a very dangerous game with a chess master, who is playing several moves ahead of us. This is not good, not good at all."

In response to that assessment, Rosovec just hung up his receiver. In the darkness of his bedroom, the bureaucrat held his hand over his eyes and began to ponder. *Now Stephan, just how different are you from those whom you replaced?* Then in answer to his own question. *Not much. But I wonder what Ostrogorsky would have done in such a situation?*

*   *   *

"So Lieutenant Callahan, in your opinion, how did the mission go?" Charlie Naysmithe asked, while Commander Tuna Cartwright sat next to him as he paged through his copy of the post-action report.

Unconsciously shifting in his seat the soldier responded.

"Well sir, first off, we did, after some initial failures, successfully locate an open desert drop point. That went by the book.

"Second, the adaptive camouflage worked liked a dream, but it was hellishly hot in that desert heat. But at night, the rig's rendered us invisible. It wasn't even fair."

This observation caused both Naysmithe and Cartwright to make a note.

"Third, the addition of infrared capability to the tactical helmets was a godsend, especially against a desert background. When used in combination with the night vision, one could clearly see who was down and who wasn't. This is a vital battlefield capability, the ability to know who is dead and who is playing possum. Simply outstanding.

"Fourth, the dedicated drone and the handy tactical screen, in combination with all our assigned GPS transponders, provided me with an almost godlike perspective of the battlefield. Again outstanding.

"We really did sucker the "bad guys," when I reported on the sat phone using the old encryption protocol. In my mind it proved two things. First of all, we now have positive proof that the encryption had been compromised, something that we had long suspected for quite some time. And second…

Pausing with a sigh.

"And second, I am truly saddened that the "bad guys" actually tried to steal the technology again. You would have thought that being turned away once would have been bad enough. Apparently not. What this tells me is that they are desperate and desperate men do dangerous things."

Pausing to reflect again.

"To date sir, we have managed to be one step ahead of them. At some point, no matter how hard we try, I fear that our luck is going to run out."

"So lieutenant, regarding the post-fire fight clean up, for the lack of a better term, how did that go?" Naysmithe asked.

Again after shifting uncomfortably in his seat, Lieutenant Callahan replied.

"Well sir, given that the "bad guys" all were wearing body armor, the clean up as you put it was a bloody mess. All of them went down to head shots. While the gathering of intel from their persons is routine, the packing of their bodies and weapons into body bags was a frankly sickening task."

Pause.

"By the time the choppers had shown up, many of the bodies had already achieved rigor mortis, which made an already sickening task, now a grisly one as well. Several arms and legs had to be broken just getting them into their body bags. Then, there was all the blood, which you really cannot see in the dark, but you sure as hell can smell. So by the time we all got back to base and got into some light, we were all covered in blood. We all looked like fucking butchers."

A long pause passed while the digital wall clock noisily ticked off several seconds.

"Thank you lieutenant both for your service and your candor."

And with that said Naysmithe fingered the tape recorder's off switch.

CHAPTER XXXIII
Precinct of the Temple of Ptah

It was not until the following January that Richards could finally tear himself away from his university's clutches and hop a flight to make a brief visit to his second homeland – Egypt. When one considered what his itinerary said, four days total in country, he had indeed a lot on his agenda.

First on the list was that promised dinner with Sharil Moussa, which turned out to be a truly memorable evening in the al-Rubayyat room at the Mena House, complete with the whirling-dervish floor show, Black Sea caviar, and a simply spectacular main meal of roast pigeon, a succulent rice and vegetable mix, fresh breads, dipping sauces, and of course that delicious sweet dessert that was a light as a feather.

"Joey, I hadn't expected you to take me seriously, but this evening has been just, well, quite unexpected." She said with a simply radiant smile.

"Well Sharil, don't you think that you just might deserve such a decadent evening? After all, by ancient Egyptian royal standards our fair was quite, how can I say this, almost meager."

"You're kidding of course! I am full to the very brim."

"Not at all and it isn't about the amount that you ate. It is all about variety. True, the caviar was divine, but their dried fish and their sauces cannot be discounted nor their cheeses, many breads, and sweet breads which are my favorite. Then there are all the roasted fowl, the ducks, pigeons, and geese. The many beers and wines. The many fruits, and finally, all those glorious flower arrangements, each a riot of color and each with their own marvelous aromas. See what I mean?"

During this description Sharil's eyes had glazed over, her head full of images painted by her well-traveled colleague.

"Yes." She said with a wistful breathiness.

"Well, can I offer you an after dinner something from the bar?"

"Why yes. Yes, that would be nice."

As the pair exited the historic room, easily half the room's eyes followed them as they made such a striking pair. The long walk through the wood paneled and white marble floored hallways to the bar that overlooks the Great Pyramid by day both broke the mood and helped clear their heads. Once so seated in a quiet corner, Richards broke the news.

"Sharil, I have something special to share with you and your father."

Smiling like a Cheshire cat and with a tall martini with double anchovy olives in her hand the Director of the Cairo National Museum said. "Ah ha! Why am I not surprised."

"Yeah I guess so. Well, here it is." He said as he leaned forward over their minute black cocktail table. "I believe that Horst Willing has located the entrance to Ptah's own tomb."

Briefly choking on her drink, Sharil's now very wide eyes told the American to get on with it.

"As you know, the Austrian Archaeological Mission is working within the temple's circuit and they hired Horst to do the surface and subsurface survey of the area. During that survey, in the northeastern quadrant, Horst detected an odd rectangular feature about ten feet beneath the current surface. Based upon what I remember during, ah, a recent visit to the area that was where the tomb's entranceway began."

"This is simply a sensational news Joey." She whispered. "Do the Austrians know about this?"

Looking down at his hands Richards said. "No they do not. And Sharil, as crazy as this may seem, I do not want any part of it. It's time to spread the wealth around. So I thought that I would clue in their director to Horst's observations and leave it at that."

"Are you absolutely sure about this Joey?"

"Yes I am Sharil. Believe it or not, my participation with the Dutch team's discovery of the Amen Re Treasury has caused a lot of friction within my academic department. To again get involved with yet another excavation could become problematic."

Now with a look of disbelief on her face. "So Joseph, if I understand you, you do not want to directly participate in an archaeological excavation, a scientific project, because you fear that your departmental colleagues will become jealous?"

"No Sharil, they are already jealous, sniping vultures, who are looking for any possible angle to criticize me."

Now with eyes blazing. "Oh, those poor, poor, babies. Get real Joseph! Do you have any idea what I have to put up with on a daily basis? The snide comments, the raised eyebrows, the snickers, and of course, all the talk about 'Oh, she is such-and-such only because of her father's influence. I believe that you Americans have a perfect expression for all of that, it's called bullshit."

Richards, now sitting back during this minor gale storm and actually blinking at Dr. Sharil Moussa's use of the colorful term "bullshit" took it all for what it was: a sharp reality check that he really needed. Adjusting the cuffs of his dress shirt Richards made up his mind. Sharil was spot on and said so.

"Thank you very much Dr. Moussa for that reality check. I really needed that. Now, would you happen to know the name of that Austria director?"

Now smiling with genuine pleasure at Richards' words, Sharil began to rummage around in her purse, then shaking her head in negation as she could not find what she was looking for.

"I am truly sorry. I thought that I had the man's card. As I best recall, his name is Ulrich Schachermayr. And if that name rings a bell, it is because he is the nephew of the late Fritz Schachermayr, the Greek historian. Listen. I will email you his particulars tomorrow."

Now Sharil leaned forward and said in a conspiratorial tone. "What I really want to know is how are you going to approach this man knowing what you know, but without giving away your rather unique inside information?"

*   *   *

On the following day, Richards awoke late in his room at the Nile Hilton with a slight jetlag hangover from the previous late night conversation with Sharil, which had extended far beyond what his body could stand.

Thank God for that taxi!

After cleaning himself up, he checked his email, and sure enough there was Sharil's promised information about the Austrian field director. Pleased, he decided on the spot to grab a taxi down to Memphis.

A few words about taxi rides in Egypt, which can best be described as a cross between getting a ride in a NASCAR racing car and the most scary carnival ride that you can imagine. First off, traffic lights are purely discretionary hindrances to forward motion. Stop signs are ignored altogether. Second, any road with three lanes can easily handle four lanes of traffic. Consequently, a taxi's passenger side mirrors are often turned in or are totally missing, i.e., have been torn off. Third, horns play a far more critical function than brakes. I think you get the idea.

Once Richards' taxi had successfully cleared the congested chaos of Cairo, the Egyptologist settled down to take in the passing scene of agricultural fields, date palms, mud brick stores and housing, cesspool canals, and the ubiquitous sprawl of garbage. Turning off the main north-south road and now heading west, Richards saw the rising grandeur of the Step Pyramid and immediately experienced a flash of *déjà vu*.

My God! He thought. The last time that I was here I was an unwilling participant in a fire-fight!

Passing under the trees that lined this road, a security check point was crossed before the taxi turned in on the right into a parking lot. Upon exiting the cab, Richards was swarmed with young children hawking "authentic" antiquities with prices to match. Moving on towards the ruins before him, next he was approached by several, again "authentic," tour guides, which he simply ignored and in the process received several multilingual assessments of his doubtful parentage. Finally clear of this usual hectoring, Richards scanning about and rather quickly picked out several military style tents. Around them several European types were standing and fiddling with an odd three-wheeled conveyance.

As he made his way over, around and through fallen limestone blocks, some plain and others inscribed with the deeply cut hieroglyphs typical of the reign of Ramses the Great, Richards now recognized the three-wheeled baby carriage as a ground penetrating radar unit.

At his approach, which the American did not attempt to disguise, three faces turned towards him and one of the blond heads simply exploded into a broad smile of recognition.

"Joey!" He bellowed. Now standing up to his full height of six foot something, the man quickly strode forward, put a true bear hug on the Egyptologist, lifted him from his feet, and said in German.

"Welcome my friend! It's so good to see you again! I just knew that you would come!"

Now recovering from that welcoming crush, Richards, now smiling, responded in German. "Yes, you as well and Horst you are looking very fit."

In response, the German proudly flexed his very impressive "guns" that were clearly in evidence in his short-sleeved shirt.

Now turning around, Horst immediately began to introduce Richards around. The first was Candice Martin, a short and smiling civil engineering student with freckles and a firm hand shake. Although not directly said, Richards judged that she was under Horst's wing as his field assistant, while she was completing her *Praktikum*. Next came Andre Gerst, announced as an archaeology graduate student from Vienna. The unspoken message here was "look out" with this one. This snap assessment was confirmed with his crisp Austrian half-handed handshake, brief nod of the head, and chilly demeanor.

Yep, pure trouble, Richards confirmed.

By this time, and no doubt alerted by all the ruckus of the initial introductions, a red-haired middle aged man appeared from under a flap of one of the tents. Again Horst handled the introduction in German, but in a far more formal manner.

"Herr Professor Dr. Schachermayr! May I introduce my friend and former kolleague vom America, Professor Dr. Joseph Richards."

As Schachermayr extended his hand with a guarded, but still curious smile, he said in English. "Velcome to Memphis Professor Richards."

Now looking around and behind the American. "But vhere is your film crew?"

Confused, Richards with his hands now on his hips, simply said. "Huh?"

"Ja, you know, National Geographic, History Channel, Discovery Channel, etc., etc."

And then Richards caught on and began to laugh so hard that he was leaning on his knees. Clearly, Schachermayr had connected Richards with the media frenzy connected with the Treasury of Amen Re's discovery and clearance.

To Gerst, he did not understand why this American was laughing so hard at his now grinning professor. He just stared hard with a stony face. Then to his great surprise, his professor began to burst out laughing himself. Vhat is going on here! He thought.

"Now that was a good one professor." Richards managed to wheeze out.

"Ja, I thought so too." Schachermayr said with a toothy grin.

*   *   *

"These are simply beautiful plots Horst, even if you did overcharge your Austrian brothers for them." Richards needled the civil engineer in his flawless German while Schachermayr and Martin looked on in amusement at his discomfort. Gerst just stiffly stood throughout it all in silence and with a rigid jaw line. Pretending to have never seen them before, Richards had just given the Austrian team his read of them thanks in large part to both Horst's and Larssen's lucid presentations. Even Gerst was impressed and the snap analysis had left Schachermayr stroking his chin while thinking deep thoughts. At that point Richards continued.

"You know, if your archaeological permits allows Professor Schachermayr, I would like to see your team attack the northeastern quadrant and in particular to investigate this particular subsurface anomaly. It looks very odd, almost suspicious to me."

At this point Gerst just could not contain himself any longer. "Und zo, Professor Dr. Richards, just vhat do you dink dhat shaft ist? A tomb?"

Deciding to make Gerst both a fast friend and a hero in the eyes of his academic mentor Richards said. "Why Herr Gerst! Why that is precisely what I think. And do you know why? Because, just as you yourself no doubt have noticed, this shaft is not a late intrusion. It is almost as if the temple's later foundation stones were laid almost over it in total ignorance of its presence. In some ways, this almost reminds me of how Tutankhamen's tomb was so built over. Brilliant idea Herr Gerst!"

Gerst, who clearly possessed a bright mind but one gummed up with an excessive ego, took Richards' ploy hook, line, and sinker. "Und I know who ist in dhat tomb!"

Now that pronouncement really caught everyone's attention.

CHILDREN OF PTAH

"Ja gut, Herr Gerst. Who might I ask?" Schachermayr demanded in a challenging if not an almost belligerent tone.

Now wide-eyed at his own self-inflicted predicament, Gerst stuttered out. "Vhy der Gött Ptah, who else?"

Richards smiling broadly then quietly asked the graduate student of Egyptian archaeology. "And why Herr Gerst do you believe this to be so?" As Richards motioned the man over to the table where the plot was displayed.

Now in potentially really deep water, Gerst suggested. "Vell, who else vould be buried vithin the sacred confines of this temple? Nein, who else vould dare such a thing?" After a brief pause then came a truly brilliant burst of intellectual energy. "Und Herr Professor, die temple's name itself says so as vell: 'der Kastle of the *ka* of Ptah.' Zo, die temple is protecting Ptah's own *ka* – his mummy!"

"Herr Gerst, for what it is worth, I have to totally agree with you." Then Richards turned to look at Schachermayr.

"Now it is your task to talk your *Doctor Vater* here into allowing you to prove that thesis."

And at that point, Richards stepped back as Schachermayr moved in to again lean over the plot, while he pinched together his lower lip between his thumb and forefinger in thought. After a few moments, the director said. "Ja, it is possible I suppose." Pause, as the atmosphere in the tent seemed to thicken with tension. "Ja. The depth ist nicht zo great." Now as the archaeologist's mind began to quicken, so did his words. "Ja. It is possible, but Herr Gerst how long can you hold your breath?" With a real look of confusion on his student's face, Schachermayr then answered his own question.

"Herr Gerst you just might need a strong water pump." He said with a smile.

*   *   *

Just before Richards left at the end of the day to return to Cairo and catch his return flight, Horst, ever the barbarian, again bear-hugged the American in his own particular form of farewell. But just before he got into his taxi it was Schachermayr, who now took him aside.

"You know Professor Richards…" Abruptly stopping himself, he shook his head and continued. "I am very sorry. Joseph, I vish to dank you for your visit. Vhile you probably do not know dhis, your visit was most providential. I am quite sure dhat Herr Gerst ist very much in your debt."

Now offering his hand. "Joseph, now do not be a stranger. Have a gut trip back zu the States und say hello to Uncle Johnny Milson for me!"

"Uncle Johnny?"

"Ja. It is a long story. Just ask him!"

CHAPTER XXXIV
Systems Check

Naysmithe stood over the retrieved portable Mark VI with his hands on his hips, all the while Callahan observed feeling like he broke something that he shouldn't have. The gear, displayed across several long work tables, was logically arranged in their functional groups: pylons and cables here, jump ring there, power pack over there, and computer at this end. In all, it was a classic example of a highly compact technology, behind which a tremendous amount of time and development dollars had been invested.

It was Charlie Naysmithe who first broke the silence. "You know, this unit has taken quite a beating and it still kept on ticking." He stated in quiet admiration with more than just a bit of wistfulness. Even though Borov's name had not been mentioned, it hung unsaid in the air.

Cartwright, now bent over low, inserted his forefinger to the knuckle into a partially shattered section of a pylon and noted. "Looky here Dr. Naysmithe. It looks like the bullet went clean through."

"Yep. You're right. Lucky for us that none of its technology was irreparably damaged. This one will be a simple patch up job. I let Mr. Mackey know that so that he can get on it."

Then moving on to the ceramic drop ring or hula hoop, Naysmithe picked it up and remarked. "Now this will require some surface refinishing. Will you just look at all of these scratches! Just what were you guys using it for? A chariot wheel?"

"You know Doc, the situation was a bit hectic out there." Callahan offered in self-conscious defense.

Naysmithe, now surveying the lot as a whole said. "But in general not bad when you consider that it just survived a fire-fight. Some dirt, grit, and dust to clean up, that's for sure, but after that the Mark VI will be a good as new."

And then a smile creased the young scientist's face.

"You know, I think that I've now got a nickname for his version of the Soap Bubble, one that Peter himself would have loved. Let's call her 'Old Faithful.' After all, it did survive an all out fire fight and a bullet hole to boot."

"Sounds good as any, Doc." A nodding Cartwright allowed.

Calli then quickly queried. "But Doc when do you think we should allow this rig out of the barn again?"

"Well, that's a damn good question. Clearly our Russian colleagues want to get their grubby mitts on it. But I really don't think that that much matters. Despite what you might say, this technology is designed to be used and not merely to gather dust. Now is each and every future deployment going to be a security risk? Damn straight it is, but it always was. But just like any other fancy tool, the Soap Bubble was built to be used. I'll be damned if we don't use it out of fear of loosing it. That's just crazy thinking in my mind." So concluded Borov's successor.

And then he added. "Tuna, what we need to do on the next deployment is not to use a sat phone. I am willing to bet that our colleagues have come to depend on our predictableness. Our deployment rules have become just too predictable, too unsecure. It's only just a matter of time before they start decrypting our other encryptions. Let's discuss this at a later date and in the meantime I want us to come up with some ideas for some other way to communicate."

"Sounds good Doc."

*　　*　　*

Due to the sensitive nature of the subject matter and some current international tensions, it was decided early on that a very select collection of individuals should meet at the Philology Annex in person. As another indication of this gathering's importance, the meeting itself was held in the conference room of the second sublevel that was secretly excavated during the rather extensive renovation of the building shortly after its purchase from the university. All attendees were to enter through the hidden outer entrance located in the gangway formed by the Philology Annex and the neighboring brownstone. Furthermore, just as with the Hourglass Seminars of old, this was an evening event.

Gathered around the longish conference table sat six men who represented a veritable who's who of both Philology Annex and Horizon Pass personnel. Charlie Naysmithe represented Horizon Pass and technological side of the issue. Paul Young and Ernst Jung did likewise for the Philology Annex and its administrative functions. Commander Charles Cartwright, and Lieutenant Callahan sat in for security. The last member was John Milson, preeminent historian and clearly chess master extraordinaire.

Per tradition and custom, Young performed as this meetings chair, and so was the first to initiate the discussion.

"Gentlemen. Thank you for agreeing to come at such short notice having travelled so far, and at such an ungodly hour."

This last caused a mild chuckle from Charlie Naysmithe.

Ignoring it, Young continued. "The reason for this Tuesday evening get together is to first ensure that Ms. Kelly is not about, or for that matter, remains totally ignorant of it. It turns out that she, is not what she appears to be."

Milson could not resist and so piped up. "You mean Paul that she is not the hottest thing next to the sun's surface?"

Knowing smiles and chuckles broke out briefly and then immediately died with Young's next words. "No John, you old horny toad! Commander Cartwright, quite by accident I might add, discovered during a security sweep that our very own Ms. Kelly is an agent of our very own government. Precisely which agency and how black, we still do not know. But that pretty face is not what it pretends to be." And so Jung concluded. "So do we manage to fire her somehow?"

"Negative." Cartwright firmly stated. "At least we know what she is and that's a whole lot better than signaling her superiors. I recommend that we just go with the flow and keep our eyes open."

"I totally agree." Milson added. "Besides, she cannot be that effective an agent as you always know when she's about and where's she's been."

"How so?" Asked an inquisitive Naysmithe.

"By her vapor trail, Dr. Naysmithe, her vapor trail. That woman just loves to drench her body in musk oil perfume."

To which broke out a generous round of chuckles.

Determined to stay on point Young pressed on.

"So am I to assume that Ms. Kelly will remain in our employ?"

All indicated in the affirmative.

"So ruled. Next order of business: deployment security. Commander, I do believe that's your bailiwick as well."

First clearing his throat, Tuna was a bit taken back how nervous he had suddenly become, as he was now the focus of this group of egg heads instead of the jar heads he was used to. At least Calli was there for moral support.

"Given what we now know of our Russian colleague's capabilities and the extremes that they are willing to go to acquire the Soap Bubble technology, any further deployment security arrangements should, no, 'will' have to be beefed up. To that end," with a nod towards Charlie Naysmithe, "Dr. Naysmithe here has provided the security team with a tamper-proof laser-based communication system. While it is a totally secure system, it is also a totally line-of-sight system. Fortunately, it is very hard not to be line-of-sight with a drone overhead. As encryption has been added to this system's transmissions, all of our communications will be secure at least for the time being.

"Additionally, I have also brought on board twelve more men to provide for injury or retirement replacements and as a backup force. This became very apparent as a result of the recent fire fight that took place at Sakkara. We literally had just exited the area in our borrowed choppers as the second 'bad guy' team had arrived on the scene. So, with secure communications available and additional troop support, I believe that we are now able to securely deploy, regardless of what our dear friends intend."

"Finally, a temporary fix for a cooling system for the adaptive camouflage is currently being field tested by Lieutenant Callahan. Calli?"

"Ahem. Yes. What we have done gentlemen is to borrow a page out of endurance auto racing. As you can probably imagine, heat in a NASCAR race car can get quite intense and their solution to 'beat the heat' was a special undergarment that is covered with a matrix of capillary-like plastic tubing through which cold water is cycled from a soft, bladder-like personal reservoir. The effect is surface cooling of the chest and back. Well, as you might expect, we took that idea, improved upon it, and now our men can actually stand in the sun and reasonably keep their cool. Frankly, I see this as a real game changer and would have been a real plus at the Amarna and Sakkara deployments. Then one of the men, a former ski bum, suggested that we incorporate some commercially available, highly breathable fabrics into the camouflaging kit. This update also turned out to be a godsend in Egypt's high temperatures."

"Thank you Commander Cartwright and Leftenant Callahan." Young then paused to take a drink of water. "Our next order of business is the next deployment of Richards and Gregorieva this time to the Egyptian Predynastic Period. Purpose: to seek out and interview a man named Ptah."

Now looking in Milson's direction.

"John I believe that you have the floor."

Sitting as he was, hands folded before him, while he examined them, a surprising tightness gripped his stomach, which frankly startled him quite a bit. John, he thought, are you alright? As the tightness seemed to pass as quickly as it had appeared, Milson shrugged it off, looked up, and began.

"Gentlemen, Commander, Lieutenant, this next deployment will confirm whether or not the human race was the subject of an extraterrestrial laboratory experiment. We know that it was attempted once by the alien known as Akhenaten. We stopped that cold at the source and dealt with his progeny. In the course of that effort, we recovered in the hanger of his space craft an amazing document, called the Annex Papyrus. Contained within the text of that precious document, Akhenaten was seeking, as was his intergalactic organization – known as the Survey Institute, evidence of what they referred to as the First Source and the Old Ones. Meanwhile, our very own Dr. Richards, stumbled upon that which Akhenaten himself was seeking, evidence of the Old Ones. What Joseph so cleverly noted was that the very spelling of the Egyptian god Ptah's name was a code in itself. Put simply, his name is a collection of glyphs that mean: male, female, and the DNA strand."

At hearing this account, most of the panel, Milson noted, had now slack jaws.

"Add to this, gentlemen, is that this Ptah would later become the patron of craftsmanship and civilization, and, I might add, this same man once made divine authored a rather surprising philosophical treatise called "The Memphite Theology." In that treatise, creation was described as a mental exercise where a thought conceived, once spoken, created matter."

"Wait a minute," Cartwright said, "that sounds to me a whole like *Genesis*."

"Indeed it does commander, indeed it does. The problem is that this treatise predates the Hebrew culture by millennia. So, I am here to advocate an interview with a god. Its purpose is to find out are we truly ourselves, or, just the children of Ptah."

After some head scratching, shifting in their chairs, and pulling of ears, Young asked for a motion. Milson uttered a motion to deploy. The motion was voted on. And the motion passed.

Now may God help you Joseph, Milson silently prayed.

CHAPTER XXXV
"God's Tomb Found!"

(Cairo) AP – The Egyptian Antiquities Organization announced today the historic discovery near Memphis of the tomb of the Egyptian god Ptah by the Austrian Archaeological Mission.

The Director of the Egyptian Antiquities Organization, Dr. Ibrahim Moussa, who was present at the opening of the tomb, was quoted as being most impressed by the find. "This is just another example that the sands of Egypt have yet to reveal all of its secrets."

The Austrian Archaeological Mission, lead by Professor Dr. Ulrich Schachermayr of the Institute of Egyptology at the University of Vienna was speechless at the discovery. "It is simply something beyond the imagination!"

Mr. Andre Gerst, a graduate student in Egyptology and member of the Austrian team, reportedly was the first to suggest the location of the historic find. "Yes, it was I who first realized that the subsurface scans revealed something truly significant. So I suggested to Prof. Schachermayr to investigate the location. And as they say, 'the rest is history.'"

Reporters on the scene described a ten-foot excavation that uncovered a stepped, stone passage that was cut deeply into the bedrock. The passage with seventy-two steps lead to a cube-shaped chamber that was filled with three inches of ground water.

Found in the center of the tomb chamber was a raised stone platform that supported an intact, but extremely fragile wooden coffin. Numerous intact papyrus scrolls, which were found in an amazingly good state of preservation, were recovered along with various grave goods.

Dr. Moussa quipped that the Department of Conservation at the Cairo National Museum would have to put in some serious overtime in order to stabilize all the artifacts. "There was recovered some fifty-six scrolls in a most fragile state of preservation, but I am quite sure that our chief curator of antiquities, Dr. Ahmed Rashid, will be able to unroll them so that we can read their contents."

The Egyptian god Ptah, considered by the ancients as the patron deity of craftsmanship and civilization, purportedly played a significant role in the theological and philosophical thinking of the ancient Egyptians.

*   *   *

"So Uncle Johnny, what's the story?"

Richards tweaked Milson, who up to this moment had had his nose buried in his morning newspaper. Squinting a bit as he looked over his reading glasses, Milson then slowly sat back into his office chair.

"Well, I see that you've finally met Ulli Schachermayr. Let me see." Now putting his hands behind his head. "He was directing the dig at Memphis wasn't he?"

"Yep!" Richards, smiling and now very pleased with himself, reversed and sat down on the guest chair in order to lean into it. "That's right Uncle Johnny. So what's the story?"

Sigh.

"Okay Mr. Private Eye. Here's the deal. Fritz Schachermayr, an extraordinary Classicist, and I were close friends. We met as graduate students at an international conference sometime back before the Earth was formed, shared a couple of beers, and we kept in touch. As time passed, Fritz got married and had three wonderful kids. One was Ulrich and the two of us bonded when he was, what, about six years old. Imagine Joseph, I was an Egyptologist, I worked with mummies, and young Ulli was smitten, much to his father's consternation. End of story. Speaking of which, have you read today's paper?"

"Nope."

"Here, read this. I think that you will find it to be rather pertinent."

And so Richards grabbed the paper and began to read.

Sigh.

"Do you believe that little twerp?" Richards remarked as he reread the article that Milson had just put before him.

"I take it that you do not entirely agree with Mr. Gerst's assertions?" Milson observed.

"Agree? Hell I was the one who first pointed out that subsurface feature to the entire team, including Schachermayr!"

"Joseph, relax, I know the whole story."

"You do?"

"Yes, I do. Ulli Schachermayr filled me in on the entire episode last night. And as for Mr. Gerst, well, if it makes you feel any better, Ulli refers to him as 'the insufferable ass.' Regardless Joseph, you have made quite an impression on Ulli and in this instance, you did absolutely the right thing. And for what it's worth, I am very proud of you. Very proud indeed!"

"But that little twerp!" Richards said as he slapped the back of his hand against the newspaper article.

"Joseph, give it a rest."

CHAPTER XXXVI
Conversation with an Old One

The deployment was scheduled for the middle of the following summer as both Richards and Gregorieva needed to achieve that natural all over tan, tune up, and pay a visit to Doc Allen to check on their mental defenses. Besides, Richards had his academic responsibilities to uphold and Gregorieva was still acclimating to her new home in Santa Fe, her job, and identity. Nonetheless, she was out running on a daily basis at Santa Fe's altitude and vowed that she would run the American into the ground. Unspoken, but on both of their minds still, was the night of the fire fight and what that had meant. Men had fought and died, all because of the orders of others to acquire something that was not theirs to possess. In the meantime, Calli Callahan successfully brought up to speed his additional troops and had integrated them into the original team. Charlie Naysmithe for his part was making sure about that special geosynchronous satellite that was now stationed over the eastern Mediterranean. To date, its testing had been flawless in all weather conditions. Well, all that the quiet and laid back genius from San Diego would say was something about the addition of a tightly focused, look-down targeting radar. And finally, several months prior to the deployment the appropriate Egyptian authorities were notified and the needed authorizations were approved.

*　　*　　*

Given that this would be an open desert, evening operation, Calli Callahan had both of his twelve-man squads in the field and in position – not that you could find any of them as they were arranged in two concentric rings around the drop point.

As for the drop point, it was easily found using the recorded GPS coordinates. In many respects, however, it took on the look of a mini Stonehenge with the four pylons in position and the venerable wooden scaffolding surrounding them. Despite the team's familiarity with the gear and its setup, it was the erection of the scaffolding while using red flashlights that still presented a challenge as the ground was uneven. In the end two pairs of socks were all that were needed to steady the wooden frame's uprights.

At the appointed time, Sgt. Osgood keyed the power switches and the drop ring began its slow rise to its operational position. The droppers, Richards and Gregorieva, waited upon the uppermost beam of the scaffolding. And as before, her wig's many tresses began to extend outwards as if she were grasping a van der Graaf device. With the drop ring secured at its operational height, Osgood gave an affirmative nod. Corporal Cooper, another of Calli's men, began to carefully probe the other side of the field with his fiber optic lens. While doing so he provided some commentary.

"Damn it's bright over there! From what I can see you guys have about a four to five foot drop max. Best of luck!"

Looking now to Calli for his own thumbs up signal, Richards saw it and dropped his leather spending money pouch through the silvery field. Then, after receiving the second thumbs up, Gregorieva dropped. With the last signal from Calli, Richards locked his bent knees together and disappeared as well.

"Okay Ozzy, perform an operational power down by the numbers." The nervous lieutenant barked. Then turning his head to his second. "Patterson, any bad guys out there?"

"No sir. Only us greenies." Was the quick reply.

"Good." He said under his breath. "It had better stay that way."

CHILDREN OF PTAH

* * *

Both Gregorieva and Richards knew that this was going to be an interesting drop, principally because they had to land and then stay low until the field closed. But on the other hand, this was also their first daylight drop into the open desert. And Corporal Cooper had been right; it was really bright, especially having come from near total darkness.

While both temporal field agents again experienced that slippery feeling during their transit through the field, Gregorieva again registered little disorientation – excepting the bright sunlight. As the first through, she quickly found and grabbed the leather pouch of their travel money and rolled to the left just as the dull thump of Richards' body had arrived. For his part, it took a good two minutes to get his head screwed on straight all the while he squeezed both of his eyes tightly shut.

"That was a most worthy hangover." He finally said as he dared to slowly open his eyes.

Gregorieva then whispered in his ear. "Be silent my brother, for we have visitors."

Now sitting up back to back, the two temporal field agents found themselves the subject of considerable interest by three pairs of very inquisitive eyes.

"They're jackals," Richards said, "desert scavengers."

And so imagine the scene of two humans surrounded by three sitting jackals with their heads akimbo in pure curiosity. Here they were just a few minutes ago minding their own business, while out on patrol looking for some tasty morsels. And then this bright light appears at high noon and out falls two humans. Most curious indeed!

Richards, now with his senses fully available, slowly reached out and carefully picked up a stone. This action brought the three as one to their feet with their attention now at high alert, their ears pitched towards them with noses twitching.

"Watch this my sister!" As Richards side armed the rock at the nearest animal, not to hit, but rather to fluster. In a flash the trio scattered and moments later disappeared over a neighboring rise.

"I thought so. Those jackals knew just what and who we were, and that rock just proved it."

Letting out a sigh of considerable relief, Gregorieva asked. "My brother how did you know that they wouldn't attack us?"

"Well, for one, we were not dead or seriously injured. For another, they are highly intelligent and clearly knew what a rock, once thrown, can do. And that means that we are not the first humans that they have encountered."

Now finally standing and brushing themselves off as best they could, Richards spit on the ground and then began gathering stones.

"Help me my sister. We must mark where we must return to."

When they were finished, they had constructed a small cairn of stones that now marked the location of their drop point. With that task accomplished, it was time to find the late Predynastic village of Mennefer and from what their noses told them, it could not be very far away. Turning towards the vast expanse of the Nile Valley to their right, the faint trails of Mennefer's many cooking fires were easy to see. As the pair walked towards those signs of habitation Richards turned on his remarkable memory and began to record what he saw.

First off, the signs of cooking fires could be seen here and there, both immediately before them and also off into the distance on the opposite bank of the river, in several places, no doubt identifying the location of other riverine villages. As for the river itself, that confluence looked untamed and wild as it was almost everywhere surrounded along its banks with thick and verdant vegetation that Richards knew was long gone by the Eighteenth Dynasty. Only here and there could be seen areas of cultivation, quite literally hard fought pockets of space cut out of the surrounding wilderness.

Now standing squarely at the edge of the Sakkara escarpment with the entire junction of the southern Delta and the northern Nile Valley in view, Richards sighed in wonder. It was simply breathtaking panorama with flocks of wild birds casting vast shadows across the river's surface and even a group of hippopotami cavorting in its currents. Then the sounds of human life reaching their ears from a rustic group of houses built of woven and bundled grasses among which farm animals wandered and children chased one another. But near this village of perhaps thirty such structures, one stood out from among the rest. This edifice, for that was precisely what it was, was built of smoothed, white washed mud brick. Its front porch roof was supported by two simple columns of bundled papyrus reeds. One would have assumed that this was the village's central temple, as its location was just west of the confines of the village proper.

Looking down the sandy and rocky slope before them, the clear demarcation between where the desert began and the furthest reach of the Nile's many inundations was unmistakable. Richards smiled that he could quite literally straddle that line with one foot squarely in the sand, while the other would sink deeply into the black, fertile mud.

Half sliding their way down the steep desert slope the pair quickly reached the vegetations' edge. Once there, Richards immediately attacked a convenient tamarisk branch and began stripping it down to a single shaft the ended in a Y-shaped fork. Gregorieva, hands on hips, quietly watched Richards' industry in curiosity and then finally asked.

"Why does my brother have interest in such a flimsy tool instead of fashioned yourself a club?"

"Because my most beautiful sister, this field before us is swarming with snakes and this is a snake stick."

And so on they continued, slowly making their way through the muddy thickets towards the cleared area of the village, ever careful of their footing and what might be underfoot. And sure enough, not thirty feet in, Richards had pinned with his forked stick a horned viper about three and a half feet long. Swiftly crushing its head with the heel of his mud-caked sandal, he then draped the dead reptile around his neck and continued on. By the time that the pair had reached the outskirts of the village, Richards had acquired no less than four deadly necklaces that surrounded his leather money pouch.

"My brother, why do you wear those frightful snakes?"

"A message, my sister, to communicate a message."

By the time that they had reached within hailing distance of the prominent white washed structure, both Gregorieva and Richards were truly a frightful sight. Both were muddy from the knees down and sweat streaked. Additionally, Richards had taken on a rather macabre look given the streams of snake blood and yellowish venom that had coursed down his chest and stomach to the waist of his once white kilt.

Now standing side by side a mere one hundred feet from the white washed building, both Gregorieva and Richards confronted a curious and oddly fearful crowd that had been gathering at their noisy and unassuming approach. Women, children and elders, all stood before them with their mouths' agape and their fingers pointing.

Gregorieva noticed it first.

"My brother, where are all the men?"

"Working in the fields, fishing, or hunting I would suppose. Let's find out."

Slightly raising his head to better project his voice, Richards called out. "We have traveled far. We seek a man named Ptah. Who among you is he?"

While all understood his simply constructed sentences and the meaning of his words, clearly Richards' accent was odd sounding to them from the gasps and giggles that it caused. Nonetheless, an old women gestured to a young girl, whispered a command, and off she ran towards village. And there the two sides stood for the next fifteen or so minutes, neither daring to move a muscle or glance away.

* * *

Rendered nearly breathless from her sprint, little Mekbet ran into the village's birthing room with the great news.

"Noble Ptah, you must come! Two strangers have just arrived from the great desert and they seek you by name!"

"Now Mekbet, take a deep breath while you collect yourself." The man said as he continued to wash the splatter of afterbirth from his forearms.

"Look, Mekbet. Our village is now one more." He said as he pointed to the still wet infant being lovingly held by its exhausted mother.

"Yes, yes, but noble Ptah, the two strangers called for you by name! And the big one was wearing a necklace of *fy*-snakes!"

Looking up into the young girl's face. "Is that so Mekbet? Are they injured?"

"No, noble one, but…"

"Then they can wait while I finish here. Or, would you rather take my place?"

Now truly torn between what she could very well perform and what was truly momentous news for their village, Mekbet hesitated. Ptah, naturally seeing this conflict, kindly suggested a solution.

"Perhaps Mekbet, we both should attend to Kawaset's needs and that of her baby boy, so that we can both see to what these strangers want. Eh?"

And so that's what they did.

* * *

"So did you see that old one instruct the girl?"

"Yes."

"Where do you think she went in such a hurry?"

"I don't know. But we'll know soon."

"But it's been almost a half an hour already!"

"Patience my sister, it is we who are the intruders into their world. A world, I might add, that does not know what a wristwatch is."

And then Richards espied a nearing movement. "Ah ha, my sister, I do believe that we have just hit pay dirt."

This assessment of Richards was based upon the slow approach of the young messenger girl, who now respectfully followed in the shadow of a bald-headed man of modest proportions walking with a forked staff. The front of his once white kilt was stained and splattered in blood, much the same as was Richards. Absolute proof as to this man's identity was made manifest as the assembled crowd wordlessly parted at his approach, and then closed formation at his passing.

Striding forward with absolute fearlessness toward the pair, Ptah then stopped about three paces away and quietly announced.

"I am Ptah. Who beckons me?"

Before Richards stood a future god, but what does a god in the making even look like? About five foot three, medium build with an ever so slight paunch, round headed with a straight nose and expressive brown eyes, in short, generic in the extreme. He was a man who could easily blend into any crowd anywhere in Europe or the Middle East. But the marked intelligence that lurked behind his eyes was definitely the initial give away that he was special in some way.

Both by agreement had their mental screens firmly in place for this moment, fully in anticipation of what could happen. For Gregorieva, the grand simplicity of the moment had brought tears to her eyes. For Richards, the sheer sound of his voice had been astounding. The calm cadence and inflection of his spoken words were a revelation. The philologist in him rejoiced. So this is what Archaic Egyptian sounds like!

Noting the odd silence of the pair before him, the true tears of joy from the most beautiful one and the clear reverence that emanated from the muscular one, Ptah unconsciously probed their minds for an answer and was physically shocked to find that he could not!

Richards, who noted the sudden widening of Ptah's eyes, smiled in understanding, and said. "Great and noble one. We have traveled far in search of you, just as you have traveled far in search of us."

This last turn of phrase brought a tilt to Ptah's head.

Now bending down to kneel on his right leg, Richards carefully removed his rather gaudy and messy reptilian necklaces and placed them at the feet of Ptah.

"We offer these harmful pests to you as a sign of our faith that we mean to make no harm either to you or your village."

This simple act that anthropologists universally understand as a gift-giving ceremony created the desired effect with the villagers' near simultaneous intake of breath.

For Ptah, however, the situation was a bit more complicated. For one, he could not use his sixth sense and so was forced to verbalize what he wanted to say – a crude and inexact task that he preferred not to use given the current level of the native vocabulary. Second, the language dialect that he was hearing, while understandable, was in itself a barrier. But finally, this heavily scared individual, clearly a warrior, nonetheless expressed his thoughts in a very remarkable and sophisticated way, with an emphasis on "no harm," or was it to be understood as "no evil?"

Truly fascinated for the first time in a very long time, Ptah responded. "The day has been a long one. Come. Refresh yourselves within my house and dust your feet."

With that said, Ptah turned and led a Russian and an American to his house – the white washed edifice, much to the utter amazement of the villagers.

At Ptah's choice of words, which both understood quite clearly, both smiled at 'dust your feet' for they were literally caked in mud.

*   *   *

The interior of the man's modest two room house was blessedly cool and once inside its shade the pair nearly collapsed in thanksgiving. Clinically noting this reaction on the part of his mysterious house guests, Ptah immediately set about getting three cups, and with a beer jug under one arm requested of Gregorieva some assistance, which she more than gratefully performed.

Now sitting on some heavy reed mats with a low table between them, Ptah made a formal toast.

"May Ra rise tomorrow, may we rise tomorrow with him, and may every thought worthy of the tongue bring forth that which is needful."

All drank deeply of the thick, cool, and refreshingly carbonated beer and so all three cups again were refilled, but before anyone had brought their cup to their lips, Richards offered a toast of his own and naturally their host was its object.

"There took form in the heart, there took shape on the tongue, the form of the god Atum. For the very great one is Ptah, he who gave essence to all the gods through his heart and through his tongue."

And while his guests again drank deeply, Ptah had not, for he had just days before written those very words, words which had taken him some 121 inundations to carefully craft, words pregnant with hidden meaning, but meaning that this vocabulary could not express in any adequate manner. And yet, somehow…

And so Ptah began formally.

CHILDREN OF PTAH

"I am Ptah. You are guests of my house. I have offered you refreshment. Now who are you and from which village do you come?"

"I am Maatkare, great one." Gregorieva said with a slight bow of the head.

And in turn Richards spoke. "I am Mayneken, great one. My sister and I have traveled far to meet you. And, we are indebted to your hospitality."

Again Ptah spoke directly. "Why Maatkare did tears come to your eyes when you first saw me?"

"Because great one, you are and will become in the hearts and minds of men even greater than you can ever imagine."

The complex linguistic transition from "are" to "will become" brought a small smile to their host's face. And so he shifted gears.

"And you Mayneken, from where do you and your sister come that is so far away?"

"Noble one, before I answer that question, may I ask how old you truly are?"

Without skipping a beat Ptah answered. "146 inundations."

"Now that is a very long time, great one," Richards observed with a smile, "and yet you appear before us as man in the prime of his life. But as to your question, how far I and my sister have traveled to meet with you, well, it is best expressed this way: 5,219 inundations."

With that answer, Ptah's truly startled eyes opened wide as both Gregorieva and Richards saw the understanding and the recognition in them.

"Why you speak so strangely, that I can understand. But what I do not is why I cannot see your hearts."

"Indeed," Richards began, "for in our many travels not everyone possesses such a gentleness of *sia* (mind) as do you. In fact, some with such a gift have even used it as a powerful and terrible weapon. So we are so protected."

Nodding in clear understanding and horror as well at the misuse of the mind, another question came to him.

"But how Mayneken do you know my own thoughts?"

"Great one, I do not, but I do know of your words. Words of wisdom that are difficult both to read and fully understand. But they are good words, full of deep thinking. Perhaps, one day, as we study your many papyrus scrolls, we will come to understand them more fully."

Surprised, the man asked. "So you have seen my scrolls as well?"

"Indeed most noble one. I counted fifty-six in all."

"Fifty-six you say? Perhaps I have written too much."

Now sitting back with his arms crossed in the unconscious body language of defense, Ptah looked up, sighed and was about to say something, but Richards stomach had gotten in the way as it rather noisily announced both its presence and its need.

Chuckling at the welcomed distraction, Ptah then announced.

"Enough talk. I will request that additional waters be brought so that we can properly dust our feet, and then, partake of an evening meal. But Mayneken, kindly take care not to lick yourself or rub your eyes as the poison of the *fy*-snake is all over you!"

* * *

The evening meal, while extremely modest if judged by the royal Egyptian standards of the Eighteenth Dynasty, for the two strangers it had been extremely tasty and filling, much to Ptah's pleasure, and that of the villagers, who had so kindly provided it. Roast duck and fresh fish comprised the main course with baked onions, garlic, and bread filling it out. Settling in and mildly buzzed by all the beer that had been forced upon them, Richards, seeing before him one very sated Ptah, decided to roll the dice.

"So noble one, now that you know from *when* we come, from *where* do you come?"

The now smiling Ptah truly enjoyed the word games that these two liked to play. So he said. "I could frankly answer that question with several possible answers and all of them would be truthful in all respects. But noble Mayneken and beautiful Maatkare, just as beer may loosen my tongue, so also does beer loosen one's grasp, one's control of the mind. And now seeing your heart, I will truthfully answer your question the way that you wish me to."

Oops! Simultaneously thought the two moderns. So we have indeed!

"As you yourself said before, I have traveled far."

To which Gregorieva responded. "Indeed noble one, you probably have, but is it true that you are one of the Old Ones?"

Now smiling even more broadly than before, the man called Ptah answered. "Ah, now that is a name that I have not heard of for a long, long time. In fact, I think that it was my dear brother Thoth, who had last used the term. From whom or where did you hear of this term, 'the Old Ones?'"

To that question Gregorieva said. "Noble one, we discovered its mention in the writings of another visitor to this place, who remarkably, was also seeking evidence of your passing, but who failed to do so."

Now with his interest truly peaked, he asked. "Now that is truly remarkable. Tell me about this other visitor."

What followed was a somewhat abridged version of the encounter with the being called Akhenaten, his attempt to improve the human gene pool through his offspring, and his attempt to philosophically influence the course of human history.

Having listened intently throughout the telling of this tale, Ptah then said shaking his head. "Such crass interference with the natural course of the body and mind is an abomination! For there is far too much that can happen that is not wished for, that is unintended. This Akhenaten was doing truly wrongful things. But the mere teaching of ideas is quite another proposition. And you say that this Akhenaten also left behind a day book of his many journeys?"

To this Richards responded as he had been cleared to read the Annex Papyrus. "Indeed noble one, for he and his kin had journeyed very far before he had stumbled upon our land."

Then the man named Ptah chose to add something that almost seemed out of character.

"To traverse the cold darkness of the stars is a very lonely and solitary task my dear Mayneken and Maatkare. It is one that truly tests the balance, the very *maat* of the mind. In some ways, I understand the desire of this Akhenaten to make many improvements. But to understand is one thing, to agree is another."

Now spreading his arms wide in a gesture that seemed to encompass the entire village. "Yet, here, in this beautiful and virgin place there is no cold darkness, only life, a wonderful abundance of life. And, in its own way, there is a peacefulness, a sublime *maat* that must be respected. The man named Akhenaten had not respected *maat* and as a consequence I seriously doubt that he even understood it."

And with that heady pronouncement a brief pause fell on the conversation, after which Richards asked. "So, noble one, if we understand you, you arrived at this place after being in the cold darkness of the stars for a time?"

"Indeed that is so."

"And then what is your purpose for being here, now, among these people?"

Again the man named Ptah smiled, but this time with a deeply satisfying one that beamed almost with a kind of rich emotional release. "Noble Mayneken, most beautiful Maatkare, do not you already see? My purpose is complete, for your very presence is the proof of it."

Moved, and at the same time stunned, by the elegant simplicity of the statement, Richards and Gregorieva both nodded in the understanding of it.

But the man named Ptah was not yet finished.

"And while I rejoice with the proof of your physical presence before me, I am troubled Mayneken that you will pay a very high price for this privilege. Even though I have yet to lay my hands upon your body, I can nonetheless see your troubled *ka*. Mayneken, you must be vigilant and shortly attend to this sickness. And for this judgment I truly am sorry."

Then turning to Gregorieva.

"As for you Maatkare, truly a worthy name, your *ka* is not sick, but instead is bright and vibrant, and for this judgment I am most pleased."

At this point in the evening, the man named Ptah began to gently rub the sides of his temples as if to relieve a tension headache, sighed deeply, and simply stated.

"I must now sleep on this."

As he levered himself up, Ptah pointed to the two raised bed frames that the villagers had so thoughtfully provided. He then staggered off to the back of his house and lay down.

Richards looking at Gregorieva then quietly said. "And what was all that about sick and healthy *kas*?"

Shrugging in ignorance and some confusion as well, she answered. "Perhaps we should consult our physician once we are safely home."

*   *   *

Just as sleep that night came quickly, so did the sunrise of the following day. Awakening remarkable refreshed and none the worse except for a few insect bites, Richards and Gregorieva found themselves alone. The man named Ptah was absent, perhaps out and about, as some fresh bread, onions, and cheese were waiting for them on the table under a finely woven linen cloth.

Reaching for the bread in order to tear it in half so that he could share it, Richards commented. "Maatkare, we must have just missed him as this bread is still warm."

With their first meal finished and their bed coverings folded, the pair decided to go exploring in order to find their kind host, pay their respects, and say farewell.

As they passed through the door way, they were greeted by a little one, a girl, with red eyes.

As Gregorieva bent down to the girl, the tears again began to flow.

"What troubles you so little one?"

Gregorieva protectively asked as she unconsciously began to stroke her head.

With a sniffle came the answer.

"The noble Ptah has left our village!"

"What do you mean?"

"Last night, while you were asleep, he came to me with one of his scrolls as a gift and said goodbye." Sniff.

"Oh come now," Gregorieva crooned. "He's just gone for a walk, or perhaps to bathe in the river."

"No! He left our village! I saw!"

Now Richards squatted down and kindly asked.

"Little one, what is your name?"

"Mekbet."

"So little Mekbet can you tell us what you saw?"

Now nodding like a bobble-headed doll, the little girl said.

"I followed the noble one into the desert, there."

And the two temporal agents now looked in the direction of her rigidly extended arm.

And again Richards gently asked. "And when you followed the noble one into the desert what did you see?"

"A bright light like Re."

CHILDREN OF PTAH

Now Gregorieva prodded. "And then what did the noble Ptah do in the desert?"

"He went into the bright light and then the bright light flew across Nut's tummy and became a star."

*   *   *

After hearing little Mekbet's account of the noble Ptah's rather stellar departure, Gregorieva and Richards left the village and made their way towards the desert in order to make their high noon departure. Richards, ever mindful, had brought along his snake stick and had to kill two more horned vipers before they reached the steep sloped base of the Sakkara escarpment.

While trudging up the sandy and rocky slope Richards swore that he heard someone behind him, but when he turned around there was no one there.

After reaching the top of the escarpment, the pair made their way into the desert and after a bit of searching, found their stone cairn marker unmolested. Sitting down next to it, Richards finally enunciated what he had been ruminating on during the entire hike.

"You know Vesna, he sort of told us that he was leaving. Do you remember that comment that he made about us being proof of his purpose?"

Thinking a bit before she answered. "I think that your right. Still, I cannot get over the fact that I actually spoke to a true alien, drank beer with one, and even slept under his roof. It's all so very, very strange. And then all that talk about sick and healthy *kas*. That frankly scared me."

"As it did me. I wonder if he was referring the Post Drop Syndrome?"

And at that moment, above their heads, a second sun disk had begun to form.

*　　*　　*

Little Mekbet just could not believe her own eyes. From her vantage point in the rocks, the friendly strangers were just sitting in the desert next to a pile of stones as if they were speaking to it.

Then, a bright light appeared above them!

And then, they disappeared into it!

And then, the bright light went away!

Curiosity not being one of Mekbet's weaknesses, she then investigated the pile of stones after the kind strangers had left and found nothing but their snake stick. This she took back to the village as evidence of what she had witnessed. In the fullness of time, the village's recollections about the departure of Ptah and his visitors would blur, but his use of a snake stick would not. So became Richards' discarded tool a much-revered early totem of Ptah that would even be buried with one of his early high priests along with some other items later discovered by an Austrian named Gerst.

*　　*　　*

There was an odd somberness among the security detail, and especially with Calli, at their retrieval. While nothing was said, nothing really had to be said. So clearly, Richards reasoned something was up and whatever it was he was determined to get to the bottom of it.

Once all the gear had been taken down and stowed aboard the helicopter and just before their departure, Richards took the big Irishman aside and stared into his eyes.

"Okay lieutenant, I have never before gotten such a vibe from you. What's up?"

First looking down at his boots and then finally meeting the Egyptologist's gaze directly, it was then that Richards saw the tightness in his eyes.

Then Richards presciently said. "It's Professor Milson isn't it."

"Yes sir, it is. I am truly sorry."

During the short helicopter ride back to Heliopolis' military airport, Richards told Gregorieva that Milson had passed away. Blessedly, the surprising level of emotional grief that the Russian expressed provided the American some cover for his own. With her sobbing head buried into his chest, he held her, and gently rocked her back and forth, all the while totally oblivious to the passage of time or his immediate surroundings.

CHAPTER XXXVII
Death of a Friend

Milson's passing had been a peaceful one that occurred during his sleep. His last day had been a full one, just like his life. Richards, his own handpicked successor, was away having just successfully dropped into the distant Egyptian Predynastic Period, the purpose of which was to interview an Egyptian god no less. Happy beyond words that their joint struggle to understand the archaic version of "The Memphite Theology" was about to be cracked by actually asking the author just what he had in mind, Milson's last mortal thoughts nonetheless had put a smile on his face.

A widower since the death of his beloved wife Alice, the discovery of his situation had taken two full days. Fortunately, his documentation that stipulated his final requests had been in the hands of Paul Young for the past four years, ever since the onset of Milson's nasty encounter with cancer.

Once the door to Milson's flat had been jimmied open, the smell alone told the tale. As soon as the coroner had completed his paperwork, what had once been Milson was cremated per his instructions and his ashes placed in the niche next to that of his wife. While Milson did not mention any sort of memorial service, his colleague Young, an Anglican, nonetheless went into high gear in its planning. A date was chosen. The university's chapel was booked as were two full floors at the Student Union's hotel for all of the expected out-of-town guests. The announcements and arrangements were sent worldwide. The only potential fly in the ointment that could foul all of these complex machinations would be a hitch in Gregorieva's and Richards' safe return.

*   *   *

CHILDREN OF PTAH

The memorial service for Professor Emeritus John Allen Milson took place within the gothic grandeur of the university chapel and to Young's great pleasure the place was absolutely packed to the gills. There were even bodies crammed in up in the choir loft.

Yes, Johnny my boy, the Dean of Humanities thought, good men are oftentimes forgotten, but not on my watch!

Even before the remembrance ceremony had begun, Young had taken up a position in the arch's shadow of the right nave, where he could easily observe in true British voyeuristic tradition the trickle of the mourners' arrival.

Let's see now, he silently mused with slitted eyes, there's Milson's departmental chair and spouse followed closely by four of his colleagues. I just wonder where the rest of them are? My God, what else could possibly trump this memorial service? The grading of papers? Library research? That seminal book review? I am going to have to have a conversation with that man about the health of his department. Perhaps all that scuttlebutt about professional jealousies centered on Richards really do have some substance.

After the passage of a few moments.

My, my, it's the university's football coach and wife. Now that's a surprise. I just wonder what's the connection there? Most likely Richards, but what about? Most curious. I always knew that John was a rabid fan of the Crimson, but this is still rather a surprise.

Then the stream of arrivals began to quicken.

Well, there's Paul Silas, the editor of our own university press and his wife, another surprise. Well, maybe not, given Milson's prodigious publication record and Richards' textbook's sudden notoriety.

Ah ha, I am so very glad to see that the word got out, for there's Commander Cartwright and wife. My, he does look quite resplendent in his uniform! I did not know that he had so many medals. Is that a sword that he is wearing at his side!

How nice, I see that Dr. Allen and wife made it too. What a fine couple they make. That man has made such a contribution to the cause in so many ways. I have heard nothing but good things about that man, and in this business, that is really something.

Ah, there is that materials scientist from Wright-Patterson Air Force base. What was his name again? Peters? Yes. Roy Peters. He's one serious looking fellow.

Now this is deliciously wonderful! The Moussas made it. How splendid Sharil looks on her father's arm. She's just as breath-taking as ever. Now I just wonder if this is their first time in a Christian church?

Young, now pausing in shock, covered his mouth.

My God in heaven! I do not believe it! There's Karlov Drazinzka and Vasily Ostrogorsky! Gads do they look old. Look at the way the pair support one another. This is probably also their first time in a Christian church. Well, perhaps not. Vasily I seem to remember had some ties with the Russian Orthodox Church.

I see that Charles Naysmithe has arrived. Is that absolutely stunning red-head his wife? No, that's Becky Stewart! Doc Allen's nurse. How intriguing…

And here comes Professor van der Boek and wife, and if I reckon rightly, those four in tow are the original members of the Dutch archaeological team from Thebes.

This next group I do not recognize; they're probably former students of Milson by the look of some of them.

There's Ernst Jung with wife and he is even early for once! Now there's a tribute to John if I have ever seen one!

Now who is this? Why it is that woman from the university microfilms department. Now I wonder what her story is all about?

What's this! Gregorieva and Richards arm-in-arm? What a handsome pair. They both look so wonderfully tanned and healthy. She must be wearing a wig, while Richards is blatantly sporting his cue ball look. I wonder if anything is going on there? Now wouldn't that be a delicious development!

Well I'll be damned! This is absolutely historic! Even that bastard Rosovec has dared to show up. I sure as hell did not invite him. Still and all, he must have felt the obligation to pay his respects as John did for Alexander.

At this point in his observations, Young ceased noting the arrivals and instead began to understand the coin of what greatness truly was. Just look how many people John had touched throughout his life, all the while the crowds just kept on coming.

*   *   *

While Milson's public memorial ceremony that had been published in the *Chicago Tribune* had been described as a high Anglican affair, the more private farewell that took place at the mortuary was a highly emotional Irish wake. With an open bar, the Russians themselves emptied two bottles of the house's best Vodka. Two full trash cans were filled to the brim with empty Silver Bullets. While toasts abounded and endless stories were told that immediately turned the man into a legend, it was Richards' farewell that took the prize and as they say "nary a dry eye could be found in the house."

In the end and after the great majority of the mourners had left, a small cadre of the inner circle still remained. These included all the Russians, the Moussas, Naysmithe, Cartwright, van der Boek, Schachermayr, and Young.

To this close cadre, Richards announced. "Folks, I wish to thank you all for waiting this out, but I think that John would truly appreciate one last farewell gift."

Stepping up to the niche which now contained the remains of both Alice and John Milson, Richards placed within it a small papyrus scroll. Then, he closed his eyes and raised his arms forming a U-shape with his palms facing forward. And then in a long dead language he began to chant to the rhythm of a plain song.

I open your mouth, so that you may speak,

I open your eyes, so that you may see Re,

I open your ears, so that you may hear of your glorification,

And I grant movement to your legs, arms, and heart so that you can repulse your enemies.

Long may you live most righteous John Milson.

The effect on those present was profound. The Russians had all witnessed this before beneath Lenin's Tomb. The Moussas were immensely proud. Van der Boek and Schachermayr were absolutely spellbound. Cartwright with considerable pride actually managed to understand most of it. Only Naysmithe and Young were left in the dark, but the streaming tears of the others expressed well the gist of what had just taken place.

Epilogue

As Doc Allen hovered over Richards' medical history, he just could not believe what he was seeing. Then he dredged up his last entry in Piankoff's. It all came down to the results of a very extensive blood panel workup; one of those all encompassing workups where the patient was drained no less than five vials worth of blood. Seemingly out of nowhere Joey's electrolyte levels had decided to totally go out of whack, just as they had done twice with the late Russian. Given that Joey had not yet noted any of the unusual symptoms, Doc Allen decided that it would be best nonetheless to handle the situation with some delicacy.

"Okay Doc, let's hear the bad news." Richards commented.

"Why must the news be bad?" Doc Allen countered.

"Because you seldom frown, Doc."

Shaking his head, Doc Allen just did not know what to say as Joey's electrolytic condition was unprecedented in modern medicine. He'd checked. But then again, Joey's many exposures to the Soap Bubble's EM field, and now recently to that far more powerful Philadelphia field, were not exactly the usual run-of-the-mill scenarios that a typical power grid technician would experience.

"Well Joey my boy, that fella' that you talked to really knew his stuff." As Doc Allen paused trying to figure out just how to explain what he had found.

"Well for starters, do you know what electrolytes are?"

"Yeah, they are elements in the blood that regulate respiration, brain function, muscle performance, a whole bunch of stuff."

"That's correct, electrolytes are critical to your bodily functions, because these minerals are substances that become ions in your blood. Once there, they acquire the capacity to conduct electricity. Consequently, your sodium, potassium, chloride and bicarbonate levels are essential for the normal operation of both your body's cells and its organs. Now, can you image what would happen if you could not regulate your electrolytes?"

"Doc, is that what the post-drop syndrome is all about? Is that what you are getting at?"

Pause.

"Yep Joey, there's no question about it. Piankoff had it and now you are displaying it. So, here's the drill. From this day forward we're going to monitor you and your ability to regulate your electrolytes. Got that tiger?"

"You got it Doc."

"It is a good thing is that your ancient buddy gave you a head's up on this, that we caught wind of this. Now we have an angle on beating this bodily EM reaction."

"Doc, this imbalance of my electrolytes, does this mean that I am washed up?"

"Naw, your situation is nowhere near that dire. But Joey, this condition is something that we have to get a handle on. It could very well mean a change in your diet. And if we cannot manage it, then it may mean that you will have to retire as a temporal agent far sooner than you would have liked."

*   *   *

And with that "guardedly happy" news I began writing down some thoughts, which over the years became several rather longish manuscripts. So that my words would be sure to reach the light of day, I contacted Paul Silas, then an associate editor of our university's press. At first he was very reluctant to take on the role as the guardian of my literary estate, but thankfully his good and generous heart finally gave in, and for that kindness I truly bless him.

CHILDREN OF PTAH

*   *   *

Twenty-seven years have passed since I, Joseph William Richards, was first hired as a green-as-grass associate professor of Egyptian philology. During my first four years of academic initiation and following the peaceful passing of my mentor, I became the first occupant of the John A. Milson Distinguished Chair, an endowed chair of Egyptology that was established in his name by a little known legal entity in New Mexico.

Before that singular honor, however, my presence among the academic faculty had been treated as something of a scandal as I had begun my career having barely turned twenty-one. Add to that my rather sudden, unannounced, and unadvertised appointment. Despite these apparent academic irregularities, my contract of employment clearly stipulated a tenured position within the Department of Near Eastern Studies at the associate professor level. Such a contract had deftly circumvented a legal irritation that the university would have endured with a certain national academic organization, as the position had not been advertised nor circulated among the usual academic circles. But with that subtle maneuver I nonetheless became the topic of wonder with a tinge of irregularity wrapped in whispers of speculative gossip. Finally there were my rather unique scholarly credentials – the philological details of which were beyond dispute, but impossible to explain as how I had acquired them as that was a highly classified subject.

Nevertheless, over the years my professional career has been an extremely full one. I, unlike some of my colleagues, gladly shouldered the responsibility of teaching several generations of students. That enthusiasm ensured a modest legacy as I was flattered to mentor to fruition five bright minds, who have since successfully continued on in various aspects of ancient studies. I found out early on that the classroom commitment required an immense amount of

347

energy and that teaching was not for the faint of heart, as it could be as grueling as rewarding. Still and all, as I reveled in the classroom I also gleaned never-ending inspiration from my charges. And truth be told, at times, I have often wondered who was really teaching whom. All I know is that I have grown immensely from the experience and along the way earned six university teaching awards. After the third such presentation my departmental colleagues began to again noticeably cool to near-arctic levels; after the sixth, well, I became an anomalous embarrassment – much like a multimillionaire who somehow backed into a whopper of a lottery win. In apparent retaliation to this campus notoriety snipping whispers began to circulate during the annual conventions about the weight of my scholarship.

As for my academic contributions, well, I have published several hugely successful textbooks on the teaching of the ancient Egyptian language – no surprise given my rather special circumstances. Translated into several modern languages, their royalties have backstopped rather handsomely my personal needs such as they are. Needless to say, my rather novel philological positions on the grammar and the vocalization of the ancient Egyptian's language have earned me both fiercely faithful followers and equally embittered, lifelong enemies. Such is the academic world.

Within academe, where delicate egos abound, I quickly discovered that there is little cause for mediation and certainly no gentlemen's middle ground. No matter how polite or cultured the audience might appear to be. And, so in order to bolster my philological claims I have written plenty of pithy little treatises and have even penned an occasional book review, but only when directly asked (read "pressured" by this journal editor or that). I performed these tasks sometimes with enthusiasm, but more often, not. Instead, what this consummate conforming nonconformist found most invigorating were not the meager tidbits found in a library's dusty card catalogue or in an obtuse footnote of a dusty journal, but rather what could be discovered on an archaeological excavation or better a topographical survey. In that environment I found that I could freely flex my intellectual muscles, get my hands dirty, all the time while I earned some hidden kernel of knowledge or subtle insight paid in the coin of honest sweat. Quite frankly, my participation early on with the Dutch team in the clearing of the Treasury of Amen Re was for me a magical time, truly my proudest moment, that, well, I simply will never forget. Nor ever would my departmental colleagues, for they were simply scandalized that I had debased myself to the level of a dirt archaeologist. Then when the Dutch project went public as to the extraordinary nature of their findings, with all the televised hoopla and cable specials, that visibility only further distanced me from my department – envious beyond imagination all. Blessedly, I had the prescience to play a behind the scenes role with the Austrian Archaeological Mission in Memphis, in spite of Sheril Moussa's strong opinions to the contrary.

So in the final analysis, this combination of relative youth, enthusiastic pedagogy, financial independence, and off campus notoriety conspired to make me a marked man, shadowed by a flock of sharp-eyed academic harpies, all who eagerly lusted to find any irregularity, who yearned to discover any academic failing whatsoever, who simply would drool at the mere hint of any ethical impropriety. In short, my success placed me squarely under the microscope.

On the other hand, my second self – the private side that will never appear in any *curriculum vitae* or in any public document, has been just as frenetic. In all, as the second temporal field operative of the Philology Annex, I have logged a total of sixteen drops out of my time. Along the way and as a direct result of those journeys, I have paid a dear physiological price. The lesson to be learned here is that powerful electromagnetic fields can be a source of seriously deleterious effects upon the male physiology in general and its electrical constitution in particular. Just how people can consciously live near and even under electrical power lines I will never know. Anyways, I am officially offline when it comes to any further drops as I am no longer up to its physical rigors, although I have been retained by the Philology Annex as a much-valued consultant. This sad state of affairs is due to my irregular ability to naturally regulate my electrolytes. The whole situation is just altogether way too quirky for an active temporal field operative. One day I am fine and full of energy; the next I struggle to just walk several flights of stairs – hardly the sort of physical condition to be in while taking on the everyday vagaries of the ancient world. Add to that, each and every time I pass through the EM field of the Soap Bubble only worsens my condition. And so after a fashion, I was put to pasture.

My successor Dr. Vesna Gregorieva, an accomplished dancer and truly gifted linguist, is now the Philology Annex's primary field operative, and fittingly, she has selected and trained a fine assistant – another female. This turn of events is only fitting as the first field operative, the venerable and crusty Alexander Piankoff, had been my able teacher and Vesna's. His premature death, however, robbed us both of his hard-earned field craft, his canny and crafty ways, items all that I had to rediscover and reinvent on my own. What a tragic loss that was and one so very unnecessary. More than once my heart wanted to propose a rescue drop to save Piankoff, but logic always overruled such a scheme so contrary to the sensible dicta of the *RUTI*, even though I know for a fact that others would have quickly and gladly bankrolled just such a fool's errand in a New York minute.

So in the end, I guess in some sort of backhanded sense of recompense, I have experienced the ancient Egyptian culture from a perspective that only a precious few other living humans could possibly possess. I also experienced firsthand nuances that the learned fields of epigraphy, papyrology, and archaeology, could only begin to infer. For instance, I know what ancient Egyptian sweet breads taste like and I simply love them. I have gotten deliriously drunk on their marvelously thick and tasty wheat beers. I became the adopted son of a high priest of Amen Re and then was burdened with the filial responsibilities of his burial. I was befriended by an Egyptian prince and even shared the intimate confidence and affections of a queen. Best of all, I thoroughly enjoyed the sensuous delights of the royal household's ceremonial "dusting of the feet."

Not everything has been all fun and games. There were those dark moments, when I performed unspeakable acts all in the name of protecting our blessed time line and continuum. My heinous crimes are many and they all began with the murder of countless innocents when I allowed myself to become a virulent germ carrier. Then there was that brutal assassination of the alien life form poising as a pharaoh. During a follow up mission I helped finished off one of his sons – a hopelessly neurotic and paranoid homicidal maniac. All of these acts were fully sanctioned by the scientific communities of several sovereign nations. The heavy sense of guilt, the personal nightmare that I was even capable of taking life so coolly and efficiently, haunts me to this very day. Yes, I suppose I could brush aside all responsibility for those actions and hide behind the institutionally imposed hypnosis and the many memory block implants that were required in order for me to do what I had to do. After all, the alien had been a powerful inline telepath and his hybrid son a cruel telekinetic menace as well. Nonetheless, I feel indelibly soiled at having performed this very nasty business on the behalf of others, all whose hands have remained spotlessly clean, their consciences completely clear.

I am rambling. I know. Of late it has become somewhat of a bad habit – such ruminations, such self-incriminations. But I have to let someone know. While my temporal adventures must remain classified, I nonetheless find myself driven to share a portion of them with someone, for they represent the most important discoveries of my life, events that totally eclipse in significance all of my public triumphs. And yes, there is always the guilt – that incredible need to come clean. So I decided to leave behind some sort of a record of my most memorable visits into the distant past. Not to mention to chronicle my brief acquaintance with a most remarkable personality.

So I sit typing on my encrypted laptop. After all, didn't even the alien pilot of the Aten spacecraft need to pass on such a memoir, the highly classified Annex Papyrus? And so must I.

By the way, my given name is not Joseph William Richards; that is just an alias, just as are all the names and organizations mentioned in these manuscripts. Similarly other sensitive details have been deliberately changed or excised altogether in order to ensure a particular individual's anonymity or protect the security of a national agency or international entity. In other instances, I see little harm in the describing that which would be obvious to anyone. Still and all, if there is anything that I have come to know and respect, it is the law of unexpected consequences. No matter how hard you try, you just can't win against the sheer randomness of chance.

A Note on the Vocalization of Ancient Egyptian

Regarding the vocalization of ancient Egyptian, the fact of the matter is simply this: the language is a very, very dead one – meaning that what it sounded like has been long lost. Its closest linguistic cousin, Coptic, is itself a dead language, but at least one that included vowels within its script. On this shirt-tailed basis, Egyptologists have carefully compared the vocabularies of the two languages and have constructed a scientific vocalization scheme to approximate what the Egyptian tongue might have sounded like. But even if the assigned vowel placements are accurate, their quality remains just as uncertain as is their emphasis or where the accent falls on a particular word – not to mention that there is evidence to suspect several regional dialectics during the course of any given dynasty. To add even more fuel to the fire, different vocalization schemes have been put forward by the dominant Egyptological schools of thought be they American, British, French, Italian or German. As a consequence, the vocalization of ancient Egyptian becomes more a matter of one's cultural preference than anything else. In short, just what the language really sounded like during a given time period and within a given region is up for grabs.

With the above caveats and considerations in mind, the author offers the following possible pronunciations for the ancient Egyptian names and words that appear in this manuscript.

Akhenaten – King of Egypt: *a-ken-a-ten*

Akhetaten – capital city built by Akhenaten: *a-khet-a-ten*

Amen Re – chief divinity of Thebes: *a-men-ra*

Ankhmes – court physician to Akhenaten: *ankh-mes*

W.J. CHERF

Atum – Egyptian god of creation: *a-tomb*

Deshret – "red land" Egyptian desert: *desh-ret*

Djoser – pharaoh of the Third Dynasty; builder of the Step Pyramid Complex: *djoe-sir*

Hapi – Egyptian god of the Nile: *haa-pee*

Hathor – Egyptian goddess of childbirth and fertility: *hat-hor*

Hatshepsut – Female pharaoh of the Eighteenth Dynasty: *hat-shep-soot*

Hesy – Memphite city elder: *hesy*

Hor – Memphite farmer: *horr*

Horemheb – Prince of Egypt and future pharaoh: *hor-em-heb*

Houtkaptah – "the castle of the *ka* of Ptah," the name for the Great Temple of Ptah of Memphis: *hoot-kha-p-taa*

Hyksos – Invaders of Egypt during the First Intermediate Period: *hick-soss*

Issi – son of the Memphite city elder: *iss-yy*

Kha en seshretou – "hall of papyrus rolls": *kha-en-sesh-ret-ou*

Kahepet – Memphite village trouble-maker: *kha-hepet*

Kawab – Memphite farmer: *kha-wab*

Kemet – "black land" Nile Valley: *kem-et*

Khnum – a god of creation: *kha-noom*

Khufu – pharaoh of the Fourth Dynasty; builder of the Great Pyramid: *koo-fu*

Maat – goddess of divine order: *maa-haat*

CHILDREN OF PTAH

Maatkare – Egyptian name of Vesna Gregorieva, assistant of Mayneken: *maa-haat-ka-ra*

Mayneken – Egyptian name of Joseph Richards, *sem*-priest of Ptah: *may-necken*

Mekbet – female Memphite name: *mek-bet*

Menes – possible name of Egypt's first pharaoh: *men-es*

Mennefer – the city of Memphis: *men-nefer*

Merimaat – second prophet of Amen Re: *merry-maa-hat*

Meryptah – high priest of Amen Re: *mary-p-taah*

Mose – house servant of Ptahesou: *mo-se*

Narmer – possible name of Egypt's first pharaoh: *nar-mer*

Nebneteru – high priest of Amen Re: *neb-net-er-u*

Nefertiti – Queen to Pharaoh Akhenaten: *nefert-iti*

Nesi – Prince Horemheb's houseman: *ne-si*

Osiris – Egyptian god of the underworld: *o-sir-iss*

Nut – Egyptian sky goddess: *noot*

Pahamneter – high priest of Ptah: *pah-am-neter*

Per ankh – "house of life": *per-ankkh*

Per medjat – "house of book rolls": *per-ma-jatt*

Perunefer – port of Memphis: *peru-nefer*

Ptah – chief divinity of Memphis: *p-taah*

Ptahmesou – high priest of Ptah: *p-taah-mesoo*

Sekhmet – goddess of war: *sech-met*

Sennufer – mayor of Thebes: *sen-nu-fer*

Seshi – chief librarian of the *per ankh* of Ptah: *sesh-i*

Sia – divine understanding: *see-ya*

Thoth – god of writing and civilization: *thoawth*

Thutmose III – pharaoh of the Eighteenth Dynasty: *thut-mose*

A Note on the Editing of Papyri & Inscriptions

The study of inscriptions, known as epigraphy, possesses well-known philological shorthand for the recording and interpretation of such ancient monuments – be they handsomely carved stone inscriptions, painted surfaces, or hastily scratched out graffiti. This methodology was first established by Theodor Mommsen, the founder of the *Corpus Inscriptionum Latinarum*, or *CIL*, in 1853. The *CIL*, which celebrated its 150th anniversary in 2003, is a vast compendium of nearly eighty volumes of inscriptions that relate to the Roman Empire. The continued study and publication of newly discovered inscriptions from this period of history is the patient and laborious task of the Berlin-Brandenburgische Academie der Wissenschaften, Corpus Inscriptionum Latinarum's staff and its able director, Prof. Dr. Manfred Gerhard Schmidt.

Needless to say, with such a ready tool available historians and philologists of other ancient time periods naturally gravitated to the *CIL* methodology of philological criticism and commentary and either wholly adopted it or did so with few exceptions.

Consequently, all of the ancient Egyptian texts contained within this book follow the *CIL*'s editorial conventions and use the following symbols to indicate:

a|bc	Breaks in the text, usually a line break
a||bc	Text located outside of an inscribed field or displaced text
(vac.)	The presence of a gap in the text
[[abc]]	An ancient erasure of text

<<abc>>	Ancient text inscribed on an erased background
abc (!)	An ancient grammatical error, misspelling, or philological irregularity of some kind
abc (?)	Uncertain reading of the text
(abc)	Either the modern explanation of an abbreviation or philological convention
a[bc]	A modern editorial addition, explanation, or change to the text
{abc}	A modern editorial deletion of text
<u>abc</u>	Letters once read by previous editors, which are currently lost or unreadable

About the Author

"Can't was killed in the Battle of Try!"

As a fifth-grader W.J. Cherf took Sister Mary Stephana's words to heart and ever since has found the confidence to take on challenges that others shy away from. When confronted with retirement, Cherf said, "Heck, I've always wanted to write a book without footnotes, to tell a fascinating tale that is so real that my avid readers would be left puzzled over what was real and what was Memorex."

To craft such a tale takes wit, a love of science fiction, and above all a deep reverence for ancient history and archaeology. All of these qualities are stitched together beautifully in his books, because Cherf has been there, dug that. This is a guy who has even seen the sun rise from atop the Great Pyramid. Cherf likes to tell a story about when he was eleven year old and had become bored with dinosaurs. While exploring the Field Museum along Chicago's water front one Saturday morning he discovered Hall N – the ancient Egyptian collection. From that time forward Cherf was terminally smitten as that truly was his life-changing "ah ha!" moment.

Needless to say Cherf's books have been generously reviewed by his readers, who have eagerly shared their joy. For an author, such sentiments are an embarrassment of riches; precious words like honey deliciously, drizzled.

Here are a few representative examples:

"Bow Tie: Two Thumbs Up! Imagine a dinner party thrown by Tom Clancy, where he sits EE "Doc" Smith next to HG Wells."

"Amazing story, fascinating detail, a fabulous read."

"Cherf has done a wonderful job combining facts from Egyptian history and a fictional story to create a compelling trilogy of intrigue and espionage."

W.J. Cherf

"What an enjoyable experience reading this series!"

At his core Cherf is a teacher and his books do just that. They are a passionate sharing of a much-beloved subject. His readers tend to be adults who are looking for an adventure, who enjoy lively description, an involved plot, and the intellectual satisfaction of learning something new.

Cherf has excavated in Israel and Greece and toured and photographed many of Egypt's ancient sites first hand. He is also a big fan of Tom Clancy and Michael Crichton. But Cherf is quick to point out, whenever he can, the four men that professionally shaped him. Rufus J. Fears first lit the fire; Edward W. Kase stoked it; George J. Szemler refined it; and Charles K. Wolfe, Jr., set him free.

With a BA in Anthropology, MA in Egyptian Archaeology, and Ph.D. in Ancient History, Cherf remains current as an elected officer of Denver's Egyptian Studies Society. He is also a member of SERTOMA – Service to Mankind, a national service organization.

Living with his beloved wife Sue, they keep Foxbat 1 and Foxbat 2 out in the garage. They enjoy playing golf, road racing (that's where the Foxbats come in), jawing around a fire pit on a cool evening while sampling craft beers, and rooting for the Cubs – clearly Cherf is a hopeless romantic. Bottom line: Cherf just, flat makes science fiction, ancient history, and archaeology come alive.

Come visit to access some sample chapters and continue following the temporal adventures of Egyptologist Joseph Richards at: www.wjcherf.com.

Made in the USA
Charleston, SC
30 September 2013